Line of Sight

A Jake Presnall Novel

GEORGE ESLER

ISBN: 0615947395
ISBN-13: 978-0615947396 (Esler Media)

DEDICATION

There are three people in particular who deserve mentioning as I celebrate my first novel. I would like to thank Kelli, my lovely wife, who supported me through this process. She also deserves recognition for not running away screaming after reading that first draft. Nick, who introduced me to this wonderful thing called the novel, and cultivated in me a love of books. And last but not least, the real-life Miss Jerry, who nurtured and encouraged my love of writing during those pivotal early years.

ACKNOWLEDGMENTS

A big thanks to Vincent Verdin, who took a cover design concept that existed only in my mind, and turned it into something that looked even better than the picture in my head. I would also like to thank Kelli, Bobby, and Craig, whose feedback was instrumental in improving the novel. Your advice and constructive criticism is much appreciated.

One

Faith Daelly glanced back and discovered that the two strangers were still following her. In a way, this was a relief; as long as she didn't lose sight of the creeps, she would always know exactly where they were. On the other hand, the longer this went on, the less likely it was that she was just imagining the threat.

The two men kept a determined pace, shouldering through the thick crowd, careful to maintain a safe distance of about fifteen feet at all times. Maybe they thought that if they didn't get too close, Faith wouldn't notice them. Or maybe it was really just a coincidence. While not usually suspicious of others, Faith couldn't ignore the fact that they kept popping up in each of the clubs that she and her friends visited that night. And there was something about their lewd glares and hungry expressions that kept triggering the silent alarm in her head.

"Everything okay?" It was Alicia's voice that snapped her attention away from the possible stalkers. She had to yell to be heard over the roar of a thousand simultaneous conversations going on around them. Faith had been trying not to burden her friends with what she hoped was nothing more than her own paranoia, but a lull in their chattering about the night's escapades had given them opportunity to notice that she had withdrawn from the conversation.

Faith bit her lip. "Those two guys back there are watching us."

"Where?"

Alicia and Stephanie both looked back, and Faith pointed them out.

The two guys were college age, but any suggestion of a higher education ended there. One was noticeably shorter than the other, clad in an oversized basketball jersey with his eyes almost invisible beneath the visor of a baseball cap pulled low atop his head. The taller one had greasy black hair that fell to the shoulders of his stained wife-beater shirt. Despite the superficial differences in attire and body type, they both had the same hollow gazes and walked with the same kind of unimpressed detachment.

Alicia didn't look particularly troubled.

"I'd be watching us too, if I were them. Taking a good look at this." She gestured to her own body and laughed. "I'll be more concerned when guys *stop* looking at me."

"Amen to that," Stephanie chimed in.

Faith sighed. "I guess. It's just that, I keep seeing them. I think they've been sticking close to us all night."

"Probably because they're too afraid to actually come up and talk to us. Guys their age shouldn't still be scared of girls. Their loss."

So the predicament that had been bothering Faith all night became just another topic for her two friends to joke around about. She pondered over this for a while. Either she was too uptight, or they were too nonchalant. It was probably a little bit of both, but there was no denying that people had been telling her that she was an excessive worrier for pretty much her entire life. The irony there was that she kept a lot of the big stuff bottled up, so the people telling her this only knew the half of it. Which led to a troubling thought: if sharing only half of her worries was enough to make people think she might be neurotic, then she must *really* have a problem. Which was itself one more thing for her to worry about.

Alicia tapped her shoulder and pointed ahead. "Now, these are the guys you really need to be worried about. Get ready, girls, we're going to hell!"

Centered in the street so that the wandering pedestrians and intoxicated tourists were forced to go around, were three street preachers clad in impeccably pressed business suits and carrying signs warning of the impending apocalypse. One of them, whom Faith took to be the leader for no other reason than because he was the one in the middle and because he had the bullhorn, was screaming, red-faced, at the crowd. Sweat dripped freely from his brow.

"Repent, ye sinners! Repent! You bring fire and condemnation upon yourselves! Turn from your wicked ways! Thou shalt not get drunk on wine!"

"Good thing we weren't drinking wine," Stephanie called to her friends, prompting Alicia to crack up laughing. Even Faith had to shake her head. How did these guys expect anybody to take them seriously, making a spectacle of themselves and hurling insults at people?

One of the three was noticeably younger than his companions, in his mid-twenties like her, and seemed a little embarrassed to be out there. Maybe this one had some sense. Could he be a first timer? He was actually kind of cute, in a traditional, old-fashioned kind of way, with wavy black hair that curled over his forehead and an olive complexion that helped emphasize his dimples. He looked like he must have some Italian in his blood.

While Faith was still studying the young street preacher, his gaze locked onto hers. For a moment she found herself transfixed by his gaze. As her path brought her closer to him, he visibly cleared his throat, and she had no trouble hearing what he said to her.

"My friend's a loud-mouthed baboon, isn't he?"

Caught off guard, she paused and laughed whole-heartedly. Alicia and Stephanie kept moving, unaware that she had stopped.

"Why are you out here, if you feel that way?" she yelled over the crowd.

He looked over his shoulder at the ringleader and then back at her. "I thought we might come out here and do some good. I wasn't prepared for this, though. This isn't doing anybody any good."

"So it is your first time? I suspected as much."

"And last. People need to know how much God loves them, and that we all need his grace in our lives. Each one of us. No one person is any more or any less a sinner than any other. But this isn't the way to get that message across."

Someone grabbed Faith's hand, and her first thought was that one of those two strangers from the clubs was attacking her. A startled cry almost erupted from her throat, but she reined it in somehow. It turned out to just be Alicia, who had come back for her.

"Come on, sweetie," Alicia said. She then turned to the young street preacher. "Peddle your hatred somewhere else, bigot!"

She pulled Faith along, and all Faith could think as she followed her friend was that the poor guy hadn't struck her as being the least bit hateful. She wanted to stick up for him, but she was still confused by his words, which had not at all been consistent with what she had expected him to say to her. As the gap between Faith and the preacher widened, and just before his face became lost to her amidst the crowd, she mouthed the words, *Good luck*.

He smiled and then she saw him no more.

"Bourbon Street," Stephanie said. "Where else can you listen to a sermon, buy a beer, and witness public nudity all at the same time?"

Around them, the sights and sounds of the New Orleans night-life rained down on the girls. The city just refused to sleep, as did the people who wandered its streets, undeterred by the early pre-dawn hour. Signs hung above doors or on the outside walls of establishments, proclaiming live music, two-for-one specials, the cheapest booze in town, the best in nude entertainment, or some combination thereof. Music erupted from strategically placed speakers facing the street. Revelers on the overhead balconies screamed, sipped alcohol, and tossed beads down below to the people walking by. The scents of perfume, body sweat, and stale urine mingled in the air to give the area what Stephanie liked to call "that sweet Bourbon Street smell."

Occasionally the girls had to redirect their path in order to avoid the strange-colored puddles that seemed to be everywhere. She didn't even want to know what they were.

"Ladies drink free! Ladies drink free!" a hawker called from a doorway.

The crowd moved with a sort of rigid fluidity, a meandering conglomeration of bodies that could form an impenetrable wall one second, and the next, an unassailable tidal surge that pushed you along whether you wanted to move or not. So many people packed into such a small space on the narrow boulevard that sometimes it was difficult to tell where one inebriated tourist ended and the next began. How much money had changed hands in the past hour along this strip? And for what? Booze that would create a temporary buzz and then wear off? She wondered how many starving children had died today in places like Uganda or Kenya.

Faith realized that Alicia was still complaining about the street preachers. She was glad she had missed most of the rant. By the looks of it, Alicia was really working herself up.

"The nerve, telling me I'm a sinner! If I've said it once, I've said it a million times, there's no such thing as sin! We die, and that's it. If there was a God, he would have zapped Bourbon Street off the face of the earth years ago."

It occurred to Faith that Alicia was evangelizing her atheist outlook on life with the same passion and intensity with which the loud-mouthed street preacher had shared his. She chose not to point this out. Sometimes you just needed to let Alicia go and hope that she would eventually get sick of hearing herself.

A young, good-looking guy with bulging biceps walked past, going the other way, and grinned deliciously at Alicia. He didn't even glance at Faith, and she felt a stab of guilt over the surge of envy that came over her. Why should that bother her? She was getting married next week, and shouldn't care if other guys looked at her like that. Maybe Alicia was curvier and tended to expose more skin, but Faith was no slouch. Blonde and well-proportioned, with the tight agile body of a tennis player, she should be the one getting the looks.

But maybe not all attention was good. Those strangers at the club had been watching her, and it gave her the creeps.

"Honey," Stephanie said, leaning close so that their faces were only inches apart. The aroma of Peppermint Schnapps hung heavy on her breath and her concealer did little to hide the pimple bubbling to the surface on her forehead. "You sure you don't want a ride home?"

The thought of climbing into Stephanie's dirty Honda Civic, of sitting on discarded candy wrappers and empty Burger King cups, was almost more than she could bear.

"I think I'll walk," Faith said. "My place is only ten minutes from here."

"I know that, silly. But why walk when you can ride?"

They badgered Faith and forced her to decline Stephanie's offer at least a dozen more times, but at long last they relented and hugged and kissed their good-byes. A moment later, Faith was walking by herself, alone in the crowd, with only her thoughts for company, and these taking on an increasingly somber note.

She never should have allowed Alicia and Stephanie to drag her out of the house in the first place. Of course, they had thrown the wedding in her face, telling her that since she was so stressed out with wedding planning, that she owed it to herself to take a night off and enjoy a relaxing, stress-free evening. She recalled too late that there was nothing peaceful or relaxing about staggering around the French Quarter, dodging drunks and puddles of vomit, and fending off the groping hands of tipsy out-of-towners.

She turned left at Royal Street and was grateful to be putting some distance between herself and the mob. Immediately, the noise of the crowd began to fade into more of a background din than the all-encompassing roar it had been just a few moments before.

A plump gray rat raced across her path, scampering along on tiny padded feet. It hissed at her and she stopped short with a startled gasp. The rodent ran along and vanished into the shadows beneath a dumpster. She cut a wide arc around that dumpster as she went by, being very careful not to pass too close. Laughter erupted from somewhere behind her, causing the hairs at the base of her neck to prickle. She knew what she would find when she looked back.

Her two stalkers were half a block behind, still leering, still muttering to one another.

She quickened her pace as a chill took hold deep in her bones. Her heart thundered against her chest. She wondered at the startled whimper that reached her ears, until she realized it came from her own throat. She tried reasoning with herself. The strangers probably meant no harm. It might be just a coincidence that they turned down the same street that she did. They might even subject her to some rude comments and suggestions, but surely that would be the worst they would do. She told herself these things and many others, but none of it helped.

Ahead, the three spires of St. Louis Cathedral were just visible in the distance, thrusting upward like so many spears into the belly of the night. The sky that served as backdrop was a deep black, the color of a death shroud, and the soft glow of moonlight that shone down did little to brighten the scene.

She darted one block, then another. A loose strand of hair fell across her right eye, and she tucked it back with a trembling hand. The rapid patter of her pursuers' footfalls told her that they were still coming, and had sped up to keep pace with her.

"Hey, baby, where you off to?"

She did not respond.

"Slow down, honey. We need to talk to you."

A heavy hand fell on her shoulder. She jerked free from its grasp and tried to run, but then one of the men seized her upper arm and spun her around to face them.

"Damn lady, easy, you got us all out of breath." The one who grabbed her was the one in the basketball jersey. He was breathing heavily. His friend in the wifebeater was in slightly better shape.

"Please don't touch me," Faith said, and pulled her arm out of

Jersey's grasp.

"A fighter." Wifebeater snickered.

She took in her surroundings. The nearest pedestrian was a block away, moving in the opposite direction. Only the darkened windows of antique shops and art galleries surrounded them, which had all closed for the evening hours ago. For all intents and purposes, she was alone. But there was no need to panic yet. Like persistent telemarketers, these guys might just need to be told no a few times before they moved along.

"We thought maybe we could keep you company, tonight," Jersey said. His flesh was pale and moist, his eyes glassy. A scar meandered down his left cheek like a cracked riverbed.

"I'm not interested. Please let me be." Faith turned to go. Her back was to the men when Jersey made the unfortunate mistake of grabbing her arm again. His fingers dug deep into her flesh, hurting her.

"You can't just walk away from us."

"And you can't say I didn't ask nicely." Faith used her free arm, judging where the creep's face should be, and lashed out with her elbow. There was a pop, like the sharp crack of a twig snapping. She felt his nose crunch under the blow, and she thrilled at the hapless whimper that came out of him, like a wounded dog.

She spun on her heel to face them. Jersey was grasping at his ruined nose, blood seeping from between clenched fingers. Wifebeater's eyes were glued to his wounded friend. That was all the opening Faith needed. She mustered as much force into the kick as she could, and her foot sailed true, burying itself in the sensitive unprotected spot where his legs joined together. He howled in pain, clutched at his jewels, and fell over onto his side. She had never kicked a man quite so hard in that spot before, but she found satisfaction in it.

This seemed like as good a time as any to get out of there, so she turned and ran. She didn't want to risk going around them to rejoin the Bourbon Street crowd, so she took off in the direction she had previously been headed, putting distance between herself and the two men. Surely they had learned their lesson, and would not bother her again.

But a moment later she heard a howl of rage, followed by the unmistakable pounding of heavy feet on asphalt, and Faith knew the chase was on. She would not play the hapless female victim who needs to be rescued. She would avoid them if she could, beat up on them a little more if she must, but she would not scream.

The rear façade of St. Louis Cathedral was coming up fast, as she continued putting one foot in front of the other as quickly as she could. The cold stone walls of the building were already visible just up ahead. Moonlight filtered through the trees and shrubbery of the little garden nestled at the back of the church, turning them into skeletal wraiths that danced and rustled in the soft breeze.

A narrow little path wound alongside the cathedral, hemmed in between the church on one side and the old museum on the other. Locals referred to this claustrophobic track as Pirate Alley, rumored to have been a favorite hangout of the pirate Jean Lafitte and his band of outlaws in a bygone era. But if she understood her history, the entrance to the Old Spanish Dungeon had been right around here. Would a group of criminals really want to congregate right outside the local jail? It was something she had often wondered, but she wouldn't waste any thoughts on that now. Tonight, Pirate Alley was her shortcut to Jackson Square where there was sure to be a small crowd, even at this hour of the night. Her attackers would be forced to abandon the chase.

She did not enter the alley so much as it rose up and swallowed her. The walls were so high and they pressed so tight on either side, that the sky above was all but blocked from sight. Darkened balconies stretched out over the alley from above, pointing like accusatory fingers. The soles of her shoes *clack clacked* along the cobblestone path and echoed off the walls.

She realized a moment too late that there was a bar located right off of the alley at the spot where she entered it. Years ago William Faulkner had lived in the building, and penned his first novel there. Now people got drunk there. In her haste she sprinted right on by, and since she didn't dare turn around and run back toward her pursuers for the safety of the bar, she would have to just stick to her original plan.

Her eyes settled on the lone street lamp that marked the approximate midpoint of the alley. Even this was famous, a landmark in its own right, appearing in much New Orleans-themed artwork and photographs. Now it called to her in the dark, like a beacon, signaling her forward.

Had she been paying more attention to where she placed her feet, she might not have tripped.

What she failed to take into account was the narrow defile running down the center of the alley, an old-fashioned French-style drain that carried rainwater away from the gutters of the surrounding buildings. It wasn't particularly wide or deep, but in the darkness the little trench all but sprouted fingers and clutched her foot as she rushed along the alley.

Faith's head slammed into the cold metal pole of the streetlamp on her way down. Her vision exploded in a firework display of lights and colors, and her ankle protested sharply and burned where she had twisted it. She sprawled across the path, feeling the murky wetness of the rust-colored sludge that seeped into her clothes from the drain. The slime assaulted her nostrils with its musty, sickly aroma laced with traces of mildew and decay.

She lay there beneath the city's most famous streetlamp for too many precious seconds, out of breath, her head throbbing, her ankle swelling.

"Got you now," one of her pursuers cackled, skidding to a stop beside her. She could not say which one it was; her vision had not yet cleared enough for her to see anything but the red glare in her skull. "We just wanted to talk to you, maybe show you a good time. You didn't have to attack us."

Attack them? Weren't they the ones who had put their hands on her?

"Looks like we got the alley all to ourselves," one of them said.

"But for how long?"

"Guess we gotta hurry then. Make her pay for what she did to my nose."

They laughed, and she hated the sound of it. Whatever they had in mind, it wasn't going to be noble, or pleasant for her to experience. If only her vision would just clear already, so she could make an attempt at self-defense. She fully intended to slam her fist into Jersey's already-broken nose the first chance she got. Whatever they accomplished, whatever they got away with here tonight, it would not come without a cost.

A hand stroked her cheek; she batted it away. Laughter rang out again. She tried to roll onto her side, but they just pushed her back over. Apparently this was some kind of a game to them.

But then she heard something else, a grating, slithery kind of noise, like something sliding toward them from the far end of the alley. Something big. The ground shook, and a sound like a small tornado whipping through the alley drowned out all other noises. She felt something like small pebbles falling down around her, striking her body and face. The ground shook with a rumble that made her think the walls were collapsing around her.

When that noise cleared, the only sound left was the retreating footsteps of her two attackers. But what had scared them off? How much danger was she in, lying here, unable to get up and defend herself?

Faith opened her eyes. Her vision slowly corrected itself, and she turned her head the other way to try to make out what had happened. A vague shape lingered nearby. Somebody standing there, maybe? It was hard to say. But as she regained her sense of sight, it became apparent that there was a person standing about twenty feet away, silhouetted by the gloom and the streetlight beyond the alley, so that all Faith could make out was an outline.

After another long, tense moment, she grasped the cold metal pole of the streetlamp with one shaking, grime-encrusted hand, and used it for stability as she pulled herself to her feet. All this time, the newest stranger made no effort to help or to hinder her.

"Thank you," she muttered.

Mocking laughter, bitter and cold, came from the stranger's mouth. "You're welcome."

Then Faith noticed the wall. It looked as though some giant beast had swiped a massive claw along the side of the cathedral, ripping away stone, and leaving a gaping sore in its place. Chunks of rock and grout littered the ground around the point of impact. What could have done that?

Then she heard that slithering noise again, as something came ever closer in the darkness. She could just discern a vaguely humanoid shape in the inky black recesses of the alley, but surely her eyes deceived her. This shape was far too large and not proportioned correctly to be a man. And it moved with a sinewy kind of grace she did not think any man could duplicate. Its features were hidden in shadows, but three tiny pinpricks of light sparkled back at her from where the thing's face should be. Its eyes, perhaps? But why three? The cold hand of terror clutched her heart even as her mind struggled to grasp what was happening.

"My pet," the stranger said, and Faith recognized the voice.

She didn't get a chance to respond, though. Another horrible wailing noise filled the alley, like that of a fighter jet breaking the sound barrier. A column of light, purple like a fresh bruise, and as wide around as a manhole cover, streaked toward her and caught her full in the chest.

The pain was excruciating. Every nerve in her body was on fire, each individual pain receptor online and flaring its indignation. The deep breath she drew scorched her lungs, and a tortured scream tried but failed to rip free from her throat.

When that moment passed, she was no longer feeling pain.

She was no longer feeling anything.

The dead husk that was once Faith Daelly would never feel anything again.

Two

The sound of a wrecking ball crashing through the front of his house roused Jake Presnall with such a start that for a moment he thought he was still dreaming. He rubbed the sleep from his eyes as his senses came back online. Not a wrecking ball. Just somebody doing his best imitation of one, and pounding on his front door with enough force to shake the pictures on the walls. His two-year old nephew was crying in the next room. The dim sunlight slanting through the window beside his bed told him it was still early. What day was it? Did he have work today?

Last night had been rough; Lucas had woken him up about every two hours, screaming his head off until Jake went to him, rocked him, and sang him back to sleep. Jake could certainly have used an extra couple hours sleep this morning, but whoever was hammering away on his door had done away with that foolish fantasy.

He maneuvered free of the twisted covers, flung them aside, and stepped out of bed. Something crunched under his foot. It turned out to be an old Froot Loop. The morsel shattered into tiny crumbs and stuck to his bare sole. Dogs liked to pee on furniture, but Lucas preferred to mark his territory by leaving little piles of snack food all over the house. At least it wasn't pretzels this time, which were surprisingly painful if they caught your foot the wrong way, or gummy bears, which felt like roach guts when they squished under his feet.

Which to tend to first? The screaming child or the person trying to take the door off its hinges?

"I'm coming, I'm coming, sheesh!" he yelled toward the front of the house as he entered the makeshift nursery that had once been his parents' bedroom. He found Lucas standing in the crib with tears and snot streaking down his face. He really needed to trade the crib in for a toddler bed, the little guy was getting big. When Lucas spotted Jake, he held out his two tiny arms.

"Uncoo!" the child shouted, squeezing more passion into that one word than William Wallace screaming for freedom in that old Mel Gibson movie. The one where that guy caught an arrow with his butt cheek. What movie was that?

"Hey, little man." Jake scooped the child out of the bed. Lucas's cries immediately died away and he rested his head on Jake's shoulder. Jake felt his soft weight and the coarse fabric of the pajama onesy, and for a moment he couldn't care less about the person beating on his door. He could smell the morning on the child, a scent he wished he could bottle and sell. You just couldn't find another aroma like that anywhere else under the heavens.

He heard the firecrackers go off in Lucas's diaper, and a different smell assaulted his nostrils.

"Toot toot," Lucas said.

Jake did not linger to reap what Lucas sowed. He crossed the living room floor, nephew in tow, trying not to notice the congealed applesauce on the wall and the milk that had apparently sat out all night on the coffee table.

He almost missed the misshapen lump under the blanket on the sofa.

"Bre!" he said, the dismay clear in his voice.

His sister did not stir. He could hear her snoring under the covers. *How long has she been here? When did she get in? Was she here when Lucas kept waking up? Did she deliberately let me tend to her kid all night?*

"You have got to be kidding me," he said under his breath as he threw open the door, at which point his blood turned cold. *Dear Lord no. Not Phil. Anyone but Phil Latham.*

"Hi-ya, Phil," he said, throwing as much fake cheer into his tone as he could. *Kill me.* "My, you're looking exceptionally handsome today! Did you finally get your new knee?"

The impish little man on Jake's porch stared up at him with his pickled face and beady eyes. His few remaining wisps of gray hair pointed every direction at once, like an unruly crowd fleeing a bomb threat. Phil stood just shy of five feet, about a foot shorter than Jake, but compensated for his reduced height with sheer tenacity and a heightened skill in the art of aggravation.

And the wheezing. Every time he sucked in a labored breath, it sounded like a Chihuahua trying to regurgitate a T-Rex's thigh bone. For as long as Jake could recall, the old man was just one startled gasp away from death, but so far, Jake had not been that lucky.

Phil pointed one crooked, gnarled finger at Jake's chest. "Young man, if you don't turn down that fragging music right now, I swear by all that is holy, I am going to go home, get my bayonet from the war, and stab you to death with it, you little scrap of crap!"

"Wow, Phil," Jake said. "That was so... descriptive." *Fragging?*

Another drawn out wheeze. The old man's breath smelled like liver cheese rubbed down with bathroom disinfectant. "Don't play coy with me, you square. Turn the music down."

"Which one?"

"What?"

"Which war were you in?"

"You trying to be funny?"

"Come on, Phil, tell me. Vietnam? Korea? The Third Holy Crusade?"

Phil threw up a middle finger. "Climb it, Tarzan! Now turn it down or I'm calling the cops!"

"Wait a minute," Jake said. "Which is it? Death by bayonet or a phone call to the cops?"

"Are you being a smart ass?"

"Heavens no, I'm just confused. You just made two entirely different threats. Am I going to die at the business end of your military rifle, or bent over some prison cot with Bubba's socks stuffed in my mouth?"

Jake thrilled at the furious glare that last comment earned him, even as it became evident that Phil had no idea what he was talking about. In the silence that followed, Jake realized that his joke had sailed right over Phil's head, taken orbit, and was last seen just off the coast of Nova Scotia leaving the atmosphere. He sighed. He hated wasting good jokes on people with no sense of humor. It was such a squandering of resources. Sometimes he almost regretted being so freaking funny.

"Look, Phil, I just woke up, and I'm not playing any music. I can't even hear any music. I think you have your hearing aids turned up too loud."

"I don't believe you."

"I don't care." And at that, Jake slammed the door in his face, for all the good it did him. He could still hear the imp wheezing out there. Normally, he would not be so rude as to slam a door in someone's face, but Phil Latham was not human, so it didn't count. Jake had bought a Bible once, just to flip it to the Book of Revelation and see if any of the prophecies about the coming of the antichrist might apply to Phil. The jury was still out on that one.

When Jake turned, Bre was sitting up on the sofa, grinning at him.

"Good show," she said, clapping. "I loved the line about the prison socks."

"I aim to impress," he said, walking right by her. "Have you been here very long? Did you hear your son crying last night?"

"Well sure," she called after him, "but you were doing such a good job with him, I figured I should leave you to it."

He ignored her and went back into the nursery. Lucas hugged him tightly and Jake wondered, for the briefest of moments, if he would ever have a child of his own. He figured there would probably need to be a girl in that equation somewhere, which made it pretty unlikely. Either way, this wasn't how he had seen his life turning out by the age of twenty-eight.

He laid the child down on the changing table. With two experienced strokes he peeled away the adhesive strips that secured the child's diaper in place. He went about the task of cleaning, drying, powdering, and securing a new diaper to the kid's bottom in less time than it took an Olympic athlete to swim a fifty.

He cradled Lucas in one arm as he went back into the kitchen and swung open the pantry door to look inside. Ever since Bre had gotten into the habit of leaving Lucas in his care for extended periods of time, which started about two seconds after the kid was born, Jake had taken to stocking up and being prepared. He perused the shelves.

"How about an apple sauce while I scramble you up an egg?" he said to Lucas.

"Want eat," Lucas said, in that munchkin voice that all toddlers possessed.

Jake placed the child in a booster seat at the table. He grabbed an applesauce, three plates, two forks, and a spoon. He gave Lucas the spoon and the applesauce and set out the plates and forks. Bre plopped into a seat across from her son, who still had not acknowledged her presence. Her hair, at one time as fair and blonde as Jake's own, was now dyed a soft shade of blue, like under-ripe blueberries, with bangs that slanted across her forehead at an angle. A mild hangover left her with heavy lids, puffy eyes, and last night's mascara smeared across her face. She looked like a Lindsay Lohan mug shot.

Jake cooked breakfast for all of them, making sure to sprinkle shredded cheese over the scrambled eggs so it would melt atop them, just the way Lucas liked it. Then he divided the cheesy eggs amongst the three plates, slid one to Lucas, one to Bre, and kept one for himself. He sat next to his nephew.

"Just like your grandma used to make for me," Jake said to Lucas.

"Needs salt," Bre said, after one bite.

"You know, my mom was the best breakfast cook in the whole world," Jake announced. Lucas flung a piece of scrambled egg that hit him square in the forehead. "Great, I think you got egg in my hair."

"Too bad he never got to meet them," Bre said. Jake could only nod. And was that actual emotion in her voice?

Jake glanced off to his right. The kitchen adjoined the living room, with an extra-wide arch connecting the two rooms. Across the way, an old family portrait hung on a nail over the sofa. It slanted a little; Jake straightened it almost every day, but it always went crooked again.

In the picture, a teenaged Jake and an even younger Bre huddled in City Park at the base of one of its famed giant oaks. Their parents were in the picture with them. They were all smiling, even Bre, who would not smile again for years after the accident. In the shot, his sister still looked like a respectable girl, unlike the specimen across the table from him now who had likely struggled for hours to squeeze into a halter top that fit her like sausage casing. Jake stared at the image of his parents, wishing, and not for the first time, that he could just step through that portrait into a world where his mother and father still lived and walked and worked and laughed.

Jake had never been able to stomach the thought of moving into their old bedroom himself, even after he inherited the house. But he had no qualms about setting the room up as a nursery for Lucas. It just seemed right, like it brought him closer to the grandparents he never knew.

"...should have been there last night," Bre was saying. Jake had no idea how much of her rant he missed. "You remember Candace, right?"

He nodded. How could he forget? Once upon a time Jake tried to hit on Bre's best friend. Rumor had it she was the easiest girl in New Orleans. Either that rumor was false or Jake needed a new mouthwash. The fallout from the incident provided Bre with an infinite arsenal of bad jokes to hang over his head.

"Well," she continued. "There was this big blowup, right? Amy texted her with this picture of Josh out in the quarter with another girl, but Josh said she was just trying to set him up because she was still mad about what happened at prom. At this point, I'm like, grow up already. That was like, what, five years ago? So Amy went and--"

Jake held out a hand to stop her. "Whoa there, cowgirl. It's too early for me to follow along with these Jersey Shore politics that go on with your friends."

"Least I have friends," Bre said. "You got any coffee?"

"I have friends."

"Yeah whatever. Coffee?"

"Not till I get to the grocery."

She snorted. "What's keeping you?"

"I'll get around to it, but right now I'm babysitting eight days a week."

"Very funny. I'll have you know--"

"Toot toot!" Lucas bellowed, and a loud fart ripped out of him. They both looked at the toddler, whose grin turned into a scowl. "Uh oh, Uncoo. Poo poo come out."

Jake looked at his sister. "You want the honors?"

"I believe he asked for you."

He huffed and puffed and went to change the child's diaper.

* * *

Later, after he had dressed for work, gelled his hair, and set off for his Friday morning commute, he sat in his car replaying their last conversation and thinking up all the snappy comebacks he could have used on Bre to get her to change the diaper herself.

He made his usual Friday morning pit stop at the Cajun Confectionary. The corner bakery was a staple in Mid-City New Orleans, probably having stood there since before the first colonists arrived in the New World. A wide picture window fronted the store, and you could stand there on the sidewalk and watch a huge silver machine that looked like something out of an old science fiction movie stretch out and press large batches of taffy. The smell of freshly baked doughnuts and hot fudge blanketed the vicinity like a protective cloak.

An impossibly tall black man loitered on the sidewalk near the bakery's entrance, one foot propped up on a newspaper dispenser machine, like he was waiting for somebody. He stood seven feet tall if he stood an inch, but he was all flesh and bones, just a beanpole in baggy jeans. His thin face framed a set of eyes that darted everywhere at once, and he studied Jake as he approached. An uneasy feeling settled in Jake's stomach when he passed him.

"Must suck for you," Jake said, as he walked past.

"What does?"

"Having all the old ladies at Wal-Mart asking you to reach stuff off the top shelves for them."

The man scowled at him and then went back to studying the area. Jake had forgotten all about him by the time he entered the shop. The first thing he noticed was that the wrong person was behind the counter. At first he paid no mind to this. Then he heard the bad news.

"What do you mean you're all out of pralines?"

Jake looked at his watch. The Cajun Confectionary had been open for all of thirty minutes.

The kid on the other side of the counter, whose name tag identified him as Adam, merely shrugged and did his best imitation of an apologetic expression. "Sorry."

"Can you check in the back or something?"

"We put them all out in front this morning. Some lady came through as soon as we opened and bought every last one."

Jake didn't want to give him a hard time. He probably got that enough at whatever college he attended. Hair full of grease and face full of acne, Adam probably hadn't won too many popularity points in high school either. A folded up magazine rested on the counter near the guy's elbow, depicting the image of a knight in full armor, sword raised high, a dragon in the background, and fire billowing all around. Adam fidgeted and kept glancing down at the book, clearly itching to get back to his reading.

"Maybe you could try a danish, those are good," Adam suggested.

"It can't be a danish. It has to be a Cajun Confectionary caramel pecan double raisin praline."

"Well, we don't have any more," Adam replied. He said it slowly, in the same voice Jake would have used if he had been trying to explain trigonometry to Lucas.

"Where's Fay, anyway?" Jake said. Adam shrugged. "She's usually the one that's here on Fridays."

Adam made a face. "She didn't show up today."

"You mean she called in sick?"

"No, I mean she just didn't show up. Boss called me to fill in. He's not happy."

That was strange. Fay struck him as being more responsible than that. She always had all of her ducks in a row, and took her job very seriously, pointless as it was.

"Fay knows I come in here every Friday. She would have saved me some pralines."

"Such is life," Adam said, probably not meaning it to sound as harsh as it came out.

Jake's eyes soaked in the sights behind the display counter. There were doughnuts, cheesecake bites, brownies, petits fours, more varieties of cake than he knew existed, cannolis, and assorted flavored fudge, but he just couldn't get excited for any of that. To settle for such would be tantamount to failure.

He perused the baked goods a moment longer, gave up on it, and then a thought struck him. "Has anybody gone to check on her?"

"Check on who?"

Jake tried not to roll his eyes. "Santa Claus."

"Why would we send someone to--"

"I was being sarcastic. Fay. Has anybody been by to check on Fay?"

Adam just shrugged, and his eyes darted down to the folded up magazine on the counter. If Jake did not get out of here soon, the poor loser was likely to start showing symptoms of withdrawal. Far be it for Jake to keep a nerd from his nerdiness.

"You know what, I'll just call her," Jake said.

"You have her number?" Adam grinned.

"It's not like that, perv." He reached into his pocket and grabbed for his phone, but found his pocket empty. "Oh, no. I forgot my phone at home again."

"How will you ever survive?"

He turned to go, wondering if he had time to race home and get his phone before he showed up at work. He checked his watch. No way. He was already running late, and he couldn't afford to be any later. He sighed and stalked toward the door. *This is really shaping up to be one crummy day.*

"Hey, check it out," Adam called after him.

Jake turned. The youth was holding up a single cellophane-wrapped item. "Is that what I think it is?" When Adam nodded his head in the affirmative, Jake felt the thrill of victory. A praline.

"Must have gotten loose and slipped behind the cannolis," Adam said. "You want it?"

"Ring me up."

Things are definitely looking up. Maybe today won't be such a bad day after all.

He had already forgotten about the tall stranger outside, who had not moved.

Three

By the time Homicide Detective Lester Rivera Junior arrived on the scene, two crowds had already formed, one at each end of the alley. Yellow crime scene tape blocked access to both the Royal Street and Chartres Street entrances of Pirate Alley, while a wall of uniformed officers at each location attempted to prevent any onlookers from getting too close or getting too good a look at what was going on.

Like Moses himself, the sea of officers parted and allowed Rivera through. The Medical Examiner awaited him just on the other side. The man cleared his throat when Rivera approached.

"What are we looking at?" Rivera said.

"You sure you want to see this? It's pretty nasty today."

Rivera sighed. "You're right. I'll just go home now and turn down my next paycheck."

"Like you'd miss it." It was probably meant as a joke, but Rivera was not in a laughing mood. He just fixed his eyes on the rotund little man. His name was Wally Perkins, and Rivera did not particularly like working with him. For one thing, he was so short that Rivera had to look almost straight down just to make eye contact, and when he did look down, it was the man's bulging gut that demanded the most attention. His hairline had long ago receded, leaving only tufts of reddish brown hair on the sides of his head. All told, Perkins did not paint a very convincing picture of bureau competence, which to Rivera was the ultimate sin.

Perkins realized that Rivera was not amused. He cleared his throat, and gestured behind him. "Tough room, I guess. This way."

Rivera followed Perkins deeper into the alley.

A few scattered rays of early morning sunshine penetrated the enclosed space, but the cold stone walls on either side of him drank in the soft glow and bathed the scene in a somber gray haze. Rivera was a thick-set bull of a man. He wasn't hitting the gym regularly anymore, and so his muscles had softened somewhat, but what he still had was more than enough to make most people think twice before messing with him. His shaved head and full mustache always seemed to conjure images of bar fights. When all was said and done, Rivera was a man who was more accustomed to causing fear than to feeling it.

Even still, Pirate Alley gave him the creeps.

Perkins led him to a sheet-covered lump sprawled across their path. Near the corpse, a huge chunk was missing out of one of the walls of St. Louis Cathedral, and rubble was strewn about the alley floor. The edges of the crater bore the singed look of something burnt.

"What's that smell?" he asked as they approached.

Perkins snickered. "We haven't identified it yet, but it's definitely coming from the corpse. A sulfurous kind of aroma, I'd say." He inhaled deeply as if to solve the mystery once and for all. The thought of inhaling corpse-stink made Rivera's skin crawl. But it did smell sulfurous, Perkins was right about that, an acrid stench that reeked of New Year's Eve and expended fireworks, and it only grew stronger as they approached. When they stopped, Royal Street loomed ahead and St. Anthony Park was just off to their right.

"Everything documented?" Rivera asked. He was looking around at the crime scene techs, who were darting to and fro, some with cameras, some with notebooks, meticulously documenting every object, every angle.

Perkins nodded. "We got everything we need. It's all yours now."

"Let's see it then."

Perkins pulled back the sheet.

There were days when Rivera just knew that becoming a homicide detective would prove to be his undoing. It was bad enough that he spent his days looking over the scenes of grisly murders and interviewing low-life scumbags, but lately he had been noticing that his faith in humanity had become yet another casualty in the war on crime. It was getting to where he was pretty sure that given the right motive or opportunity, there was nothing that human beings were not capable of.

Not a very pretty thought.

And what he saw beneath that sheet only reinforced his disdain.

The girl had been young and pretty at one time. It was hard to find any beauty in what he saw sprawled across the cobblestone path, however. Her face was clean enough, if you could somehow overlook the expression of pure terror forever captured in the sightlessly staring eyes and curled lips. Her mouth was frozen in a sneer, like she had died with a scream about to rip from her throat. Judging by the look of the rest of her body, it was pretty clear she had a lot to scream about. The little clothing she wore looked like it had gone through a fire, most of it having burnt away, leaving her all but naked. The skin of her chest and stomach was dark, shriveled, and cracked in several places; the meat that peeked through looked a lot like overcooked pork.

"Crazy, huh?" Perkins said.

"What am I looking at?" Rivera finally blurted. Maybe if his diminutive guide corroborated what he was seeing it would not seem like an illusion.

Perkins gestured to the center of the victim's torso. "Just what it looks like. Victim suffered from advanced tissue necrosis resulting from deep thermal trauma to the ventral cavity."

Rivera could have choked the man. "Maybe you missed the part where I didn't go to medical school."

The little man giggled, a surprisingly girlish sound. "Sorry. I forget myself sometimes. The victim received a severe burn injury to her middle torso. It not only killed her, but seems to have completely dried out the tissues, like she was left too long in a hot oven."

To demonstrate his point, Perkins rapped one gloved knuckle on the victim's torso. It produced a hollow clicking noise, like the drumming of fingernails on plastic, not at all the sound one would expect when thumping a human chest.

"What could have done this?" Rivera said.

Perkins cleared his throat again. Each time he did that, it was more annoying than the last. "We actually have not figured that out yet."

"Of course not. What about that hole in the wall?"

"Well, you may have noticed that the rubble on the alley floor is charred, and the perimeter of the hole is blackened as well." Rivera nodded; he had noticed this as well. "In most cases, a fire or explosion would have produced more widespread damage, and there would be other evidence, such as shrapnel, more spread out."

"But?"

"But this is nothing like that. It bears the mark of a more focused, localized kind of blast. If this were a science fiction movie, I might think this was the work of some kind of heat ray."

"A heat ray. I'll be sure to put that in my report. Do we have an ID yet?" Rivera asked.

Perkins gestured to one of the nearby crime scene investigators who happened to be holding a small red handbag. "Will?"

The tech stepped forward. Perkins introduced him. "This is Will. One of the best guys I've got. We plucked him right out of the air force, servicing jets and air bombers. You'd be surprised how often that kind of technical know-how can come in handy on some of our cases."

Rivera observed the young man before him. He stood a good foot shorter than Rivera, with short-cropped hair, black-rimmed glasses, and the hint of stubble on his face that would need to be shaved soon.

"I'll take your word for it," Rivera said. He gestured to the handbag. "Did that belong to the victim?"

"We think so," Perkins said. "It was found a few feet away from the body."

Will handed a small sliver of plastic to Rivera. It was a State of Louisiana driver's license.

"Cash and credit cards are present," Will said. "The killer wasn't interested in robbing her."

"Faith Daelly," Rivera read from the driver's license. Overhead the sun began to show itself more fully and a sudden gust of heat was already sweeping through the alley. Rivera felt a flush around his neck, and the beginnings of perspiration at his brow. "We'll need to work up a full profile, find out what we can about her and how this might have happened. Witnesses?"

The examiner shook his head in the negative. "There were some old drunks sitting out by Jackson Square said they heard a loud sound, like a tornado, ripping through the alley."

"Like a tornado?"

"Their words, not mine."

"Are they still around?"

"We gave them coffee and donuts. They're not going anywhere."

"I'll need to talk to them."

"Of course."

Rivera clicked his tongue. "Do we have a time of death yet? Or know what time they heard this *tornado?*"

Perkins grimaced. "Hard to say. Their perceptions of time don't seem to coincide with ours, to put it as mildly and politely as I can. Not long, though. Maybe four or five AM. They don't know what time they heard the noise, just that they heard it. Said they didn't pay much mind to it at first. Not until somebody found the body and police started showing up."

Rivera gaped. "So they heard what sounded to them like a tornado in the alley and never bothered to check it out?"

Perkins shrugged. "You have to understand, they live out here. They see and hear all kinds of craziness, every day. One lady said she woke up the other night to some guy making out with a mop. She said he'd just rounded second base and was heading for- -"

Rivera cut him off. "Any idea from the state of the body what time she might have died, then?" He really did not want to hear about the nocturnal mating rituals of the New Orleans homeless.

"Never seen a body that looked like this before. We can't really tell out here. Maybe once we get it back to the lab, run some tests."

"The handle or the head?" Will said.

Perkins just looked at him dumbly. "What?"

"Which end of the mop was he making out with? The handle or the head?"

Rivera sighed. "I'll want the results of those tests as soon as possible."

"Of course," Perkins said.

"She didn't die before Eleven PM," Will chimed in.

"Oh yeah?" Rivera turned his gaze back to the tech, who showed him a cell phone.

"This was in her bag. Looks like she made three phone calls to the same number last night. The last one was at Eleven PM."

"That doesn't really narrow the window a whole lot," Rivera said. He gestured for the phone. Will handed it to him. He scrolled through the recent call log, noting that she had in fact made three calls very close together the previous evening. Her address book listed the contact name "JAKE" but with no last name. No matter, he had this Jake's phone number and could trace him down easily enough with the resources at his disposal.

"I think I'd like to talk to those witnesses now," Rivera said.

Perkins nodded to another technician who had been standing silently throughout the duration of the conversation. The other man placed the sheet back over Faith Daelly. A disappointed sigh rose from the nearest crowd. Rivera gritted his teeth and looked across at all those excited loiterers, some with smart phones held high to try to catch video footage of the scene. Was this what society had come to? These people were so concerned with other people's lives, when they should have been living their own. It disgusted him. And any one of these people could be the next corpse whose murder scene Rivera had to investigate, or even the next killer he had to bust.

These were sick, sick times he lived in.

But they kept a homicide detective employed.

The Medical Examiner led the way.

"I'll tell you one thing," he said, shaking his head. "I don't think I'll ever look at beef jerky the same way again."

Four

A human skull grinned at him. The many awards, certificates, degrees, framed magazine covers, dusty leather volumes, and medical implements hanging on walls or arranged in precise formation around the spacious office criticized, even mocked him. *Look at us,* they all said. *Look at what you will never have. Respect. Prestige.*

"Buzz off," Jake said under his breath, in response to those scoffing voices.

"What was that, Presnall?" Doctor Maurice Joseph Peter Cherry barked. Jake's boss always made it a point to use his full name whenever he introduced himself to someone. And when he was quoted in medical journals, he always insisted that the writer of the article use his full name at least once. Even the degrees and certificates stretching across the wall bore the name "Maurice J.P. Cherry, M.D., PhD." A devout Catholic, at least on Sunday mornings, Dr. Cherry insisted on giving his Confirmation name, Peter, equal weight to his middle name.

"Nothing, sir."

He had been at work for almost half a day now, and up until Dr. Cherry asked to see him in his office, he optimistically believed that his tardiness might have gone unnoticed.

Dr. Cherry favored him from behind the polished desk. His chair was made of genuine leather and when he leaned forward it creaked invitingly. He folded his smooth, hairless hands atop a spread of medical journals that bore titles and headlines that were nonsensical to Jake's untrained brain. The doctor's gray hair was parted to one side in the most

God-awful comb-over this side of Trump Plaza. "Do you enjoy being a perennial underachiever, Presnall?"

"No, sir." His pulse raced as his employer berated him. Dr. Cherry never referred to him by his first name, instead always referring to him as Presnall. It felt demeaning, which was probably why Dr. Cherry favored the technique.

"Then why do you constantly put me in this position to have to speak to you as such?"

There was no satisfactory answer to that question. Jake knew that Dr. Cherry enjoyed the act of making subordinates feel subordinate.

"You have a simple job here," Dr. Cherry continued. "Get here on time. Drive around. Pick up blood samples. Deliver said samples to the lab for testing. Fax results. Fill in with lab work when required. I could train my dog to do your job, yet I pay you to do it." He fixed his squirrel-colored eyes on Jake, sized him up, found him lacking. That one simple gaze possessed a certain ruefulness, as though he were chastising himself for ever expecting anything of Jake in the first place.

Not all doctors were pretentious. Jake knew that. And it was entirely possible that Dr. Cherry had made life better for hundreds, maybe even thousands of patients throughout his career. But he also knew that the man had left a slew of broken and defeated nurses, medical assistants, lab techs, interns, and residents in his wake who would love nothing more than to shove the man's stethoscope right up his--

"Are you paying attention, Presnall?" Dr. Cherry's grating voice snapped him out of his reverie.

"Yes sir."

The doctor rattled on. "You are skating on thin ice here. If you can't perform your duties efficiently and in a timely manner than someone else will. Are we understood?"

"Yes sir."

"If you give me any more reasons to fire you, I may do just that."

"Yes sir."

Somebody knocked tentatively on the office door. "What is it?" Dr. Cherry yelled. The door opened a crack. The receptionist stuck her head in cautiously, as though afraid there was a hungry dinosaur lurking in the office. And maybe she was right. A petite brunette with adorable dimples and hair pulled back in a tight ponytail, she adopted an apologetic expression.

"Yes, Kate?"

She looked at Jake. "Visitor for you."

"For me?" Who would be visiting him at the lab? And should he apologize to Dr. Cherry for the disruption?

"It's a cop," she added.

"A cop?" Dr. Cherry eyed Jake, his expression full of disdain.

"Yes sir," she replied.

"Are you in trouble with the law and failed to disclose this to me?" He glared at Jake who shrugged and shook his head. "What was I just saying about giving me any more reasons to fire you?"

"I have no idea what this could be about," Jake said.

Dr. Cherry regarded him with no shortage of skepticism. "Get to it then," he said.

* * *

The brooding detective in the lobby would have been hard to miss, even if Jake hadn't already known he was there. He must have been pushing fifty, but his hulking frame and the fiery intensity in his eyes probably intimidated most guys half his age. A bushy mustache almost completely hid from view the grim line that served as his mouth.

"Jacob Presnall?" the detective said, upon sighting Jake. The dull reception area lights reflected off of his shaved head, and the sport coat pulled tight around his colossal shoulders looked like it would rip clean in half if he moved just right. Every muscle in his face was tensed, as though he were preparing for a sucker punch.

"Most people just call me Jake," he replied, and held out his hand.

"My name is Lester Rivera, Junior." He did not take Jake's hand or even acknowledge the gesture. For a moment, Jake felt awkward, his arm just dangling out over empty space. Finally, he dropped it back to his side. Rivera continued. "I'm a homicide detective for the New Orleans Police Department. I have some questions for you. I think we should step outside."

"What's this about? Is something wrong? Is everybody okay?" Jake said.

"I think it would be best if we stepped outside."

Jake noted the stares they were getting from the other people in the lobby. A couple of elderly women made no effort to hide their interest. A mother with a small toddler on the far side of the room was watching the exchange out of the corner of her eye while pretending to read a magazine. A guy about Jake's age, maybe a couple of years younger, twenty-six or so, was looking down at his lap, but had his head cocked at an angle to suggest he was listening attentively. The lab offered a variety of diagnostic tests and services, and these people had either been referred from neighboring clinics or perhaps just needed job-related drug screening. Which meant that they were probably very bored, and Jake did not care to serve as their afternoon entertainment.

"Okay, then. Outside," Jake agreed.

They stepped out into what was shaping up to be a blistering day. Jake's body was adjusted to the air conditioning inside the lab, which somebody kept setting to sixty-eight degrees. So as they passed through the glass double doors into the blinding glare, the heat that smacked him in the face might have been birthed from the very bowels of hell itself. Once they were alone on the sidewalk, and the door closed behind them, Rivera turned toward Jake.

"Do you know Faith Daelly?" Rivera said.

He thought about that for a moment. "No. Should I?"

Something changed in Detective Rivera's demeanor. It was subtle, but it was there. Before, he had been merely standoffish. Now there was something predatory about him that Jake did not like at all.

"So let me get this straight? You claim to have no relationship with Faith Daelly?"

"I don't think so," Jake said. He racked his brain, and still came up with nothing. The last name sounded vaguely familiar. Where had he heard it before? He certainly did not know anybody named Faith. Or did he? The detective's hard stare was making it progressively more difficult to concentrate.

"What's this about?" Jake asked again.

Rivera straightened his back, thrusting out his chest. He inhaled deeply, as if savoring a scent in the air that he found to his liking. Maybe fear.

"What were you doing last night, at approximately eleven o'clock?" Rivera said. Jake noted that Rivera had yet to actually provide any information, even though Jake had now asked twice.

"Sleeping, I guess."

"You guess?"

"Or trying to."

"Alone?"

Jake sighed. He thought about the cold spot next to him in his bed every night; it had been a very long while since anyone had filled it. Bre probably had not come in until much later.

"I had my two-year old nephew over. What does that have to do with anything?"

"Can anybody corroborate that you were at home sleeping at that time?"

Jake took a step back. "You mean, like an alibi? Wow. Is this an episode of Law and Order?"

Rivera's nostrils flared and he closed the gap between them in two bounding steps. Jake noted that he possessed a speed and grace not typical of a man of his size. They stood almost nose to nose, except that, at about six and a half feet tall, Rivera was a good six inches taller than Jake. He exhaled, his breath heavy with the reek of old coffee.

"I don't usually let people get this close on a first date," Jake said, even as his palms grew moist.

"This a joke to you?" Rivera asked.

"I just don't have any idea what you want," Jake said, "and I'm starting to feel like I just stepped into a cop show on TV. And my mouth starts running when I'm nervous. No telling what's going to come out of it."

"Do you feel like you have something to be nervous about?"

"Other than the big, hulking detective in my face? No, everything else is peaches and lollipops. Look, I was baby-sitting my nephew last night. My sister can vouch for me."

As Rivera continued to study him, Jake felt like a field mouse scurrying around under the watchful gaze of a hungry eagle.

"Faith Daelly," Rivera offered, "is the name of a murder victim that we found this morning. We believe she was killed shortly after she made three unsuccessful attempts to contact you."

"Contact me? No. There must be some mistake."

"A mistake that she called you three times in the span of an hour and had your name in her contacts?"

"Look, my phone was on silent last night, I didn't want it waking up my nephew. And I forgot it at home this morning anyway. But I never talked to any Faith Daelly last night."

"What about your name in her contacts?" Rivera asked.

"I don't know. The only person who I know for a fact that was supposed to call me last night was…" He paused for a moment. The wheels were turning. Could it be? Is that why the last name sounded familiar? "Fay."

"Fay?"

"Yeah, Fay, this girl I know. She works at the Cajun Confectionary, a bakery in Mid-City."

Rivera crossed his arms over his wrestler's chest. "You mean Faith Daelly from the Cajun Confectionary?"

It made sense. That must be why the last name sounded familiar. She must have said it once. Reality set in. Fay was Faith. And Faith was dead. His throat went dry. A cold tingle spread up his arms. Dead.

"I know her as Fay," Jake said. "I've never heard her go by the name Faith."

"So then you do know the victim?"

"I guess so."

"And you admit to speaking with her last night?"

"I never spoke to her."

"She called you three times."

"My phone was on silent. I just told you that."

"What was the nature of your relationship with Faith?"

Jake drew a breath and ran a hand along the back of his neck to wipe away some of the perspiration that gathered there. He might just as well have not bothered; fresh beads of sweat immediately replaced the ones he smeared away. The heat of the day was only part of the reason for the outburst of moisture.

"I didn't know her that well," Jake said.

"Apparently well enough that she felt comfortable calling you three times at eleven PM on a Thursday night."

Jake started fidgeting. He rubbed his fingers together. Sometimes he did that when he was thinking, as if he needed to move his body in order to focus his thoughts. He realized the gesture made him look nervous. He hoped the gesture did not also make him look guilty.

"Furniture."

"What?" Rivera raised an eyebrow.

"We were supposed to get together today and I was going to look at some furniture she was going to sell, to see if I wanted any. She's getting married." He caught himself. "Was getting married. She didn't want to move in with her fiancé until after the wedding. And she wasn't going to be needing much of her old furniture anymore."

"So your story is that she was calling you at eleven PM the night she died to talk about furniture?"

"I don't know if I like the term *story*. It makes it sound like I'm hiding something. But my *guess* is that is why she was calling me."

"Has Faith called you before last night?"

"I don't think so," he replied. "Not that I recall. I just gave her my number last week when we first talked about the recliner she wanted to sell to me."

Rivera paced the sidewalk and glanced out to passing traffic. Jake leaned against the side of the building, resting his head against the unyielding stone exterior. He tried to relax his tensed neck muscles, but it took some additional convincing from a gentle self-massage that he applied to himself with one trembling hand.

Could this be happening? Could Fay (Faith, he reminded himself) really be dead? And not just dead, but murdered? And did this detective really come to the lab to interrogate him about the case? Was he a suspect? That was downright absurd. He lived a quiet, boring life. He worked at a blood lab as a courier and tech, for crying out loud! He came home and played video games and had few friends and seldom went out. His life was not exciting in the least, had never been exciting. Sure, there had been days and nights, when the boredom of it all set in, when the relative pointlessness of his existence had come over him in a rush, that he had fantasized about being in the center of some action, of having a name people would recognize and glorify, of having something, anything, break the monotony. But a murder investigation was never the subject of his fantasies. A murder investigation was definitely not preferable to boredom.

His thoughts returned to Faith, and he felt like a jerk for standing here feeling sorry for himself. Faith was dead. Her situation sucked far worse than his did. And while he could not rightfully call her a friend, she was sweet and sincere and certainly did not deserve the fate that had befallen her. He thought of her easy smile, of her lively eyes, of the way she sometimes teased him about how he applied way too much gel when he spiked his fine, blonde hair.

"Assuming for a moment that your story checks out," Rivera said at last, returning from his impromptu stroll and no doubt choosing the word *story* because Jake had specifically said he did not care for the term, "is there anything you can tell me about Faith Daelly that you think I might find useful?"

Jake mulled that one over.

"She was getting married next week." Jake imagined the unlucky fellow somewhere who had probably, in just the past few hours, gotten the news that his fiancée had been murdered. The poor guy must be devastated. Jake had once received similar news, years ago, about his parents. His mom's best friend, a lady named Miss Jerry, who had subsequently become something of a mother to him in her own right, had been the one to have to break the news to him and Bre. It had not been a very good day for any of them.

Rivera nodded in a way to impart that he already knew about the wedding. Heck, he'd probably already spoken to the fiancé.

"She has a sister," Jake offered. "A younger sister, if I recall. I've never met her, but Fay- err, Faith, mentioned her a few times. She works at some restaurant in the Quarter. Other than that, I don't really know anything about her. I have no idea who would want to kill her."

So many lives that would be affected.

Rivera continued to stare at him. His upper lip twitched slightly. It made his mustache wobble. It seemed like there was something more he wanted to say. Instead he simply stood there with his arms folded across his chest for another moment. Then he reached into his jacket pocket, pulled out a small plastic case, and removed a business card from it.

"My card," Rivera said, eyes fixed on Jake. "If you think of anything."

Jake took the card. "Okay."

"I'm sure we'll be speaking again. Soon." Rivera dropped the case back into his pocket, flashed the most artificial smile Jake had ever seen, hopped into an unmarked sedan parked nearby, and drove off. The car was so nondescript that Jake immediately forgot what it looked like. Jake watched him go. Then he glanced back down at the business card that he still clutched in one trembling hand.

He almost failed to register the very tall black man across the street, who was trying really hard to *not* look interested in what had just transpired between Jake and the detective. When Jake looked back up, the man was gone. He couldn't have imagined it, but at the same time there was no way a person could move fast enough to have completely disappeared from view in the time that it took Jake to look down and then up again.

And as much as he would like to conclude that it had been his imagination, he knew he had seen the guy before somewhere, and recently at that. The brief glimpse left an impression in his mind's eye of someone extremely skinny, in a tight shirt and very baggy jeans.

Someone he had seen before. But where? And then it hit him. The tall man he had teased about his height.

The same man who had been waiting around outside the Cajun Confectionary.

Five

The old, busted water heater lay discarded on the curb, a terrible eyesore in an otherwise well maintained neighborhood. Garbage pickup would not come and claim it until Saturday. Rivulets of rust-colored water still seeped from the winding crack that circled its base. When Miss Jerry called him earlier that week, in a panic, Jake had rushed over to find that same rusty sludge all over her laundry room floor.

It just seemed wrong somehow. Everything eventually broke and let you down. Nothing lasted. Shouldn't something be eternal? Anything?

He wished he could be in a better mood. Was there ever a more delightful point in the week than that moment when you pull into your own driveway on Friday afternoon, all those prospects and possibilities of a weekend away from work dangling in front of you? Yet, joy eluded him this day. A voice in his head enticed him to just cross back over the street, go home, and crash on the sofa. In light of the day he'd just had, he would have been completely justified in doing exactly that. But if he didn't check on Miss Jerry, who would? Bre?

Fat chance of that ever happening.

Before proceeding to the porch, Jake hauled Miss Jerry's garbage cans to the curb and left them beside the old water heater. He also noted a screen that was hanging crooked off of one of the windows. He'd have to fix that before Monday. The front of her house could also use a good scrubbing. He wondered how expensive it might be to rent a pressure washer for a day and whether or not he had enough money in his account to cover it.

Jake climbed the steps and knocked on the door.

When the old lady answered, a wide smile spread from one side of her face to the other. A pair of spectacles dangled around her neck by a thin chain, rising and falling with each breath. Her hair, swept up in a classic bouffant reminiscent of Lady Bird Johnson, was a shade too dark to be natural. She dyed it regularly, self-conscious of the gray roots that kept rearing their ugly heads.

"Jake!"

"Hey, Miss Jerry."

It almost defied physics how somebody with such tiny arms could engulf Jake with them the way Miss Jerry did. Her head barely cleared his chest, adding that extra bit of maternal warmth to the embraces he had come to love so much. For many years after the loss of his parents, that hug was his primary solace. She was more than just an elderly neighbor to Jake; she was his second mother.

Jake stepped back and took a long, deep whiff of the scent that drifted through the open doorway. "Meatballs?"

She beamed. "Simmering on the stove. I cooked extra because I figured you'd be coming by to check on us. Missy and I were just about to sit down and eat. Would you like to join us?"

"Should I do the polite thing and pretend to decline so I don't put you out of your way?"

"You could," she teased, "but when have you ever turned down food?"

"You know me so well."

Miss Jerry backed away from the door so Jake could enter. Stepping over her threshold was like marching headlong into a more peaceful, bygone era. Most people would probably note the floral-print wallpaper in the hall, the faux-wood paneling in the living room, and the hand-knitted doilies on all the furniture, only to say that the house needed to be updated. But the decor suited Miss Jerry to a tee.

He waited for her to close the door. "Miss me?"

"Like you have to ask. Every time I use the hot water, I think of you. Thank you so much for changing that water heater for me."

He shrugged. "Nothing to it."

His chest swelled when he spotted the fifteen-year-old girl standing in the doorway to the kitchen. Missy's eyes widened at the sight of him. Her hair spiraled around her face in wide, curling locks. The fabric of the calf-length sundress she wore was the color of freshly mown springtime grass.

One glance at it evoked images of new life and fresh starts.

"Hiya, Papaya," Jake said.

Missy gushed and ran to him. She giggled like a little school girl the entire time. Although physically an adolescent, her mental age was much younger, on account of that one extra chromosome in her DNA.

Jake made sure to keep one hand behind his back, the one that clutched the little surprise he brought for this girl who had been like a second sister to him all these years.

"You have to love that exuberance," Miss Jerry said. "When she's excited to see somebody, she acts excited. Most girls her age wouldn't let you know what they're feeling for all the gold in Fort Knox."

Jake wondered if Miss Jerry was referring to his sister. He still couldn't fully comprehend why Bre never connected with her on the same level he did.

"What's behind your back?" Missy sang. Her face radiated with anticipation. Nothing got by her.

With a flourish, he brought his concealed hand forward, revealing the praline he purchased that morning from the Cajun Confectionary. Missy's eyes practically bulged out of their sockets, and she chortled again. The sound of it was light and airy, and all the innocence in the world resonated in that one simple noise. She hopped in place, up and down, up and down, then turned to her grandmother.

"Can I have it, Gram?"

"As soon as you finish supper, dear." Missy groaned. Miss Jerry shook her head and favored Jake. "I swear, it's a good thing she has you in her life. Otherwise, I don't know where the child would go to get her sugar fix."

"That's what I do. Sorry it's only one today. It was... their last one."

Miss Jerry must have read something, either on his face or in his tone of voice. She spoke slowly. "I hope you didn't go to any trouble."

"It never is any trouble."

They proceeded to the kitchen, where Jake retrieved glasses from the cupboard and poured tea for everybody while Miss Jerry dished the spaghetti and meatballs onto three plates. Next came several thick slices of buttered garlic toast, fresh from the oven, with Parmesan cheese melted right on top of them. When they were seated, Miss Jerry nodded to Jake.

"Would you say Grace for us, please?"

Truth be told, he never really saw the point, but Miss Jerry was old school, and so Jake humored her on these things. The three of them held hands. Jake led the prayer. "Bless us O Lord, and these thy gifts, which we are about to receive, from thy bounty, through Christ Our Lord. Amen."

The meatballs were heavenly. Miss Jerry would have put them on early this morning and let them simmer all day to really draw out the flavor. She also refused to cook with canned sauce, but chose instead to begin with fresh, organic tomatoes that she blanched, seasoned, stewed, and pureed to form the base of her tomato paste, which won by a landslide in her church's spaghetti cook-off a few years back. When Jake wanted pasta, he normally popped open a can of Ragu.

"How's she doing?" Jake said. He meant Missy, whose eyes never strayed from the praline that now rested on the table right next to her plate.

"Just wonderful. She's been..." She paused to address her granddaughter. "Slow down, dear. The praline isn't going anywhere." Missy paused in mid-bite with an oversized meatball engorging one whole cheek. It was a wonder she didn't dislocate her jaw. Miss Jerry turned back to Jake and continued. "I think the child is trying to choke herself. What was I saying? Oh, yes. She's been singing her Disney songs and playing with that little drumstick of hers. She waves it like a baton, directing her own imaginary orchestra."

Jake chuckled and sipped from his glass. "You make the best iced tea."

"That's because it's brewed from actual tea leaves. The day I buy a can of flavored sugar, mix it with water, and call it tea, they might as well throw me in my grave and cover me with dirt."

He wiped his mouth with the back of one hand and set the glass down. "Nah. You're going in a shrine, Miss Jerry. Or under an altar."

"Such a charmer."

"Like I said, I... Holy cow, is that what I think it is?" Jake bolted from his seat and crossed to the other side of the kitchen in order to examine more closely the object that caught the attention of his trailing eye. "How did I not notice this sooner?"

An old photograph, snapped almost twenty years ago and frayed around the edges, peeked back at him past the Pillsbury Doughboy magnet that secured it to the refrigerator.

"I found it yesterday, looking through some old boxes," Miss Jerry said.

His mind traveled two decades back in time. For his mother's fortieth birthday, Jake's father planned a surprise party for the ages. Roland Presnall rented a historic plantation house that had been refurbished as a reception hall and invited all of their closest friends and family. Jake could still see the astonished look on his mom's face when she entered that room and the assembled crowd greeted her with a loud shout. Connie Presnall, being who she was, immediately started crying of course, and everyone shared a good-natured laugh about it afterward.

The photo on Miss Jerry's refrigerator showed Jake, his parents, and Bre, who was only three or four on the night of the party, sharing a dance together. At the time, it felt like nothing in the world would ever tear the family apart. Little did they know...

"I can't believe how long it's been," he said, and returned to his seat.

"Time does have a way of trickling by," Miss Jerry agreed.

They dined in silence for the remainder of the meal. Jake's mind was still back there with his family, and Miss Jerry must have recognized this, because she did not speak to him until later, as they cleared the table. Jake gathered the plates and brought them to the sink. He turned on the faucet. Missy retreated to the living room with her praline, leaving the two of them alone.

"Good thoughts?" Miss Jerry asked tentatively, breaking the ice.

"Ma'am?"

"Are you thinking good thoughts?"

He smiled and began to rinse the plates. "I am now. That night is such a great memory for me. The whole family together. I needed that pick-me-up. It's been a rough day."

Miss Jerry retrieved the butter and placed it in the fridge. "I didn't want to say anything, but you seemed really down when I answered the door."

"Was it that obvious? I thought I did a pretty good job of covering it up."

She came to stand next to him by the sink as he scrubbed the plates with a soapy sponge. "You forget, I watched you grow up. It's not that easy to hide these things from me."

"You'd think I would know that by now."

"Is there anything you'd like to talk about?"

There was no use playing coy with her. He rinsed the plate he was holding, turned off the water, and put the sponge down. She followed his motions with a wary eye. Finally, Jake turned to face her.

"A detective came to see me at work today. A homicide detective."

"A detective? What on earth for?"

"There's this girl that works at the place where I buy the pralines. She was murdered last night."

Miss Jerry's hand went to her mouth and her eyes widened. "Heavens! I'm so sorry. Were the two of you close?"

"Not really. More like acquaintances. But I'm pretty devastated for her. She was getting married next week." Jake paused, noting the look of horror that crept into Miss Jerry's features. "The detective wanted to ask me about her, but at first I was confused, and denied knowing her, and now I think he suspects I might have had something to do with the killing."

She shook her head. "That's insane. I know you. You wouldn't do anything like that. Did you tell the detective you wouldn't do anything like that?"

"Well, sure. But I don't know if he believes me. So not only am I sad for my friend, I'm scared this cop is going to come after me."

"Nonsense. If he really thought you did something to that girl, he would have arrested you."

Jake shrugged. "I don't know. I guess so. They need evidence, right? To make an arrest?"

Miss Jerry's nostrils flared. "Don't you worry. I've got some second cousins that are lawyers. If that mean detective tries anything, we'll show him."

Jake forced a smile. The cousins she referred to practiced family law, but the sentiment was sweet, all the same. But she had a point. There was no way anything incriminating would stick to him. He was at home with Lucas all night, and, depending on what time Bre staggered in, she could corroborate that. Then again, she probably wasn't nearly sober enough at the time to be any kind of a decent alibi. He was getting too far ahead of himself, though. He was innocent. Detective Rivera, if he even thought it worth his time to investigate, would see that. This mood was probably just Jake's nerves acting up. It's not every day a homicide detective gets in your face and insinuates that you might be a murderer.

But no matter what Jake told himself, that hollow pang in his gut, the one that told him things were about to go from bad to worse, never let up.

He helped himself to another glass of tea. He sipped and made a face. That was weird. The same tea he had been raving about just a few moments ago, suddenly tasted very bitter.

Six

He would come to wonder later, had he not been so preoccupied with feeling sorry for himself, would he have sooner noticed the man following him? The sun dipped toward the horizon, casting shadows across the earth as Saturday afternoon slowly gave way to Saturday evening. A few scattered clouds hurried across the sky with no regard to the world below them, while above them the sky had become an inky blue.

Jake plodded, shoulders hunched, hands in the pockets of his tattered jeans, head cast forward, eyes on the pavement in front of him. One foot in front of the other.

He knew the streets of Mid-City well. He was no stranger to strolling the neighborhoods. He knew he was headed in the direction of the French Quarter, but he never actually intended to walk that far. But as his thoughts carried him, his feet did likewise, and he ended up travelling much farther than he realized. No matter. He could walk around the French Quarter just as easily as he could his own neighborhood.

But no matter how far he walked he would never outpace his thoughts. Fay was dead. Faith, he reminded himself. Somebody had killed her, and now there was a police detective who thought Jake might be the guilty party. He kept picturing that look on Rivera's face as Jake had tried explaining himself. He didn't buy it. But what does he have? A few phone calls. So what? But it wasn't just the Faith thing. One of these days, Dr. Cherry was going to fire him. The blood lab was not exactly a dream job, but it paid the bills. Mostly. Some months he had to prioritize which ones to pay.

The sky continued to darken, turning the color of wilted violets. The fast moving accordion riff of a zydeco tune wafted over from the next street and caught his attention. Live music. Part of him wanted to go find where the band was playing, but mostly he just wanted to feel sorry for himself.

He paused, noticing the display window of a novelty doll shop. He peeked through the thick glass at the dolls arranged nearest the pane. A sign hanging above the storefront boasted that all the dolls were handmade, and Jake could believe it. The facial features were so realistic as to be borderline creepy, and the miniature clothing they wore was hand-stitched and looked like the miniature versions of actual name brand outfits. As he glanced about, he thought about Missy, and how much she would love one of these dolls.

Then he saw the price tag hanging off of one of them.

Maybe Missy would rather something else. He turned to go.

And that was when he saw the reflection in the glass, peering back at him. Standing about twenty yards back, the tall man from the Cajun Confectionary regarded him with a grim expression.

Jake spun on his heel to face the man.

There was nobody there. He had disappeared again, just like outside the blood lab.

Jake started walking again, faster. His quickened pulse pounded in his temples. What to do now? He looked all about, examining the faces of everyone he passed, wondering why this guy kept showing up everywhere he went. This had to have something to do with Faith. It couldn't be a coincidence. The thought made him shudder, and the streets he knew so well became alien and menacing to him. Each darkened window was a sniper's nest, each doorway a potential ambush in the waiting. An attack could come from any direction at any time.

So this was what paranoia felt like.

Jake kept going. He tried to find solace in the crunch of rubber on concrete that accompanied his wide, bounding steps. The air grew cooler and a gentle breeze nipped at his neck, carrying with it the smell of boiled seafood. He could practically feel a malevolent glare aimed at him from somewhere nearby.

Enough of this. He quickened his steps. His strides grew even wider. He acted like he was in a hurry to get somewhere, and did not stop to look behind himself again for several blocks. A drunk staggered into his path, and Jake almost barreled over him. He swerved around him, but did not slow down, did not stop. This might work if he could somehow lull the tall man into a careless mistake.

Then, all at once, Jake ground to a halt and whirled in a complete one-eighty.

The tall black man stopped short, about a half block back. Their eyes met. Uncertainty flickered in the man's eyes when he realized that he had been caught. They stood like that for a while, Jake and this man, appraising one another.

Then the man turned and started marching back the other way. Jake knew he should just go about his own business, and let the man go about his. Now that he knew Jake was on to him, he might even leave him alone. Maybe Jake could just call Rivera and let him know what happened. But what could he tell him that would help anything or anybody?

Jake was giving chase before he was even consciously aware that he was doing it. Why? He had no idea, other than his blood was racing, his face was hot, and he wanted to know why this guy was following him. What would he do if he caught up to him? *One thing at a time.*

There was no place for subtlety. Jake took off at a full sprint, hoping to overtake the man before the man had a chance to realize Jake's intentions. But it did not work out that way. The tall man began running also, and the chase was on.

Now it was a race through the streets. Slower moving, half-drunk tourists became obstacles to be avoided and dodged. Potholes and puddles of urine became hurdles to hop over. The man cut often from one side of the street to the other, so that dodging the moving vehicles became a part of the process.

Up ahead, the stalker cut through an alley. Jake cut into the same alley moments later and emerged onto another street. It started to feel like someone was breathing fire into his lungs. He was almost ten years removed from high school when he had tried out for the track team. Back then he was in much better running shape, and could have probably caught this guy easily. But, like the famous book title, that was then and this is now.

It went on that way for what felt like a century. Sprinting up and down streets, cutting through alleys, dodging ill-positioned bystanders. All the while Jake never seemed to gain any ground.

The chase came to an abrupt halt after the man ducked into yet another alley. Jake rounded the corner about four seconds later.

And found no trace of the man anywhere.

The alley came to a dead-end about thirty feet ahead. Just three walls, with no doorways or windows or any other means of egress to be seen. A dumpster sat near the far wall, and several discarded beer bottles dotted the landscape, some broken, some intact.

The dumpster, then. It was the only place he could be. Either behind it, or in it.

Jake waited a few moments to catch his breath. No sense rushing into the alley. If the man was hiding in the dumpster, it's not like he was going anywhere without Jake knowing about it. Slowly the sharp stab of pain in his sides began to fade. He then crept to the dumpster, trying to maintain some element of surprise, and to not give away his exact position. The stench of decaying meat filled his nostrils as he made his approach.

The dumpster was wide and low, the paint flaking from the rusted metal in several spots. Two plastic flaps along the top sat on hinges, and a sliding door at one side provided the only ways in or out of the receptacle.

A quick peek around the sides revealed that Jake's stalker was not hiding behind it. He had to be inside the stinking thing.

Jake flicked one of the plastic lids over, and jumped back as he did so, expecting the man to lunge upward as his refuge was disturbed, like a platoon soldier from a camouflaged jungle pit in one of those old war movies his dad used to watch. His every nerve on high alert, Jake repeated the gesture on the second flap, but again, nothing happened.

His inner voice told him to just quit while he was ahead and get the heck out of the alley.

He moved forward again, in a half crouch. This was the moment of truth. He was strong, right? He could fight this dude if it came to it, right? Ignore the very real possibility that the stalker had a weapon. Ignore the very real possibility that the stalker was almost certainly a much more experienced fighter. Ignore the fact that this was probably the guy that killed Faith.

And ignore the fact that he had no idea what he intended to do when he actually exposed the man.

He rose to his full height and peeked down inside the dumpster.

Three garbage bags, a few loose items, and one hell of a stench; those were the only things that greeted him from inside the dumpster. Even in the poor lighting he could see that the man he chased into this alley was not hiding within.

But there was nowhere else he could have gone. Where was he? Jake glanced around again, looking for something he might have missed, like a hole in one of the walls, some means of climbing over one of the walls, or anything that would have provided a means of escape.

But there was nothing. He was completely and utterly....

Alone, was the first word that came to mind to finish that thought. But then a better one revealed itself.

Trapped.

He groaned and smacked himself in the head as he turned toward the mouth of the alley.

Yep. The tall stalker guy was standing there, alright. Eyes ablaze. Fists clenched. Directly between Jake and freedom.

Seven

Jake's mind, completely at odds with his will, conjured up images of all the gruesome and painful ways that he might die in the alley.

"No sudden movements," his pursuer said, "And keep your hands where I can see them."

What if he just grabbed his cell phone from his pocket and called 911? Maybe he could get the call off before Beanpole attacked, assuming he was not carrying a gun. But would he have time to properly explain his predicament to the operator? He could always ask Beanpole to hold off from killing him while he made the call. That's it. Just remind him that it's rude to interrupt someone while he is on the phone.

You know you have a problem with your mouth when even your inner voice is sarcastic to you. But there was another problem. He was not exactly sure where he had ended up. He had chased this man for blocks, winding up and down streets and through alleys, paying little attention to the specific streets they traversed. He could be in any alley in the city for all he knew.

"Get down on your knees," Beanpole said.

"This isn't some kind of come-on, is it?" Jake blurted.

"Sorry to break your heart, junior, but I don't swing that way. Just shut up and do what I said."

Jake could have done as he was told. Instead, he rushed the guy. In retrospect, it probably was not the greatest idea he ever had. At least this way he might have an element of surprise.

The space between the two men was about ten yards. Jake ran

headlong as fast and hard as his rubbery legs could carry him. He prepared to strike. Beanpole lazily side-stepped his pathetic assault and struck him in the neck with a knife-edge chop. Jake felt a flare of pain and cried out, dropping to the ground. The cold cement jarred his knees. Fire erupted along his right side.

Before Jake could make any attempt to reorient himself, Beanpole straddled him from behind, wrapping one skeletal arm around his neck in a chokehold, and wrenched back on his head. For a moment Jake feared that he meant to snap his neck or choke him to death. Jake was certainly in no position to stop him.

"I'm going to overlook that miserable excuse of an attack," Beanpole said, wrenching harder on Jake's throat. "But you try something like that again and I might have to hurt you."

Jake choked out a garbled surrender. The words did not sound intelligible. Beanpole must have gotten the point, though, because he released the hold and backed away. Jake lay there for several moments, collecting himself and trying to get the oxygen flowing properly in and out of his lungs again.

"Did you have to go for the neck?" Jake finally wheezed. "A simple sweep kick would have dropped me."

"Yeah, but I couldn't have you busting your head on the ground," Beanpole responded. "I need you conscious."

Jake worked himself to a sitting position and leaned against the alley wall. The brick was hard against his back. He massaged his own neck. "I think you interrupted the flow of blood to my brain."

"I don't think your brain needed it all that much."

"Talk about insult to injury," Jake said.

The shadows played games with Beanpole's figure, making him appear more sinewy than lanky, and granting him a sinister aura. Jake just hunkered down while the stench from the dumpster filled his nostrils and the unyielding concrete assailed his aching limbs.

"Who are you?" Beanpole said. His voice was high pitched, but he had impeccable articulation, like Chris Rock doing a James Earl Jones impression. His accent almost sounded British.

"Who are you?" Jake said back to him.

Beanpole regarded him for a long moment, chewing his lips. Finally he said, "My name is Najac."

That caught Jake by surprise. He had expected the man to say something like *I'm the one asking the questions here, punk.* He had not at all expected him to actually answer the question.

Jake squinted in the growing dark. "Don't take this the wrong way, man, but what are you waiting for? You're going to kill me, right?"

"Why do you assume I'm going to kill you?"

"Call it a guess."

Najac sighed. "I gave up some information. Now it's your turn."

Jake drew in a breath. "I'm twenty-eight years old. I live alone. I hate cats. Once, on a dare, I licked some bird poop off the ground and-"

"Shut up, would you? I don't care about your life story."

"You said you wanted information."

"Not that kind of information. I want to know about Faith."

Jake's next sarcastic comment died on his lips as the seriousness of his predicament, held at bay only temporarily by his smart mouth, crashed over him once more. This situation was no joke. He was trapped in this alley with this killer. He had no way of calling for help. Even if he screamed, the alley would probably muffle the sound and Najac could just kill him and slip away. That was assuming, after the blow to the throat he had just received, that he was physically able to scream. His heart pumped ice water through his arteries.

"What about her?" Jake said.

"Did you kill her?" Najac asked.

That seemed like an odd question, coming from a killer and all.

"No," Jake said. "Seems like you'd already know the answer to that."

"What were you doing at Faith's workplace?" Najac asked.

"I was training monkeys to work a sewing machine," Jake spat. "What the hell do you think I was doing there?"

"I think you were casing it," Najac replied.

"Casing it? Do people still say that?"

"What's your name?" Najac asked again.

"Jake." He figured there was no harm in giving up his first name at this point. Withholding the information would not provide him with any advantage. Besides, there was no telling how much Najac already knew about him.

"Do you know Faith Daelly?" Najac said.

"Knew," Jake corrected.

"The detective," Najac said. "Why'd he come see you yesterday?"

"To ask me the same kind of questions you're asking me," Jake fired back. "Just without the knife chops."

"Why?" Najac insisted.

"Why do you need to know?"

"What did he want with you?"

"Why do you care?"

They stared each other down. Najac's nostrils flared and his shoulders rose and fell in rhythm with his deep breaths. He stood looking down at Jake with his hands balled into fists. An expectancy hung over him, like at any moment he might explode.

"This is going nowhere," Najac said at last, breaking the silence after nearly a full minute.

"Did you kill her?" Jake asked.

Najac stood there, feet planted, arms at his sides. Slowly, his fists unclenched.

"You really just asked me that?" Najac said.

"I did."

"Did you have anything to do with what happened to her?"

"No. Why would you think I did?" Jake spat.

"The detective-"

"The detective wanted to know why Faith called me three times Thursday night!"

"That's it?"

"That's it."

As so often happens at dusk, it seemed to go completely dark all at once. Jake found he could no longer see clearly in the alley. He could barely discern Najac's features now. That made Jake's chances of winning a fight against this guy even more unlikely.

"So you're just caught up in this by mistake?" Najac said.

"And you're what?" Jake said. "Investigating what happened to her so-"

He never got the chance to finish his sentence. A loud hiss filled the alley. And there was another noise underneath the first one, like the sound those little flexible straws made when you bent them, only amplified so that it was more like a thousand straws bending all at once.

"What the-" Najac looked about him and threw a glance back toward the mouth of the alley.

But the sound was coming from above.

Jake tilted his head back, cast his eyes in the direction of the top of the opposite wall and saw something that his brain refused to comprehend. A wriggling, writhing mass twisted and contorted as it glided smoothly down the sheer surface. Nothing should be able to scale down a vertical wall like that. Najac followed Jake's gaze and muttered something under his breath that Jake did not catch, but the tone of voice was unmistakable.

Najac was scared.

Jake rose to his feet and started to make a break for it. But before he took two steps he saw that his plan was hopeless. The writhing mass sliding downward would reach the ground well before Jake cleared the alley, and its angle of descent would put it well ahead of him, effectively cutting off the only means of escape.

All at once the mass crashed to the ground with a resounding impact. Somebody screamed from outside of the alley, maybe a passerby that was happening by and caught a clearer view of the thing that had landed there. It rose into an erect posture and turned to face them.

It was some kind of creature. But Jake had never seen anything like this before. What at first appeared to be a great big knot of coiled wriggling ropes was in fact a humanoid form, covered in squirming, rope-like protrusions that seemed to grow out of its very body. As the protrusions writhed, they produced the sound Jake had moments ago compared to that of many straws bending. But the hissing noise coming from its mouth was louder, if it could even be called a mouth; it looked more like a narrow slit in the creature's face.

Najac reached a hand and pulled Jake backward, away from the creature. That one simple motion likely saved Jake's life because just then one of those coiled rope-like protrusions shot forward and almost swiped him where he stood. Jake had just the briefest view of the appendage up close and he almost gagged on his tongue to find that it was actually a long, slithering, pale snake, complete with eye slits, gaping mouth, and pointed fangs.

"What the--"

Najac tackled him, cutting him off in mid-speech, interrupting him from uttering a word he usually reserved for only the rarest and most desperate of situations, like when the New Orleans Saints lost a football game.

"Get as far from it as you can," Najac yelled.

Jake did not need to be told twice. He was on his butt after being tackled, but he used his elbows and heels to scamper backward across the hard ground in an attempt to distance himself from the creature, knocking discarded beer bottles aside in his haste.

The beast had the yellow, slitted eyes of a reptile, and its head reminded Jake of a great big lizard, except its maw did not poke forth nearly as far. A small glittering jewel, maybe a diamond stud, was embedded in the flesh of its forehead. The creature stood upright on two legs, and Jake could see now that the many writhing snakes were, in fact, a part of its body. They were the color of eggshells, and as big around as Jake's wrist. Some cascaded like a waterfall down its shoulders, as if the creature was wearing them like a shawl. Other snake limbs grew out of the beast's upper arms and wrists. These arms were powerfully built, but disproportionately short, considering the beast's size. The snakes were in constant motion, twisting and snapping from one direction to another, so that the creature was a constant flurry of motion, a thrashing mass that squirmed like the legs of an overturned cockroach.

"Why have I never seen one of these things on Animal Planet?" Jake screamed.

Najac moved to take up a protective stance between Jake and the monster. "I'm going to assume that was some kind of rhetorical question," he yelled. "Now get back and try to stay out of the way!"

Having spoken those words, Najac surged forward. Jake couldn't believe it. He was actually charging the monster!

The snake monster poised to meet the attack head-on. When he was still several yards outside of the creature's range, Najac leapt into the air.

And vanished.

What?

Did Jake see that correctly?

In the span of the same heartbeat, Najac reappeared, directly in front of the monster, still in mid-leap. Jake gaped, mouth open, as Najac leveled a powerful looking dropkick dead-center on the beast's chest. He had all the force of his body weight behind him, and the sound of the impact was thunderous in the enclosed space.

But he only succeeded in driving the monster back a half of a step. It shrieked its anger, and several snake limbs rushed forward to counter attack. But Najac's feet had not even touched the ground before he vanished again, reappearing that same instant behind the monster. He dropped to a crouch.

Several more snake limbs lashed backward. Jake wondered in that moment if the monster could see whatever the snake appendages saw. If that were the case, then it could probably see in 360 degrees around itself, and there would be no sneaking up on it. Najac made a funny little noise in his throat, even as he disappeared and reappeared again, at Jake's side.

"It's strong," Najac said, his voice strained, his tenor rising noticeably. He was moving a little less gracefully now. "I don't know if I can stop it." He studied the dumpster near the back of the alley, and Jake noticed his shirt was ripped and blood dripped from the spot beneath the tear.

"It got you," Jake said.

"I wasn't fast enough." Najac moved toward the dumpster. Behind them, the creature hissed and slid forward, cutting short their maneuverable space. A stray light cast from above reflected briefly off of the jewel stuck in the thing's forehead.

Jake moved in step with Najac, not wanting to be left behind. They moved closer to the dumpster and farther from the monster. But there was no reasonable expectation of escape from this alley. Not unless they could get around the monster somehow.

"What is that thing?" Jake said.

"A loa."

"A what?"

"A spirit god. I think it's Damballah, with the snakes and all."

"You know its name?"

"Damballah's supposed to be a good guy though. Maybe it's someone else."

"You lost me at spirit god. And why are you talking like you know this Dambana guy personally? Do you visit him at home? Play drinking games together? Organize play-dates with the kids?"

Najac threw a glance back over his shoulder. "Damballah. Not Dambana. And stop talking. I'm trying to think."

Even though the loa stood on two feet like a man, it still managed to slither toward them in a way that was more in line with a true snake. It was taking its time, sizing them up, studying them with a level of intelligence in its reptilian eyes that gave Jake the creeps.

"Maybe I can get around it and distract it, make it chase me out of the alley," Najac said.

"Why?"

Najac cast a dubious look at Jake. "So you can escape, stupid."

"Why do you have to call me names?"

The loa kept coming. Its progress was slow and methodical. Apparently the thing was in no hurry. Maybe spirit gods could afford to have more patience about things than humans. Give the thing a smart phone though and it would probably be swerving through traffic and cursing at the steering wheel with the best of them.

A still hush came over them all. The creature had stopped in its tracks and gathered itself to its full height, somewhere in the neighborhood of eight feet tall. Tall enough to smack its head on the average doorway, but not quite tall enough to date a Kardashian. When it stopped, Jake and Najac froze in place as well, like they were all just playing a game. One, two, three, red light!

The sound that echoed through the alley then could loosely be described as a crackle of static, a kind of malevolent white noise. The air around the loa shimmered and distorted, and a phosphorous purple light resembling a semi-transparent cloud appeared and gathered around the spirit god's head.

"Down!" Najac cried, and tackled Jake. If he took a few more hits like this, Jake might have to join the NFL Players Association.

A purple blast erupted from the loa's mouth like so much projectile vomit. It shot toward them in a column of light and noise, and the sound that it made was like a freight train coming off its tracks. If Najac would have hesitated for even a moment before tackling Jake, then Jake would not have made it; the ray crossed the distance between them that fast.

Thanks to Najac's quick thinking, however, the blast flew harmlessly over their heads. It struck the wall at the back of the alley, and the column of brick simply exploded in a cloud of light and smoke, spewing fragments of stone and plaster all over the place. Jake covered his head and balled himself into a fetal position as the rubble rained down around him. Some of the shrapnel struck his prone form, and pain flared at multiple points across his body.

When the dust settled, he sat up. Beside him, Najac rolled onto his side, his face bloodied, a wicked looking gash running haphazardly across his forehead.

The loa watched them with those unblinking eyes. It almost seemed surprised that they were not dead.

That was when Jake noticed the pool of light flooding the alley. The purple vomit blast had left a wide and uneven hole in the previously solid brick wall where it struck. The light was spilling through the hole from a well-lit room on the other side. He realized that he was looking into one of the many clothing boutiques that could be found all over the French Quarter, and the screams of the frightened patrons wafted through the opening.

"Looks like we have our way out of here," Jake said.

Najac did not immediately respond. He grimaced and struggled to rise. Jake hooked an arm around him and half-carried, half-dragged him toward the opening in the wall.

"It might be a tight fit but we can make it," he said. Najac nodded.

Behind them, the loa hissed and resumed its slithering pursuit. Jake chanced a look back. It was moving much quicker now. It meant to stop them before they escaped.

"It's coming fast!" Jake screamed.

Najac shoved Jake toward the hole with a strength that seemed at odds with his current condition. He meant for Jake to go first. The hole was about four feet off the ground and was just large enough for him to squeeze through. Jake wiggled into the space; the sharp edges of the bricks around the jagged perimeter of the hole dug into his flesh, but he managed to push himself through.

It was a clothing boutique alright, but not what you would call a traditional one. The nearest wall display boasted rack upon rack of black leather bodysuits that no self-respecting female would want to wear to grandma's house. Beside that display, a long table held the accessories: whips, variously sized chains, spiked collars, and other bizarrely shaped objects he didn't even want to know about. Many of the patrons gunning for the front door of the shop were clothed in either leather or latex. Realization dawned on Jake.

"I can't die in an S&M sex shop! What'll Miss Jerry think?" Jake muttered.

Najac did not have to squeeze through the hole. He stuck his head in, and did his little trick again, disappearing and reappearing in the same instant, but now on the other side with Jake.

"You're going to have to teach me how to do that," Jake said, as Najac stooped to pull him to his feet.

"Come on," Najac said through gritted teeth as he reached for Jake. "That wall is not going to be able to stop Damballah."

"What are you talking about? It's a solid brick-"

A mighty crashing noise shook the whole building and seemed to vibrate in his very teeth. Another noise just like it followed the first. Jake chanced a look back. The thick muscular arms of the loa pounded at the wall, dislodging entire sections of mortared brick. The many snake limbs went to work, dashing forward, tearing bricks away in their many mouths. In the time it would have taken Jake to unzip his pants, the size of the hole in the wall had doubled.

Najac pulled him forward, breaking the trance that threatened to take hold. Jake got his feet moving again. The front entrance of the shop was a carrot dangling right in front of them. Almost there. Almost to freedom. Surely the creature would not pursue them through the streets.

Again, that sound like white noise gathering, followed by a loud rumbling. It was easy to imagine an angry rhino charging through the store, trampling things underfoot as it went. A purple glow bathed the immediate area as the creature fired off another blast, and the front of the store simply exploded in a maelstrom of shattering glass and screeching metal. Najac grunted. A smell like burnt matches filled the air.

They reached the ruined storefront, but Najac's eyes were wide and he fell headlong amidst the debris that had once been the tinted glass double doors. Jake tried to tug him along, but it was like moving dead weight.

"Come on!" Jake screamed. He pulled and yanked and wrenched, but to no avail.

He looked back. There was no sign of the creature, but the entire back wall of the store seemed to be missing. Every hair along his entire body stood straight. Where was the loa? He believed he could sense it watching him from some hidden corner, waiting to strike. They couldn't just rest here, waiting for it to kill them. They were so close! He felt like he was in one of those bad horror movies, where the hapless teenaged girl is almost out of danger, having almost escaped the haunted house, but stops short in the doorway to take one last look back, and pays for her stupidity with her life.

"Come on!" he called again, yanking harder.

Curious pedestrians were already gathering in a loose semicircle several feet away. Some of them were the store's previous customers. It might have been funny in a different context, the sight of all of those people in black latex standing amidst people dressed normally.

He fell beside Najac.

"Come on," he said again, weaker, a note of pleading in his voice.

Najac was lying on his back, staring up at the starless night. He was breathing so fast that Jake half-expected him to birth a baby at any moment. The entire right half of his body looked disfigured and scarred. The burnt smell lingered.

He leaned over. Najac fixed his eyes on him, a trickle of blood running down one corner of his mouth.

"Listen up fool," he said. Even in death, still with the name calling. "Four."

"Four?"

"Four. Nine. Myrtle. Happy. Go. Lucky."

"No offense, but you might want to just conserve your energy," Jake groaned. Why was nobody coming to help? Why were they all just standing there? Had anybody even bothered to call for an ambulance?

Najac retched, a horrible gurgling noise, but nothing came up. His face grew pale, his cheeks tight. "Take this."

One weak hand went to his neck, and lifted what looked like a silver chain with interlocking clasps from his neck. He held it out. Jake took it, feeling confused. Excited murmurs passed through the crowd.

"This chain," Najac said, coughed, and then tried again. "This chain. Don't lose it. Special. Wear it. Line of sight. Wish you were somewhere else." His breaths were becoming more ragged, his speech more broken as his life slipped away. He pointed to the chain. "Put. On." Jake did as he was told, even though it was the stupidest dying request ever. Not 'scatter my ashes someplace pretty.' Not 'make sure my family is safe.' Najac wanted Jake to wear his jewelry.

Najac nodded almost imperceptibly when the chain was fixed around Jake's neck. "Line. Of. Sight. Wish. Somewhere else." He grabbed Jake's hand and squeezed. Jake squeezed back, as if Najac's chances of survival rose in proportion to how much pressure Jake applied. A racking sound came from somewhere deep in Najac's chest.

He moved his mouth to say something else.

The sirens of an approaching squad car drowned out the dying man's last words. The flashing red and blue lights lit up Jake's peripheral vision the same as the loa's purple light had done.

When he looked back down, Najac was gone, his final words unheard.

Eight

A rough voice screamed at him from many thousands of miles away.

Lights flashed, shapes whirred by, people murmured, the smell of dirt and blood and sweat and burnt things assaulted from all directions.

He was still seated by Najac's corpse. He looked up to see the barrel of a gun. The black hole seemed so tiny compared to the purple blast of the loa. He pondered on that rather than the fact that the gun was pointing at him and a man dressed in a police uniform was screaming for him to move back.

Someone grabbed him from behind, dragged him backward. The hands were rough, unsympathetic, the finger tips digging into his flesh. The pain they caused blended into the other aches.

There were voices, lots of excitement. Squad cars everywhere, angled in random arrangements up and down the street. There were fire engines also, and ambulances. Half the emergency personnel in the city must have been congregated right here on this dirty little street. The night was aflame. Gawkers emerged from every direction.

Someone in uniform asked him questions, and he said things that later he would not be able to recall. Somebody led him to a curb and made him sit. An officer loitered nearby. Jake sat with his head in his hands, his elbows resting on his knees. He sat there, mute and dumb as the cacophony of noises around him drowned out the sound of his heart slamming against his sternum.

Police officers scurried about in every direction. Najac's body was simply left in the street where he went down. At least they had the decency to cover him with a sheet. Jake tried not to look at that sheet, at the contours of the shape barely concealed beneath it. For the moment nobody seemed to care much about Jake, they were just scampering around him, performing various tasks like putting up the crime scene tape and photographing the site. There were almost as many uniforms represented in the motley bunch as there were spectators, and each one clamored to make his own voice heard over the din of everyone else's.

Jake became aware of a young girl standing by, close enough that she could have reached out and touched him. Maybe it was just a trick of the colored swirling lights that caused her skin to appear pale, but her raven-colored hair stood in sharp contrast to it. She stared at him. The officers were keeping people back, not allowing them within the circle of the crime scene tape, so he could not fathom how this small girl had gotten past all of them. Maybe her size allowed her to slip by unnoticed. She couldn't be more than thirteen. He told himself he didn't care. But there was no ignoring the intent way she gazed upon him.

She took a shuffling, half-step forward and whispered in his ear, struggling to be heard over the murmurs and loud voices all around. "I have information about Najac, but you need to come with me right now," she said. Jake just stared at her. His mouth hung open. He felt stupid. He had trouble comprehending what she had just said. She cast another glance all around before elaborating, more urgently. "You're in trouble, you know. Big trouble. They're not going to just let you go now. Come with me. I can tell you about Najac."

He did not mean to bare his teeth like a cornered dog. He did not mean to practically growl his response, but he heard himself doing just that. "Who's not going to let me go? What are you talking about? I don't have anything to do with this. I don't even know who these people are!"

She knelt down, put her eyes at his level. Those eyes were far too world-weary and experienced for such a young girl. What exactly had she been through in her short life to cause her face to look like that?

"I know this is confusing for you. But you have to get up and walk away with me now."

"The cops told me to stay put."

"The cops are going to pin this murder on you."

"There's no way. All these witnesses!"

"Witnesses who aren't sure what they saw other than two people running, a flash of light, and you leaning over a dead body. Get your ass up and come with me now!"

Jake rose to his feet and she looked hopeful. She took a tentative step away from him, nodding with her head in a direction leading away from the ruined store. She flagged him with one arm. He stood transfixed, uncertain if this was a wise move. Her eyes were pleading with him in the red glow of all the squad car lights. And then he made his decision.

Jake rushed to the nearest officer, blubbering all over himself. "Officer! Officer! This girl says she has information about what happened here!"

He pulled at the officer's sleeve and pointed behind him, not caring what he must look like, what kind of picture he painted. The officer looked at him impatiently and threw a glance over Jake's shoulder.

"Who?"

Jake looked back. Of course, there was no trace of the girl. *Come on, Jake,* he told himself. *You've seen enough of these kinds of movies to know how it goes.*

"Look buddy," the officer said, "Just sit back down. The detective will be here soon. He's the one who is going to have the questions for you."

In a stupor, he allowed the officer to lead him back to the side of the street where he was again assisted in sitting, even if more forcefully this time. He gazed about in all directions, but could find no trace of the young girl. Had he done the right thing? She was just trying to help. Maybe he should have trusted her words. Maybe she really did know something that would have helped him. But there were too many variables, too many scenarios, and no clear right answers. He hated situations like this.

He looked to the crowd. Several people on the far side of the tape eyed him enviously, as if jealous of him for getting to be on the exciting side of the tape. One woman in particular caught his eye, a tall shapely beauty with hair as dark as that of the young girl from a moment before, who stood silently, watching everything that was going on. She looked familiar somehow. Next to the woman was a short man with red hair and thick glasses, snapping pictures with his phone, looking like he was having the time of his life. And next to him a gaggle of off-duty strippers gaped at everything going on. A bright flash of light shone in his face and he looked up to see one of the crime scene investigators snap a picture of him.

He stopped scanning the crowd. It just depressed him. He exhaled and looked front and center. Somebody was standing there, towering over him. His eyes followed the trail upward starting with the feet, then the legs, the torso, the face.

Detective Lester Rivera glared down at him.

"I gotta admit, Presnall, you're making this too easy on me."

When he saw the stupefied expression on Jake's face, Rivera added, "Come on. Two victims in three nights. Same modus operandi. The first victim was calling you right before she died and then you're actually spotted at the scene of the second murder, arguing with and chasing the victim."

Jake hung his head low. This was not looking good. Another man, presumably the Medical Examiner, gestured to Rivera. The detective looked back to Jake. "Stay right here. I have about a thousand questions for you." He turned to face the other man.

Jake found himself wishing he was anywhere but here, anywhere but in this spot. Which got him to thinking about Najac's final words, at least the ones he had been able to discern: *This chain. Don't lose it. Special. Wear it. Line of sight. Wish you were somewhere else.* He had to admit, it didn't make much sense. And right about now he wished he was somewhere else, anywhere else. He looked again at the crowd gathered outside the perimeter of the crime scene tape, scanned their hopeful faces. To be over there, on the other side, far from this mess.

Something happened. Najac's chain, still fixed about his neck, grew warm against his skin, a bizarre and painless heat. If he still had his wits about him, he might have immediately ripped it off his neck.

Instead, something bizarre and wondrous happened. With his eyes still locked on that spot outside the perimeter of the police tape, he felt that he was growing smaller, just dwindling where he sat. Only that wasn't really it. It was more than just a shrinking. The sensation was more in line with being shoved through a very tiny opening, more like he was being condensed than anything else.

The feeling spread and engulfed his entire body, and he began to feel drawn out, stretched, like silly putty. All this without actually moving from his spot on the side of the street. His body felt like it was many miles long, flowing freely at the speed of a white water rafter through a pipe the length of the United States but the width of a nickel. And then the journey ended, the sensation of motion stopped, his stretched out body seemed to pull itself back together and the bizarre crushing sensation released him, and he found himself sitting just as he had been before. He had not moved a single iota.

But he was no longer seated within the perimeter of the crime scene.

Now he was sitting in the middle of the street, well outside the perimeter, behind the onlookers. He would have to stand up and peer over their shoulders to view the crime scene, to see the spot where he had just been sitting. A great panic overtook him, a disorientation unlike any he had felt before. What the hell had just happened? He bolted to his feet. An excited fervor rippled through the assembled onlookers.

And then Rivera's voice rose clearly over the ruckus. "He's gone! He's fled the scene! Bring him back here!"

Jake panicked. Should he rush back over there and show himself? What were the odds they would play nice with him now? This was serious. He was in over his head and he knew it. So far this weekend he had been almost fired, all but accused of a murder, accosted by a snake monster, watched a man teleport, and now was facing the very real possibility of becoming the victim of a good old fashioned police beat-down. He felt his body shaking and he could not steady it or his breathing.

So he did the only logical thing.

He ran.

Nine

Rivera could have throttled Perkins when he interrupted his questioning of the Presnall kid. The little punk was thoroughly freaked out, reeling from all of the lights and sounds, clearly dazed. The perfect time for Rivera to press him and get what he needed. Nevertheless, he'd had to give the medical examiner his attention.

This new victim showed the exact same cause of death as Faith Daelly. The main difference, as the examiner pointed out, was that while Faith's main trauma was to the center of her torso, with the extremities relatively unscathed, this guy seemed to have taken all the damage to the right side of his body.

"Why the difference?" Rivera asked, after Perkins pointed this out to him.

The little man took a long, deep breath. "Well, in keeping with the heat ray analogy, it looks as though he was struck on the side during the pursuit, whereas the previous victim was standing still and hit directly in the center of her torso. Her death was instantaneous, more than likely. It looks like this guy's life dragged on for a few more seconds after he was hit."

Rivera absently scratched at his mustache, feeling the coarse hair against his hand. He didn't want to know what that must have felt like for the victim. Those final agonizing seconds must have been hell for him.

"Do we have an ID yet?" Rivera asked.

"The kid said it was something like Najat or Najam or something like that."

At the mention of "the kid," meaning Presnall, Rivera turned to glare at the latest thorn in his side. That was when he found him missing.

"He's gone!" Rivera yelled. "He's fled the scene! Bring him back here!"

Immediately, several uniformed officers hopped into action, spreading out, scanning the crowd. Rivera himself raced to the edge of the masses, noticing their excitement and the audible crackle of electricity that surged through them like a power line as the action kicked up again. Morons. They should be home with their families or something. Not gawking at dead people and cops, hoping to catch a little of the excitement that was missing in their lives.

The officers fanned out, searching for the runaway.

The kid wasn't making things easier on himself. Just the sight of him, with those mocking eyes and metric ton of hair gel plastered to his head, got Rivera's blood to boiling. Even still, he could not yet be sure if the kid was telling the truth about his involvement with Faith Daelly. He was almost willing to give him the benefit of a doubt for the time being. But that was before he turned up at the second murder scene. And now that he had fled the scene...

There was definitely something big going on here, and one way or another, Jake Presnall was somewhere near the center of it.

The kid should have done as he was told. Now he was in for it. And Rivera was all too happy to dish it out. After he found him, of course.

* * *

Jake had a head start on his pursuers and the advantage of having somehow teleported outside of the immediate vicinity of their perimeter. He kept his head low and tried to scurry away like the frightened rat he was, all the while hoping to preserve whatever advantage he had in the matter for as long as possible.

If he could just stay out of sight long enough to--

"Over here! Over here!" A bystander spotted him and promptly began screaming and hopping up and down, drawing the attention of others nearby.

Jake gave up the attempt at stealth and sprinted for the nearest cross street, rounding the corner and giving everything he had to the effort of putting distance between himself and those who would be after him. He had no way of knowing if the screamer had managed to get the attention of any of the cops. The side street was much narrower than the previous street had been, and the buildings on either side pressed in much closer. The only foot traffic that he could see consisted of a trio of tourists rushing toward the excitement, apparently to see what all the fuss was about. They did not spare a second glance at Jake; they had no reason to care about him.

He made it to the next street over without incident and tucked his hands in his pockets, head down, and walked as fast as he dared without drawing any undue attention his way. Shops, diners, motorists and other pedestrians passed him by in a blur. He chanced a glance back and saw that a squad car had turned the corner in his direction a couple of blocks back, lights on top flashing.

He ducked into a small walkway between two shops that clustered close together. He finagled his way along the path and threw himself to the ground behind some discarded boxes just as the car passed him by. The cruiser slowed, and from his position Jake could just make out the shape of an officer who appeared to be straining to see into the narrow space. A moment later the window rolled down and a flashlight beam flicked his way.

Jake ducked his head just as the spotlight flashed over his position. He tucked himself into a ball and tried to keep as low a profile as possible, while the beam lingered in the area, bouncing around and illuminating all the dark corners of the tiny space.

The light hovered over the discarded boxes for so long that Jake started to panic, thinking they had spotted him. A lump rose in his throat as he considered his next move. But after another moment, the light flicked off, and the cruiser moved along. He counted to thirty before he dared pick his head back up.

He made his way to the next street, a bit more deliberately, a bit more cautiously. This street was even more off the beaten path. The pedestrians and the music were more subdued. The scene was a tad more peaceful. Jake tried to appear nonchalant as he tucked his hands into his pockets and kept moving.

* * *

"This is ridiculous! How hard can it be to find one little punk?"

Spit actually flew from Rivera's mouth as he hollered the words. He grinded one foot on the rough asphalt beneath him and leveled his gaze squarely at the man standing in front of him. The young deputy was practically a baby, and was noticeably intimidated by Rivera's outburst.

"We'll get him, detective," the deputy replied. "He couldn't have gone far and we're spreading out to cover the perimeter. Plus he's on foot and we have cars."

"On foot! How do you know he's still on foot?"

"We have no reason to think he could have made it to a vehicle, sir," the deputy said.

Rivera was already sliding his phone from the holster on his belt and flipping it open. He forgot all about the deputy the moment he turned away. The night was going to run longer than he originally anticipated. As he headed toward his sedan he called home.

Maxine answered on the third ring.

"Yeah?"

"Yeah we're running late tonight."

"Okay then." Then, almost as an afterthought, "Everything okay?"

"Yeah we just got this guy that--"

"Okay then."

She hung up the phone. Rivera stayed on for a few extra seconds, listening to the dead line in his ear. Problems all around. Then he slipped the phone back into its holster.

He started up the car and wound a crisscrossing pattern from street to street, alert for any signs of the suspect. Revelers and drunks and colorful people of all types hobbled to and fro, as if they were all attendees of the same massive, city-wide party. And in this city that was pretty much the case.

One thing Rivera did not spot was any sign of Jake. He passed other cruisers as he searched, and as the minutes ticked by, he lost hope that they would find him in the immediate vicinity. The punk had slipped by somehow. The perimeter the officers had set up had probably been too little too late.

He slowed to a halt at a street corner. He looked left and then right. He smelled warm doughnuts. There was a bakery on the right-hand side at the corner. He desperately wanted to pull over for some coffee. Somehow he resisted that urge.

Near the corner, tucked back in an out of the way alcove, a cluster of four homeless people dozed in a loose pocket beneath the awning of a long abandoned building. Two of them huddled under blankets, sleeping. Another simply lay on his side facing the building, body covered by a thick tattered coat and a flimsy blanket. Another lay nearby wearing only pants. They were all either asleep, unconscious, or dead.

Rivera punched his steering wheel and continued along.

* * *

Jake listened to the car roll by. Even from a distance he recognized Rivera's car. He crawled to his feet after a long moment. He considered giving the sleeping homeless guy his coat back. He felt bad about leaving the guy just lying there with his bare chest exposed. He was shocked the man did not wake up when he took the coat in the first place. He tried not to think about what kinds of life forms might be crawling around on the old raggedy garment. In the end, he decided the coat might come in handy. It modified his appearance. He pushed his guilt aside and continued on.

He had no idea where to go. His house was out of the question. That was the first place they would look, right? The question was, how hard were they going to look? Was it possible they would try for a while, then call off the search? Or would there be a large-scale manhunt? Would his face be all over the news?

He really should have just stayed put in the first place.

The coat tickled his skin as he walked, and he could almost imagine little ticks and mites crawling around on him. Whenever he noticed a squad car creeping up, he found a way to duck out of sight.

He kept mainly to the narrow little side streets, having no idea where exactly he was headed. He needed a plan, but right now he had none.

Jake nestled in for the night beneath a nice little overpass that was every bit as comfortable and luxurious as the downtown Hilton. At least that's what he told himself as he squeezed himself in between two of the metal girders that supported the structure. Every time a car drove by overhead, the whole thing shook, and it sounded like a plane was landing on his head. He tucked himself as far back into the recesses as he could, several feet of solid cement substituting for a ceiling, hoping to remain unnoticed until morning.

His attempt to hide himself failed. After a short while he became aware of a man seated nearby on a similar cross-section of metal pilings, staring at him.

"You didn't knock," the man said.

Jake tried to ignore him.

"You didn't knock," he repeated.

Jake studied him. His face was pockmarked and full of uneven patches of stubble, and he had those crazy Steve Buscemi eyes that freaked Jake out. He was wrapped in several layers of dirty clothing.

"Was there a door?" Jake finally asked.

"You can't just come into a man's house without knocking."

"Sorry."

"It's okay. You can stay. I like your jacket."

"Thanks."

The man withdrew two sticks from among the many folds and pockets on his person and began vigorously rubbing them together. Jake leaned his head against a concrete piling. Just like the Hilton, alright. Another car rumbled overhead, and Jake was sure that the entire structure was going to come down on him.

"You must be new," the homeless man said.

"Something like that."

"You want to see my roach collection?"

"No thanks."

"Okay."

The man kept rubbing his sticks together. Jake wondered if he was trying to start a fire. He dismissed the thought. The guy just obviously liked rubbing sticks together. He smiled a strange maniacal kind of smile as he worked. Jake closed his eyes.

His mind drifted. He wanted to feel sorry for himself, but the first stray thought that popped into his head was about Miss Jerry and Missy. Would they have to see his face on the news? It would break Miss Jerry's heart. She would be scared and heartbroken and worried. He hated that his decisions were potentially going to cause her grief. He could only hope that he would get the chance to make things right.

At some point, during his reveries, his lids grew heavy and he dozed, lulled by the repetitive scratching of the two sticks rubbing together, only to be jerked awake by a sudden dream flash of the snake monster attacking him from the shadows.

They sat like that for a while, Jake coasting in and out of slumber but never actually falling completely asleep. After about an hour or two the man looked directly at him, but seemed surprised, as if he had forgotten Jake was there.

"Oh, hi!" he said, grinning. "I like your jacket! You must be new!"

"Sure."

"You want to see my roach collection?"
Jake sighed. It was going to be a long night.

Ten

Maxine Rivera did not look up when her husband staggered into the kitchen, groggy from a broken night of sleep. There was coffee in the coffee pot, enough for him to have a cup. That was something, at least. He fetched a mug from one of the newly installed cabinets and splashed a measure of hot liquid energy into it. Rivera looked over at his wife. She hunched over the kitchen table, her back to him. Several open manila folders surrounded her. Stacks of papers spread out and covered almost the entire tabletop. He said nothing as he sipped. Weak, just the way she liked it, and just the way he hated it. It looked like dirty pond water in his mug. He drank it anyway. That was a battle he lost a long time ago, like a cold case, still haunting him.

He set the mug down on the countertop next to the tiny porcelain ballerina that forever curtsied by the sink. Such a bizarre place for such a decoration, but that was another battle he had lost. Rivera could not even recall where Maxine had gotten the thing or why it was so important to her that it stay in the kitchen, out of place, alone, when it would have been so much better suited to one of the varnished shelves in the den or even in the bedroom. The painted-on face was locked forever in a grimace. Rivera commented once that the ballerina's shoes must have been laced too tight. It was one of his few attempts at humor, but Maxine had not been amused.

Rivera made his way to the bathroom, showered, dressed for work, and rubbed some oil on his head. He came back into the kitchen thirty minutes later, found his wife in basically the same position as when he left except now she was scribbling something on one of the papers and had a calculator in the other hand. Undoubtedly she was working on some super important, need-this-yesterday, the-world-is-going-to-end official business matter for the Community Center she directed, a place for the dispassionate youth of the area to congregate until they were old enough to congregate in jail. Over the past few years Rivera had hauled a few of her kids in on murder charges. Was she really making a difference? He had asked her that once, but he could not bring himself to agree with her answer.

He helped himself to the contents of the refrigerator. He wolfed down a cold bagel and chased it down with the remainder of his coffee-scented water. He poured himself the little bit of remaining coffee, just so he would have something to sip on in the car until he could pull into a gas station on his way to Headquarters and throw it out in favor of something better.

His eyes fell across the memo stuck to the refrigerator with a magnet from some restaurant or other. It was a reminder, meant for him, about a presentation at the Community Center this Wednesday at 10am. Maxine was hosting an event meant to encourage local businesses to help sponsor the center, or something like that. The memo was on the official Community Center stationary (who knew there was such a thing?) and read like a business proposal. Very formal. No "Love, Maxine" or "xxoo" at the bottom. He almost groaned audibly. That was going to be painful to sit through, but Maxine had told him several days ago, in an equally formal tone, that as the director's spouse and a positive force in the community, his presence would be advantageous for the center. He read between the lines: Show up this time, or sleep on the sofa for the foreseeable future.

Rivera was already thinking ahead, mentally reviewing his caseload, when he exited the kitchen through the backdoor of the house. He did not bother to tell his wife that he was leaving. He trusted that the soft click of the door latch and the jingle of his keys as he engaged the deadbolt would announce his departure. Maxine still did not look up. Behind her, the tiny glass ballerina continued to dance alone.

Eleven

Two thousand years or so after Jake fled the murder scene, the sun rose again over the city of New Orleans, ushering in a dull and dreary Sunday morning ripe with the promise of scattered showers throughout the day. As soon as his eyes popped open Jake caught a whiff of urine. He sat up and located the puddle lying nearby, making a mental note not to step in it. The second smell that hit him was the odiferous stench of the homeless guy's coat he had stolen the preceding evening.

Stealing clothes from homeless people. He pushed aside all the implications of the statement.

Apparently he had been too wound up and strung out on his own adrenaline last night to notice a lot of things. The stench of the coat was only the beginning of the surge. His body ached, particularly his right hip and the left side of his neck. He recalled the knife edge chop from Najac and the subsequent fall to the pavement. There had also been the chokehold. Najac had tackled him a couple of times after that. The snake god Damballah (seriously?) had fired a death ray at him and a wall had fallen on him. A cop had dragged him forcibly from behind to get him away from Najac's corpse. He had run farther and harder than he had in a very long time, exercising muscles he had forgotten existed.

So, yeah. He was a big bucket of sore.

But at least he survived the night without being arrested, killed, or having to look at any roach collections.

The vagrant from last night was gone. Hopefully Jake would never see him again. In the place where he had been sitting, Jake noticed wood shavings. That guy sure loved to rub sticks together.

Jake collected his bearings, stood, and stretched. It was the start of a new day. But what to do with that day?

"Hi, you must be new," someone said. The voice came from off to his right. He turned and there was the Steve Buscemi guy again, returning from some unknown errand.

"I slept here last night," Jake reminded him. "How do you not remember that?"

"Oh. Did you knock first?"

"No, I'm sorry."

"It's okay. Want to see my-"

"No thanks."

"Okay."

"Look, Steve," Jake said. "Can I call you Steve?"

"Whatever rocks your X-Wing."

"I have no idea what that means. I'll just call you Steve. Why are you here?"

Steve got this far off look in his eyes and he inhaled so long and hard Jake kept waiting for one of his lungs to pop. He seemed he was recalling some long forgotten era of bygone times and better days.

"Many years ago," he started. Jake leaned forward. "There was this big explosion known today as the Big Bang. It was the beginning of space, time, and matter as we know it and the start of the universe."

Jake shook a hand at him. "No, Steve. I don't mean how did we get to be here in the universe. I mean, how did you come to live under this overpass?"

"Oh, I don't live here."

Jake sighed. "That's a relief."

"No, this is just my summer house. I'm on vacation. I live under a different overpass."

"Don't you have anywhere to go that's not under an overpass?"

"Like out in the sun? It's too hot for that."

"No I mean, like a shelter. Or a relative's house. A place with a real bed."

Steve's eyes twinkled. "Yes! I had a house once! With a bed!"

"Why aren't you there?"

"That house is long gone," Steve said. "Long gone."

"What happened?"

Jake waited for an answer but Steve just sighed, mulled over to a cross-section of concrete piling, pulled himself onto it in a sitting position, withdrew his sticks, and started rubbing them together again.

A new voice came from far off to the left.

"What do you think happened? You think he chose this?"

Jake turned his head in time to see a new man gliding smoothly over to where he stood. The man appeared good-natured enough; close-cropped brownish red hair, neatly trimmed beard, and a face that appeared at once friendly yet sad. It was a face with more lines in it than should have been there. He could have been anywhere between forty and sixty. He dressed modestly in khaki shorts and a striped polo shirt, untucked. The shorts and the shirt were both faded and well-worn. It was easy to imagine the man had worn this particular outfit for several days in a row yet he somehow managed to appear rather clean and well kempt.

The man stepped directly to Jake and offered his hand. They shook, and the man looked deeply into his eyes.

"I'm Corben," he said.

"Jake."

"Nice to meet you, Jake. That's Bogart," he said, gesturing to "Steve."

"That his real name?"

"Probably not. Maybe he just likes Humphrey Bogart. I don't know. He told me to call him Bogart, and that's what I call him."

Jake favored Bogart with a glance. He had not looked up or acknowledged Corben's arrival. He merely sat there on his little perch, rubbing his two sticks together.

"You look the part," Corben said, sizing up Jake, especially the coat. "But you're new. You have that displaced look all about you. Like you don't feel you belong here."

"I don't belong here," he said. "I have a house and a car and a life."

"We all have lives, Jake," Corben said, smiling. "Question is, how are you going to spend it?"

"Are you homeless too?" Jake asked.

"Wouldn't be down here if I wasn't."

"How does that happen?"

"There's all kinds of ways it can happen," he said. "In my case, my wife and I split and I came down here for a fresh start. Didn't have much of a life savings. Had some job prospects lined up but one by one they fell through. I was staying with a friend until he moved. I lived out of a hotel for a while until it got to be too expensive. Then I lived out of my car for a while. One day I come back and the city's done impounded it. I've been just trying to make due ever since."

"Make due? Why don't you call somebody from back home to come get you?"

He shrugged. "Don't think I didn't try. It's amazing how wound up people get in their own lives to lend a little assistance to another human being. The ones who should have been the first ones to help... They had the grandest and most sophisticated excuses of all." He paced a few steps. "But it's not so bad, really. There's shelters that feed us and give us a place to bathe. We can wash our clothes. I've taken to doing odd jobs for people who can look beyond a man's circumstances and see the person underneath. I'm able to earn some money. I use most of it helping out some of my brethren."

Corben turned and leveled his eyes on Jake. "What about you? What brings you to my neck of the woods?"

He had a decision to make. He recognized that. He could spill his guts or he could make up a tale that did not have quite so many horror movie elements. And for some reason that he would never be able to explain, having known this man for less time than it would take to eat a sandwich, he knew he needed to trust somebody with the story. He threw caution to the wind and spilled his guts.

Jake hardly knew where to begin but he told the tale, modifying certain parts somewhat. For instance, he told him about the attack in the alley that killed Najac, but left out the part where the attacker was a demonic snake god. For reasons he could not explain even to himself, he disclosed to Corben about the silver chain he wore on his neck and Najac's dying words and even the teleportation. Bogart stopped rubbing his sticks together long enough to listen.

He did not know what to expect in the way of a reaction when he finished reciting his story, but Corben surprised him.

"Sounds like that chain's got some kind of mojo. You better figure out how it works."

"What? You don't think I'm nuts?"

Corben exchanged a lingering glance with Bogart. Then he chuckled. Jake could not help but think that he was on the outside of some kind of private joke.

"Son, we've seen some stuff out on these streets you wouldn't believe," he said. "Maybe one day I'll tell you some of *our* tales."

"Creepy," Bogart agreed. "Strange city. Lots of ghosts."

"Ghosts are only the half of it," Corben agreed. "I wouldn't be surprised at all to find out that your little chain has some kind of charm worked on it. But if your story is true, and the cops really do think you killed this girl, you need to utilize every advantage you can."

"So you believe in the supernatural?"

"Sure. Don't you?"

"Not until last night."

Corben chuckled again. "You were one of those 'show-me-proof' types, I bet. Looks like you got your proof."

Jake nodded his agreement, wondering what this man would have said if he had told him about Damballah.

"Okay, let's go over these last words again. What did this Najac fellow say?"

"Something like four nine Myrtle Happy Go Lucky."

"And after that?"

"He said the chain was special. For me to wear it, and something about line of sight and wishing I was somewhere else."

"Okay, and you said when you teleported you were wishing you were somewhere else, right?"

"I was wishing that I was outside the line of police tape."

"So maybe that's how it works. Try it now. Wish yourself out of here."

"I can't believe I'm having this conversation."

"Speculating on how you got here or what might have been won't change your predicament. Trust me, I know. All you can do is deal with the situation at hand. Conserve your thinking for finding solutions to your problem. Don't waste time thinking how ridiculous it sounds or wondering how you got here."

"I can do that. You know, you don't talk like a homeless person."

"What's a homeless person sound like? While you're at it, tell me what a black person sounds like too. And an Asian person. Hell, let's sit down and stereotype everybody that's not like you."

"Sorry. I didn't mean any offense."

"None taken. People spend too much of their lives on the lookout for things that they can get offended over. Now shut up and solve your problem."

Jake closed his eyes. Could he really just wish himself out of here? Where would he like to go? Hawaii? Cozumel? The women's shower at World Fitness Gym?

He settled for the comfort of his own living room. That was a start. He pictured it in his mind's eye. He saw the cozy and well-worn little sofa he loved so much. He saw the little doorway leading to the hallway where his mother had marked off his growth over the years with a black Sharpie. He pictured it and he wished himself there.

Nothing happened.

He opened his eyes.

"It didn't work. This is stupid," Jake said.

"Try again, son. Nobody gets anywhere in life by quitting the first time they try something."

Jake sighed. He wanted to throw something. Instead he closed his eyes again and wished. He felt like Dorothy with the red ruby slippers, saying, "There's no place like home." He pushed the thought aside. It was unproductive and made him feel even sillier.

Again, nothing happened.

"It's not working," he said.

Corben scratched his chin and leaned against a piling. "Interesting."

Bogart grinned and hopped down from his nest. "You should leave your eyes open!"

"Why?" Jake asked.

"So you can see where you're going! You're always supposed to watch where you're going!"

"It's easier for me to picture my house with my eyes closed," Jake said.

"Maybe he's on to something." Corben scratched his chin again. "Maybe we're trying to start too fast. Why don't we try a simpler experiment? Maybe you can just teleport yourself right over there next to Bogart?"

"Sure." He closed his eyes and tried to wish himself over to a spot next to the man.

"Eyes open."

"Right."

Jake opened his eyes wide and stared at the spot on the ground. He imagined himself there. He strained his eyes as if he meant to pop them out of their sockets and send them flying over there. Try as he might, nothing happened.

"This is dumb. I probably imagined the whole thing."

"That's your discouragement talking," Corben warned. "Shape up. Stop making excuses and make it happen."

"Why? Why do I need to imagine myself walking over there? It would take me five seconds to walk over there and I don't need some magic chain to do it!"

"Is that what you're doing? You're imagining yourself walking over there? Is that what you did last night? Did you imagine walking away from those cops or did you just wish with all your soul that you were away? Don't put so much emphasis on the physical act of locomotion. Forget the walking. If this works, you don't need to walk. Just concentrate and make yourself be there."

Jake grunted. Probably not the most mature reply, but it was how he felt.

He settled his eyes on the spot. He did as instructed and tried to push aside all thoughts of walking, crawling, scooting, and any other physical means of movement. He stared at the spot and simply allowed his mind to believe it was already there. He pictured himself there, tried to see what he would see if he were already there. In that moment he wanted to be there.

He felt the chain grow warm at his neck again. He recognized the sensation. Soon he felt other recognizable sensations, like being squeezed through a tiny opening, compressed and stretched out, travelling at great speed through a very long and very thin pipe. When he reached the other end of the imaginary tube, he snapped back together like a rubber band. The experience was disorienting, and he stumbled, falling to his knees.

He heard Corben mutter something that sounded like approval. Bogart cheered and started jumping up and down. At first he could not figure out why. Then it hit him. He'd done it.

He looked up at Bogart, then back to where he had been an instant before. He had crossed a distance of about five yards without taking a single step.

"Holy crap! Holy crap!" Bogart was screaming.

Corben smiled.

Things did not just fall into place after that. The successful hop was followed in short order by many more unsuccessful ones. He grew frustrated again, and required Corben's constant encouragement and advice to keep going. He tended to default to viewing the hopping as an extension of physical locomotion and it required great deals of patience and practice to wrap his head around the fact that he was not physically crossing the empty space. Finally the jumps began to come more and more easily to him, and with every successful attempt his excitement grew.

"This is so cool!" he exclaimed after jumping from one end of the enclosure beneath the overpass to the other side.

Bogart was skipping in place and clapping.

"I think I'm ready to try to make the jump to my house now," he said.

The hops were getting easier and easier. He'd done it successfully about a half-dozen times in a row up to this point. Jake had no reason to think he'd fail to teleport himself to his house. He pictured it in his mind and tried to will himself there. He tried again. And again. And again. He threw his hands up in the air.

"I'm never going to get it!"

Corben tapped a forefinger to his chin. "Perhaps you can't just hop anywhere you want?"

"What do you mean?"

"Well you said that this Najac's instructions included the phrase 'line of sight,' right?"

"Yeah."

"Maybe you need to see where you're going. You know, physically be looking at the place you're trying to go."

"Well that's stupid, what good is a teleportation power if I can only use it to go someplace I could just as easily walk to?"

"I don't know," Corben said. "I'd be willing to bet if I went out and stood on this overpass I could see a pretty good ways. Heck, you could just look down the street and see a good mile or so down. Imagine being able to travel such a distance in the time it would take you to think the thought."

Jake tossed that around in his head. "Yeah, I see your point."

Corben grinned. "Most people do once they come to their senses."

They shared a laugh over that one.

"The question is," Corben continued, "now that you have a pretty good working knowledge of how this thing works, can you put it to use in your current predicament?"

In response, Jake vanished.

* * *

Corben was right, Jake realized. This little power could prove handy. He jumped first to a grassy place outside the cover of the overpass. He regained his equilibrium a moment later. It was getting easier to regain his senses after a jump but the complete disruption in his sense of space and distance was still unsettling. He next hopped about a block away, within sight of a long avenue that wound through the French Quarter. Careful to stick to places that seemed to be unoccupied or shadowed or out of sight of pedestrians, he hopped many consecutive times, crossing a great distance in a very short span of time until he was about a block away from his house. By his estimate about thirty seconds had passed since he stood there staring eye-to-eye with Corben.

This was frickin' awesome.

He desperately needed to get into his house, but he did not want to just walk up to the front door, in case somebody was watching the place. He figured he could go to the next street over, locate the house whose backyard butted up against his own backyard, and come in that way. With the chain to guide the way, it was easy.

A moment later, he used his key to let himself in through the backdoor.

It did not look like anybody had been here since he left. Likely the police would come eventually, but they would need a warrant and they probably had not been able to secure one yet. At least, that was what his experience watching cop shows told him. And since he knew he could believe everything he saw on TV, he was good to go.

The first thing he did was lose the homeless guy's jacket. He could not deal with the smell of it any longer. He searched the house to see if there were any snake gods hiding behind any of the doors, but everything seemed fine. He took a chance and showered quickly, throwing on a fresh pair of jeans and the first T-shirt he grabbed that did not smell like bodily functions.

He did not want to get caught here but he also took a risk and prepared a quick bowl of instant oatmeal. A guy's got to eat. It took him a few minutes longer than he would have liked to find what he had come back here for. But there it was, hidden beneath some pens, scissors, Velcro, screwdrivers and other debris in the kitchen knick-knack drawer. It was a yellow square-shaped piece of paper with a sticky strip along one side.

A Sticky-Note.

But this Sticky-Note was special. It had an address on it.

Faith's address.

She had jotted down the address when they first discussed the purchase of the furniture she was selling. He was going to come over to take a look at it. That was probably what she was calling about on

Thursday night. Why the late calls? Maybe some people were just night owls and assumed that everybody else was, too. Who knew?

The unmistakable noise of tires slamming to a halt on the pavement outside reached his ears. He should have fled immediately but curiosity got the best of him and he peeked out the front window. Three police cars, lights flashing, had arrived one after the other, two from one direction, and one from the other. They parked at an angle from one another so that they formed a letter V in front of his house.

Then he saw Phil Latham across the street, waving frantically from his front porch and pointing at Jake's house. He had a phone in his hand. Had he caught sight of Jake and phoned the police? If so, then perhaps news of the previous evening had spread. They might even be showing Jake's picture on TV for all he knew. Phil was probably all too happy to try to bust him. He'd have to repay the favor sometime.

He slipped the paper with the address into his pocket. It was time to leave.

TV cop shows had taught him more than just that police need a warrant to enter a house. They had also taught him that if you were going to investigate a murder, you always pay a visit to the victim's residence.

He left the way he came.

Twelve

In the movies and TV shows, when the investigators visited the place where the murder victim had lived, it was always an insightful experience. Something extremely useful and interesting would turn up or a compelling character would be on hand to dispense a crucial clue or some other plot information. Jake stood in the little one-bedroom apartment and felt more than a little disappointed that none of those things happened for him.

He felt like a pervert when he noticed a stack of Faith's undergarments on the dresser. They were neatly folded but had yet to be put away. The covers were pulled tight on the bed, a throw blanket adding an extra splash of color, the pillows fluffed and tastefully arranged. Faith must have really liked kittens. At least a dozen stuffed animals, all of them of the feline persuasion, took up residence on the bed and on her dresser. A poster hung on one wall, depicting one of the furballs lying on its back looking up at the camera. The caption underneath read: "CUTENESS – There is no such thing as too much."

Bridal magazines occupied every available horizontal surface, and the cover of each one looked just like the cover of the next; women in white dresses posing in front of shrubbery. The magazines bore titles like "Bride," "Dream Wedding," "Modern Brides," and "Tie the Knot." Business cards of videographers, florists, bakeries, and jewelers were taped to the mirror.

Faith had been on top of her planning, that was for sure.

But no helpful old ladies showed up to give him cryptic warnings. He found no creepy masked man rummaging around in Faith's underwear drawer, carrying an envelope conveniently marked "CLUE."

This investigation thing kind of sucked.

What he did find was Faith's planner, stashed in her sock drawer. Imagine that. An entire drawer dedicated solely to socks. Pardon the pun. There were socks in more colors, sizes, and shapes than he had ever imagined existed, some that ended just under the ankle bone, and some that could have stretched right up to Jake's neck. His socks at home usually stayed on the dryer where he could get to them quickly. He owned about four pairs, and he was pretty sure at least a couple of them didn't have holes on the bottom.

In the planner he found two phone numbers for Faith's sister. Faith had mentioned Fleur a time or two. He didn't know much about her, other than that she worked at a restaurant in the French Quarter, and that she would be a good person to talk to about Faith. The battery on his smartphone, which needed recharging every seven or eight minutes, had run out of juice the night before and was useless to him now. So he used Faith's home phone, being careful to punch in the code to block the number from showing up on Fleur's Caller ID; he didn't want Fleur seeing her dead sister's number when he called. The first number turned out to be a disconnected cell phone. The second rang through to what he assumed was Fleur's apartment.

An Asian girl answered the phone. At least she sounded Asian. He recalled Corben's comment about stereotyping different people groups based on what they sounded like. But she did sound Asian. It wasn't Jake's fault.

"No," the girl said, when he asked if Fleur was there. He pegged her for a roommate. "She's at work."

"Work?"

"Yeah. Who's this again?"

Under the circumstances, he didn't think he should give his real name. "Her friend Ralph."

"You want me to tell her you called?"

"Sure. She works at that restaurant, right?"

"Louis' Bistro."

"Yeah, that's the one." So smooth.

He hung up, congratulating himself on a job well done.

He still wished somebody would show up and dispense some critical plot information. When that did not happen he decided to go to Louis'

Bistro.

* * *

The bistro in question turned out to be a dingy little diner off the beaten path (if there was an off the beaten path in the French Quarter) where only the locals knew to go but where occasionally a wandering tourist might stumble by.

He leaned back in a booth by the window and waited for a server. Eventually, a short and spunky teenager with spiked red hair meandered over. Not red as in natural red. Red as in "the fire engines called and they want their paint-job back" red. Her puffy cheeks lent her the appearance of a weather balloon. According to the tag pinned to her shirt, her name was Destiny.

"Can I get you something?" Destiny asked.

"Actually, I was hoping for Fleur. Is she working today?"

"We don't usually do requests."

"Please?" He flashed his best and brightest smile, which, considering his status of single, probably wasn't that great.

She sighed. "I'll send her over. It might take a while."

At least she hadn't screamed and run for cover when she saw Jake. Maybe his face wasn't being shown on every television screen in the city, like he'd imagined. He perused the menu until Fleur came over. The first thing that struck Jake about this girl was how utterly calm she looked. Her skin was smooth, her face serene, no trace of redness or puffiness about her eyes, no worry lines or creases or bags hanging under them. This was somebody who looked both well rested and well put together, not someone whose sister had been dead less than seventy-two hours.

When at first she did not say anything but merely appraised him with those focused eyes of hers, he launched into his first question. "What's the difference between your Crab Stuffed Eggplant and your Eggplant Crabmeat Stacker?"

She narrowed her eyes and said, simply, "Who are you and what do you want?"

He studied her for a moment. All in all, she was pretty, but not in a way that made him immediately want to jump on her. Rather, she was pretty in the way that he wanted to photograph her, blow the picture up to poster size, mount it on his wall, and decorate the rest of the house around it. Her rounded face was cherubic, not a blemish to be seen. She had dyed her short-cropped hair a very soft and very attractive shade of pink. Her thin lips puckered slightly, and under the cover of gloss, glistened in the reflected light. She had the slim yet well-toned body of a tennis player, and smelled faintly of lavender. The only thing that really messed up the look for Jake was the piercings, two or three in each ear (lobe and top), as well as a tiny stud in her left nostril. Celtic-style tattoos were visible on her arms, and they disappeared up her sleeves.

"Destiny said you requested me specifically," Fleur said. "That's not really something we do here, usually."

"So she told me," Jake added. "I guess it just wasn't her destiny to wait on me today." He waited. And waited. Somewhere there might have been a cricket chirping. Fleur did not look amused. "That was a joke," he said.

"I'm tired of people and their senses of humor."

"What possible reason could you have for hating a sense of humor?"

"Well, for one thing, my parents thought they were hilarious. My name's Fleur Daelly, for crying out loud."

He thought about it for a moment. And then he got it. "Oh, like fleur de lis."

"So you're a genius as well as a comic. Yippee. Now will you order already?"

"Sure, sure. Sheesh. How is your Smoked Duck Quesadilla?"

She took a deep breath. "Do you like duck?"

"Yes."

"Then you'd like it."

He nodded in agreement with the logic. "I guess I'll take that. With a Coke."

"I'll be in the back putting that in, and thanking all the gods of all the religions all over this messed up world for giving me the privilege of taking your order today." And then she spun on her heel and was gone. She never even asked if he wanted an appetizer. He felt a little put out.

Fleur returned with the food a short while later. She brought the Coke and the quesadilla at the same time. He noted that the two tortilla shells that made up the quesadilla were practically kissing each other, and wondered how in the world they possibly could have stuffed roasted duck in there. Fleur plopped the plate onto the table, a little rougher than was necessary, and turned to leave without ever saying a word.

"Whoa, one second, please," he said.

She spun around slowly, a smile frozen on her face that clearly did not represent how she truly felt. "Yes?"

"Would you mind joining me for a moment?"

"Yeah, that'll be the day."

"I don't mean like that," he said. "I'm not coming on to you. I wanted to ask you some things."

The already spiteful eyes now turned suspicious as well. "Things about what? You're not a writer researching the *eccentric types* who work in the French Quarter, are you?" She made little quotation fingers when she said "eccentric types."

"Heavens no. Writers. Gross," he replied.

"Good. I get about three of them on a good day, six or seven on a bad. I usually have to physically show them where they can shove their notepads."

He fidgeted a little bit when he said, "I had some questions about Faith."

Her facial expression did not change one bit. A still lake on a calm day beneath a clear sky showed more variation. Even her eyes maintained that pleasantly detached yet subtly spiteful look.

"What could you possibly want to know about her?" Only the voice gave her away. It sounded pinched, as if someone were clutching her windpipe.

"Well, I'm trying to figure out-" he began.

"Are you a cop?" she asked.

"No."

"Private investigator?"

"Not exactly."

"Then leave me the hell alone." She turned to go again.

"I'm a friend of hers," Jake said. "I knew her from the Cajun Confectionary."

She paused. In the drawn-out moment that followed, he was suddenly aware of his posture, of the smell of French fries wafting across the air, of the sounds of plates and silverware clinking together at the other tables. He swallowed several times while waiting for her to say something.

"What's your name?" she said, turning back to him.

"Jake." He figured he should give his real name this time. "I'm sorry for your loss."

She stepped closer. "Thanks. But what do you want? Not to console me. You don't know me."

"I'm trying to figure out who might have killed her."

She drew in a long breath and narrowed her eyes at him. The hard line of her jaw told him that she was clenching her teeth. "Why?"

"I want to help her."

"Why?"

"Because it's important to me."

"Why?"

"Because I don't trust the cops to get this one right."

"Why?"

He closed his eyes and grabbed the edge of the table, knowing how this was going to sound and having no idea how she was going to take it. "Because they think I did it." And then, opening his eyes and seeing the look on her face, he added, "they think wrong."

"So you're a suspect in her murder?"

They say honesty is always the best policy. Jake wasn't so sure. But he went with it. "Yes."

"Why?"

"It started out simple enough. She called me three times the night she was murdered."

"Why?"

"You say 'why' a lot."

She didn't appreciate the joke. "Why?" she repeated.

"Because I expressed an interest in buying some of her furniture that she needed to get rid of before she let her apartment go. And a detective showed up to ask me about her. I got confused and said I didn't know her, because he kept saying Faith and I only knew her as Fay. So he thought I was lying to him."

This answer seemed to satisfy her somewhat. Fleur plopped down into the booth across from Jake. She folded her hands on the table before her and pursed her lips.

"That sounds like a pretty weak reason to end up as a suspect."

Jake mulled that over. "Let's just say that things went from bad to worse after that."

"So you don't really give one good crap about Faith. You just want to clear your name?"

When she put it like that, it did sound kind of selfish. But what else was he to do?

"Look," Jake said, leaning toward her. "I do give a crap. But normally I could afford to let the police do their job and wait for them to catch the bad guy. But since they're gunning for me... I need to help them out a little bit."

Fleur sighed. "I already spoke to the cops. The real cops. The ones who might actually solve this. You're just some guy."

"Thanks for noticing. Listen, I-" he began.

A large man, his hair a greasy black mane of tangled locks cascading well past his shoulders, stopped at their table. His body was vaguely shaped like a great big potato. His eyes bore holes into Fleur. She actually cringed. It was the first time her tough shell had cracked since Jake had first laid eyes on her.

"Sitting when you're supposed to be working? What did I tell you about socializing on my time?" the big man howled.

"I'm sorry, Louis. I'll get back to work immediately," she said.

"No you won't. Look, I'm sorry about your sister, but this just isn't working out with you being back so soon and all. I want you to take a couple of weeks off. Go home. Go be with your family. Just do something away from here."

"I can't take a couple weeks off, I need the work," she said.

Louis just shrugged, letting her know that wasn't his problem.

She gasped, and threw a spiteful look at Jake, who suddenly wanted to melt into the seat. He realized it had been selfish of him to bother her at work. He could have cost her the job.

Her expression remained intent, bordering on defiance, but she was clearly rattled. If she had been barely holding it together before, this might be the final crack in the eggshell that spilled the nasty slimy part all over the counter. Scrambled egg metaphor. Jake ate a lot of scrambled eggs.

"Actually," Jake said, springing to action. He had no idea what he was going to say when he opened his mouth. He just needed to say something. "Fleur here was helping me. I'm not a friend."

Louis scowled at him. Fleur threw him a furious glare that was surely meant to convince him to shut his mouth.

"Helping you?" Louis boomed.

"Yes." Think fast, Jake. "I was asking about booking your restaurant for a gathering."

"A gathering?"

"A big gathering."

Louis's eyebrows squinted lower and lower until it appeared they were trying to make babies with his eyelids. He studied Jake. Then he said, "We don't do parties."

"Well, yes," Jake said. He coughed into his hand. Stall. Buy time. Think. He coughed again. "Well, I didn't say a party. I said a gathering."

"Same difference."

"Come on Louis. You're a smart man. A businessman. I mean, that's your name on the door outside, right?" Jake the Schmoozer was emerging. Look out. "I'm not talking some kid's birthday party here. No Spider-Man decorations and confetti everywhere. No! I'm talking a few dozen of the leading healthcare executives in our area meeting one evening for a corporate outing. We'd like to reserve the whole place."

He could see the wheels turning as Louis allowed himself to consider the possibility. Never mind that the best *corporate outing* he could deliver would be a few people from the office shooting back a few beers. Nevermind that the healthcare executives in question were probably the receptionist at the lab and a few of the lab techs. Nevermind that he did not even have the authority to negotiate such an event.

"For me to turn away my regular business for an evening would be costly," Louis said. He still looked skeptical. His black eyes bore an uncertain look that suggested he might even be trying to calculate just how much it would cost and finding it difficult to compute.

"Certainly." Jake went for the kill. "That's just what your lovely waitress here was telling me." He gestured to Fleur. "I have an operating budget of about fifteen thousand dollars. I was planning to have lunch here today and then go talk to the manager at Galatoire's of hosting our soiree there. Fleur has convinced me that your establishment might make for a more intimate occasion."

Louis looked back and forth from Jake to Fleur. He still seemed uncertain. Hopefully the dollar signs would blind him to the fact that a guy in jeans and a T-shirt was claiming to represent a major healthcare network. Fifteen thousand dollars was probably more money than he might take in during a week at the restaurant, and Jake was dangling this possibility in front of him like a carrot. He almost felt guilty for playing with the man's emotions like this, but he was, after all, fairly desperate.

"You don't look like a doctor," Louis said. He clearly wanted to believe Jake's story but was finding it hard to reconcile with the old adage about something that sounded too good to be true.

"I never said I was a doctor. I'm-" Think. Think. Think. "An HIT analyst." He didn't even know what HIT was, but it seemed to be the buzzword in the medical community these days. Dr. Cherry sure talked about it often enough.

"Well, okay, then. Please, let's discuss this after you finish your meal. Good job, Fleur." Louis still looked quizzical but he moved away from the table, slowly and uncertainly.

Fleur fixed her gaze on Jake. "Don't you think just because you bailed me out of a problem that you caused me that I'm going to feel grateful to you."

He mocked surprise. "I wouldn't dare!" She watched him. Finally he said, "Look, just help me for a few minutes. Please."

She sighed. "Two minutes."

"Did Faith have any enemies?"

"Good Lord, you've got to be kidding me. She was a pastry baker, not a CIA agent. What kind of enemies do you think she had? You think the people over at Krispy Kreme offed her?"

"Fine. Anybody that might have had a grudge against her?"

She rolled her eyes. "See my previous reply."

"Okay, okay. Was she involved in anything illegal or shady? Something that maybe might have backfired against her, like a bad drug deal?"

"Now that you mention it," Fleur took a moment to collect herself. Jake's pulse raced and he leaned forward again. Fleur continued. "She was running this massive criminal empire from behind the cash register at the bakery. Lately there's been some in-fighting. Turf wars. Chaos on the streets. Innocent doughnuts have been tortured. I bet one of the usurpers did it."

Jake sighed. This was going nowhere. He decided to call her on it. "Why are you back at work? Your sister just died. When's her funeral? Tomorrow? Tuesday?"

"Tomorrow."

"Tomorrow. It's been like what, three days? Why are you not more affected by this? How are you able to sit here and be so brash about her death and her killer?"

This time she actually smiled. "Now that's more like it. Now you're asking respectable questions. You kind of suck at this investigation thing. No offense."

"None taken."

Her expression softened a tiny bit. "I'm not very emotional to begin with. I've always caught flack for it. And I knew that if I just stayed home today I would go nuts thinking about it. I need to move. To work. To stay occupied. So here I am. At work."

"Were there any old grudges where Faith was concerned? Jealous ex-boyfriends or anything?" Jake asked.

"You're getting better at this every second."

"That sounded almost like a compliment," he retorted.

"Dallas," she said.

"Houston."

"What?" She favored him with a disgusted look.

"I thought we were naming cities in Texas," he offered.

"Idiot. Dallas is her fiancé. Was her fiancé. Whatever."

He tapped his fingers on the table, his quesadilla long since forgotten. "You suspect her fiancé?"

"He hasn't seemed right about this."

"I wouldn't imagine that he would."

"It's more than that. Like the way you can sometimes look at a small child and just know that they did something wrong because their demeanor is off somehow. That's the impression I've been getting from him. Plus, he creeps me out. Always has."

"Why?"

"He runs a dog training school here in the city."

Jake shrank back. "Wait a minute? You mean Dallas Lasserre? The Dallas Lasserre?"

She looked rueful. "That's him. You know him?"

"I've lived in the city more than three minutes. Yeah I know about him. Ex-LSU football jock who, for some reason that I hope makes sense to somebody out there, opened up a dog obedience school."

She almost smiled. "That's him. He specializes in teaching unusual skills to the dogs. Things you don't see every day. He can get a dog to do just about anything. They use his dogs at sporting events sometimes for entertainment."

Faith had mentioned the wedding at least ten times every time Jake was around her. How had it never come up that she was engaged to Dallas Lasserre?

"What is it about him that makes you suspicious?"

"Anybody who can train a dog to wipe its own butt is already suspicious."

"Point taken. But what else?"

"He's been off lately. Even more than usual. He had zero interest in the wedding. Even insinuated a few times that he didn't want to get married at all. And then there's his ex-wife."

"What about her?"

"She's been missing for a long time. Eight or nine months. Something like that. It bugged the hell out of Faith. Sometimes I think she suspected Dallas did something to her. Faith went over to Dallas's place one day, before the ex-wife went missing, and found the ex-wife there, and started to get angry. Then she realized that they had been fighting. She jumped in. The ex-wife stormed out and disappeared a day later."

"No one has seen his ex-wife in all this time?" Jake said.

"Not even her family knows where she is. She's gone. Dallas didn't want to talk about it. He blew up at Faith one day when she pressed him about it. If you ask me, he did something to his ex-wife."

"What do you think he-"

She looked at her watch and sprang to her feet. "Two minutes are up."

She walked away and would not come back. Then the real fun began when Louis showed up to go over details about the fake corporate outing. Jake had no choice but to speak to the man, to continue the charade that spared Fleur her job. He reluctantly gave up information such as his name and where he worked, how many people were in his office, etcetera. By the time he got out of there he was more grateful than ever for his newfound teleportation ability. He couldn't wait to put distance between himself and the cramped little diner.

And yes, the quesadilla tasted as bad as it looked.

Thirteen

"They call him the Dog Whisperer," Corben said. He scraped one final plastic spoonful of cold baked beans from an aluminum can.

Jake nodded. He knew about Dallas Lasserre's nickname. "Yep."

There was no brand name on the can. No fancy packaging. Just a generic white label that read, simply, "Baked Beans." Corben chewed his lips and kept his eyes trained on the can, as though memorizing its every ridge and contour. "And I don't know who films his commercials. Most low budget pieces of work I've ever seen. I guess you could say they're unintentionally funny."

"Do you watch a lot of television, Corben?" Jake said.

A wry little grin spread across his face. "Sure, when I stay at the shelters."

"When they have room at the shelters," Bogart added. The crazy little runt had found two fresh sticks and was vigorously rubbing them together, blanketing the pavement in wood shavings.

Monday morning marked the second time in as many days that Jake woke up beneath an overpass. He'd found Bogart resting on a steel girder that crisscrossed the one Jake was on, his head draped uncomfortably close to Jake's shoulder. He wished, and not for the first time, that he would have thought to grab a few blankets and pillows from his house when he was there, but did not dare return now. For some reason, maybe his own stupid pride, he refused to sleep on the ground, as if that would be a new low even for him in his current predicament. So instead he wedged himself into a cross-section of support beams that more or less afforded him a chance to stretch out. When he woke, his back was stiff and sore, and several distinct muscle groups ached.

Corben returned a short time after that with the canned goods, singing the praises of a nearby church that could often be counted on to provide assistance to the needy. The cans had those little tabs with the lids that popped right off, so no can opener was necessary. He'd offered Jake a can of corn, but Jake refused. Probably his pride again.

"So what's on the agenda for today?" Corben asked, after a while.

"Well, I'd like to go talk to Dallas, but today is Faith's funeral, so I guess that's out."

"You probably don't want to bother him in the middle of that," Corben agreed.

"And I can't go to work. Not looking and smelling like this, and certainly not if the police are looking for me. Dr. Cherry surely knows I'm wanted, by now."

Corben shook his head. "You know, you were asking me before how I ended up on the streets. Now you've got your own story."

Jake thought about that for a while. Corben was right. Just a few days ago his life was typical in many ways. Now he did not have a home he could sleep in, or a job he could go to, and he was sleeping under an overpass. Sometimes it really is as simple as that.

"You know," Jake said, "I used to look down on people in your predicament."

"You mean *our* predicament?"

That gave Jake a moment of pause. He didn't want to admit it, but this was his predicament now also. Sleeping on the streets. And he was still a person. So were Corben and Bogart, and all of those other unfortunate souls he used to drive past and pretend they weren't there. "Yeah, I guess so. Our predicament. Sleeping under bridges and on the steps of old buildings. I forget these are just people, with tales to tell." His pride felt rather foolish now. "You know, on second thought, I think I will take that corn."

Corben grinned and exchanged a look with Bogart. Jake couldn't help but feel that he had passed some test. He accepted the can, and the plastic utensils, and started eating. After a few bites, he regarded Corben again. "I can't just hang out under an overpass all day, though. There's got to be something I can do today to help my cause."

"Well there is another lead you can chase down," Corben said.

"What would that be?"

"That guy that was following you. What was his name?"

"Najac."

"Najac. Right. Well, he was following you for a reason. Based on what you told me about him, he obviously thought you were involved with the murder."

"Yeah?"

Corben pointed a plastic fork at him. "You need to figure out what his involvement was in all of this. Was he a friend of this girl that died, or did he get mixed up in it for some other reason?"

"But he's dead. I can't just ask him," Jake said.

"Actually-" Bogart tried to chime in.

Corben cut him off. "You need to make some sense of those last words of his. Figure out what he meant. He was obviously trying to tell you something."

"Couldn't we just get Malecc to do his-" Bogart began again.

"None of that," Corben said, favoring him with a hard stare. Bogart fell silent. Corben returned his gaze to Jake, who had no idea what just happened, and didn't care. "Najac had a reason for following you around, it clearly has something to do with this girl, and that assassin that came after him had something to do with her too."

Jake took another bite of corn. It was good thinking. "You said to make sense of his last words. But how am I supposed to do that? *Four nine myrtle happy go lucky.* That's what he said."

"Maybe it's a code. It must mean something to somebody."

Jake huffed and blew out a long breath. "So I'll just walk up to everybody in the city and tell them *four nine myrtle happy go lucky* and see if they respond?"

Corben frowned. "You know, you could meet me halfway here. I'm trying to help you."

Jake felt the sting. "Sorry."

The truth was, he had been puzzling over those last words. The only thing that made even a little sense was that perhaps the numbers stood for letters. So assuming a straightforward A-equals-1, B-equals-2 code, *four nine* could be D I. But *D I happy go lucky* didn't make any more sense than it did before. If *myrtle happy go lucky* was some kind of phonetic alphabet, that could give him M H G L. So if he put it all together he would get D I M H G L. Were those some sort of initials? Maybe an anagram? He couldn't seem to arrange those letters into any other words. The whole thing just made his head hurt.

"Do the initials *D I M H G L* mean anything to you?" Jake asked.

Corben shook his head in the negative.

"Great," Jake said. "I don't get it. A riddle. Why did he have to die with a riddle? Why couldn't he just tell me what he wanted me to know?"

Corben grew uncharacteristically silent. Not even Mr. Know-It-All had an answer for that.

It got to be too much. Jake hopped down off the girder and stalked across the concrete, stepping out from the shade of the overpass into the glare of the sun. Bogart yelled something to him, but Jake ignored him. He just kept going, walking parallel to the street as cars flashed by. He knew he was too close to the side of the road, that at any minute some idiot motorist could veer a little too far over and clip him. And with his luck lately, it wouldn't surprise him in the least if that actually happened.

Corben was running after him, yelling something.

Jake exerted the mental effort necessary, and suddenly found himself two blocks farther along the street. It was getting easier to teleport now that he had gotten used to the physics of it. He didn't even get dizzy or break stride, but his sudden appearance startled a roaming dog, which immediately took to growling and barking at him. The confused pooch found itself barking at empty air a moment later as Jake hopped again.

Now he was standing in front of a little diner. A few pedestrians strolled by but they weren't facing him, and nobody paid him any particular attention. He looked at a bank several blocks away, and beamed himself there, but did not linger there. He immediately hopped several blocks along another little side street, where he flashed by a row of lower income housing. For a while he just beamed himself randomly all over the place, hitting any spot where his eye happened to fall. The chain he wore was warm against the flesh of his neck.

He could hardly contain himself. To put it simply, this was exhilarating. Amazing. Unbelievable. Jake could be anywhere he wanted to be. He just had to look where he was going. The buildings, shops, houses, parks, schools, restaurants, playgrounds, and everything else whirred by him in a blur, he was hopping so fast now. He felt like a pinball bouncing around the gameboard, except the pinball had to actually travel from bumper to bumper; Jake could just be there. One second he was on a sidewalk, then he was up in the high branch of a tree, then he was down on a park bench, then a gazebo in the middle of a pond, then some stranger's front porch, then inside of a parked car, then somewhere else entirely. He never remained in one place for more than a second or two, and if anybody noticed, he was gone so fast that they would probably just rationalize what they had just seen anyway.

He was having the time of his life.

But one question kept nagging him: *Why a riddle? Why did Najac leave me a riddle?*

He paused when he found himself gazing at the downtown New Orleans skyline from a neighborhood many miles away. An idea presented itself to him. Was there any logistical limit to how far he could teleport? Did he dare try to push it that far? The rooftop of one of those distant high-rise buildings beckoned to him, calling for him to give it a shot. But if he didn't do this right, he could end up a very unfortunate splat on a sidewalk far, far away.

He took a deep breath, held it.

This was it. Time to find out how far he could push this thing. He focused on that rooftop, willed himself there, and relished the sensation as space and time parted for him.

The next thing Jake Presnall saw was downtown New Orleans spread out before him like it was his own personal kingdom. He had made it. He was on the roof of the high-rise building. But he was too close to the edge, and up here the wind gusts were so much stronger than at ground level. They tried to heft him over the side and to his death several hundred feet below. Only the waist-high ledge saved him; he pressed against it, regained his balance, and was finally able to back away, lucky to be alive.

When the initial fright and shock passed, the majesty of the sight overcame him. It wasn't exactly the same as gawking from the Empire State Building observatory from eighty stories up, but it was pretty stinking impressive. Clusters of buildings great and small encircled him, but he was higher than all of them. Traffic flowed and meandered along the streets and boulevards, and he was able to appreciate it in a way he could not do when he was a part of it; it almost seemed its own organism, flowing, moving in waves, winding around bends and turns, alternately starting and stopping in procession. The stink of its exhaust could not reach him here. Barges and ships coasted along the mighty Mississippi, reflected sunlight glittering off the surface of the water. The river snaked its way around the city, crisscrossing back and forth as though it could not make up its mind which way to go; in its wandering it formed the distinctive shape from which New Orleans drew the nickname *Crescent City*. A foghorn cut through the air from one of those barges, and he almost imagined he could hear the calliope music from a tour ship that chugged along. He wanted to stand here forever and savor this.

A voice from behind snapped him out of it.

"Are you a ghost?"

Jake turned toward the sound, surprised to find he was not alone on the rooftop. A man wearing a yellow hard hat stood just a few yards away, pudgy on the sides, face full of stubble, a cigarette dangling from his gaping mouth. His eyes all but bulged out of his head.

Jake tried to play it cool. "A what?"

"I saw you appear out of thin air."

Jake answered by beaming himself a short distance along the roof, so that he was behind the poor sap. He heard the startled gasp and knew he had shocked the crap out of the guy. Hopefully, he did not cause him to question his sanity. But Jake couldn't let the guy spot him again. He lost himself amidst the many tall air-conditioning units, generators, and other electrical equipment that dotted the rooftop in no particular pattern or order, forming a maze of sorts.

Time to get himself down now.

He crept as near to the building's edge as he dared, fixing his eyes on the sidewalk far below. Again he felt like the wind was trying to sweep him away. There was a bus stop a few blocks along, and the four other people waiting there did not notice when a fifth person just poofed into existence among them. He found this odd until he noticed that every single one of them was texting. In that phone-induced haze, oblivious to the world around them, they probably would not have noticed if a T-Rex rounded the corner and started eating them one at a time.

He looked back at the building, which, only a moment before, he had stood atop. With the proper creativity, his new chain could certainly tip the scales of fate back in his favor. He could do this. He could figure this out. He could solve the whole freaking mystery.

Something about the building unsettled him. An uneasy feeling climbed into his gut as he looked back at the sandstone façade. But why? A series of wide concrete steps climbed to the front entrance, where four sets of double doors opened into a glassed-in lobby that was elegantly furnished in marble and dark stained wood. The windows were all tinted in a reflective coating that turned them into mirrors, and in their reflection he could see himself and the buildings behind him. The address of the building, etched into the exterior in wide, four-foot letters above the doors, greeted him. Something about those numbers tickled at his psyche.

A few seconds later, it hit him.

Of course.

Four nine myrtle happy go lucky.

Najac had not left him with a riddle. He'd left him with an address.

Fourteen

Myrtle Street ran roughly south-southeast until dead-ending near the river in an area of the city commonly known as the lower Garden District. Jake traced the street into a neighborhood that had seen better days. It consisted mostly of old warehouses, long since abandoned or burned down, and a smattering of residences that could have been transplants from an old apocalypse movie about a civilization struggling to survive after a horrific bomb blast. It would almost be preferable to sleep another night under the overpass than in one of these houses. Empty lots hunkered everywhere, with weeds as tall as toddlers, crumbling piles of bricks, and rusted metal railings the only clues as to the structures that once rested there.

He was looking for an address: 49 Myrtle. He was sure of it. He still was unclear on what "Happy Go Lucky" meant. Maybe he was supposed to act happy when he found the address? There was no telling, but it seemed so obvious now that he thought about it, that Najac, with his dying breath, was giving him a place to go. Undoubtedly he would find somebody at 49 Myrtle Street who could help him.

During the search, Jake drew more than his fair share of wary glances from suspicious passersby, people who knew on instinct that he was an outsider, and so he dared not rely too heavily on his teleportation to speed up the search. No telling who was keeping an eye on him. Needless to say, he did a lot of walking, and by the time he collapsed, exhausted, on the stoop of a long-since closed-down corner store, his legs ached, sweat dripped freely down his neck, and his face was flushed.

He came to a very sobering conclusion as he sat on that stoop: All of the houses had three-digit addresses. There was no 49 Myrtle Street. It did not exist.

He used one sweaty palm to pull at the collar of his T-shirt and let some air circulate against his chest and back.

How could he have been wrong? He had felt it in his bones that this was what he was supposed to do. But that was before he had gone up and down the street several times, checking and re-checking his discovery, unable to believe it.

He should go. There was no point dawdling here. The house was not going to magically appear in front of him. But he hated to admit he had gotten his hopes up for nothing. The remnants of his elation from when he thought he had cracked the code still haunted him. A wispy little bird sat on the skeletal branches of a dead pecan tree and sang a mournful tune. A strange scent wafted past him; maybe something dead inside the old store, or perhaps something stuck in one of the sewer pipes. Either way, he knew what it really was; the smell of defeat.

His mind wandered back to the night of Najac's death, and he replayed it from memory. How could he have misinterpreted the message, if in fact, it was an address?

"Listen up fool," he said. Even in death, still with the name calling.
"Four."

"Four?"

"Four. Nine. Myrtle. Happy. Go. Lucky."

"No offense, but you might want to just conserve your energy," Jake groaned. Why was nobody coming to help? Why were they all just standing there? Had anybody even bothered to call for an ambulance?

He still remembered that moment clearly. The name, the numbers. He had not forgotten or transposed any of that information. He was sure of it. And then it hit him and he wanted to smack himself in the head.

The second time Najac said the word *four* Jake had just assumed he was repeating himself because Jake interrupted him. But what if he actually meant to say it twice? What if the address was not 49 Myrtle Street, but rather 449 Myrtle Street?

He jumped to his feet, reinvigorated, and headed off toward the 400 block.

The house stood more or less alone, a crooked two-story structure with loose shingles and a sagging porch. Whatever color it had once been, years of exposure to the sun had bleached it to the color of eggshells. It looked about one good sneeze away from just falling over on its side. Screwed in place over the warped front door, three faded plastic numbers identified it as 449. Of the surrounding houses, only a few cracked foundations and piles of debris remained, the dwellings that once stood upon them having given way long ago to the unstoppable forces of time and decay. Lots of privacy here. The nearest house was all the way at the other end of the block.

Jake tried not to fall through the wilted porch as he crossed to knock on the door.

The bare-chested man who answered the knock eyed Jake with a hard suspicious glare. His abdominal muscles bulged through his skin as though they were trying to rip their way free. He towered over Jake, looking down upon him, his body glistening under a faint sheen of sweat, and a dim musty odor came off of him, as though he had missed his last shower or had been in the middle of working out.

Jake adopted his most upbeat smile. "Hi," he said. "Does the term 'Happy Go Lucky' mean anything to you?"

The sweaty man didn't even flinch.

He simply hauled back and punched Jake in the face, completely without warning.

As Jake fell backward, excited murmuring drifted out of the darkened doorway and footsteps rushed him. He landed hard, his head spinning, his lip burning where it had no doubt been split, and he felt rough hands grabbing at him. There were more people now, upon him, hoisting him to his feet, carrying him along. They dragged him into the house, slammed and locked the door behind him, and he was too dazed to do anything about it.

* * *

When he regained his composure he found himself sprawled across the floor in what must have once been a child's bedroom. The walls were painted a soft pink, and he recognized the glow-in-the-dark star-shaped decals affixed to the ceiling. As a kid, he had once had some just like that. Otherwise, the room was bare; any furniture that may have once filled the room was gone.

He pulled himself to a sitting position, noting the spiteful glares of the three men who stood over him, staring down at him. A fourth man stood back by the door, as though guarding it. He was a bit older than the others, with thinning gray hair and a stringy beard. The smell of incense hung heavy in the air, and there were strange symbols painted along the walls and floor; stylized images of serpents and shamans and saints and other signs that were unintelligible to him. A cold chill crawled down his spine.

He noted a dingy window to his left, and, grateful for his newfound ability, focused his eyes on a spot of grass visible through cracked glass, and willed himself to be there.

Nothing happened.

His hand flew to his neck. The chain was gone.

The bare-chested man who had punched him lifted one arm, and dangled the chain. "Looking for this?"

Funny how the brain works in times of stress; Jake found himself wondering how many crunches it would take to get abs like that.

The man by the door said, "Maybe you could explain where you found this chain."

Jake shrugged. "Craigslist."

Nobody laughed.

The older man stepped forward. His weathered face and hanging jowls made him look like a bulldog. His mouth seemed permanently etched into a frown. Jake scooted back away from him, until his back was flush with the wall.

"Who are you?" Jowls asked.

"Who are you?" Jake shot back.

Jowls made a face that looked a lot like a snarl. Sweaty man shook his head slowly. The other two guys exchanged glances. Jake noted that these two were identical twins, with the same ebony skin, medium builds, and eyes the color of dead grass.

"You might want to answer the questions we ask you," one of the twins said.

The sneer never left Jowls's face. In fact, it appeared as though the man had never smiled, not once, in his entire life. After another moment of silence, he said, "You, boy, just stepped in a big pile of stink. So why don't you just make this easier on all of us and tell us what we want to know?"

"What's to know?" Jake said. "Other than that you're a bunch of murderers?"

One of the twins laughed, but he was the only one. Jowls just looked angrier, which Jake would not have thought possible only a few seconds ago.

"Now why would you go and make a rash accusation like that?" Jowls said.

Jake looked around. "The Bates Motel you live in, for one thing."

Sweaty man even laughed that time.

"How did you know to ask for me?" Jowls asked.

"I don't know what you mean."

"You asked for me by name. How did you know my name?"

"I still have no idea what you're talking about," Jake said.

"They call me HappyGoLucky," Jowls said. "Because of my sunny disposition."

That certainly cracked up the other three men, but Jowls only continued to glare at Jake, waiting for a response. Jake looked from one face to the next, trying to keep up.

"Wait, that's your name?" Jake said. "Now it makes sense! Then you must be the one I was sent for."

"Sent?"

"By Najac."

It felt as if all the air had been sucked out of the room, as the four men standing before him each took deep breaths and held them. So they did know Najac. Now he was getting somewhere.

"What do you know about Najac?" HappyGoLucky asked.

"He sent me to you."

"Oh yeah?"

"With his dying breath."

Perhaps he misjudged or maybe it was just a poor choice of words, but all at once the glares of the men turned murderous and the four tensed in unison, as though they meant to attack. HappyGoLucky continued to study Jake for several more seconds. He breathed deeply in and out, his thick chest expanding and contracting in rhythm. After another moment, he trudged over to the bare-chested man, and took the chain from him, then stood holding it.

"Ifé, you may want to get the Mother," HappyGoLucky said at last, then turned back to Jake. The sweaty man nodded and backed out of the room, making sure to keep his gaze fixed on Jake until he was gone.

"So what now?" Jake said.

HappyGoLucky pursed his lips. "Boy, you know you're in trouble, right?"

"What else is new?" Jake said. "Trouble is all I've had for days."

"Did you hurt our friend?"

"Did I what? No!"

HappyGoLucky came near again. "Not many people know we're here. We've been careful to keep it that way. You coming here and asking for me is pretty suspicious by itself."

"I told you, Najac sent me here."

"So you did."

"Yes."

"Why would he do a thing like that? And why would he give you his chain, I wonder?"

"He was dying."

HappyGoLucky fingered the chain. He rubbed one link between thumb and forefinger and, said, almost absently, "What happened to him?"

"I met him Saturday night. I was walking in the French Quarter. He started following me. We were... Well, we were arguing. Then something attacked us. He got hurt. He gave me this address and your name and that chain and then he died and I've been on the run ever since."

HappyGoLucky exchanged glances with the twins. Their expressions remained set and spiteful but it seemed a trace of uncertainty might have crept in as well. The older man leisurely walked back over to Jake. He dropped the chain into one pocket.

"Attacked by whom?" HappyGoLucky said.

"Some kind of snake monster," he answered, watching their faces for a reaction. To his surprise, their expressions reflected curiosity more than skepticism. He wasn't sure what to expect, but something told him to speak the truth.

"A snake monster?" HappyGoLucky asked.

"He called it a loa, I think. He said it was a snake god. He called it Danwaga or something like that."

"You mean Damballah?"

"Damballah! That's it!"

"That's impossible," HappyGoLucky replied in a flat tone completely devoid of even a trace of uncertainty.

"You act like you know this creature," Jake said, studying their faces. Their expressions remained neutral. A fresh surge of ice swept through his body, turning the blood cold in his veins.

"Mother is ready," came a soft, feminine voice from the doorway. The three men were still crowding Jake in, which prevented him from seeing the speaker. HappyGoLucky grunted his acknowledgment, but seemed a bit disappointed by the interruption. He wore a thoughtful expression. But then he stepped back and turned to the sound of the voice, and Jake saw her.

It was the young girl that had tried to help him the night of Najac's murder.

"You!" he blurted, pointing at her, his hand trembling.

The girl gasped and took a step backward out of the room. HappyGoLucky glanced from one to the other, reading their reactions.

"You two have met?" he asked.

"She was there!" Jake said. "She was there! When Najac was killed! She knows I'm innocent!"

HappyGoLucky regarded the small girl for a long moment. "Is this true, Lita? You know what this guy is talking about?"

Her expression hardened. She threw a bitter look in Jake's direction, as if he had done something wrong and she wanted to scold him for it. But she sighed and looked HappyGoLucky in the eyes. "I was there. I followed Najac." She pointed a finger at Jake. "Najac was following him." She started fidgeting, and fingered a tiny little ring that she wore on the pinky of her right hand.

"And why haven't you told us anything about this?"

"I was scared."

"Scared?" His voice became harder, his tone sharper.

Lita met his eyes, and her adolescent defiance flared. Her face went rigid and she balled her fists. "Yes, scared. Najac died! Do you think that was an easy thing for me?"

Something in HappyGoLucky's demeanor changed and he reached as though to pat her on the shoulder. She jerked away from him, her nostrils flaring. His mouth tightened into a hard line.

"We shouldn't do this in front of this one," he said, gesturing absently in Jake's direction.

"Agreed," said one of the twins.

"Fine," Lita said, looking around. She fixed her stare on Jake again. "I want to talk to him, though."

HappyGoLucky shook his head. "Out of the question."

"I wasn't asking," she said, and even Jake was taken aback at the certainty of her tone. He had never heard a girl of her age speak with so much confidence.

HappyGoLucky stomped out of the room.

Lita stepped toward Jake, who remained sitting against the far wall. She took measured steps, watching him closely. The twins tensed, as if waiting for Jake to make some kind of move. Lita stopped them dead in their tracks with a cold scowl that even Jake felt. How did one so young and seemingly innocent wield such influence over people like this?

She stopped when she was still several feet away from Jake. He had time to take several long breaths before she addressed him directly.

"Why did you sell me out to the cops the other night?" she asked.

"I was scared out of my mind." She nodded and sat down facing him. Up close, she didn't smell much better than the tall sweaty man, whom HappyGoLucky had called Ifé. He wondered if she was related to one of these men somehow, and how was it she came to be a part of this group. Another thing Jake noticed was that she seemed almost as nervous as he felt. She kept running her hands through her hair and playing with that ring on her right hand. Its band was plain and tarnished, like something won from a candy machine that would turn your skin green if you wore it too long.

"Najac thought you were involved with killing that girl in the French Quarter the other night," she said. Jake nodded. He already knew that. She continued. "Were you involved with killing that girl?"

"No," he said, with absolutely no hesitation.

She nodded. "I didn't think so. I didn't see him get hit, but I saw you and I knew you weren't the one who killed him."

Jake shivered. "Did you get a look at the thing that did that to him?"

She shook her head slowly from left to right. "Nope."

"He called it a loa."

"A spirit god," she said.

Jake almost laughed. "Of course. I keep forgetting that apparently I'm the only person in the world who has never heard of a loa before now." He used his palm to massage his forehead. "I don't know what freaks me out the most, that I saw someone get killed by a snake monster, or the fact that no one seems to bat an eye when I start talking about snake monsters." When she did not respond, Jake added, "Why did you offer to help me?"

She fixed those dark eyes of hers on him. "I knew you didn't kill Najac. But I figured you were mixed up in all this somehow."

"Mixed up in what?"

She shrugged. "I wish I knew the whole story. But Najac was pretty interested in that girl that died. He wouldn't tell me why. He said he thought somebody was twisting our teachings."

"What do you mean by twisting?" Jake said.

"We're a peaceful group," she replied.

He rubbed his sore jaw. "Yeah, I noticed."

"They were just being safe when they hit you," she said, a hint of derision in her voice. "I haven't been a part of this group long. But I can tell you that they are the real deal. And they don't go out looking for trouble or hurting people. The fact that they have been operating for as long as they have and nobody even really knows that they are here should be enough proof of that. But Najac died and they're all freaked out. And then you just show up asking for HappyGoLucky."

Jake appraised the girl for a moment longer. "No offense, but how did you get mixed up with these people in the first place? I mean, you're what, like thirteen, fourteen years old?"

"Thirteen," she said, looking away, as if the secrets of the universe were painted on the walls. Jake looked at the symbols and markings. Maybe the secrets of the universe *were* painted on the walls. "I guess sometimes one thing leads to another and you find yourself someplace you never thought you would end up."

Jake swallowed hard. He knew all about that.

Lita continued. "Let's just say I was wandering the streets with no place to go when I met Najac. I slept wherever I could and just made do. I really don't want to explain how I ended up that way." She fidgeted with the hem of her skirt while she spoke, and for the first time she actually came off like a thirteen-year-old, just a lost and frightened little girl. "Najac started bringing me food and blankets and stuff. One day he said he had talked to his people, and that I could come stay with them for a while if I thought I could handle it."

"If you thought you could handle it?"

"He was concerned I might freak when I saw their set-up."

"Oh." He felt foolish for not understanding that intuitively.

"So here I am," she continued. "They took me in, and at first it was weird, but I like it here. When I offered to help you the other night, I was going to bring you here."

He scratched absently at the floor. "Well seeing as how I ended up here anyway, I might have just taken you up on your offer and saved myself the trouble."

She said nothing, just started playing with the ring again. Jake decided to ask her about it.

"Interesting ring," he said.

She looked down at it. "Thanks. I guess I fidget when I'm nervous." Then, as an afterthought, she added, "My dad gave it to me."

"Your dad? Where is he? Why are you here instead of with him?"

The door opened again, before she could reply, and HappyGoLucky re-entered the room.

"It's time," he said, his face as stone sour as ever.

Jake stood. A concerned look etched its way onto Lita's features.

"Good luck, Jake," she said. Some part of him wanted to grab her and flee this place, to return her to wherever she had come from, to save the day for her. But of course she was here voluntarily and was not in any apparent danger and would probably view such an act as kidnapping rather than saving. But there was that part of him that instinctively sought to protect and cherish children, which was ironic considering he himself had none. He thought of Lucas. He thought of Missy. And now Lita, too.

"Thanks," he said, and moved forward to hug the child.

She shrank away from him and scurried out of the room.

"She doesn't like to be touched," HappyGoLucky said. "She must like you though. I got a little too close to her once and she kicked me in the giblets."

"So," Jake said, "has this Mother person told you I could leave?"

"That remains to be determined. We're going upstairs now."

"Upstairs? For what?"

This time HappyGoLucky did smile. It was a bizarre and alien expression on his face, and completely out of place, like Satan showing up for Sunday School.

"You ever been to a voodoo ceremony?"

Fifteen

They led him from the room, down a shadowy hallway, up a creaky staircase, and to the upper story of the old house. At some point, these people had knocked out all but the load-bearing walls of the structure, opening the entire upstairs into what amounted to a single, spacious, poorly lit room.

"This is a joke, right?" Jake asked along the way. "Voodoo? Are you for real? Is that even real?"

Nobody answered him. Jake was surprised to spot about a dozen other people already present, busying themselves with various tasks. A trio of women were in the process of closing the curtains over the broken windows, ushering an even darker gloom into the space. The only light in the room came from the stray beams of sunlight that somehow managed to sneak in through the drawn curtains. Then the same trio of women began lighting candles on an altar that ran along the far wall, spanning the entire width of the room. The flickering flames they produced chased away some of the shadows, but created new ones that that crept and danced along the walls. Several other items littered the bizarre altar: flags, bells, rattles, jars, pots, a very large wooden crate, statues of Roman Catholic saints, and a framed picture of St. Peter holding a large key.

HappyGoLucky noticed Jake eyeing the portrait and said, "St. Peter, who holds the key to heaven."

Standing near the altar, smiling at Jake with all the warmth and grace his own mother used to bestow upon him, was an older woman, not quite elderly, with wide brown eyes and skin the color of the deepest night. Her features were sharp and focused, and her eyes studied him with a vast intelligence. Her grayish hair was pushed back with a pearl-encrusted brocade clip and spilled over her shoulders in a wave. She wore a purple gown with a golden-colored sash tied about her waist, with only her bare feet visible beneath the hem line.

The Mother.

"This is he," the Mother said. She continued to smile.

HappyGoLucky stepped forward. "He claims to be innocent. He claims to have been-"

"His claims are known to me," she answered, cutting him off in an authoritative yet not unfriendly way. HappyGoLucky merely nodded and stepped back. Jake looked about and saw all his other friends here as well: Ifé, the twins, Lita, as well as an assortment of other unsavory characters he had not yet met.

The Mother stepped closer to Jake, that smile never wavering. Her eyes appeared at once loving yet stern. She reached for him and he flinched away. Undeterred, she placed her hands to Jake's temples. There was nothing to do but let her go through with whatever this was.

"So, you reading my mind?" he asked. "What number am I thinking of?"

"There is much angst in your mind, child," she said.

"It's called the modern age. We're all angst-ridden."

She looked into his eyes and continued to hold her hands to his head. Her fingertips felt like she had been soaking them in ice water for just this very occasion. She smelled of incense, but another scent lurked beneath the first, a musty aroma, like that of an old library book. She continued smiling at him the entire time that her fingertips massaged his temples, until finally she stepped back with a self-satisfied expression plastered to her face.

"So, which number?" Jake said.

HappyGoLucky gritted his teeth. "Mind your manners, boy."

"He is merely unconvinced," the Mother said. She alone appeared unoffended. Everybody else in the room glared vehemently at him, as though infuriated by his disrespect.

"You can't blame me for that," he replied, making sure everybody in the room heard him. "Voodoo? Seriously?"

"Give it time," the Mother said. "Arrange yourselves."

The assembled moved into a loose semicircle around the perimeter of the room, facing a central point right before the altar, where the Mother stood. Her smile was gone now. Her eyes shone with an eerie determination as she gathered herself, puffing her chest out, straightening her posture, flaring her nostrils. To Jake's untrained eye she was doing a great job of putting on a show.

Two large barrels rested in a corner of the room, with a thin sheath of animal skin draped over them and fastened into place. Two men he had not noticed emerged from out of the shadows to take up position behind these makeshift drums, and began pounding out a steady beat with their hands. They played in perfect tandem, their emotionless stares glued intently on the Mother, who cocked her own head back and allowed the beat to wash over her. Slowly at first, but with ever increasing rapidity, she began to gyrate, shaking her body with increasing abandon in a way Jake would not have thought her capable.

"The gods hear us!" she called out.

It was all Jake could do not to groan outright.

The old woman ceased her gyrations and approached the altar. Her head held low, she scooped a particular glass jar filled with clear liquid and then spun to face the assembled. They all wore identical enraptured expressions. She dipped her hand in the jar and flung wetness about the room, once in each direction.

"Papa Legba," she chanted. "Ouvri barrie pou nous passer." She recited this incantation with each dip of her hand into the jar.

"Water," HappyGoLucky whispered to Jake. "Just water."

"Really?"

"For Papa Legba."

"Of course. I knew that."

The drummers now took up a chant of their own: "Eyia, houn'to-a he! Delai commandé!"

Now the Mother flung the last of the water amidst her assembled crowd, gently placed the empty jar back onto the altar, turned once again to face her audience, and raised her hands over her head. With closed eyes and upturned face she cried out, "O Legba! Commandé! Vié Legba! Commandé. Commandé-yo."

Now the crowd joined in: "Legba lan oum'phor moin! Legba lan oum'phor moin! Legba Congo nan oum'phor moin!"

"Are you with us?" she whispered.

The candles flared with renewed intensity, the flames rising several feet into the air. Jake almost fell backward but righted himself in time. Thick plumes of smoke rose from the engorged flames, and the intensity of the heat in the room doubled. A parlor trick. Right?

The congregation members fell to their knees as one and cried out, their moans lacking any hint of articulation. They were primal moans, an expression of awe and pleasure. Jake alone remained standing, and stepped backward, away from the circle of worshipers, toward the nearest wall. The Mother watched him, a hint of a smile playing at the corners of her mouth. When she turned her eyes up toward the ceiling, the smoke from the candles gathered near her, enshrouding her in a kind of cloud. Those had to be some kind of trick candles; regular candles just didn't put out that much smoke.

The Mother called out in a loud voice, "Holy Mary, Mother of God, pray for the saints! Danbhalah-Wédo, assuage your children! Danbhallah-Wédo, we are all angels!"

As one, the congregation shouted, "Hail Mary, hear our prayers! Holy Angels, we are on our knees at the feet of Mary! Saint Rose, hear us! Saint Anthony, hear us! Saint Peter, give us the keys! Saint Joseph, charm our eyes!"

The flames of the candles receded until they were again only about an inch tall, and the excess smoke began to clear. A hush descended over the room. Nobody chanted. Nobody sang. Even the drummers ceased their beating. It seemed for a long while that they had all stopped breathing.

And then Jake felt it.

It was as if the available air in the room had been cut in half, like a presence of great mass had entered and filled much of the void. The hairs at the base of his neck prickled, and he felt a cold shiver run up both of his arms. Physically, nothing in the room had changed. Nobody had come or gone. Nobody had moved. Yet someone or something had joined them and was even now hovering above and among them. Someone sighed. He could not tell who made the noise because he was suddenly on his own knees, not in worship or deference, but as under a great pressure, like a heavy hand on his shoulder was pressing him into the floor. He heard the sigh again, and realized it was coming from his own lips. He was the one breaking the silence. He gathered his strength and gazed up, locked his eyes on the Mother, who stared back at him, arms outstretched, palms turned upward as if she expected to catch raindrops in them.

A young man rose from the crowd and moved forward. The Mother stepped aside. A plate rested on the altar, on which lay two pieces of pound cake. The young man removed this plate, bowed before the Mother, and crossed to the far side of the room. There, he knelt before a statue and placed the cake at its feet.

"An offering for Saint Expedite," the young man called, as he gently arranged the plate and then stepped away.

Jake studied the statue. It depicted a young man with curly brown hair, dressed in blue leggings and cloak with a red cape overflowing past his shoulders. His left hand was pressed to his breast, his right hand held high while clutching a crucifix. The face was calm, peaceful. Jake had never heard of Saint Expedite.

"Saint Expedite, hear our prayer," the Mother called, then stepped before the statue and dropped to one knee. "You who are our defender in urgent causes and prompt solutions. You who protect and heal, you who accomplish. Please hear our cries. One of our number has been attacked and murdered. Please answer us. Please expose his attacker, please show us the answer. Please grant us vengeance in this matter. Great Saint Expedite! Hear our urgent plea!"

The rest of the assembled began to pray fervently from their positions on the floor. They fell prostrate and cried out, their voices ringing with anguish. Whatever else they may be, their pain was real, the pain they felt for the loss of one of their own. Their prayers intermingled in the air and became an offering unto itself for this saint, this silent statue holding its cross. The clatter of sobs and shouting filled the air. Some voices rang with hurt. Others roared with anger. There was no chanting now, no ritualistic repetitions in languages he could not understand, these were the voices of men and women making known their hurts and worries.

Gradually the room went silent once more, one snuffed-out voice at a time until at last only the sound of labored breathing and a few muted sobs could still be heard. Something about this abandon of pretense and the laying bare of emotional turmoil touched at Jake in a way he had not expected.

The Mother moved toward the large crate that rested upon the altar. Jake had earlier noticed this box, had wondered what its purpose in all this might be and what it might hold. It looked like he was about to find out. As one, the congregation sighed, the sound of it pregnant with expectation. Whatever was in that box sure excited them. The eagerness was plain on their faces, and the invisible presence in the room seemed to move toward the front of the room, where it gathered and waited.

She flipped open the lid, opened the box, and reached in.

Cries of excitement and jubilation arose. Apparently this was the part of the ceremony to which they all looked forward. Despite himself Jake found his own curiosity piqued.

And then she withdrew the biggest snake Jake had ever seen.

As she pulled the creature free of the box, the beast seemed never-ending, coils upon coils slipping free of the confined space like one of those trick handkerchiefs that circus magicians liked to pull out of their pockets. Jake was no zoologist, but this thing had to weigh a ton and this old woman was handling it like it was no heavier than a wash cloth. It was as thick around as Jake's calf and long enough that the Mother could drape it across her shoulders and stretch it from wrist to wrist. She held it lovingly, cradling it in her arms, before doing something that really grossed Jake out.

The Mother lifted the snake's head close to her own until they were nose-to-snout. The snake seemed to be looking right at her. Then she stood completely still as its forked tongue shot forward several times and flicked across her face. Her body convulsed, spasms racking through her. More gasps and mutterings from the assembled. The crowd was really getting into this now. Many started muttering under their breaths rhythmically in what sounded like more chants. The drummers resumed their beat.

The Mother moved the snake slightly to one side and it licked her face again. Again she convulsed. Her eyes closed. The snake watched her but did not move, did not try to slither away or to fight her. Without any great spectacle beyond the face licking, she placed the snake back into its box and closed the lid.

The Mother turned to face the crowd. From his place near the back of the room, Jake could have sworn her eyes were now yellow, slitted, and very, very reptilian-looking. Surely it was a trick of the light? His pulse quickened and his breath caught in his throat.

"Who are you?" HappyGoLucky blurted.

The Mother's head snapped in his direction. It was a curious motion, like a stop animation movie, and it gave Jake the creeps.

"I go by many names," she answered. "Aida Wedo. Erzulie."

"Erzulie," HappyGoLucky repeated, and fell on his face.

Apparently this was a name that meant something to these people.

"Mother Erzulie, what would you tell us?" somebody screamed.

The Mother stalked toward the semicircle of her followers. She moved in a very curious manner, her legs slithering more than striding, her upper torso undulating from left to right, her arms swaying with the motion of her hips.

"I would tell you to beware," she responded. "Old powers have been renewed. Battle lines have been drawn. Desecration of the old ways has been uncovered."

"Desecration?" moaned somebody from across the room. Now the Mother's head snapped in that direction.

"A desecration of the worst grade. And there looms above you all a great shadow."

Just like that Jake's skepticism flooded back into his mind. Was this for real? He sat and waited for the supposed goddess to proclaim some dark prophesy and to hail the coming of "the one" who would save them all.

But she surprised him. She slithered right on over to him and looked down upon him with those serpent eyes. How had she done it? Contacts? But when had she put them in? Jake had been staring at her this whole time, and had never once seen her put anything in her eyes.

"This one means us no harm," she announced. He sat upright with a start. "His story rings of truth. No harm will befall us at his hand. He is an entrusted brother."

Entrusted brother?

At that she strode away, making her way back to the front of the room where she promptly fell on her face and did not move for several seconds. Nobody went to help her. Nobody cried out in alarm. She stood again finally, faced them and smiled. Her eyes were normal. That was some trick! Neither did she continue to undulate like a gypsy princess. Whatever had come over her was gone. In fact, the presence that had loomed over the room for the last several minutes seeped away, and with it the pressure Jake had felt all that time.

The candles spontaneously extinguished, plunging the room into near darkness. The muted light filtering through the thick curtains at the windows bathed the room in a soft magenta glow. The trio of women moved to pull back the curtains and expose the room once again to the light of the sun.

The ceremony was over.

HappyGoLucky found Jake a moment later, as the group began dispersing and many of the others disappeared back downstairs.

"Well?" he said, his face expectant.

Jake had no idea what to say about what he had just witnessed. A moment later, the Mother glided over to stand beside HappyGoLucky, and she smiled at Jake.

"They tell me you were proclaimed innocent," she said.

"What do you mean, they? You just said that yourself."

She chuckled. "That was not me, child. When I am mounted I have no recollection of what transpires while the gods give voice."

"Sounds like a frat party," he said.

"Not that kind of mounting, fool," HappyGoLucky said. "A loa can mount a human host like a jockey mounts a horse. When that happens, the loa is in control. The host has no awareness of what transpires until the loa dismounts. Afterward, the host relies on the rest of us to tell her what happened while she was gone."

Jake looked from one face to the next. "Well, I can't say you people don't believe in all this."

HappyGoLucky looked shocked. "Don't you? Didn't you just witness it for yourself?"

"I witnessed something, that's for sure."

The Mother placed a hand on HappyGoLucky's forearm. "The child remains skeptical. That's fine. We don't need to convince him otherwise."

"Great, can I go now?"

"First, I would have you take something from me," she said. She pulled one sleeve up, and Jake noticed a small sack that was tied about her wrist by a thick strand of chord.

"Take this," she said, removing the sack and handing it over.

"What is it?"

"To ward off evil. That bag contains a gray powder made from snake vertebrae mixed with some silver dust. I *fixed* it myself. Something evil hangs over you, and you will need that protection."

He held the bag close to his face and examined it. "Fixed it?"

"Mixed the ingredients and cast the protective wards over it," she clarified.

"Thanks?" he said, making a mental note to dump it as soon as he was away from here.

"I guess you should have this back too," HappyGoLucky said, and Jake almost jumped for joy when he handed back the silver chain. He must have read the incredulity all over Jake's face because he was quick to add, "If Najac gave that to you, then it stays with you. As much as I would like to have it, I believe it's yours now."

He took the chain and clasped it once more about his neck.

"There's still something I don't get," Jake said. "What's the connection between Najac and Faith? If he was investigating her death, then why? Did he know her? How did he know what happened to her?"

Before they could answer, a shout arose from downstairs, and all at once there seemed to be many muffled voices bickering at one another.

"What the-?" HappyGoLucky said as he turned to head down the stairs. It sounded like quite the commotion was taking place down there.

HappyGoLucky went down first and Jake just instinctively followed. He didn't look to see if the Mother was behind him. As he descended, the front door came into view, visible at the end of the long hall that stretched the length of the house's ground floor. The door stood wide open. The frightened woman who stood frozen with her hand on the knob was visibly trembling. Many others were yelling nervously.

Several police officers stood just outside the door in a huddle on the front porch. In the doorway, first and foremost among the officers, stood Detective Rivera.

"Oh crap," Jake muttered.

Rivera had his gun drawn faster than Jake could even process and respond to what was happening. Once he saw that gun pointed his way his knees buckled.

"Hold it right there," Rivera said. "Don't you so much as move a nose hair."

Jake stood perfectly still, his every muscle tensing, even as he fought against the urge to ask the detective if it was possible to move one's nose hairs.

Rivera stepped farther into the house. The others gave him a wide berth, none quite willing to step in his way. "On your knees. Hands on your head," he said.

"I really don't think-"

"I said on your knees!" he roared.

Jake complied. He sank to the ground, slowly placing his hands on top of his head.

Behind Rivera, more police officers filed into the house, weapons drawn. They all seemed to notice the strange symbols and markings painted on the floors and walls, and a few of them appeared quite frightened. Even Rivera seemed uneasy as he took it all in.

"Seriously, Presnall?" he said. His eyes fell on one wall in particular, to a crudely drawn picture of black witch doctors with bone necklaces about their necks dancing over a large kettle. Everywhere the eye traveled there were stylized circles painted that seemed to be comprised of individual symbols linked together, with swirling lines and shapes of stars and hearts within them. And everywhere in between, serpents, serpents, and more serpents.

"What the hell kind of whacked out crap are you into?" Rivera said, stepping forward. He gestured to one of the officers and nodded to Jake. The officer withdrew a set of handcuffs and approached, timidly, as if expecting somebody at any second to curse him.

"I can explain this," Jake said, his voice strained.

"You'll get your chance at the station," Rivera replied.

The officer slapped a cuff on one of Jake's wrists, pulled his hands down and behind his back, and cuffed the other. It seemed to Jake that he clasped the steel unnecessarily tight.

"Get up," Rivera said. The officer standing behind Jake helped pull him to his feet. All around Jake, the cultists looked on, concern etched on their once impartial features.

"What in the hell have we stumbled into?" Rivera asked as he relaxed his poise ever so slightly, looking around anew. "Check the place out," he said to the officers. Not a one of them looked excited to go deeper into the house. Jake could not blame them. The house exuded creepy. He could see that now. His previous trip through here had been rushed and he had not been in full control of his senses. Now he could clearly appreciate the gloominess, the way the many boarded-over windows and lack of indoor lighting afforded it the look of something you might ordinarily see in a haunted house movie. Couple that with the strange symbols and the hushed faces looming in the shadows and he could see why this might be a scary place to explore. Undoubtedly these officers had all seen more than their share of horror movies and right about now it was easy to believe that the things they saw in those movies could be possible.

"What is the meaning of this?" a voice bellowed from the staircase. Jake turned to see the Mother emerging into view and all at once about half a dozen guns were pointed at her.

"Not another step," Rivera said.

She kept coming.

"I said, hold it!"

She came to a stop at the bottom of the staircase. "You cannot come into my home like this. I have not seen a warrant."

Rivera eyed her. "I don't need a warrant, lady. Your friend here opened the door and let me in." He gestured to the girl who still stood by the door. "And when I came in I found a wanted fugitive on the premises." He gestured to Jake. "So you will do as you are told, is that understood?"

"I take orders from no man," the Mother replied.

Great time to play the feminist card, Jake thought.

Rivera just glared at her. "I am not giving orders as a man. I am giving orders as a homicide detective under authority of the New Orleans Police Department. You will do as instructed or you will be arrested for hampering an active investigation. Is that understood?"

She bared her teeth and took another step forward.

"How many people are in this house?" Rivera barked.

"I have not counted."

"I want everybody outside now."

"You cannot legally demand such a thing," she said evenly. Jake had no idea if that was true or not.

"Lady, you are trying my patience," Rivera said.

The situation only grew tenser from there. Rivera continued to glower at the Mother. The Mother continued to openly defy Rivera. The other members of the congregation continued to loiter on the periphery like so many frightened shadows. Even HappyGoLucky was silent. Nobody quite knew how to proceed, it would seem. Tempers flared. Police officers flexed. Everybody stood tensed and waiting to see what would happen next. Something would have to give.

They did not have to wait long.

At that moment, a deafening wail sounded throughout the house, and one entire wall crashed inward upon itself. Almost everyone present, law officers included, dodged or dropped or in some way cowered. A fresh burst of light entered the house through the spot where there was no longer a wall. Debris and rubble settled. The cops trained their guns in that direction. Nobody fired. Not yet.

Then the loa, the thing they called Damballah, the hideous snake creature that had killed Najac, stepped through the hole, hissed, and charged.

Sixteen

Once, when he was a boy, Jake stood up to the neighborhood bully. The moment could have been plagiarized right out of "A Christmas Story," with Jake playing the role of little Ralphie. Minus the snow, of course. New Orleans rarely saw snow. But the situation was the same. Titus was a kid who back then stood just shy of three stories tall and was built like someone destined to play in the NFL. At least, that was the way it seemed to Jake and his friends as they cowered in fear. Titus was ahead of his time, relying more on threats of violence and psychological warfare rather than on wedgies and arm twisting, but he was not above throwing a sucker punch or shoving some hapless kid to the ground.

One day Jake had enough and socked Titus. It was as simple as that. The bully had the audacity to make a very unchildlike comment about Bre, insulting her honor as it was. This was back when she had honor. Had he waited a few more years before making the same comment, she probably would have jumped his bones right there in the street. But at that delicate age the comment shocked and upset her so Jake just hauled off and hit him. He packed everything he had into that one punch; all the frustration and months of torment and abuse all came out in one cataclysmic frontal assault.

Titus took the blow like a championship boxer, returned one of his own, bloodied Jake's lip, and walked off laughing. Jake looked up at the sky from where he lay on the ground. Bre forgot the insult and giggled at his misfortune before skipping away without a care in the world.

The encounter taught Jake two very important lessons. One, Bre was the worst sister in the world. Two, when facing down certain demise by a bigger, stronger enemy, caution is always the better part of valor.

In other words, when Jake saw the snake creature charge, he ran like hell.

Those who were closest to the creature never stood a chance. Three of the voodoo cultists happened to be within easy striking distance of the beast and they went down first, their screams drowned out as the snake appendages lanced out and cut them down with ease and grace.

The police officers finally opened fire. Gunshots rang in the confined space, and Jake had no idea that the retorts could be so deafening. The movies never portrayed that. The sound of the blasts bounced off the walls in a crescendo of noise so great that it became impossible to tell how many were actual gunshots and how many were merely the echoes. For a long while he thought his head would explode, with his hands cuffed behind his back so that he could not even muffle his ears against the noise. He saw the snake creature strike a glaring blow with one of those short but powerfully built arms, and the nearest officer went down, not to rise again.

Detective Rivera practically yanked Jake off his feet as he tossed him into the waiting arms of the nearest officer, who happened to be the same man that had cuffed him.

"Get him outside, Perez, away from all this," Rivera barked. The officer nodded.

Perez marched Jake through the front door of the house, across the porch, and away from the screams and crunching noises behind him that were probably the sounds of bones and bodies being smashed and twisted. He noted four squad cars parked in front of the house, their red and blue beams flashing round and round.

"They don't stand a chance against that thing," Jake said as Officer Perez pulled him along to one of the parked squad cars.

"Shut up," Perez said.

Jake tried to protest further, but Perez forced him inside the car and slammed the door shut behind him. He found himself face down on the seat, and struggled to a sitting position, which was no easy feat for a man in a confined space with his hands cuffed behind his back. Perez was facing the house, as if trying to decide whether to guard his captive or rush back to the aid of his friends inside, who were likely being ripped apart at this very moment.

Jake slammed his shoulder into the car window repeatedly in a failed attempt to get Perez's attention, but gave it up when he realized Perez was not going to turn back around and face him. His eyes were fixed on the house, his attention unwavering, as the sounds of a small war drifted across the space.

Jake could think of no worse way to die than to just sit in that car, wait for the loa to kill everybody inside the house, and then come for him. He was a sitting duck like this, and it was all he could do to not completely lose his mind and give in to utter panic.

What was that old saying about desperate times?

He scooted across the seat, away from Perez, and peered out the window to the ground beside the squad car. He felt that familiar ring of heat around his neck, and then he was sitting on the ground beside the squad car, thanking his fortunes that HappyGoLucky had returned the chain to him before the police showed up. Getting up with his hands cuffed behind his back was awkward to say the least, but Perez was so focused on the house that he did not notice his captive was free until Jake rammed his shoulder into the small of the officer's back with all the strength and momentum he could muster. They landed in a heap on the ground together, where Jake's leading shoulder took the brunt of the impact and flared in protest.

Jake rolled over and hoped the old trick from the movies really did work. He tried to work his hands over his butt and down the back of his legs to get them in front of him. It turned out to be harder than it was always portrayed. The most difficult part for him was getting his wrists past the backs of his calves. His legs simply did not want to stretch that far, but after much wriggling that would have made any earthworm proud he finally worked his hands free. He was still cuffed, but at least now his hands were in front rather than behind him.

Perez stood over him, gun drawn and pointed right at him.

"Crap," Jake muttered.

"Don't move, creep!"

"Such original cop dialogue," Jake said.

"I mean it."

Rather than reply, Jake hopped again. He wished he could have seen the cop's expression when he vanished from right in front of him. But he did not travel far. He reappeared right behind the startled officer and charged him again. This time Perez was not so quick to get up.

"I am so sorry. You probably don't deserve this," Jake said, as he fumbled for the keys to the cuffs. The stupid belt around the cop's waist had about as many compartments as Batman's utility belt. He kept expecting to come across some smoke bombs and a boomerang, but that never happened. He did, however, finally locate the keys, which he used to unlock his cuffs. Perez, for his part, appeared to still be out of it. Jake figured he had a few seconds before the officer regained his senses and started shooting.

The question now was, did he run away or did he rush back into the house?

But there was no question, really. People were dying and he did not think he would be able to look at himself tomorrow if he just walked away today.

He mounted the sagging steps and crossed the porch for the second time as he rushed headlong back into a situation that could easily cost him his life.

The inside of the house reminded him of a scene from a war movie he had seen recently. Not one of the classics that always took place in the jungle; modern war movies were set in places like Afghanistan or Iran, and always seemed to involve a firefight inside a dilapidated old house in a dusty village. That was what the inside of this house now looked like. Entire sections of walls were shattered, with plaster and wood chippings everywhere. What little furniture there had been was smashed and scattered about. A curious dust lingered in the air. Insulation hung like stalactites from places where entire sections of ceiling had fallen in.

And the bodies.

Dead and dying people were everywhere. Some of them wore police uniforms. A couple of officers were moaning and dragging themselves along the floor, their bloodied faces twisted in pain. Near the large hole through which the loa entered the house lay the three mangled bodies of the cultists who had been the first to fall. He recognized one as being one of the women who had lit the candles upstairs, and another as the corpse of one of the twins.

Other than the sounds of pain that surrounded him, the house had grown eerily silent. Either the loa had finished its work and left the premises or it was lying low somewhere just waiting to ambush its next victim. Jake thought that the silence was worse than the ruckus.

And then, a new sound, coming from upstairs, like something being dragged across the floor.

It looked like he was going up.

He took the stairs at a snail's pace, unable to avoid the faint creaking of each and every footfall. He dared not teleport; the thought of accidentally materializing blindly right in front of the loa was not a pleasant one. As he ascended, more and more of the upper floor came into view.

The altar was in pieces. Heaps of broken wood lay everywhere, amidst the remnants of all the various implements that had been so meticulously arranged on the altar only a short while ago. Nearby, adjacent to a smashed statue, the Mother was trying to drag herself toward the steps. She groaned with the effort, but she was not making any progress; her entire body below the waist was twisted at an unnatural angle. Yet she smiled when she saw Jake.

Jake knelt at the old lady's side. Somehow that grin on her face was making this even worse, and he felt a tightness in his chest, a swell of emotion he would not have expected to feel for this woman who was little more than a stranger to him.

"Are you alright?" he asked. Dumb question, but obligatory.

"Never better," she croaked.

"I'm going to try to get help."

"No time," she said. "I won't be long of this earth. And it's still here somewhere. I can sense it."

"What is it?" he asked. He remembered what Najac told him, but he wanted to get confirmation from the Mother. He figured she was the authority on the matter.

"Loa."

That answered that.

She continued. "Spirit god."

"Damballah? Najac said it was Damballah." Jake Presnall, voodoo expert.

She grimaced as a sudden wave of pain wracked through her broken body. "Not clear. But he's powerful. And dangerous. I didn't have enough time to try to counter him."

"There's a way to counter him?" Jake asked. "You mean, like kill him?"

Her eyes focused on Jake. "You can't kill a loa."

"But you said you could counter him?"

"Try to send him back," she corrected. "The spirits need host bodies." Jake recalled just a short while ago when the Mother had supposedly been 'mounted' by some being called Erzulie. "Sometimes," she continued, "they don't leave the host body right away. The host starts to change physically. Become more like the spirit dwelling within."

It sort of made sense, in a way that made absolutely no sense. If you followed the twisted logic and assumed that people could be mounted by gods and all that. If some person had been mounted by a serpent god and the serpent god refused to leave, the person would over time take on serpent-like qualities. Or something.

"How can I send it back?" Jake asked.

"You can't." Sadness in her eyes. "Only one with *the power* can work the spells."

The power. Meaning a voodoo priestess. Of which he knew only one. And she was about to die. Great.

"What can I do?" he pleaded.

Before she could answer, a rough voice called out, "Don't move!"

He looked up and saw Detective Rivera standing at the top of the staircase, his gun trained on Jake.

"Just a minute," Jake said.

"Put your hands where I can see them!" Rivera barked.

"This is really bad timing."

"Do it now!"

Jake had no choice but to comply. He half expected Rivera to shoot him anyway. The man was quaking with visible fury. He bared his teeth, and his face was a shade of purple not normally found in nature. Jake couldn't blame him. How many of his friends had just been butchered downstairs?

"Detective Rivera, this is-"

"How the hell did you get loose? Again?"

"This lady might know how to stop that monster!" Jake screamed.

That gave Rivera a moment's pause. The Mother tremulously moved one hand and dropped it on Jake's leg, getting his attention. He glanced down at her.

"No use," she said. "Can't. Cast. Counter. Spell." She was slipping. Her sentences were growing as short as her breaths.

"Why not?"

"So. Much. Don't. Know."

Rivera just listened to the exchange. He was uncharacteristically silent, appearing indecisive for the first time since Jake had met him.

Jake was about to press the Mother further but never got the chance.

A section of floor ten feet away simply exploded upward in a shower of wood bits. The loa came through the floor like a volcano blowing its top. Debris went everywhere. Jake tried to shield his face as he fell to one side. He rolled to get clear, and even Rivera fell back.

And there it stood, the being everybody kept calling Damballah. The snakes about the creature's body writhed and twisted, slithering over one another in a mad dash to kill something. The loa's eyes were reptilian and slitted, its skin pale and muscular. A stray gleam of sunlight glinted off of the jewel in its forehead as it darted forward. It hefted the Mother into the air and tossed her into the nearest wall like Miss Jerry's paperboy tossing the morning paper onto the porch. There was a loud snapping noise, and that was the end of her.

"No!" Jake screamed, unable to tear his eyes off of the poor woman's corpse.

Rivera wasted no time, as years of training took hold. He adopted a firing stance and popped out a couple of rounds into Damballah, who promptly turned, gathered himself, and vomited one of those awful purple blasts like the one that had killed Najac.

Rivera barely had a chance to react, and could not have known what was about to happen. But when the energy began gathering around the creature's head as it had in the alley, Jake knew what was coming. By the time the light appeared, Jake already had a running start, and beamed himself to the detective's side. He reappeared just in time to yank him from the path of the blast, which cascaded past them both. It struck the far wall and caused it to explode, leaving a sizable hole in the drywall.

Rivera looked up at Jake, surprise etched on his features. Jake realized he was lying on top of the man like a lover.

"Get off!" the detective bellowed.

"I guess you like dinner and a movie first?"

"Get off!"

Jake slid off of the detective.

Damballah raged about and charged again. The flimsy floor shook under its determined strides. Jake rolled clear as the beast slammed one massive foot down, clearly aiming for Jake's head. There was a crunching noise and its foot actually broke through the floorboards and disappeared from view. With one herculean jerk it tore free, leaving behind a crater.

That was when Jake felt the fingers close around his neck. The sheer strength of that grip was mind boggling. His feet kept working, as though they thought they could separate themselves from the rest of his body and escape on their own. But he had not been fast enough. The creature had him. The shock and surprise dumbfounded him for the moment or two it took for the creature to spin him around and lash out with its snake appendages. It was time that would have been better spent teleporting out of the creature's grasp, but his mind was blank and the thought did not even occur to him.

The bite did not come. The snake veered aside at the last moment. Damballah narrowed its eyes and peered at him more closely. It pulled him nearer so that their faces were only about two feet apart. Up close Jake got a good whiff of an antiquated earthen smell that rolled off of the beast, as if it had been sleeping under a pile of mud. The jewel on its forehead glittered in the lights that came through the cracked windows. It took Jake a moment to realize what was happening.

Damballah was studying him.

Rather than just killing him outright, something about Jake had interested it enough to cause it to pause and appraise its prey.

Jake realized what it was that had caught the creature's attention, when, with its free hand, it clasped and began to finger the silver chain about his neck. Could it sense the chain's special properties? There was no way to know for sure, but there was no denying that the creature was uncannily interested in the chain.

Jake did not want to sit around while the creature decided what to do. He teleported away.

Or at least, he tried to teleport away.

Just at that moment when Jake felt his body being stretched out over many miles, like it did every time he beamed himself somewhere, it felt like he slammed right into a brick wall, only to bounce back to his original location. Disoriented, he tried again, and met the same resistance. Something was blocking him, and the realization was terrifying. The loa started making a clicking noise in its throat, with a certain repetitive quality and tone that Jake recognized even though he had never heard a sound quite like that ever before in his life.

Damballah was laughing at him.

In some mysterious way, Damballah was cancelling out the chain's power. And even worse, Damballah *knew* that it was cancelling out the chain's power.

The fingers about his neck tightened. His usable air supply dwindled. The loa could have snapped his head from his shoulders with the same effort that it took Jake to pop a can of Coke, but it was savoring this moment. It was watching him struggle and gag, and it was enjoying it.

It all came to him in a flurry then. He would never know what truly happened to Faith Daelly. He was pretty sure this creature was what had killed her, but he would never really know why. He would possibly go down on record as a fugitive from the law who had died during a botched recovery attempt. His memory would be tarnished. Miss Jerry would be devastated. Lots of people, like Dr. Cherry and Phil Latham, would feel vindicated in their distrust of him.

He would never have a real life. No wife. No children. As he felt his life draining away, he was surprised how much regret he felt at the thought of never starting a family. How could he have never realized how much that meant to him? It wasn't a coincidence that he had the relationship he had with Lucas and Missy. That part of him that desperately longed for a family of his own saw something in them for which it yearned night and day.

He flailed as the usable oxygen in his bloodstream was depleted. It was one of those panicky writhing kind of things, and in his struggles he felt a pressure against his leg. Something lumpy in his pocket. It was the small pouch that the Mother had given him. Supposedly some kind of ward she had come up with against evil. Maybe it warded off magic, but it apparently did not stop somebody from choking you to death.

But wasn't Damballah at least somewhat magical? Hadn't some form of spell accounted for his "mounting" of the host he inhabited?

Jake was just seconds away from loss of consciousness when he plunged a hand into his pocket and pulled the small sack free. If the creature holding him noticed this it gave no indication. Likely it figured whatever resistance Jake could muster was no threat to it.

Damballah continued to hold him there, choking out his life. Its mouth hung open, revealing rows of sharp teeth. Jake threw caution to the wind and plunged that little sack into the creature's gaping maw, then pulled his hand back sharply, fearing the thing would snap its jaw shut and he would lose it.

The result was instantaneous. The loa's eyes widened, its body jerked, some kind of squeal came from deep in its chest, its grip slackened, and suddenly Jake was free. He dropped to the ground, collapsing and choking. The soothing flow of oxygen felt good in his lungs and he gasped it down as quickly as he could, even while having the good sense to roll clear of the thrashing mass above him.

Damballah was not a happy camper. It stomped and heaved, trying to dislodge the ward.

Jake glanced over just then to see Rivera taking a shooting stance. He held his firearm outstretched and fired off several shots at the loa. Maybe it was the ward that was making Damballah vulnerable, but the bullets penetrated the creature's flesh and spurts of orange blood erupted with each hit. Damballah screamed, a high shriek that was full of shock and anger and pain. Rivera emptied his clip, and orange goo was dripping freely down the loa's chest, and yet the creature stood, staggering. It hadn't gone down, but it was showing weakness.

Then Jake realized that the loa had chosen a very unfortunate place to stand. Still out of breath, he nevertheless gathered himself up for another assault. He rose to his feet, eyes locked on his target. The St. Expedite statue, minus its head and one arm, rested on its back not very far away. Jake went for it.

He hoisted that statue high above his head, estimated its weight at about thirty or so pounds, took a half dozen brazen steps toward the loa, and chucked it right into the creature's chest. Normally he might have feared getting this close, but the loa was still staggering, off balance. The many serpentine appendages flailed about in disarray, none seeking to strike.

The sudden blow of the heavy statue had the intended effect. The creature toppled over backward. But it did not land on the floor. Damballah had been standing over the hole that it had created when it erupted into the room like Mt. Vesuvius blowing its top. The beast fell through its own crater, through the floor, and fell an entire story before crashing to the ground floor below with a shriek, a grunt, and a loud, cartoonish splatt.

Jake sank to his knees and crumpled over on his side. He struggled to catch his breath. For a moment at least they had a reprieve. With any luck the creature would be dead. The Mother had said it was impossible to kill a loa, but there was no harm in having hope. At the very least they should have a few moments to collect themselves.

Rivera knelt over him. "Good move, Presnall," he said as he checked for injuries.

"That sounds a little bit like a compliment," Jake rasped out in reply.

"You're a jerk."

Jake thought he saw a smile wanting to form on the detective's lips, but Rivera quickly snuffed it out. Satisfied with the results of his search, Rivera stood and peered down through the hole into the abyss that lurked below.

"I'll be damned," he said.

"What?"

"It's gone."

From a distance came the sound of multiple sirens blaring, signaling the arrival of more cops. There were lots of them, and they were getting closer.

Officer Perez staggered onto the second floor landing, gun held at the ready. Rivera turned to face him.

"One job, Perez. I gave you one job. Watch Presnall."

"Sorry," he said. "He escaped."

"Yeah, he seems to do that a lot." Rivera threw a glare down at Jake that was one part aggravated, one part awed.

"He attacked me," Perez said.

"I was just trying to get back in here so I could help," Jake said.

The angry scowl on Perez's face did not abate. He simply looked to Rivera for some sort of decision or answer.

"Did you catch sight of that thing down there?" Rivera asked Perez.

"I didn't see anything," he said.

"You would have had to walk right by it to get up here."

"I didn't see it."

The sirens were right outside. Jake heard the sounds of multiple cars arriving on the scene, brakes squealing and car doors slamming, voices barking at one another.

Rivera paced back to Jake. "I'm going to see you off to the hospital to get checked out. But you're under arrest, you know that right?"

"Arrest? You have to know I'm innocent after that!"

Rivera sighed. "Yeah, probably, all things considered. And you did just save my life. But you have outstanding warrants from the other night and you did assault an officer today."

Jake stretched out and stared at the ceiling. He could not believe his ears.

"But I'll see what I can do," Rivera continued. "We'll observe the formalities, and we'll try to take care of this."

Jake stole a glance at Rivera. The detective was offering to help him?

"You can't be serious. He attacked me!" Perez demanded.

"Like I said, we'll observe the formalities."

Perez fumed.

"People died today," Rivera said, turning to the obdurate officer. "Go downstairs! Take a look at the bodies! Then come back up here and tell me about your wounded pride!"

Perez looked like he had been slapped. For a moment shame passed over his features like a shadow cast by a rolling cloud. It quickly dissipated. He steeled himself and stalked away. The sound of many voices downstairs could now be heard.

"Lucky for them that they didn't get here sooner," Rivera said. "Or there would be more bodies to sort through."

Seventeen

"I have no idea how to respond to this."

Rivera spun to survey the damage in light of this new and most welcome news. In his line of work, the good news came so infrequently that it was always harder to receive that than the bad news. Around him, the carnage still looked like carnage, but it was as if a heavy drapery had been pulled back from a window and shed some extra light on it all. The house was still trashed, entire walls still seemed to be hanging on by only a single wooden stud, there were still pools of blood and broken bodies scattered about, but the news was good. Really good. It just did not make any sense.

"All of them?" Rivera spun to once again face the diminutive Medical Examiner.

"All of them. They're all alive. All of the officers who reported to the scene. They're all injured, sure. Some worse than others." He removed his glasses, wiped them on his shirt, and placed them back on his face. "But every one of your guys that went in there is going to be able to go home to their families."

Rivera, not typically an emotional man, did not trust himself to speak for a long moment. His chest swelled under the significance of this news. His guys. Alive. All those wives who would not need to receive *the visit.* "And the people from the house?"

"Dead, most of them. Some of them managed to survive. Probably because they had the good sense to go down and stay down."

Rivera exhaled and unclenched his fists. He scratched his head and tried to puzzle it out.

"That can't be a coincidence, given what we were up against."

"Yeah, about that. Listen-"

"I don't need the patronizing doctor speak about mass hallucination or battle stress or whatever it's going to be," Rivera said. "I'm not even worried right now about that creature, or whatever the hell it was. I'm trying to wrap my head around how in all that carnage in there, not one officer died. Not one. I saw people cut down. I saw all kinds of stuff I wouldn't have imagined. That thing was not messing around. It went through that place like a bulldozer, attacking without discrimination, but it only killed the people from the house and it let the officers live?"

"Statistically-" Perkins started.

"Statistically my ass. There were fourteen people in that house when we arrived. I had nine officers with me. That's twenty-three people in all, not counting myself, and that monster cut through the whole lot of them in less than three minutes."

"Are you complaining?"

"I'm grateful as all hell. I'm the last person that wants to see one of our boys go down. But this is not a coincidence. It's as if that thing was showing restraint, like it knew who its targets were and wouldn't or couldn't kill anybody else."

The Medical Examiner simply regarded him silently. Rivera knew that look. He hated that look. It was the look medical professionals gave to people when they were filtering their words and actions through some sort of mental encyclopedia of medical knowledge, categorizing them as though all people could just be sorted neatly into little columns in which what they said meant nothing because the medical professional alone knew better. Perkins was not looking at Rivera as a colleague, but as a subject, a person to be analyzed. He was sizing Rivera up, determining what type of trauma response he was exhibiting, trying to "decode" his words as though he were not competent enough to accurately report what he had witnessed. It was a patronizing look. Rivera fought down the urge to just punch him in the face and break his nose.

He did not bother bouncing any more thoughts off of Perkins. The man was limited by his knowledge. Perkins thought his vast education made him smarter, and to an extent that was true, but it also boxed him in, forced him to view everything, all of life, through a narrow little lens, as if the only things in the world that were real and true and meaningful were the things that he could recreate in a laboratory somewhere. So-called intellectuals were always saying stuff like that. But people knew better.

The entire world was Rivera's laboratory. It had to be. The real world was where he had to work.

Rivera had taken philosophy in college. He remembered the professor trying to convince the class that any meaningful knowledge should be falsifiable, that is, there must be some way to "test" a theory in order for the theory to even be worth considering. Some of the people in the class bought into that, but he had immediately realized that this was a self-defeating philosophy, because it was itself a theory that could not be tested or falsified. Yet narrow-minded scientists and science majors used that type of thinking every day to pre-emptively limit what they perceived to be the realm of physical possibilities, to disavow the existence of anything that they could not directly observe under a microscope. Perkins obviously fit into this category. To people like him, powerful emotions like love and devotion were nothing more than random chemical and hormonal releases. They ignored reports of anything that even sounded supernatural, insisting there was no evidence for such things, even as they were ignoring what would be construed in any other situation to be evidence. They vehemently insisted that there was no such thing as God, that the universe had somehow created itself, and then non-life had just spontaneously produced life, and that these early life-forms then began evolving and becoming increasingly well-formed and complex.

It was a load of bull. Rivera was not a superstitious man, he had never claimed to see a ghost, nor was he particularly spiritual or religious. He chose agnosticism over atheism because he knew in his heart that the concept of a God figure was not as farfetched as some believed, that it actually explained a whole slew of issues more accurately than did naturalism, and thus he saw no reason to rule the possibility out preemptively. What he lacked was even the foggiest idea how to sort out the world's religions and determine which, if any, had discovered any actual truth about what lies beyond this world. He knew better than to subscribe to any of that new age crap about how all religions were equally valid because they all pointed the way to nirvana. Anybody with half a brain should be able to spot the problem with that logic. One religion says God created the universe and exists apart from it. Another says God *is* the universe and we are all part of his body. Another says we all get to be gods of our own universes if we're good enough. They could not all be true. Not when they all believed very different things. Any perceived similarities were at best superficial, a result of a universal objective hard-wired into the human condition, such as the call to live morally and upright. No. Rivera knew that all the world religions were not equally valid. No doubt they all possessed sparks of truth. But if there was a single religion that had stumbled upon absolute truth, then by definition, any religion that disagreed with it was wrong.

Rivera knew all that. What he did not know was if absolute truth had ever been discovered, or how it would be recognized if it had been discovered. So rather than puff himself up and pretend like he had all the answers, he walked the middle road, nestled comfortably in agnosticism, the shrugging of shoulders and the firm belief that he knew nothing.

Which is why he hated it so much when he got that look from guys like Perkins, guys who thought they did have all the answers and who had already decided far in advance what the finished picture of the universe simply *must* look like.

The Medical Examiner was great at looking at dead bodies and determining time and cause of death. Outside of the morgue or the crime scene, however, he was just another cog in the machine and his opinions and thoughts did not count any more than did Rivera's own. But since he would never see it that way, he was less than useless for this case.

Rivera would have to talk this out with somebody else. And he thought he knew who that person would have to be. He was going to have to look at Jake Presnall in a new light. But he did not have to be happy about it.

Eighteen

Jake remained in the hospital for the remainder of Monday evening and most of Tuesday while the doctors ran their tests and determined that other than the bruises on his neck and the various cuts and scrapes he had sustained, he would be fine. He spent all that time handcuffed to his hospital bed, most potential visitors being turned away. It was just as well. Apparently he was being highly sought after by reporters. The police had used the media for the past few days to try to catch him, he was told, even showing his picture on the news. But it wasn't until he had been found at the scene of the "Myrtle Street Massacre," as the media so cleverly dubbed it, that he became suddenly interesting to the reporters.

He was allowed a single visitor on Tuesday, in the presence of a uniformed officer. Miss Jerry entered the small hospital room tentatively, her demeanor stiff, as though she was steeling herself so as to appear strong for Jake's sake. But when she leaned over to hug him, the officer stepped forward, using a restraining hand to prevent the physical contact.

She lost it. She began sobbing, and it seemed she would never stop. The anguish on her face and in her voice was almost too much for Jake, who had been mostly successful keeping it together up until now.

"I've been so scared," Miss Jerry said at last, once the worst of it had passed.

"I wanted to let you know I was okay, but had no way to do it," Jake offered.

She nodded, using a tissue from her purse to wipe the tears from her cheeks.

"Are you okay?" Miss Jerry said.

"Just a little beat up and tired, but that's it," Jake said.

"The cops have been to your house."

"I figured."

"They interviewed me about you. That was how I found out how bad it had gotten. I've never been so afraid in my life," she said.

Jake wanted to crawl away and die. He tried to envision Miss Jerry, who was going through her own problems at home, finding out about the trouble he was in the way that she did. What must that initial shock have felt like? Could he have handled things differently these past few days and spared her this unnecessary agony?

"I thought I might never see you again," she said, after a long silence. With a great strain of effort, she added, "I thought you might die out there."

He tightened his grip on the cheap hospital sheet. This was all his fault.

"I know. And I'm so sorry." What else could he say?

"Where have you been?" she asked, her voice trembling again.

"Under an overpass," he said. She made a choking sound in her throat. He elaborated. "The guy they thought that I killed. It turned out that he was part of some sect out on Myrtle Street. That was where I was when it all got blown to bits."

"Why would you go there?"

"Looking for information." Stupid, now that he thought about it. "Where's Missy?"

"She's waiting at the nurse's station with one of the nurses for a minute. I wasn't sure what kind of condition you were in and didn't want her to get upset."

He smiled. "That was probably for the best."

Miss Jerry begged the officer to just let her hug Jake once before she left. To his credit, the officer actually looked somewhat sad about it, but he was still obliged to refuse. Sniffling once more, Miss Jerry finally left the room, and a part of Jake was glad that she was gone. He hated for her to see him like this, cut up and bruised, handcuffed to a hospital bed. It was better for him to be alone.

Tuesday evening, Jake was transferred into police custody. A line of photographers and reporters waited outside of the hospital. Requests for comments whizzed by like bullets around everybody's heads, as the photographers snapped away with their expensive little cameras. Boom microphones were lowered over Jake's head. The officers escorting him did their best to keep the crowd at bay.

He spent Tuesday evening in lockup. Not his finest night. He spent most of that time being glared at and was unable to sleep for fear of what condition he might find himself in when he awoke. The following morning a couple of officers with unreadable expressions and large bellies came and unlocked the gate, beckoning him forward.

They led him into a small room, perhaps the same room in which he gave his statement the preceding evening. Detective Rivera joined him shortly thereafter and sat across from him at a small table before a pane of what could only be a two-way mirror.

"First of all, no talking about monsters," Rivera said.

Jake nodded. This conversation was almost certainly being monitored. Any observers would interpret Rivera's command as nothing more than the logically grounded cop refusing to entertain fantastical tales.

"You're being released," Rivera told him.

Jake laughed. A great big invisible giant removed its hand from Jake's chest and allowed him to breathe easier. He felt the reduced weight all the way down in his bones.

"At this time no charges are being brought up against you for your assault on Officer Perez or your little disappearing act, although the investigation into the murders of Faith Daelly and Najac Petion is still open."

"Wait, you don't still think I-" Jake stammered.

"Until a murderer is caught, the investigation remains open." Rivera stared hard at him. The expression was clearly meant to silence him. Jake obliged. Rivera continued. "At this time you are not being brought up on any charges for either murder."

He was escorted to see a desk sergeant who out-processed him and returned his personal belongings, including his silver chain. Even though he did not have to do so, Detective Rivera offered to drive him home.

Once they were alone in his car, Rivera turned to face Jake. "Spill it," he said.

Jake spilled it. The whole story. He told Rivera how Najac had followed him, about his first encounter with Damballah, the silver chain, teleportation, living on the street for two nights, the voodoo sect, the second encounter with Damballah, all the way up to the point where Jake had been arrested. Rivera stared out the front windshield while Jake told the tale. He did not comment, interrupt, or ask any questions. Jake wondered at times if the detective was even paying attention.

Jake finished speaking. Silence hung in the air between them. Rivera refused to make eye contact. He rubbed one open palm across his forehead, as if to hold his head together.

"You do know how this all sounds, right?" Rivera said at last. He still faced the other way.

"You saw that thing at the house," Jake said. "You saw it bleed orange. And don't forget the fact that you saw me teleport."

"There is that," Rivera admitted. "And I'm not one of those people who would dismiss something that I know I saw just because it didn't fit in my preconceived notions of the universe. But still." Rivera seemed to be looking for the right words to express his next thought. "This is just a lot to swallow," he added at last.

Jake did not immediately respond. He suddenly found the cuticles on his right hand utterly fascinating. But he finally gave voice to something that had been bothering him for days. "The thing I don't get is how did you know I was at that house?"

"I didn't know you were there, exactly. We got an anonymous tip."

"Really? Who?"

"Emphasis on the word anonymous," Rivera said.

"Oh yeah. Right. Well, what did they say?"

"Somebody said they witnessed a scuffle in front of the house, and that it appeared as if a bunch of people took somebody prisoner and dragged him into the house. This witness also said that the guy who got attacked looked like the guy on the news who was being sought after."

"That would have been me," Jake said.

Rivera nodded. "Which is why I showed up."

"What about the other people that were at the house? The voodoo people?"

"Dead. Most of them. Two survivors. Old guy and a young woman."

"Old white guy?"

"Yeah."

That had to be HappyGoLucky. He'd survived. He had been the only old white guy there, from what Jake had seen. But something else struck him and made him suck in a breath. He thought of Lita, sitting on the floor of the old house, confiding in him, looking so lost and alone for one vulnerable moment. Rivera had said a young woman survived. Not a teenage girl. And everybody else was dead. Which could mean only one thing.

"Lita," he said.

"Lita?"

It felt like a mule had just kicked Jake in the gut. "There was a young girl there. She was thirteen. Lita. I take it she wasn't the other survivor?"

"No, this woman was about twenty."

Jake hung his head.

Rivera wore a puzzled expression as he worked it out. "We didn't recover the body of any teenage girl."

Jake blinked. His mouth opened and closed several times. "Then she's not dead?"

"Sounds like this girl is unaccounted for."

Jake looked out of his window. "Then she's not dead. She's missing." Relief coursed through his veins, a tangible and physical thing, even as a fresh worry reared its ugly head. Where was she? "She must have escaped during the attack. We need to talk to HappyGoLucky."

"Who?"

"The old white guy."

"He's still out of it. Not unconscious, not comatose, but too doped up to do us any good."

Jake continued to stare out the window. They were parked near the street. The sidewalk that wound past the parking lot was cracked and uneven. Strands of weeds tried to grow through the cracks, tried to forge out a life amidst impossible circumstances. Somehow they made it. Weeds always did.

"I haven't had a chance to tell you about Dallas Lasserre," Jake said.

"You mean Faith's fiancé," Rivera said. "The significant other is pretty much always a suspect until ruled out. Common procedure. I've already spoken to him."

"Do you know about his ex-wife?"

Rivera turned and looked at him. As he did so the seat creaked under his weight. "What ex-wife?"

"Faith's sister told me that Dallas's ex-wife went missing a little under a year ago, within twenty-four hours of dropping in unexpectedly on Dallas and getting into a huge argument with him about something. On top of that she thinks Dallas has been acting funny lately."

"When did you talk to Fleur?"

"You know her?"

"Of course I know her. I'm a homicide detective. She's the sister of the victim. She was one of the first people I talked to. What the hell are you doing talking to her?"

"I went to ask her-"

The detective's tone grew hard again, regaining the stern edge that had been there the first few times they met. "Let's get something straight. I am the detective. I interview people. It's called detective work. When you do it, it's called hindering a police investigation. Are we clear?" Jake did not say anything at first. He was too shocked by the change in tone. Rivera leaned in closer. His breath smelled faintly of old coffee. His skin glistened with a slight oily sheen. "Are we clear?"

"You know," Jake said, "they sell little wipes that you can rub your face with to take the oil off." The look on Rivera's face told him that he did not appreciate the humor. "Just tell me," Jake added. "Yes or no. Do you know about the ex-wife?" He could see that the answer was no. There was no need to wait for an answer. He continued. "For reasons you might have guessed, this is very personal to me. I knew Faith. I have a right to offer my condolences to her sister and talk to her about whatever I want."

Rivera kept up the tough cop façade for another moment and then backed off. He sat straight. Fixed his collar. Scratched his forehead. He stared hard at the dashboard as if the answer to the case was etched into it.

"Tell me about the ex-wife," he said, after letting out a deep sigh.

"That's pretty much all I know about her. She dropped in on him, got him riled up, then disappeared. Nobody has seen her in months, not even her family. She just vanished. According to Fleur, Dallas started acting funny. She said he's been really disinterested, enough to even make Fleur wonder if he still wanted to go through with the wedding. She seemed to think he was hiding something. When Faith tried to press the issue, he blew up at her."

"I didn't know any of that," Rivera admitted. "I've talked to Fleur and Dallas both. The subject of an ex-wife never came up. I'm waiting for background checks on the both of them, though. I'm sure I would have learned about the ex-wife angle soon enough, but still. This is good information. If it's true." He must have seen Jake's chest puff up at the sound of the begrudging compliment, though, so he quickly added, "But I still don't want you impeding this investigation."

"I just want to make sure whoever did this gets caught."

Rivera started up the car and drove him home.

They sat in silence most of the way there. Jake watched the

pedestrians and the other motorists that they passed along the way. Most of them looked self-absorbed, but not in a bad way. Just people deep in their own business, worrying about their own problems and going about their own routines. He figured that each one of those people out there, like himself, probably thought that their issues were a big deal. End of the world type stuff.

Of course, they probably weren't being chased around by snake monsters.

Then again, maybe they were going through things that were even worse. How could he know? He thought about it. Everybody had a story to tell.

All those people. All those problems. In a hundred years they would all be dead. Every one of them. Another hundred years after that, they would not only be dead, but completely forgotten. Nobody living on the planet at that time would even have a memory of them. Whispers in the wind.

Jake thought of his own situation. No kids. No wife. No prospects for either.

He would probably be forgotten long before that. Not a great thought.

As they neared Jake's house, Rivera cleared his throat.

"Just sit tight until you hear back from me," Rivera said. "Don't go looking for any more trouble. You see anybody suspicious, or God forbid, any monsters, call me. You still have my card, right?"

"At the house," Jake said.

Rivera nodded. "Good. And remember what I said. Stay out of trouble."

He dropped Jake off in front of the house and sped away. Jake waited until he was out of sight. He couldn't just go back to a normal routine after what he had been through. Not yet, anyway. Rivera had only said not to go looking for trouble. Technically, he didn't think that what he was about to do could be called looking for trouble. Technically, he would just be looking up an address. Technically, he would just be going to pay his respects to a grieving fiancé. Technically.

Then again, it was always the technicalities that got you.

Nineteen

When Detective Rivera pulled up to Dallas Lasserre's house in his unmarked sedan, right about the same time that Jake was ringing the doorbell, Jake knew he was busted.

"Oh damn," Jake muttered under his breath. He thought he heard footsteps from within the house, possibly descending a set of stairs.

And what a house it was. When Jake first laid eyes on it he had whistled appreciatively, then added, "Wow." Just in case the whistling was not enough to indicate his approval.

The other houses along the wide oak-lined street were nice. Dallas Lasserre's house was grand. Superficially, the stately two-story piece of architectural wonder had a lot in common with its neighbors: A wide porch, thick columns supporting an overhanging eave, arched windows, marble-textured stucco exterior. Yet it possessed a majesty the other houses would have envied had they been capable of such an emotion. The place oozed symmetry. The lawn was more lush and verdant than all the others in sight, and each blade of grass looked like it might have been individually trimmed by hand to affect a type of immaculate precision that bordered on obsession. A stone walkway leading up to the front door was lined with glazed pots in which dazzlingly pink blooming bougainvillea overflowed. Off to one side a varnished gazebo stood flanked by stone benches near a cascading fountain. It was a lot to take in.

"Remember that little bit I said about staying put?" Rivera barked as he barreled up the walk.

Jake shrugged. It was a "what can I say?" gesture.

"Get out of here," Rivera said. But before either man could say or do anything more, the door opened. A grim-faced man stood facing them. He was as tall as Jake, but with much wider shoulders and the general physical appearance of someone who was passed his prime but hadn't gotten the memo. He sported a full beard and mustache that blended in perfectly with his black hair. Seated beside him in the doorway, one on either side, were two chocolate-colored Labrador Retrievers. The dogs appeared aloof but suspicious, eyeing Jake and Rivera with gazes that were so intelligent as to be eerie.

"I'll do the talking," Rivera warned.

Jake couldn't promise anything, so he kept silent and allowed the detective to infer what he would from that.

Dallas looked surprised to see them standing there. He recognized Rivera right away but gave Jake a curious glance. Jake had only before seen him in commercials. Compared to the confident, heavily made-up face he had seen on television, the man standing before him was deflated and sunken. In the commercials he was always dressed impeccably in pressed shirts and crisp slacks. Standing before them this morning, in gray sweatpants and a wife beater T-shirt, Dallas did not exude the same kind of confident swagger that was part of his trademark television persona.

He waved them into the house with barely a second glance.

Jake's first impression of the interior matched his first impression of the exterior: meticulous neatness approaching compulsion. They crossed through the foyer into the warm living room which oozed with its own symmetry. The room was painted in soothing earth tones. Expensive looking tapestries hung from the walls. The books on the bookshelf were carefully arranged by size and binding type. The curtains hanging from ornately carved rods at the windows looked like they had been recently fluffed by Martha Stewart, so that every crease, fold, and wave appeared to have been placed there deliberately. The floor was done in peach-colored eighteen inch porcelain tiles that complemented the earth tones of the rest of the décor very well. The room was thick with the scent of cleanliness, as if it was scrubbed and swept hourly such that not one particle of dust had ever been permitted to land on any surface.

"Miley. Pillow," Dallas said. One of the Labradors complied by pacing across the room, retrieving a cushion from a futon in the corner and carrying it in its mouth to a thick leather recliner. The dog dropped the pillow into place on the seat and Dallas sank into the recliner. The

Labradors stretched out at their master's feet.

"Please tell me you did not name your dog after Miley Cyrus," Jake said.

"Miley who?"

"Thank God."

Dallas gestured to his guests. "Make yourselves comfortable."

"One second," Rivera said. He placed a heavy hand on Jake's shoulder, guided him, a little more forcefully than he needed, back toward the foyer, farther away from Dallas. Once they had distanced themselves, he gritted his teeth and spoke to Jake in a hushed yet urgent tone. "Look. There's nothing I can do about you being here now. But you better behave yourself. This man is grieving. You start anything, and I will throw you out on your ass. Are we understood?"

Jake met his eyes and looked away under the glare of the fiery determination that he found there. "Sure. You detective. You talk. Me Jake. Me quiet."

Rivera released his shoulder and they turned back to face the sunken man on the recliner.

"Everything okay?" Dallas said, eyeing them warily.

"Just needed to iron something out," Rivera said.

"Like I said before, make yourselves comfortable."

Rivera remained standing, taking up a vigil across from the recliner near a window that featured a dazzling view of the gazebo outside. Jake took a seat on a beige-colored sofa, noting that his butt had never been more comfortable. On a coffee table before him rested several books, artistically arranged like a museum display. He noted the titles of two of them: "101 Ways Your Dog Will Know You Mean Business" and "Canine Training Essentials."

Yawn.

"I like the trick with the pillow," Jake said. "I guess you have to have the furniture cleaned for dog drool pretty often."

Dallas looked at him blankly.

Rivera glared at Jake, his entire countenance shooting little daggers in Jake's direction. Jake decided to shut his mouth. This was probably what Rivera had meant when he said to not start anything.

"Would you like a beverage?" Dallas asked.

They both declined, Rivera probably out of principle. Jake was just scared that it would be the dogs that fetched the drinks, and he didn't like his tea sweetened with slobber.

"Have you found anything more?" Dallas leaned forward as he spoke. Jake noted what appeared to be genuine hopefulness in the man's eyes.

"Actually, Mr. Lasserre, I'm here to ask you a few more questions," Rivera replied.

"Sure." His eyebrows knitted together ever so slightly, puzzling over the tone of Rivera's voice. "Anything I can do to help your investigation." His voice broke off and he looked away, then stared at the window. When he looked back, his eyes were moist, his voice shaky. "Whatever it takes to help find who did this."

Jake knew bits and pieces of Dallas Lasserre's history, seeing as how the man was a regional celebrity. He was originally from somewhere out west, but had come to Louisiana on a football scholarship and played two seasons for LSU before abruptly dropping out. Even in college he had something of a taste for discipline and order, finding the football coaches to be more fascinating case studies than the other players. Somewhere along the way he discovered a knack for taking that love of discipline and channeling it into dog training. It was said by many satisfied customers that the man had a real gift, and so his services were always highly sought after by people with too much money on their hands and enough free time to think of ways to spend it.

"So why'd you only play two seasons?" Jake did not have to specify that it was a football question. Dallas figured that out all by himself.

"I took a semester off my sophomore year after my dad's funeral. I meant to go back the next semester, but you know how it goes."

"Once you were out of the rhythm, it was hard to go back?"

Dallas nodded.

"Do you train other kinds of animals?"

He shook his head from side to side. "Dogs only, I'm afraid."

Rivera was studying Jake, sending out another silent warning. He obviously didn't want Jake speaking at all, but he just couldn't help himself. It's not every day you get to meet a television personality.

The detective cleared his throat and all eyes were back on him. He fixed his gaze on Dallas. The dog trainer looked casually back at him, his expression now more curious than it had been only moments before.

"Mr. Lasserre, when is the last time you spoke to your ex-wife?"

Dallas's back jerked upright. He hadn't seen that question coming. His face bunched up, a curious blend of emotions playing at his features.

"What has she got to do with this?" Dallas said.

"We understand that her whereabouts may be currently unknown."

"That's one way to put it. I really don't want to talk about her."

Rivera turned to peer out of the window, and spent a few seconds with his back to the others, and began drumming his fingers on the windowsill. Dallas alternated between watching Rivera's back and glancing questioningly at Jake, who in turn just stared at the floor, trying to decide what his role in all this should be. Was he really expected to just sit there quietly? Aside from the rhythmic clicking of Rivera's nails on the polished wood and the steady humming drone of the air conditioning, the room was fairly silent. Jake had time again to inhale and savor the clean air. It smelled of pine, the next best thing from camping out in the untamed wilderness.

Rivera turned back to face the room. His eyes darted over Dallas. "I was hoping you could tell me a little bit about the nature of her visit to New Orleans eight months ago, and what happened after that."

Dallas cleared his throat. "How do you know about this?"

"It's my job to know things, Mr. Lasserre. Would you please tell me about the visit?"

Dallas turned his palms upward. "Look, she just stopped in. It was no big deal."

"Really? From what I understand the two of you had a pretty big argument."

"So?"

"So what happened?" Rivera insisted.

"Why does it matter? What does an argument I had with my ex-wife almost a year ago have to do with my fiancée's murder?"

"That's what I am trying to figure out."

Dallas chanced a glance at Jake, who was mostly successful in keeping the smirk off his face. Then Dallas seemed to get it. His eyes shone with understanding. His face went a shade of red. He looked back at the detective. "I'm a suspect. You suspect me."

"You're the fiancé," Rivera corrected. "It's only natural that I come to you for information. This probably won't be my final visit, either. Get used to seeing my face. Now please answer my question."

Dallas sighed and shifted in the chair. Both of the dogs looked up at him as if they expected a treat. "For what it matters, I wasn't expecting her," he began. "I had not spoken to Elizabeth in a very long time. It got back to her somehow that I was engaged. She was a little peeved that I didn't bother to tell her. I didn't think it was any of her business. There had been little to no contact between us since the divorce. The marriage didn't last very long and we made a pretty clean break of it. Why should I seek her out to tell her I was getting married?"

"What happened after you argued with her?"

"Faith came home. Elizabeth left. I haven't spoken to her or seen her since then."

"Did you know she was missing? Did you know that nobody in her family has seen or heard from her since then?"

Dallas sighed. "Like I said, I hardly ever spoke to her to begin with. It wasn't until a while later that I found out she was missing. Her sister called me to ask if I knew anything about it. She often went off for long stretches at a time, doing God knows what, but they had never gone so long without hearing from her before. And frankly, I'm surprised that they even cared."

"Why is that?"

"You would have to meet them to understand them. Elizabeth is not well liked in that family. If they were looking for her, there was probably some other reason beyond care and concern."

"So," Rivera summarized, "your ex-wife comes to you specifically to pick a fight with you. Then she disappears without a trace. Nobody ever sees her again."

Dallas narrowed his eyes. "I didn't do anything to her," he said. He looked from Rivera to Jake and back again.

"What did Faith think when she saw the two of you together?" Rivera asked.

"I don't know what you mean. It's not like we were in the bed together. We were standing in this room, arguing. Obviously, Faith wanted to know what we were fighting about. I told her what had happened. They got into it with each other. I had to break them up before it came to blows. Faith called her some unflattering names. Elizabeth stormed out. End of story."

Rivera was silent for a few seconds. He appeared deep in thought. Or maybe he was just trying to use the silence to intimidate Dallas. If that was the case then it wasn't working. Dallas stared back, waiting for the next question. He wore an expression of expectancy.

Rivera's phone rang. He pulled it out of his pocket, flipped it open, and held out one finger to signal that he would try to be quick.

"Rivera," he said into the phone. He listened for a few seconds as someone on the other line spoke. "When?" He nodded a few times, like the person on the other end could see him. Finally he flipped the phone shut.

"Any more of your questions?" Dallas asked. "I found them so very insightful."

Jake noted the sarcasm. "Are you sure you didn't name your dog after Miley Cyrus?" he asked.

"Miley who?" Dallas said again.

"Good man."

Dallas rolled his eyes. Rivera hoisted Jake to his feet, guiding him toward the door.

"Thank you for your time Mr. Lasserre. I'll let you know if we find anything. Let's go, Presnall."

Jake noted the look on the detective's face and he recognized the eagerness to get going. That phone call must have been important. Jake did not bother speaking to Dallas again and Dallas did likewise. He saw them to the door and very unceremoniously closed it after them.

As soon as they were clear, Jake said, "How come you call him *Mr. Lasserre* and I just get *Presnall?*"

"Seriously? That's what you're worried about?"

"I just think I should get at least as much respect from you as that guy does. He's just as much a suspect now as I was, right?"

"He doesn't piss me off every five seconds, like you do. So he gets the mister in front of his name. Now shut up about it."

Jake rolled his eyes. He bumbled along after the detective as they strolled away from the house. "So what do you think? He's clearly the killer, right? He killed his ex-wife eight months ago and now he's killed his fiancée too? Like some kind of serial killer thing, right?"

"Let's try not to jump to conclusions," Rivera answered.

"Like you did with me?"

Rivera stopped short and turned to face Jake. They were standing near the street. A lawn sprinkler one yard over spun merrily and hissed as it released a steady spray of cool mist over a patch of thirsty grass.

"Swallow your pride, Presnall," Rivera said, then opened the door of his unmarked sedan and climbed behind the wheel. He leaned over, peered up and out of the passenger window at Jake, who hesitated, not sure what he was supposed to do now. Rivera added, "You coming?"

Jake hopped in, scratching his head. "Don't get me wrong, it's just that my boss, Dr. Cherry, he always calls me Presnall. And it's kind of demeaning, you know?"

"Are you still dwelling on that?"

"Yes, as a matter of fact I am. Whatever happened to guys talking about their feelings?" Jake said.

"That's crap. I happen to know that for a fact."

"It wouldn't kill you to open up, you know? Maybe you wouldn't be so grumpy all the time."

"I'm about to kick you out of my car."

"So? I have a magic necklace."

Rivera started the engine. "If I had a nickel every time I heard that one."

"You'd have about fifteen more cents to drop in your little 401k, or whatever you cops put into. So where are we going, anyway?"

Rivera put the car into reverse and backed out of the driveway. He switched it into drive and pulled forward. They sped off. "Hospital. Your guy's lucid. HappyGoLucky."

Twenty

A gruff voice, lacking any semblance of good will or patience, met Rivera's gentle yet insistent knock. "Might as well come the hell in! Everyone else has!"

Jake and Rivera entered the room to find HappyGoLucky sprawled in a small bed that did little to contain his girth. A nurse hovered over him, checking vitals on a monitor which loomed beside the bed. A clear tube, secured by medical tape, ran from his arm and disappeared into a cluster of equipment. He wore one of those oversized hospital gowns that were little more than aprons. A bandage crisscrossed his face, concealing one eye and most of his head. His left arm and right leg were heavily bandaged.

"Looking good, homey," Jake said.

HappyGoLucky visibly sneered. "Bite me."

The nurse sighed and retreated from the room. Jake watched her go. He turned back to HappyGoLucky. "She looked thrilled to be here. You been charming her with the same witty banter you used on me, I take it?"

"Bite me twice," HappyGoLucky replied.

Rivera cleared his throat and stepped forward. "I'm Detective Lester Rivera of the NOPD," he said. "I was hoping you could answer a few questions for me."

HappyGoLucky turned his head away and stared at the far wall. "Just what I want to do when I wake up from near death. Answer questions."

Jake stepped forward. "Lita's missing."

"Good," HappyGoLucky said, unmoving. "That means she got away."

152

"You're not worried about her?"

"She'll take care of herself."

Rivera chimed in. "What happened at that house?"

There was no answer. The question hung in the air like a house fly that just would not leave. For a long moment nobody spoke. HappyGoLucky's deep breaths and the occasional beep stemming from one of the monitors made the only noise. The silence grew increasingly tense.

"I need some information," Rivera insisted.

"Tough."

"If you don't cooperate, I'm sure there are all kinds of nasty charges I can bring you up on."

"Whatever. I just lost people that were like family to me. I almost died myself. You really think I care anymore? I couldn't stand cops to begin with, and that was before a bunch of them busted in our house like a cavalry charge." He finally turned his head back to face them and looked directly at Jake. "And you! The Mother said we could trust you. Now you're with this guy, telling him God knows what about us."

Jake had had enough. His hands balled into fists. "I'm trying to figure out how to stop that monstrosity that attacked us back there!" he spat. "That's the second time it tried to kill me."

"And thank you so much for leading it right to our doorstep. We can't thank you enough!"

Jake's mouth fell open. He had no reply. But Rivera did.

"I don't think Jake was the intended target," he said. HappyGoLucky looked up at him with a healthy dose of skepticism, but there was something else there, an iota of doubt. "Both times Jake has been attacked he was in the presence of someone from your group. Both times the creature attacked and killed people from your group. Yet here Jake stands. I had several police officers with me when we went in that house, and that creature did not kill a single one of them."

"So?" HappyGoLucky tried to sound tough and unfazed, but his voice had raised a timber, and Jake could see wheels turning and the doubt taking hold.

"So that shows incredible restraint," Rivera elaborated. "That thing could have killed anybody it wanted to kill. Yet it only incapacitated my guys and killed your guys. I think it was after you and your group the entire time. Jake just happened to be present both times. Which means you're all still going to be in danger. Including this young girl Jake was telling me about."

"Lita," HappyGoLucky said. Her name rolled off his lips like he was watching her from far away. "She's all alone out there."

"Yes," Rivera agreed. "She is."

Every aspect of his body language changed. He released the tension in his muscles, allowing his body to grow lax. His face softened, a pained expression passing over his features. He bit his lower lip and ran his good hand through his oily gray hair.

"You've got to help her," he said at last.

"First we need to know what we're up against," Rivera said.

"A loa. A spirit god. But you already knew that. I guess what you mean to say is that you need to know how to kill it."

"The Mother said you can't kill a loa," Jake said. "But she said there are counter spells to send it back to wherever it came from."

HappyGoLucky blew out a long breath. "Look, Jake, you were there when Erzulie mounted the Mother. When a loa comes in, it's in. It stays as long as it wants to stay. But they usually don't stick around very long. A few minutes normally, sometimes an hour, but hardly ever longer than that. They grow bored after a while and leave. And they never seek to do harm."

"Never? That thing left a lot of dead bodies behind."

HappyGoLucky sighed. "That's the part I don't get. The loas are not murderous spirits. They don't go around trying to kill people. Especially Damballah. That's who that was, you know. Damballah. One of the most powerful and often invoked loas we know about. He's a serpent god. Besides Papa Legba and Erzulie, Damballah is at the very center of everything we do. He's benevolent. He's a good guy."

"Not anymore," Jake said.

"So it seems," HappyGoLucky agreed. His fingers worked at the edge of the linen bed sheet and he stared down at his white knuckles. "Just make sure Lita is safe."

"We don't know where she is," Jake said.

"Find her."

"Do you know where she would go?"

"No clue. She came to us one day and we took her in. She was a runaway or something. It was either we help her or she lives on the street, so we helped her."

"What was she running from?" Rivera asked.

"Her parents. She hated them. Most teenagers do, if I'm living in the right century. But she really hated hers. I think they abused her. Or at least one of them did. I can't say for sure, I'm just going off comments she made. And the fact that she never lets anybody touch her, not even a hug or a handshake."

Rivera's mouth became a hard line. "And nobody thought that any of this should be reported? An underage girl? An *abused* underage girl?"

HappyGoLucky closed his eyes for a moment. "You probably know the stats on teenage runaways better than I do. But even I know that if a kid doesn't want to live at home, there's little anybody can do to stop her from leaving. And like I said, I don't know for sure she was abused at all. It's more a suspicion."

"Anything else?" Jake asked.

"Najac sure took to her. Sometimes you would think he was her uncle or something. When we found out he died, she changed."

"How?"

"She grew sullen. Upset. Moody. More so than usual, I mean. And she was close with the Mother also. The Mother really took her under her wing and started showing her stuff."

"What kind of stuff?" Rivera asked.

He smirked. "Simple stuff. How to make gris-gris. You know, little talismans for bringing luck, or protection against evil. She taught her some of the prayers and some of the old songs. Nothing big, but Lita had fun with it. We all liked her, but Najac and the Mother were particularly fond of her. But they're gone now and I'm laid up, so you've got to find her and protect her."

"Which brings us back to Damballah," Jake said. "Look, I get it. They mount. They stick around until they get bored. But the Mother said there were counter spells."

"There are ways you can encourage a loa to leave," he replied.

"Great. That's what we need."

"But you need to know something about how the loa was summoned in the first place. And even then, you have to have the power to do it. I don't have the knowledge or the power to help you there."

"Who would?"

"Whoever summoned him. Which may very well be the body he's inhabiting right now."

"Which does us no good."

HappyGoLucky stared up at the ceiling and bit his lip. Jake could see the wheels turning as he worked it out in his head. "Your best bet is to find Lita, hide her, and hope that loa gets bored and dismounts that poor soul he's riding right now. There probably won't be anything left of that guy's mind by this point. He'll probably be catatonic by now."

"That's your advice? Hope that it gets bored?" Jake asked.

"I know it sounds anticlimactic. But that's why the mountings usually don't last this long. Loas get bored. Maybe the killings are keeping this one focused. Maybe if he goes a while and can't find any of his targets, he'll get bored and leave."

"That's a lot of maybes," Rivera said.

"There's more," HappyGoLucky said, his voice taking on an ominous timber.

"Oh?"

He looked right at Jake. "Do you remember back on Myrtle Street, when you were asking about the connection between Faith and Najac, and why would Najac even be investigating her murder?"

Jake shook his head up and down.

"The cops showed up and interrupted before the Mother could answer. But there's something else you need to know. The Mother had been getting visions. For about two weeks leading up to the murder. Visions about Faith."

"What do you mean by visions?"

HappyGoLucky took a deep breath and let it out slowly. Jake could see the strain on his face. By the looks of it, he would be drifting off to sleep again any minute.

"She would just see the girl," HappyGoLucky said. "The Mother might be sleeping, or taking a walk, or in the middle of a conversation, and then bam. A vision would hit her. She started seeing that girl all the time. We think the visions were coming from Erzulie."

"You mean the spirit that mounted her during the ceremony?" Jake said.

"One and the same. They had something of a rapport, those two. But that was the only time the Mother had ever received visions like that. It was tough, but we eventually were able to figure out who the girl was. The Mother always seemed to see her in a bakery, so the Mother started checking out bakeries. Imagine our surprise when she said she had located the girl. Some of us had been thinking the visions weren't real. But by then we knew better."

Jake leaned forward. "And so you kept tabs on her. That's why I spotted Najac outside of the Cajun Confectionary."

"Of course. We figured there must be some reason the Mother kept seeing her. We wanted to know why. We wanted to find out if there was some connection. The day she died, the Mother... she felt it. She woke up screaming. Najac went to check it out."

"And followed Rivera right to me," Jake finished. "That's why he came after me."

HappyGoLucky didn't answer immediately. His eyes were half-closed. Jake figured he would probably be in and out for as long as he was on painkillers. They tried to prod him further, but his answers came out in garbled murmurs. It was all Rivera could do after that to get him to provide a thorough physical description of Lita for a missing child alert that he intended to put out on her.

Finally, he answered them no more, and drifted off into sleep.

They loitered momentarily in the hallway outside the door to HappyGoLucky's room. The hall stretched out in both directions and the nurse's station was visible. The evidence of typical hospital business went on around them: Doctors marching along the hall, nurses scurrying about, papers passing from hand to hand, the rapid-fire clicking of keyboard keys as transcribers typed. Jake rubbed his eyes. At some point during all the excitement the sun had dropped and the moon had risen, and he was starting to feel the strain and exhaustion of the past few days. The visible signs of fatigue were not lost on Rivera.

"What next?" Jake asked.

"You go home and sleep," Rivera said.

"I can't do that. You heard him. We have to find Lita."

"Wrong. The proper authorities will locate the girl. Even if I wanted your help finding her, you can barely stand up."

"What about the other survivor from Myrtle Street? The woman you told me about?"

Rivera shook his head from side to side. Jake caught his meaning. She hadn't made it.

"Now go home. I'll call you later," Rivera said.

"Sorry. I'm kind of invested."

Rivera looked like he wanted to pull all the hair out of his head, but with no hair to pull, the gesture just looked awkward. "Look, why are you so hell-bent on being in the middle of this, anyway? It seems like you would be happy to bow out gracefully, now that you know I'm not gunning for you anymore."

Jake stood there a moment, unclear what to say in response. He met

Rivera's eyes for a moment, then glanced back at the closed door to HappyGoLucky's room. He kicked at the floor with one foot, then shifted his weight and kicked with the other.

"Well?" Rivera said.

"Look," Jake said. "In all seriousness. I have a personal stake in this now. I've faced that monster twice. For all I know it's just going to pop up and try to get me again any second. And I don't exactly have much else going on. The truth is..." He trailed off, unsure of how to finish the sentence.

"The truth is?"

Jake met his eyes again. "My dad used to always tell me that one day I would do something important. That I'd be somebody. That I was going to make a difference." He dragged the fingertips of one hand along his forehead, gently massaging it. He needed a moment to stall, because he felt tears trying to emerge. He really did not want to cry in front of Rivera.

To his credit, Rivera did not prod him to go on. After a moment, Jake was ready to continue.

"My dad used to tell me a lot of things like that. And to be honest, so far all I've done is prove him wrong. Make a difference? If I dropped off the earth right now, maybe three people would notice. And one of them is a two-year-old. If it was up to me, I'd have nothing. I only have the house I have because my parents left it to me when they died. A girl I was dating three years ago helped get me on at my job, which I've probably lost by now. I'll probably lose the house sooner than later. I haven't actually earned anything for myself, and I can't even hold on to the stuff that's been given to me."

Rivera stood there, looking uncomfortable for the first time since Jake had known him. Apparently this heart to heart stuff was not his cup of tea.

Jake plodded on.

"Besides, we're actually getting somewhere, finally. How can I back out now?"

Rivera sighed. "So this is about your father?"

"Partly, yes. And about me."

A wry little grin twisted Rivera's features. "I can't say I wouldn't do the same for my old man. He's partly the reason I became a police officer." Rivera looked away for a moment, as if deciding whether or not to say something. He must have made up his mind. He looked back and hit Jake with it. "What happened to your parents?"

It felt like a large block of ice had suddenly melted in the pit of Jake's stomach. This was his least favorite topic. He worked his mouth, but nothing came out at first. Finally he found the words.

"It was a car accident. My junior year of high school. Dad took Mom out for their anniversary that year. Our neighbor, Miss Jerry, was watching me and Bre so they could spend the night out. Dad pulled out all the stops. Dinner, movie, hotel in the French Quarter. They looked forward to it for weeks."

One tear managed to break through to the surface, and it trailed down his cheek. Jake barely noticed. He had cried for his parents before, sometimes in the presence of others. It was the only time that the tears did not embarrass him.

"It stormed that night. I don't guess I need to really say much more than that. I'm sure you know as well as I do what a little rain does to the drivers of this city."

Rivera nodded. He looked genuinely pained, even while trying to hide it.

"My wife and I are having problems," Rivera said.

Jake looked up, stunned. "What?"

"You said it wouldn't kill me to open up. So here it is. And this is completely against my nature to talk about, so I'm going to say it once and I don't ever want it brought up again."

Jake nodded, unsure how to respond.

Rivera continued. "You mentioned earlier about how I always seem so grumpy. But you don't understand what this job can do to a person. I thought I could handle the stuff I would see. I thought wrong. And my wife, who should get me better than anyone, doesn't seem to understand that, and things have gotten bad between us. Between my job and my home life, everything sucks. So yeah, I'm miserable."

Jake bit his lip. "I can't believe you're telling me this."

"Seemed only fair. You told me your painful little secret. This is mine. I go after murderers. I visit horrific crime scenes. And even when we do bust the bad guys, they always seem to manage to get off on technicalities or the D.A. can't make a case. I don't want to be one of those people who whines about everything, but everybody needs to vent from time to time, and the person who should be there for me won't talk to me. She stopped caring long ago. So I simmer. And that makes me a hard person to be around."

"No offense, but have you tried talking to your wife?" Jake said.

"I try to talk to her every day."

"No, man. I mean really talk to her. I'm sure this didn't happen overnight. There's gotta be a reason."

Rivera's face reddened. "Of course there's a reason! It's called a lack of appreciation. Or lack of respect. Or lack of consideration. Whatever you want to call it, it's the same thing. She just doesn't care."

"I can't imagine-"

"Okay, Presnall. Therapy session's over. I opened up to you. Let's move on. The girl. Lita. You want to be a contributor on this? Fine. Any idea where we could find her?"

Jake was silent for a moment. He wanted to press the other conversation farther, but even a cursory look at the defiant expression on Rivera's face was all it took to know that the door had closed on that one. He shook his head. "She lived on the streets before she took up with those people. She may be back on the streets now."

"And?"

"If that's the case, I know a couple of guys that could probably help us find her."

"These two people you hunkered down with under the overpass?" Rivera said.

Jake nodded. Something in his gut told him that if Lita was on the streets somewhere, Corben and Bogart would be able to find her.

"We need to get in touch with them."

"Okay."

They walked down the corridor together, past the nurse's station, then rode the elevator down to the main floor. The lobby was spacious, and the exterior wall facing the parking lot was made entirely of glass, which only made it look that much bigger. There were benches organized around a little fountain, and one of those back-lit directories like one often saw at the mall. People mulled about. During this time, neither man spoke.

Just before they exited through the automatic sliding door into the moonlight beyond, Rivera broke the silence.

"For what it's worth, Jake, I'm sorry to hear about your parents."

Twenty-one

Thursday morning started off innocently enough for Lester Rivera. He woke up to an empty bed, splashed some cold water on his face, brushed his teeth, took a hot shower, and stood under the sizzling spray far longer than necessary. The steam reddened his skin by the time he stepped out and dried off using one of the plush designer towels that Maxine insisted on purchasing last year. To Rivera a towel was a towel, and he would rather not spend the extra money for the name printed on the label. But the arguments were already so bad by that point that he opted not to risk causing a major skirmish over bath supplies.

Another battle he lost even before it began.

Truth was, the towels were quite nicer than the ones his family used when he was a kid, but he would never admit that to his wife.

He dressed briskly, buttoning a work shirt and tucking it into his pants as he studied his face in the mirror. Fresh worry lines crisscrossed his features and dark circles adorned his eyes. That would be due to the trouble he was having sleeping at night. Every time he drifted off, he saw that monster from the Myrtle Street house, spitting purple light at him. The dreams did not frighten him exactly, but they unsettled the part of his brain that kept trying and failing to comprehend what was going on. This was not a typical murder investigation. He could keep an open mind as he worked, but eventually, he would have to explain this to somebody in a way that would not cause one of his superiors to put him out to pasture for psychiatric evaluation.

The circumstances forced his department to put quite a spin on

Monday's events in order to keep a media firestorm from igniting around them. Reporters got wind that many of the injured officers were rambling about some kind of snake monster. In response, an NOPD spokesman told the media that the officers were ambushed in the house, at which point the poor lighting and overall trauma of the event precipitated the fantastical reports that came out. No officers were killed, the spokesman elaborated, redirecting everybody's attention away from the strange tale. It was amazing how easily the whole mess disappeared under the proverbial rug.

To add insult to injury, ever since Wednesday he had this unmistakable feeling that he was forgetting something important. He racked his brain about what it might be, but came up with nothing. Still, the feeling persisted.

A palpable tension in the air greeted him the moment he walked downstairs and entered the kitchen. Someone other than a trained investigator with long years on the force might have missed it, but Rivera's sharpened senses kicked into high alert. His wife hunkered in her usual spot at the table with forms and ledgers spread out around her. She clutched a coffee cup in two slightly trembling hands, her fingertips white along the edges. She faced away at an angle. A worried expression creased what little of her face was actually visible to him from where he stood. Another emotion played at her features as well.

Bitterness?

It was hard to say. She sat there and stared across the kitchen and out of the little window that overlooked the backyard. There was an old-fashioned wooden swing out there, big enough for two, varnished to a caramel-colored sheen. Once upon a time the two of them would go out there in the evenings and pass hours beneath the open sky as the stars winked at them. How long had it been since they had last done that?

He couldn't remember.

Rivera crept to the coffeepot and glanced at it. Empty. Maxine didn't leave any for him this morning. Had he done something wrong? The answer to that question must be yes, but he still couldn't pinpoint it.

"I made enough coffee for us both, but I ended up drinking it all." Maxine's voice startled him, so accustomed had he grown to the silence. He peered back at her. That nagging feeling in his gut returned, and he was sure that it was related to whatever was going on with Maxine. She still would not turn to face him.

A single bead of water dripped from the kitchen faucet behind him. It was something he'd been meaning to look at. Every ten seconds or so, another one plummeted and struck the metallic surface of the sink. Plink. Plink.

"I think we need to try separating," Maxine said.

It was as if a cold hand had just reached out and slapped Rivera across the face. He leaned back against the counter and tried to catch his breath. For a moment, his lungs would not function properly. Then he braced himself.

"Is that so?" He couldn't take the venom out of his voice. It was just there.

"I think it would be for the best." She took a sip of her coffee. She still did not turn to face him. Another globule of water broke free.

Plink.

He had no intentions of having this conversation with the back of her. He circled the table, and did not stop until he faced her, glaring down at her from on high, his footsteps a little too heavy, his voice a little too harsh.

"Best for who?" he said.

"Both of us."

"And you decided this all by yourself?"

She smiled then. The expression was neither happy nor sarcastic; just mournful, and ripe with melancholy. A wave of grief washed over her face. "I had help."

"Help? From who? Who have you been discussing the private matters of our relationship with?"

She did not answer him. A moment later he realized why. She meant him. He was the one who had helped her decide. He could read between those lines. It was a gentle rebuke. She was telling him that this was his fault, at least partially.

"Oh," he said. "So that's it, then? I have a little trouble at work and you want to bail on me?"

"This isn't about your job."

"Like hell it isn't!" He leaned closer toward her. She still would not meet his eyes. She just kept staring out of that damn window. "This has everything to do with my job! What is it this time? The hours? The late nights? The stress? Or maybe you can try something new this time. Maybe you can accuse me of having an affair. One of the women at the station. Oh wait. You've done that already too."

Maxine did not take the bait. She responded calmly, in a reassuring voice that he probably did not deserve. "I know you're not having an affair. You'd have to stop thinking about only yourself for more than five minutes if you were going to pull off an affair."

"That's it, then? I'm too self-obsessed? I'm a narcissist? Is that what you're going with?"

Maxine shook her head. "You know it's been a long time since things were good between us. I think this could help. A trial separation. I can go stay with my mom. I want you to take some time and think about it. We don't have to rush this."

"There's nothing to think about," Rivera said. "The last thing I need is to give that woman the satisfaction of taking you in to get you away from me. I can already see the look of victory on her face."

"I believe narcissist was your word," she said.

"Jesus!"

Rivera wanted to throw something. He stormed over to the refrigerator. His eyes stung with the frustration that welled up inside of him. He needed an outlet. Maybe some punk today would try to take a shot at him, and give him an excuse to put him down. That might help. That might help a lot.

He opened the refrigerator, reached for the bag of bagels, and pulled one out. He took a bite out of it cold. Suddenly starving, he felt like he could probably eat about three times his normal morning fare.

He slammed the refrigerator door shut.

And then he saw it.

In his shock, he swallowed the bite of bagel without fully chewing it, and almost choked. He looked again at the door of the fridge, just in case he had not seen it correctly.

But there was no denying what he was looking at.

The memo for the community center fundraiser stared out at him like an accusatory eye.

The fundraiser that had been yesterday. At ten o'clock.

The one he had completely forgotten about.

Now he knew the cause of that nagging feeling he had been having. It was his brain trying to tell him that he screwed up big time. While he was driving around town with Jake, interviewing persons of interest in the Daelly murder case, his wife had been waiting for her husband to show up and lend his support to her cause.

"Oh crap," he said.

"Now you remember," Maxine responded. She turned to face him at long last. She put the coffee mug down on the table. Her hands were no longer shaking. She was completely sure of herself. "When you didn't just immediately rattle off an excuse, I figured you forgot all about it. Even though I've had that memo up there for weeks. I don't know what would have been worse. If you had stood me up because you were doing something that you thought was more important, or if you had just plain forgotten. I guess it doesn't really matter."

Rivera felt like a kid who had been caught behind the shed with his dad's nudie magazines. The shame rose to the surface first, a bitter reminder of his shortcomings. But another emotion quickly drowned it out.

Irritation.

He had almost died the other day. His wife had no idea how close she came to becoming a widow. And she didn't even know it because she wouldn't let him talk about his work at home anymore. It was just like the evening of the Najac Petion murder. Rivera called home to let Maxine know that he would be running late. That was considerate of him. He had done his duty as a husband. And what had he gotten in return? She'd cut him off in mid-sentence and hung up on him.

"I don't need this," he said, surprising himself because he had meant it to come out sounding angry and stern, but instead he got deflated and weary. "Do you even have any idea what happened to me this week?"

"Do you have any idea what happened to me yesterday?" she echoed back at him.

He had no response to that. The bagel in his hand hung forgotten. For all the hunger he had felt a moment ago, he was sure he would never need to eat again. His stomach was clamped tight.

The faucet dripped again. The sound was maddening. He threw a glance over his shoulder, and just wanted to break the stupid thing. His eyes settled on the little ballerina figure next to the sink. Her expression was as pained as ever. He tore his eyes away from the scene before he lost his mind and destroyed the room. The frustration within him had reached a crescendo, and he would either need to distance himself from all of this or risk going into a berserk rage that would end up requiring him to remodel the kitchen.

"I need to go," he said. He tossed the bagel into the trash and headed for the back door.

"Just think about it today, and let me know," Maxine said.

He left.

The faucet dripped again.
Plink.

Twenty-two

Jake's Thursday did not start out much better. Now that he need not fear being arrested for showing his face in public, he decided to go make sure he still had a job to return to. Jake would rather gouge his own eyes out with hot fireplace pokers than go crawling back to Dr. Cherry, but he also couldn't afford to be out of work right now. Even with the job, he was barely making ends meet. Thanks to the stupid economy, he could end up being out of work for quite a long time. So he bit the bullet and went to see his boss.

Dr. Cherry leaned back in his chair, fingers steepled beneath his chin as he pondered Jake's fate. He wielded all the power right now, and the smug look on his face showed that he knew it.

"As I recall, you were being wanted by the police for a grisly murder," he said. "Now you want to come back to work for me?"

"It was a misunderstanding," Jake said, standing across from the desk. Dr. Cherry had not invited him to sit. He never did.

"You failed to show up for work several days in a row without so much as a call," Dr. Cherry continued.

"I was a little indisposed," Jake said.

"Yes, I suppose being a fugitive can have its inconveniences."

Jake tried to maintain his composure but there was not much he could do about the drumming of his heart, pounding much harder and faster than usual. As little as a week ago he would have stood here in front of this weasel of a man and felt intimidated. But in the past six days he had been attacked by voodoo cultists, fought against rebel spirit gods, lived on the streets, and narrowly escaped a massacre with his life intact. Maurice Joseph Peter Cherry suddenly seemed far less intimidating and far more of a jerk than he ever had before.

But he needed this job. Above all else, he had to remember that.

Jake sighed. "It was a misunderstanding. Not only did I not hurt anybody, but I was a victim. The police only suspected me until they figured that out. They are not pressing any charges against me. I've been cleared."

Dr. Cherry allowed him to say his piece. He regarded Jake silently as he spoke, even while showing no interest whatsoever in Jake's explanation. Any receptive speaker could clearly tell when the audience was paying attention and when it was utterly disinterested. Dr. Cherry fit into the latter category.

Jake stood motionless as the other man leaned forward, casually placing his hands palms-down on the desk as if he meant to push himself to his feet. But rather than standing, he only used the gesture to convey a sense of importance, as if the words about to come out of his mouth were going to be completely revolutionary and momentous.

"You're trouble, Presnall," he said at last. "Nothing but trouble. It wasn't but last week that I warned you not to give me any more excuses to fire you." Jake opened his mouth to protest but Dr. Cherry silenced him with a single wave of his arm. "Regardless of whether you are guilty or innocent of whatever tomfoolery went down this weekend, you are still trouble. This kind of thing doesn't just happen to anybody, you know."

"Are you suggesting this is somehow my fault?" Jake asked. He could not completely keep a snide tone out of his voice.

"Here's a friendly tip," Dr. Cherry said. "Some drivers are just more prone to getting into traffic accidents than others. Even if they never actually cause the accidents, something about the way that they drive, the way that they handle their vehicles, maybe even the chances they take on the road, makes other drivers more prone to run into them."

Dr. Cherry drummed his fingers on his desk for a moment before continuing.

"So even though they technically are not at fault, these drivers nevertheless seem to attract problems on the road, and hence their premiums go up after an accident, even if another driver was at fault."

"So you're saying that even though it wasn't my fault, it's still my fault, then. Is that it?"

"I am saying that you're trouble. Which is why, as I have stated, that just last week I was threatening to fire you. Again, these kinds of things do not happen to just anybody."

Jake felt the hot tears trying to swell up in his eyes as the frustration mounted, but he refused to give any indication of that in front of Dr. Cherry. He tried to control his breathing and focus on the rise and fall of his lungs within his chest so that the wave of emotion would pass. More than anything he just wanted to jump across this desk and commit murder. He had not asked to be questioned by a detective in a murder investigation and he had not asked to be followed by and subsequently suspected in the murder of a practitioner of voodoo magic.

But then again, what if Dr. Cherry was right? What if Jake had brought this on himself somehow? He experienced a moment of doubt in which he tried to trace back how he had landed in this mess. It all came back to Faith. He had given her his cell number because he had expressed interest in purchasing used furniture from her. She had tried calling him the night she was murdered. That was all it took. Rivera showed up asking questions, but even then nothing would have probably come of it had Najac not started following him and then been killed in his presence. From that moment on everything spun completely out of control. But was Jake in any way to blame? Could he have responded differently somewhere along the way and saved himself a whole lot of grief?

Dr. Cherry took a deep breath and then surprised him. "Look. I'm a fair guy. I'll tell you what I'll do."

Jake leaned forward despite himself. He need not have gotten his hopes up.

"I'll give you a chance to interview to get your old job back," Dr. Cherry continued. Jake felt his spirits dwindle. "When you did not come in on Monday I figured you were no longer interested in working here so I was working on getting an ad in the paper to hire your replacement. I'll allow you to apply for the position. Beyond that, I cannot make any promises."

Jake's mouth fell open. Dr. Cherry was going to *allow* him to interview for his own job, and, even more maddeningly, he acted like he was doing Jake some huge favor in the process.

"You might be on to something," Jake blurted reflexively. "The way some people conduct themselves probably does make others more prone to hitting them."

Dr. Cherry smirked. "Is that some sort of veiled threat?"

"No," Jake said. "Like you said. Just a friendly tip."

That comment elicited a faint chuckle.

"You're free to fill out an application at the front desk," Dr. Cherry said. "I'll consider re-hiring you. You can go now."

Dr. Cherry flicked his wrist and flipped open a medical journal in one continuous dismissive gesture. Jake lingered only a moment, stunned. There was little more to be said, and Dr. Cherry had already all but forgotten he was even standing there. In a daze he turned and left the office.

"Kindly close the door behind you," Dr. Cherry called from behind.

He closed the door. He walked through the corridor, back into the lobby, past Kate at the reception desk, heard her say something encouraging to him, but the fog that descended over him kept him from really comprehending any of it. He just put one foot in front of the other, headed for the front door, and wondered what in the world he was supposed to do now.

Outside, the light from the sun assaulted his eyes. He blinked and tried to let his eyes adjust, and then started walking along the street to where he parked his car a block down. He paid no attention to the large white delivery truck parked directly behind his car. He paid equally little attention to the man who got out of that delivery truck, holding an oversized gas station road map.

Jake meandered along the sidewalk in no particular hurry. Hands in his pockets, eyes on the ground, he walked the walk of the dejected and beat-down. The sun overhead was still blaring, and beads of sweat collected at the base of his neck and along his hairline. He was busy reflecting on what a miserable failure he was and paid no heed at all to the short Latino man with the map until he almost barreled over him.

"Excuse me," Jake said, sliding aside to let the man pass.

"Permiso, señor. You know where to find Bienville Street?" the man asked him.

Jake stopped and appraised him. The man was a little shorter than he was, but with a solid build, all lean muscle and sharp angles. His brow furrowed down over his eyes, his mouth was a thin line. Something about him was off. He gestured to the map. "Map no help. Cannot find." He laughed and shrugged. An alarm went off somewhere in Jake's mind, but he lacked the practical experience that would have warned him to heed such an alarm.

The blow came from behind. A powerful strike to the back of his head sent him reeling into the man who had just asked for the directions, and his flailing hands tore the map as he fell. The man was unconcerned about the map. He grabbed a hold of Jake as he staggered forward, and brought a knee sharply into Jake's gut.

Jake dropped to the pavement before he even knew what was happening. The pain blared all throughout his body, as if the nerves in his head and stomach were broadcasting the sensations to all the other nerves in his body and they were all equally aflame. Everything went a hazy shade of red for a moment and then they hauled him to a standing position, dragged him several feet, and tossed him. He found himself in an enclosed space, out of the sunlight. He looked back just as the Latino man with the furrowed brow lowered the rolling door of the delivery truck and locked it in place, sealing Jake inside. It slammed shut with an audible crash.

There were lights mounted in the ceiling of the truck above him, little fluorescent tubes that did not completely chase away the shadows. The sparsely furnished cargo area was mostly empty. It was just Jake, assorted sharp and blunt objects, and two rather large Hispanic men who looked experienced in the art of dishing out pain.

Twenty-three

"You're dead," one of the Hispanic men said. A bench ran along one wall of the interior of the truck. The man who spoke was seated on this bench. A metal railing was mounted higher up. On the opposite wall, at about chest height, there was a rack on which hung an assortment of power tools, hammers, pliers and blunt objects of various shapes and sizes. The sitting man smiled, his expression almost paternal. His khaki chinos were freshly pressed, along with his V-neck shirt of red silk that couldn't quite conceal several strands of coarse black chest hair that spilled over the top. He added, "At least, you could be dead. It's up to you."

A complete sense of panic, unlike any he had felt in his entire life before this point, threatened to overtake Jake. When he had faced the loa, the entire struggle had a surreal quality to it, and he always had the option of teleporting away. Even when the beast had held him and blocked his attempt to hop away, there had not been an adequate amount of time in which to allow the fear to really take hold.

This situation was different. He was trapped in this enclosed space with these two men who had all sorts of painful toys at their disposal. And there was nowhere for him to go.

The second man, who stood facing Jake, was simply a brute, with thick greasy hair slicked straight back. He wore jean shorts and a white T-shirt, with the sleeves cut off at the shoulders, revealing arms so thick as to make a young tree trunk envious. Those arms were folded across his barrel chest, and in his eyes Jake read a desire and an appreciation for causing pain.

"What do you want?" Jake gasped, trying to regain his senses. His head was still reeling from the blow he had taken, and his lungs still struggled to regain the breath that the initial attack knocked out of him.

The engine roared to life and a second later the truck started to roll. The standing man grabbed hold of the metal railing to brace himself against the initial lurch that accompanied the movement. The two men back here with Jake were not the same two men who had attacked him outside. The other two must have been up front, in the cab. That meant at least four attackers.

"Where are you taking me?" Jake said.

The man on the bench giggled and crossed his legs. The dim light cast by the trio of light tubes overhead lent a demonic luminescence to his already dark complexion. "Where we are going is of no consequence," he said. "You and I need some time to have a little discussion. I hear that you have been sticking your nose in business that does not concern you. So now you have to decide whether to keep that nose."

As if to demonstrate that the suggestion was not to be taken figuratively, he nodded to the beefy man in the white T-shirt. The man reached across the narrow space from his position, and grabbed a rusty pair of pruning shears from the rack. Jake's body went rigid when he saw those dull blades in the big guy's grasp.

"These babies are great," the sitting man said. "Eduardo here can snap a branch as big around as my wrist with them. A nose shouldn't be much trouble for him. Now don't get me wrong," he added, placing a well-manicured hand to his chest in mock resignation. "I'm no monster. I do not enjoy hurting people just for the sake of hurting people." He paused and thought that over for a moment. He smiled and winked, as if he and Jake were in on some joke together. "Well, maybe I do enjoy it a little."

"So what then?" Jake asked.

"Nothing major. You will tend to your own business, and stop poking around in matters that do not concern you."

Jake nodded. "I can do that."

The sitting man smiled and sat forward, clapping his hands together. The sound retorted like a gunshot in the enclosed space. Jake jumped. The man positively beamed. "Good for you! A quick learner! I had a feeling we might not have to resort to violence with you."

Jake let out a relieved little breath.

The smile dropped from the man's face. "Of course, my boss

requested that we resort to violence anyway. Just to prove the point."

Jake's mouth hung open. His throat went very dry, very quickly.

The speaker noted his reaction. He added, "But you should feel good about yourself. Because of your eagerness to cooperate we will go easier on you than we previously planned. We'll let you keep the nose. A finger from each hand should satisfy the boss."

Jake scooted himself backward across the space, until he felt the cold metal of the rolling door of the truck against his back. There was nowhere else to go. The sitting man snapped his fingers, and Eduardo nodded and started forward with the shears. He approached Jake with a look in his eyes that bordered on professional detachment, as if he was making a copy or sending a fax rather than approaching an unarmed man in the back of a delivery truck with a set of pruning shears. The truck was rolling smoothly now, and he was able to cross the distance confidently without stumbling.

Jake looked about the cargo area, full-blown hysteria about to set in. He wished for a window through which he could gaze out and teleport himself to safety. He realized that one of the things that sucked about having an ability like his when in danger was that if you could not see your means of escape, the ability could not help you.

Jake put an extra couple of feet between himself and Eduardo by sidling along the rolling door to the farthest corner of the cargo area, but at most that only bought him an extra second or two. Eduardo continued to close the distance. With a few quick strides he had crossed the gap between them. Jake was still cornered. And he had nowhere else to go.

"A little hint about Eduardo," the man on the bench said, "the more you run the more into it he gets, and the more into it he gets, the more painful it ends up being. It's best to sit still and take it like a man."

New Orleans being the city that it was, and home to the worst drivers in the union, Jake kept hoping that another motorist would cut off the delivery truck, forcing the driver to slam on the brakes, which would in turn have sent Eduardo sailing into the rolling door and possibly injuring him.

That didn't happen.

So from his position on the ground, Jake aimed the stiffest kick he could manage at Eduardo's kneecap. Eduardo turned out to be much more agile than he appeared, and easily pulled out of range. The kick missed its mark entirely. Eduardo grunted, and in a fit of anger, swung the pruning shears at Jake like he meant to bludgeon him to death with them. It was all Jake could do to roll to one side. The shears struck the wall of the truck where his head had been only a moment before. The sound they made was loud and metallic and reverberated all around the truck.

"Oh, yes," the sitting man said, as if it had just occurred to him, "and attacking him is all the provocation he needs to extend your sentence, so to speak. I'm afraid you've just given him all the excuse he needs to remove all ten of your fingers, instead of just two."

"Will you shut up?" Jake screamed back.

The man adopted an affronted expression and gestured to himself with an open hand. "And here I am trying to assist you out of your predicament. Tsk. Tsk."

Eduardo was now standing directly over Jake. He was completely penned in by the big man, whose expression remained indifferent. Jake would not have the space he needed to roll clear again. The next blow, however it might come, would get him.

But then something occurred to Jake. Maybe he could not teleport himself out of the truck, but that did not mean the ability could not still prove useful. The truck was not exactly huge, but there was enough space to move around. He fixed his gaze on the front wall of the truck, which would also be the wall separating the cab from the cargo area. Jake did not wait for Eduardo to take another swing. He just willed himself to be there, out of the big man's range.

From his new vantage point, Jake was staring across the truck at Eduardo's back. The smiling man was sitting off to Jake's right, his eyes still turned toward the spot where Jake had been. The rack of tools and blunt objects was right over Jake's head.

Eduardo grunted, and the sitting man gave a startled cry. They had just watched a man vanish. Jake could have bet sensitive parts of his anatomy that they had never seen anything like that before.

Jake had only a moment to act. He pulled himself to his feet as quickly as he could. The movement attracted the attention of the sitting man, whose head snapped in Jake's direction. Jake would not have time to reach for a weapon if he would maintain the element of surprise. He extended himself toward the sitting man, and punched him square in the jaw with all the might he could muster.

Pain exploded in Jake's fist. It had been ages since he had punched anybody. But he managed to send the man sprawling. He toppled off the little bench and fell to the floor of the truck. But he responded like a man experienced with violence. There was no confusion, no hesitation. He immediately began collecting himself.

But Jake could not worry too much about the leader just yet. Eduardo spun around, and eyed Jake with an expression that hovered somewhere between curiosity and contempt. He was probably still trying to puzzle out how Jake had escaped him, but ultimately he just wanted to hurt him, so he was probably willing to kick Jake's tail now and gather intelligence later.

Jake's right hand was still sore, so he sent a left hook at Eduardo's jaw.

Eduardo absorbed the blow with little more than a slight turn of his head. In fact, he seemed amused by the attempt. He responded by thrusting the shears in a stabbing motion aimed at Jake's face.

As much as Jake would have loved to stand there and take a pruning shear to the eye, he had anticipated some form of counter, and had already teleported off to one side of Eduardo. Instead of finding the soft tissue of his face, the shears found nothing but empty air.

Eduardo's eyes went wide when he at last understood that he was dealing with something beyond the realm of the ordinary. He turned his head in Jake's direction, fear beginning to touch his face.

"Diablo," Eduardo muttered.

Jake did not know much Spanish, but he knew the word for *devil,* well enough. The awe in the man's voice and the subconscious half-step backward that he took presented Jake with an opportunity to take advantage of the involuntary display of deep superstition.

And so he teleported himself again, this time to the other side of the big man. Eduardo's face became clouded with fear when he spun around to now find Jake standing on the other side of him again. Eduardo backed into the rolling door, cowering the same way Jake had done only moments ago.

Jake milked it for all it was worth. He began spouting gibberish, making up the words as he went, and waving his hands dramatically through the air.

"Ventus solicitus admiray cosovo bippidy boppity boo," he began his faux chant. Eduardo slinked farther away, trying to distance himself as much as he could. In his panic, he dropped the shears. They hit the floor with a sharp clatter.

"No, por favor," he said. "Por favor!"

Jake almost felt guilty for exploiting this man's superstition. Almost. But Eduardo had, after all, been about to remove Jake's fingers with a set or pruning shears. It was kind of hard to feel deep remorse for somebody under those circumstances.

The leader, who had watched the exchange, added his voice to it. His serenity and former sense of refinement were gone. Now he just looked like any other angry thug. The best part for Jake was how that meticulously slicked back hair was now all a mess.

"Fool! He's no diablo," the leader screamed, quaking with fury.

But Eduardo was too far gone in his paranoia to listen to reason.

So the leader raised one shaking hand, which turned out to be clutching a 9mm Glock handgun.

"Let's see the devil bleed," he said, and fired.

The first two bullets came out hot on each other's heels. Jake did not wait around to see if the leader was a good shot. As soon as he saw the gun, he teleported out of harm's way, clear to the other side of the truck again, by the front wall. Eduardo had no such technique for evasion. One of the bullets struck him in the stomach. The big man cried out and clutched at the wound. A ring of crimson red began to spread across his white shirt.

The look of fury on the leader's face redoubled.

At that moment, the delivery truck swerved violently, throwing all three men to the ground. The sound of the gun blasts must have jarred the driver of the truck, causing him to involuntarily jerk the wheel. It didn't matter. The truck immediately righted itself, but the sense of confusion that the jolt added to the situation worked in Jake's favor, as the leader lost his grip on the gun when he fell.

Eduardo did not rise again. He lay on his back, clutching his bleeding stomach, his face already growing pale. Jake had always heard that gut shots were the worst ones, pain-wise. Jake did not envy him.

The leader's reflexes were clearly more honed than Jake's own. He was already crawling across the floor trying to reach the gun while Jake was still taking stock of what had just happened. He was still sprawled in one corner, feeling wobbly from being thrown down during the violent swerve of the truck.

In a fair race, the leader, who was already trying to reach his weapon, would have clearly had the advantage.

But this was not a fair race.

Jake teleported himself to the location of the gun, reaching it a half-second before the leader did. But the leader was not willing to lay down and just let Jake win. He set upon Jake, swinging a fist that connected with Jake's jaw. Payback for Jake's earlier sucker punch, he figured, as he saw stars and flopped onto his back, the gun once again skidding out of reach.

The leader lunged across Jake's body to reach the gun. Jake sank his teeth into one of his ankles. The man screamed and tried kicking free, but Jake held on like a stubborn pit bull. He hooked his fingers along the waist of the man's expensive pants and yanked him backward, away from the gun. The leader wailed with animal rage and kicked again, this time with his free foot.

The blow connected with Jake's forehead. His vision exploded in a flash of red and his head snapped back. There was a sharp jarring pressure at the base of his neck at the point where it bent back. He came to a rest on his back, staring upward at the ceiling without seeing or comprehending it.

In a daze, Jake was dimly aware of the sound of the leader scratching his way forward again. In a moment he would get his hands on the gun, after which it would be all Jake could do to try to evade the barrage of bullets that would be coming his way. He tried to force himself to care. His swirling vision caused the ceiling to dance before his unfocused eyes, spinning lazily like a carousel running through its rotations with no end in sight.

Then the man got his hands on the gun. Jake heard the triumphant grunt that accompanied the small victory. In the next second or so he would probably start shooting.

Jake backpedaled, trying to put distance between the two of them. At the same time he tried focusing his vision so he could teleport into a different corner out of the line of fire. But how long could he just keep teleporting from one side of the truck to the other before the man started shooting wildly? There was a pretty good chance that at least one shot would strike Jake if he tried something like that, regardless of the power of the chain.

Then his back hit the wall and he had nowhere else to go. He was leaning against the front wall again, beneath the rack of weaponry, and his vision had still not cleared. He had a brief moment to wonder whether or not his line of sight ability would work if he was unable to focus his vision. The next moment, the leader pointed the Glock in Jake's direction and began shooting. The bullets rained in a steady stream of automatic gunfire.

It was now or never. He did his best to focus on the farthest empty corner, and tried to will himself there. For a half-second he thought that it might work. First there was the familiar sensation of being stretched out and pulled along, only this time it felt like a heavy anchor was attached to his feet, weighing him down from behind even as the rest of him tried to rush ahead through time and space. It was not a very comfortable feeling. Somewhere in between the front end and the back end of his body, it felt like someone was ripping him apart at the middle. He thought of that movie where the girl was tied between a trailer and a truck and split into two pieces when the truck took off.

He could hear the bullets whizzing by, but the sound seemed to be coming from two different directions. He couldn't tell if he was still against the wall, or if he was in the corner across from the wall, or stuck in some kind of limbo between the two points. Or was he in both places simultaneously? It kind of seemed that way. Time as he knew it had ceased, so he was able to ponder these things as he hovered there, somewhere on the edge of reality.

Then again, he had always heard that a person's last moments could feel like an eternity, so maybe that's all this was. Maybe he was dying. Maybe the bullets had found their mark after all, and he was having some kind of hazy, semi-out-of-body experience.

Then the teleport failed and he was jerked violently back to his original location. It left him feeling disjointed for a moment, and everything seemed wrong, all equilibrium lost. He was sliding along the floor and hitting a wall, or was he sliding along a wall and hitting the floor? It was hard to tell because suddenly up, down, left, and right, lost all meaning, and blended one into another. There were noises, the sounds of things shattering, and things flew by his face as gravity itself seemed to no longer be relevant.

Several seconds later, everything went deathly still.

Jake lay in a heap, panting and in pain, having no idea what had just happened.

After a few more moments he started to put it together. The disorientation had nothing to do with his failure to teleport away. The directions had physically changed for real. He was lying flat on his back on one wall of the truck, and the floor rose above him to his right as if it were a wall. But how could that be? For what felt like a hundred years, he wondered how he could lie across a wall and stare at a floor that rose up above him. But then he realized why.

The truck was lying on its side.

Tools and debris were strewn about. It was a miracle he had not been killed by a flying sledgehammer or errant nail gun. The leader was sprawled out on the other side of the truck. He was not moving. Eduardo was either dead or unconscious, it was hard to tell. There were bullet holes from one end of the cargo area to the other, including along the wall that separated the cargo area from the cab.

Jake had no idea if he was seriously injured or not. He felt numb. That probably was not a good sign. He was covered in blood, but had no idea where the blood was coming from, or if the blood was his own.

The leader moaned, and blinked his eyes several times.

That was just great. Jake really could have used a little breather, but it didn't look like he was going to get one.

He could hear noises from outside the truck, excited mumblings of many people. Of course, if the truck had flipped on a public street, there would certainly be pedestrians flocking to the scene to check it out. There could already be a crowd, for all he knew.

The leader sat up and glanced around. His wits were returning to him faster than were Jake's own. Jake had no choice but to get to his feet. His legs wobbled and hardly wanted to support his weight. He leaned against the floor-turned-wall to brace himself as he learned how to walk again.

But the simple fact was that he was still locked in this truck with these people. Unless someone pulled the door open or he thought of something that had not occurred to him yet, he would end up once again locked in mortal combat with his attacker.

Then it hit him.

The dim fluorescent lights that had served as their only illumination had been damaged in the wreck, and were no longer working. Yet, Jake realized, he could still see about him well enough. This new source of light was coming through the holes in the cab that the leader's gun blasts has punched into it. Sunlight was entering the truck at slanted angles through these openings, little beams of light like spotlights in the dark.

Sunlight.

Holes in the cab.

The leader had provided him with his means of escape.

Even as the leader started to crawl toward him, Jake turned and pressed his face to the front wall and used one of the bullet holes as a peephole into the cab. Through the tiny space he was afforded a limited view of the smashed cab of the truck. He moved to another such peephole a few feet to his left, closer to the ceiling of the truck. This provided him a higher angle, through which he could see the smashed windshield, and the daylight beyond it. He could just make out the silhouettes of some of the bystanders.

A moment later he was standing among them.

There were some shocked gasps in the crowd as the bloodied, staggering, weakened man appeared out of thin air in their midst. Some people jumped back, alarmed. He heard startled curses. Somewhere in the distance came the blare of sirens, approaching his position.

"Hey man, you okay?" someone shouted.

"Where that dude come from?" came another voice. There were additional voices, but they blended into a single cacophony of sound and the particular comments and questions went by him, unheeded.

He stepped closer to the overturned truck and thought he had a pretty good idea of what had happened. The leader's gunshots had penetrated the wall to the cab. One of them must have struck the driver, who then lost control of the truck. Amidst the wreckage, the driver's prone and twisted body showed no signs of life. In the passenger seat of the cab, the other man was struggling to free himself. It was the man who had originally distracted Jake by waving the map in his face.

Someone grabbed Jake's arm. Jake almost lashed out, thinking it was another attack.

It was just a bystander, trying to help him.

"You don't look so good, man," the bystander said. "Why don't you come over here and sit down? Wait for help." The pinched face of a middle-aged man in a jogging suit surveyed Jake.

Jake permitted himself to look around. He recognized the area. They were on Magazine Street, somewhere near the river, just shy of the entrance to the Audubon Zoo. They had been headed toward the river when the truck overturned. Where had they been taking him? Or had they just been following a pre-arranged route, only to dump him somewhere when they finished with him?

Jake allowed the nervous jogger to lead him to the curb at the side of the street. The gathered bystanders parted to let him through. Some appraised him with concern, others curiosity, others excitement. This was perhaps the most spectacular thing they had ever witnessed. The man in the jogging suit nudged him into a sitting position. He heard the sirens turn onto the street a short distance away. The unmistakable aroma of gasoline, leaking from the truck, assaulted his nostrils.

He throbbed in about a million places. His head. His stomach. His neck. Everywhere in between. Above all else he wanted to get up and leave the site, to be nowhere near this spot when the authorities got here.

And as luck would have it, he knew a good way to accomplish that.

Twenty-four

Jake winced when he pressed the ice pack to his forehead. No matter how many times Rivera insisted that he go to the hospital to get checked out, he just kept refusing. He had spent enough time in the hospital this week. The ice pack would have to do.

"Besides," Jake said after Rivera had broached the subject for the umpteenth time, "You needed to know about what just happened."

Rivera sat back at the creaky old desk and rubbed his temples. The detective was even more tense than usual, and the shockwaves of it practically oozed out of his pores. Around them, officers scurried about. Nobody looked at Jake twice, with the exception of Officer Perez, who scowled at him the first time he caught sight of him and then about fifty times afterward. There was no love lost there.

Jake hunkered down in an ill-formed plastic chair next to Rivera's desk, which was on the third floor of the 8th District Police Headquarters on Royal Street. Rivera did not have his own office, and he seemed none too happy about that. His desk occupied a corner of a large bullpen of a room. Other desks littered the same space, separated by five-foot cubicle partitions that artificially cut the room into segments. Cheap plastic nameplates hung from the partitions indicating who sat where. At least Rivera could say that his segment of the room was noticeably larger than most of the others.

"You know, this isn't my only case," Rivera said, although Jake thought his voice lacked conviction. He continued to massage his forehead with his thick finger tips.

183

"But it's the only one where you get to spend so much quality time with me," Jake quipped. When no response was forthcoming, he shifted his weight in the chair, more uncomfortable than ever. The cheap plastic just didn't match up right with his body. "That was a joke."

"In case you haven't noticed, jokes aren't my strong suit."

"That's news to me," Jake said, feigning innocence with a little shrug of one shoulder. The smell of burnt coffee wafted over from a nearby cubicle that had been equipped as a snack area.

"Here's what I've got," Rivera said, his tone gruff as he collected himself.

Rivera slid two mug shots across the desk to Jake. Jake recognized in one picture the overly polite man who had tried to shoot him to death, and in the other, the man with the map who had originally distracted Jake so that they could get the jump on him.

"Luis Mendoza and Alvaro Amador," Rivera said. "We had no records on the other two, but these guys have been getting around and getting busted for a while now. Mostly petty stuff, but also some violent offenses, aggravated assault, assault with a deadly weapon, that kind of thing. A bit of drug trafficking too. Apparently they work as a crew, and offer their services to anybody who needs things done."

"Services?" Jake said. "Like hitmen?"

"So far as we know they've never killed anybody. More like enforcers."

"Oh." Jake pondered that over for a moment. "So somebody hired them to attack me? The leader, Luis, said I had been sticking my nose in places where it didn't belong, so that makes sense."

Rivera nodded. "Between your infiltration, if you can call it that, of the voodoo house, and the people you've been talking to, you ruffled somebody's feathers. Interrogation hasn't really yielded anything from them, though. They're not talking. And the truck they used came up as a stolen vehicle. I was hoping we could trace it back and try to get lucky."

Jake sighed. "So it's a dead end?"

"Maybe that one angle. On the other hand, there's the Meullions."

"The who?"

"I've been doing some digging on Dallas's ex-wife. Her name is Elizabeth Meullion. Her father is Dennis Meullion, mother is Caroline, sister is Bernadette. She was married to Dallas Lasserre for just over a month. Dennis happens to own Avery Industries, a company that manufactures and distributes ATM machines. Elizabeth was busted once at age fourteen for shoplifting from a high-end novelty shop, but other than that her record is clean. Elizabeth's last known employer was Nolan-Avery Enterprise, a subsidiary of Avery Industries. Apparently she was a Project Manager on some digs."

"Digs?"

Rivera ruffled through a stack of papers. "I don't know everything about it yet, but it looks like Dennis Meullion is a big fan of relics and historical artifacts. He is purported to have a little collection going, and he set up Nolan-Avery Enterprise as a means of sponsoring archaeology excavations around the world."

"That's random," Jake said. "An ATM guy sponsoring archaeological digs."

"The rich often have expensive hobbies," Rivera said.

Jake sighed. "And here I can barely afford to keep my lights on." He thumbed through some of the papers Rivera had slid across the desk toward him. He studied a photo of Elizabeth Meullion, taken at the site of an excavation. The caption at the bottom of the paper indicated she was somewhere near Jerusalem when the photo was taken.

But it was not the caption or the background that captured Jake's attention. It was the woman herself.

He was sure that he had seen her before, somewhere.

Even with the dusty, arid backdrop of an excavation site providing the context, the woman in the image radiated elegance. Her jet black hair, high cheekbones, and graceful neck lent a regal aspect to her stature. Jake was willing to bet that Elizabeth wanted for nothing growing up, the beneficiary of a wealthy family who could gratify her every material whim. Even though the photo lacked color, there was no discounting those dark, striking eyes that practically transcended the paper and bored through him. But why did she look so familiar? Did she just have one of those faces? Or had he brushed past her someplace?

"And nobody knows where she is?" Jake asked the obvious question.

"She's never been reported missing, but it's as if she dropped off the face of the earth eight months ago. No credit card purchases, no bank transactions, no paid bills, no cell phone records, nothing. She just abandoned the project she was working on, came back to New Orleans, met up with Dallas Lasserre, and then vanished."

"Like she's at the bottom of a hole somewhere," Jake said.

"Or hiding."

"Hiding?"

"Your friend, Najac Petion? Do you want to guess who his last employer was?"

Jake looked at Rivera blankly.

Rivera answered his own question. "Nolan-Avery Enterprise."

Jake shot forward, leaning in toward Rivera. "He worked with Elizabeth Meullion?"

Rivera chewed his lip and drummed his fingers on the top of the desk. "She was his project manager on the Jerusalem excavation she was working on last year. Up until he abruptly quit and took off."

Jake's mind raced. "Wait a minute. So Dennis Meullion is connected to Najac and to Elizabeth. Now Elizabeth is missing and Najac is dead. And Faith Daelly is indirectly connected to all three by being engaged to Elizabeth's ex-husband."

"Exactly."

"And presumably Dennis Meullion would have the resources to try to find Elizabeth. I mean, after all, he's partially in the business of finding things that have been lost." Jake felt the color drain from his face. "Or he might even be involved somehow. Maybe something happened on that Jerusalem dig, something which would explain why Elizabeth and Najac abandoned it and came back here in the first place. The only part that doesn't fit is how Najac ended up hanging out with those voodoo people."

"It does bring up a whole host of questions."

"You've got to talk to Dennis," Jake said.

"I tried to contact him today. His secretary said he's unreachable this evening. He's hosting some kind of banquet at his downtown office." He must have seen something etched on Jake's features then, because he was quick to continue. "A private event. I'll go speak to him at his office tomorrow."

Jake smiled and fingered his chain. "I have something that gets me into private events."

Rivera just stared at him until he looked down. "Don't be stupid."

Jake did not respond immediately, but it was not because he was feeling abashed. It was because when he looked down his eyes fell across something else on Rivera's desk that he had not noticed before. Instantly, he thought his heart was about to explode out of his chest.

"What the hell?" Jake pointed to a stack of photographs to which Rivera had not yet called his attention.

Rivera followed his gaze. "Photos from the crime scene the night

Najac Petion was murdered. What's the…"

And then Rivera stopped talking because he saw it too.

Jake grasped the second photo out of the stack, which had been partially exposed by the way the photos scattered when Rivera was going through his notes. All of the pictures depicted the crime scene, neatly documenting angles, distances, that sort of thing.

But this particular photo showed Jake sitting on the curb looking forlorn and dejected. The picture had been snapped moments after the police officer dragged him off to the side and sat him down to wait for the detective, who had turned out to be Rivera. Jake recalled the photographer invading his personal space to take the picture. He had sat there, feeling screwed. The crowds were pressing as close as they could, elbowing, clawing, trying to get a better view.

Except for one woman. One woman who had been merely standing there scowling at him, a sort of angry expression on her face. Jake would have never remembered her, except there she was in the photo, clear as day, in the background. The angle with which the photographer took the shot happened to capture her perfectly. And now Jake knew why Elizabeth Meullion looked so familiar to him a few moments earlier.

"It's Elizabeth Meullion," he said, barely able to breathe. "She was there that night, at the murder scene."

"I'll be damned," Rivera said.

Just to emphasize the point, Jake held the two photos beside one another. The black-haired beauty at the Jerusalem archaeological dig. The black-haired beauty in the background at the murder scene. There was no doubt about it, they were one and the same. And suddenly, Jake found it impossible to contain himself.

"Her dad has to know something," Jake said.

And then Jake was sprinting across the bullpen toward the stairs. If he waited for the elevator Rivera would have time to catch him. So he went for the stairs. He knew he was being impulsive but then again he had been attacked numerous times in these past few days, and he wanted answers. He could not bring himself to wait until tomorrow and find out secondhand. Dennis Meullion had questions to answer and he was going to answer them tonight.

"Presnall, get back here! I said I was going to talk to him tomorrow!" Rivera screamed behind him.

Rivera yelled something else, but Jake could not make out the words. He was already through the doorway and into the stairwell, charging blindly ahead into the next potentially deadly situation. But what else was new? Lately, those were the only kinds of situations Jake Presnall could expect.

Twenty-five

"Name, please?" The two girls at the registration table spoke in unison and then giggled to one another. Obviously these were very intelligent creatures. They wore short skirts and button-down blouses with plunging necklines. Their sprayed-in-place hair swirled and looped in complicated formations like bridesmaids who just stepped out of the salon and were headed for the church. Their smiles were delicious, but were just a part of the job, as fake as their fingernails.

The buxom brunette to Jake's right deferred to the bubbly blonde on his left. Other than the stark differences in hair color, they could have been exact clones of each other.

"Name, please?" The blonde repeated the question. She still wore that same plastic grin. Her pale, powdered skin invoked images of porcelain dolls.

It would be a bad idea for Jake to give his real name. He also couldn't just stand here and look like he was trying to make up a name on the spot, so he blurted the first thing that came to mind.

"Phil Latham." He had to choke back the bile.

The blonde flipped through her guestbook, running a long, slender finger down the length of each page.

"Latham. That's under L."

How very astute of her. It occurred to Jake as he waited, that unless there was about to be some kind of miracle in his life, she was not going to find the name Phil Latham listed among those of the legitimate guests.

He obviously had not thought this through well enough. Silly him for thinking he would be able to just show up and walk into the party. Who knew there would be a whole setup, with a guest list, registration table, guards, the works? All those police and detective shows on television had let him down again.

For that matter, what about the fact that the office building in question had its own ballroom? Located just a few blocks off of Canal Street in downtown New Orleans, smack in the middle of the city's busiest commercial area, the building looked more like a high-rise hotel from the outside. And who knew? Maybe that's what it used to be? Dennis Meullion must have been a very successful man. The size and scope of the place made it easy enough to locate, at least. Well, that and Jake's mad search engine skills. When he stopped home to change and freshen up after leaving Rivera, Jake had looked up the address to the building from his computer.

The blonde raised her eyebrows and tried to look apologetic. "I'm sorry. I don't see your name on the list."

"There must be some mistake." Jake tried to adopt an air of assured confidence. Taking into account the extent of his acting ability, it probably came off more like an air of assured constipation. But there was no room for second-guessing himself now. If he started doubting, he was finished. They would see straight through the ruse. On the other hand, most people were dolts. If he just looked the part and sounded the part, it would work. It had to.

She looked down again; maybe the name Phil Latham magically appeared on her little paper in the past five seconds.

"There is nobody named Latham on this list."

This was simply an obstacle. The grand ballroom was his ultimate goal, temporarily off limits to him behind a set of varnished oaken double doors. If he could just get in there. Every time someone entered or exited, he caught a glimpse of linen-clad tables, flickering votive candles, and meticulously dressed well-to-do socialites. The upbeat crescendo of orchestra music wafted through the walls. The aroma of seasoned beef, most likely prime rib, enticed him. If he did get in, he was sneaking a plate of food for sure.

The blonde raised her eyebrows in his direction. She was waiting for some kind of response from Jake. He shook off the orgiastic food-riddled fantasies that danced through his head.

"Clearly someone has made a mistake. Couldn't you just let me through?"

She shook her head. "Sorry, sir."

She didn't look sorry, though. Jake could tell the only part of this that bothered her was that he hadn't left yet. But this stand-off at the registration table had dragged on too long, and he realized he had caught the attention of a security guard who stood sentinel nearby. The powerfully built man studied him with hawkish eyes that peeked out of a tight, protruding face like that of a predator on the hunt. His skin was black like onyx, and he had the most massive neck Jake had ever seen.

Jake swallowed and kicked it up a notch.

"This is an outrage! My company is worth millions! I flew all the way here from Los Angeles! I was assured there would be no problems!"

All of that was a lie, of course. Jake was playing the part of the angry rich guy who was accustomed to getting his way. For a moment the ploy seemed to work. The ladies looked at him and then at each other. Were they intimidated? Please, let that be the case! Then the brunette went and shattered his delusions when she cast an anxious glance over her shoulder to the guard. He cracked his neck and stepped forward.

"Is there a problem here?" The guard's hard voice conveyed solid discipline and training. The closer he came, the more intimidating he looked. He stood a good six inches taller than Jake, and his muscles strained the stiches of a dark suit that could barely contain him.

"Yes, there's a problem with this list," Jake said. "My name was supposed to be on it, but some buffoon has left it off."

The guard studied him for one extra-long moment. Then he unclipped a handheld radio from his belt and brought it to his mouth. "I need Anderson at the registration table for guest verification."

Jake nodded and stepped away, like he was satisfied this whole situation was being straightened out. Inwardly, he was freaking. If somebody came forward to fact check, his flimsy story would shatter faster than an old aluminum shed in a hurricane.

As he waited, three gentlemen stepped forward to take his place at the table. Their business suits and shiny black shoes stood in sharp contrast to Jake's discount store khakis and red polo shirt. As underwhelming as his choice of attire was, at least he hadn't shown up in the tattered jeans and bloody T-shirt from the delivery truck beat-down. He could picture the look on everyone's faces if he tried to get in wearing that! Luckily for Jake, there was a social media tycoon out there in the world who had proven that millionaires could indeed dress like bums.

The brunette located the names of the trio of businessmen with no trouble. Jake felt a pang of envy. When the guard opened the ballroom doors to admit the gentlemen, that aroma of slow-cooked, exquisitely seasoned beef called out to Jake again. He had a decision to make. When this Anderson guy made it over here, Jake would be discovered. Meanwhile, the registration girls were preoccupied with another set of guests, and the guard was exchanging pleasantries with the three gentlemen.

This meant that, for the moment, nobody was watching Jake. Even better, he had a clear line of sight into the ballroom. Better still, line of sight was all he needed.

All the familiar sensations encompassed him as the silver chain grew warm against his neck. An instant later, Jake found himself inside the ballroom. One thought persisted: hopefully nobody saw that.

He reappeared in a far corner of the room, away from the largest clusters of guests. A woman who happened to glance over did a double-take, as though puzzling out whether or not that guy in the red polo was standing there last time she looked. Confusion registered on her pampered face. One tense moment later she disregarded whatever she thought she saw and returned to her previous conversation. It looked like he was good to go.

An oppressive stuffiness threatened to overtake him, a sensation that likely had to do with the amount of wealth packed into the room. It was like a sentient creature, a presence that rejected him and wanted him gone. The room even kind of smelled like money. The guests walked, talked, and carried themselves with an air far above that of mere mortals. Or maybe that was just Jake's self-consciousness getting the best of him.

Jake strode casually amidst the crowd, trying not to notice that he was the only man present who did not seem to be wearing either a tuxedo or some fancy Italian three-piece suit with an unpronounceable name on the label. He drew no shortage of critical glares. But no one challenged him about his choice of attire; they merely appraised him and then disregarded him, as if he simply did not exist. He tried not to dwell on the implications. Dennis Meullion was around here somewhere, and Jake needed to find him.

A podium and several lush chairs were arranged on an elevated stage off to one side of the room. Jake hoped he was long gone before they commenced with the smug, self-congratulating speeches that were sure to follow. A long row of buffet tables lined the adjacent wall. Servers were stationed two to a table, because after all, the party-goers could not be expected to get their own food. The aromas of many varieties of roasted meats, gravies, steaming vegetables, pastas, and seafood hung heavy in that direction. On the opposite side of the room, the chamber orchestra performed its ambient musical arrangements. Two dozen men and women entertained the crowd with flutes, saxophones, trumpets, drums, violins, and cellos. A mob of stiff-backed couples waltzed in lazy circles on a hardwood floor. And at every point in between, little tables were arranged in rows and columns, bedecked with linen tablecloths and adorned with flickering candles.

It was going to be extremely difficult to locate his guy in all of this. In addition to the plethora of activity, these people all looked the same to Jake. They dressed, acted, spoke, moved, and carried themselves with identical swagger. It was just a great big swirling mass of suits and ball gowns.

He paused at a spot near the center of the room, just beside the dance floor, and scanned the crowd. The shoes of the men squeaked on the hardwood, and the women's heels clicked their own melody. The distinctive aroma of au jus sauce was stronger here.

Lost in a sea of bodies, Jake continued to scan faces...

A woman caught his eye. This wasn't just any woman, but quite possibly the most beautiful creature he had ever seen. She loitered off to one side, laughing at something said to her by a man old enough to be her father. A strapless satin dress clung to her many juicy curves, and the flimsy fabric vividly highlighted each ample attribute. A pearl-laden brocade clip drew the vibrant blonde hair back from her head and allowed it to spill out over her shoulders in a cascade of tightly-wound locks. As Jake watched, she sipped daintily from a champagne glass, and the sight of that delicate throat bobbing up and down in a swallowing motion intoxicated him. It was all he could do to keep his mouth from hitting the floor.

Before he could break off the leer, the lovely creature glanced away from her conversation partner and her gaze happened to fall upon Jake. She took in the sight of him, her eyes lingering just long enough to make him self-conscious of just about every single one of his features: his clothes, his skin, his posture, his face. Part of him wanted to rush over to her, kneel before her, and start a new religion to worship her. The other part of him wanted to douse himself in gasoline and ignite himself just to escape the piercing scrutiny of her eyes.

The older man whispered something in the woman's ear, and she turned her attention back to him. For a few moments longer, Jake remained where he was, transfixed. He shook his head to clear the cobwebs and tried to recall what it was he had been doing. Oh yes. He was searching for a man. Time to get back to it, then.

He moved along, but he was still a little rattled and off balance. He bumped into several people as he tried to regain his faculties.

"Excuse me," said a man wearing a monocle.

"Pardon," said a different man with a Trump-style comb-over.

Jake ended up near the orchestra's section, and found himself fascinated by the violinists' expert tracings of bows on strings. The music was slow and melodious, not intended to be the focal point of the evening, but rather something that blended into the background. He took a deep breath and allowed the tune to help clear his mind.

The scent of linen and honeysuckle overcame him a moment before a soft female voice whispered in his ear. "I can stand and listen to them for hours."

He turned. And there she was. The incredibly sexy blonde goddess he tried to avoid. She smiled, and the candlelight from the nearest table reflected in the gloss on her lips. The glossy satin fabric of her dress parted where a suggestively located slit ran up her left leg just past the knee.

"Me too," he said. Lamest reply ever. "Their music is wonderful." He hoped he sounded like he knew what he was talking about.

She appraised him with eyes the color of storm clouds, and sipped again from her champagne glass. "I don't listen for the music so much as the symmetry. The coordination. The absolute choreography of it. All those individual instruments with their own sounds, blending with the sounds of others. The discipline. The timing. Each member knowing exactly what to do and when to do it, and the stir they create when they all fit together."

Jake could not help but think that she was alluding to a different activity, and he began to feel his own stirring sensation. He tried to steady himself with a deep breath, and the goddess grinned, proud of her handiwork.

She continued, clearly enjoying that she was making him squirm. "It's earth-shattering when people move together in harmony, each knowing exactly what to do, isn't it?"

"Mmm hmm," he choked miserably.

"What's your name?"

"Jake Presnall." He extended his hand. Did he really just give his real name? Whoops. Her charms and innuendo had him off-balance. She grinned as though the idea of a handshake amused her, but she took his hand in hers anyway. Her skin was impossibly soft, and melted into his like warm butter.

"I'm Bernadette," she said. Jake gulped. That was a name he recognized. And although there was always the chance that the name was a coincidence, he knew in his gut he was speaking to the sister of Elizabeth Meullion.

"I came over here pay you a compliment," Bernadette continued.

"Oh?" Why couldn't he get it together? Was he always this much of a dolt around girls?

"I was impressed by your attire. It's so boring hanging out all night with people whose only concern when they get dressed is to show off how rich they are."

Was that supposed to be a compliment? Wasn't she in effect saying that he was dressed like a bum? He supposed it could be interpreted either way. He was still puzzling that out when she did something that further unnerved him; she folded her arms tightly across her chest, emphasizing certain attributes that were already hard to miss. He looked away, feigning fascination with the orchestra.

"Nice party," Jake said lamely. He needed to find a way to steer the conversation toward Elizabeth.

"It's boring to me. My father seems to think that because he is such a big shot it would devalue his name if I associated with the rabble, as he calls them. So he insists that I come to these parties. He's always trying to introduce me to his younger associates. He wants to make sure I date within acceptable circles." She sighed and sipped her champagne again, swirling what little bit was left in her glass while she stared off into the distance.

He realized, with a sort of bittersweet awareness, the true reason why Bernadette picked him out of the crowd. Her father only wanted her to date well dressed, established, successful businessmen, and of all the people in this room, Jake fit that motif the least. It was the bad-boy-on-a-motorcycle factor, corporate edition. Like hundreds of billions of girls before her, Bernadette had zeroed in on the guy least likely to impress her father. She was using him. If someone else showed up right this very moment in cut-off jean shorts and a rubber ducky inner tube around his waist, Bernadette would be gone from Jake's side in a flash.

Bernadette slipped her empty champagne glass onto the tray of a passing busboy and grasped Jake's hand, leading him toward the dance floor. At once he noticed that the casually dismissive glances of the businessmen turned into what looked more like wishful glances.

They reached the dance floor. She pressed herself against him and rested her arms on his shoulders, forcing him to take her by the waist. Up close, Bernadette's skin looked even more magnificent, unblemished and cream-colored, like the pale petals of a white rose. And her smell was intoxicating, a scent of springtime, wild orchids and fresh breezes. His head spun. He should be investigating, not dancing.

And of course, he was dangerously close to getting caught in the middle of some kind of family feud, with all of the accompanying politics and bickering.

He decided to just put it all on the line.

"I'm looking for your sister Elizabeth," he said.

Bernadette stiffened and pulled back from him. The music continued to swirl by, dancing couples swaying in time with the tune. Bernadette stood still, staring at him, her eyes darting and accusing.

"Elizabeth? What about her?"

"I'm just trying to figure some things out. I don't want trouble," he said.

Her eyes narrowed. "Who are you? How you did get in?"

An amused voice reached Jake's ear from behind. "That's precisely what I was wondering." The voice sounded at once smooth yet dangerous, like a scorpion tail dipped in honey.

Jake spun to meet the eyes of an older male version of Bernadette, a blonde-haired gentleman in his mid-fifties who stood completely at ease in a business suit that looked very Italian and very expensive. A smile that did not quite reach his eyes lined his impeccably tanned skin.

"Hello daddy," Bernadette said.

"Hello, Bernie," the man said, not for one second looking away from Jake to greet his daughter. His gaze bored a hole into Jake's face like a focused laser beam.

The man stepped forward, and offered his hand to Jake, who took it, speechless.

"I haven't had the pleasure of your acquaintance," the man said, his voice taking on the tone of thinly veiled hostility cloaked in faux pleasantries. "I am Dennis Meullion. This is my party. And who exactly would you happen to be?"

Twenty-six

Jake's throat went dry and his palms grew damp. Dennis Meullion's sharp icy glare dissected him like a frog carcass on a biology lab tray. Those eyes picked over him, sized him up, evaluated him, and neatly categorized all of his shortcomings.

"Your friend must have a speech impediment." One side of Meullion's mouth curled upward. He spoke to his daughter, but his eyes never wavered away from Jake.

After a moment, Jake recalled how to speak. "My name is Jake Presnall. Nice to meet you, sir."

"Jake Presnall," Meullion parroted. "I'm afraid I'm unfamiliar with that name. I will need to rectify that immediately. Bernie, will you excuse us, please?"

Bernadette started to protest, but a sharp glance from her father silenced the objection before the first word could spill out. She cast one lingering wary glance at Jake, and then retreated.

"Let's walk and talk, shall we?" Meullion placed a hand on Jake's shoulder and guided him in the opposite direction, much like a parent directing a stubborn child. Jake went along like a bridled horse. Meullion led him to a nearby bar where a stooped, aging gentleman in a tuxedo served drinks. Two guests awaiting service saw Meullion coming and graciously stepped aside. Meullion took no notice of the gesture and failed to acknowledge those who paid him the kind deed. He merely moved straight to the front of the line as though it were his rightful place.

Meullion turned back to Jake. "Champagne? Or do you prefer soda?"

Something about his inflection on the words champagne and soda stung like a verbal slap, a not so subtle attempt at contrasts meant to suggest that Jake did not belong with people of this caliber. So even though Jake actually would have preferred the soda, there was no way he was going to give this guy another reason to despise him.

"Champagne is fine."

The bartender filled two glasses.

Meullion withdrew a billfold from his jacket and slapped a fifty in the bartender's tip jar. He made a show of it, for Jake's benefit, and beamed almost good-naturedly as Jake took this in. The bartender nodded and thanked him sincerely, but Meullion did not see this because he had already turned away. He led Jake back out into the thick of it.

Jake decided to take the initiative. "Sir, I was not trying to hit on your daughter."

"My boy, you worry yourself too much. I merely wished to introduce myself to the man who would dance with my beloved daughter at the event to which she arrived with another." A bit of mirth touched Meullion's face. This was a game to him, making Jake squirm. A game that he enjoyed playing.

"I didn't fully understand the situation."

"No, clearly you do not," Meullion intoned, a statement of cold, solid fact.

Jake gulped. "I know this is going to seem random, but I actually came here tonight for the sole purpose of speaking to you."

That at least elicited two raised eyebrows. Meullion cocked his head slightly to one side. "Is that so? Well, you do have an interesting way of getting my attention."

"I was hoping to ask you about your daughter," Jake said.

"It seems to me that we were discussing my daughter."

"No sir. I meant your other daughter."

For one clear instant something passed over Meullion's face, a shadow dancing at the edges of his features like something seen from the corner of one's eye. But it passed just as quickly, leaving behind an expression that was merely stern, and lips pressed into a hard line.

"You mean my step daughter." Something about the unnecessary emphasis on the word 'step' made Jake uneasy.

"Have you had any contact with her, any contact at all, in the last eight months or so?" Jake asked.

"You've got some brass ones kid, I'll give you that, blindsiding me with this."

"I'm not trying to drag up bad memories or anything. I know she's been missing, but I saw her the other day and was wondering if you-"

Meullion grabbed Jake by the arm, and there was nothing soft or tentative about his grasp. Jake's champagne glass, still full, almost fell to the floor.

"What do you mean you saw her? If you're jerking me around-"

"I mean exactly what I said. I saw her." Jake pulled his arm free of the older man's grip. "And I was hoping maybe you knew something about where I might find her. I really would like to speak to her."

"Wouldn't we all?"

"So then you haven't seen her?" Jake asked.

Meullion sighed. "What's it to you?"

Jake had to decide how much to tell. "There was this murder and I-"

"A murder?"

"Yes, and-"

"And do you represent any particular law enforcement agency?"

"No, but-"

"Then I'm afraid I'm going to have to ask you to leave my party."

"I just need to-"

"Now." Meullion's tone was edged with an unimpeachable note of sharp finality.

Jake took a deep breath and tried to steady his racing heart. "Maybe I'll try your wife then."

Meullion grabbed him by the collar, subtly enough to not draw attention, but forcefully enough to let him know that he had crossed a line. "Listen here, you little piss-ant. If you bother my wife or ask her about that whiney brat she raised, I will use the resources at my disposal to destroy your life. Are we understood?"

Jake did not know what to say. He silently returned the hard gaze that was pointed at him, and Meullion released him with a slight shove.

"Leave this place, or I will see to it that you are arrested within the next two minutes."

Three security guards made their way through the crowd and came to a halt nearby. Jake recognized the tall black guard who had questioned him outside by the registration table. He stood between the other two, out front, like he was their leader.

"Is there a problem here, Mr. Meullion?" The tall guard's eyes never left Jake. He was itching for a fight, if Jake read his body language correctly. Muscles tensed, hungry look in his eyes, balled fists, these weren't signs of a peacemaker.

"Yes," Meullion sneered. He plucked the champagne glass from Jake's hand. "See to it that this piece of rabble is removed from my building immediately."

"Yes sir." The security guard stepped forward and grabbed Jake by the arm. "Let's go."

"Oh, and Curtis?" Meullion called. The tall security guard turned back to face his employer. "We're going to sit and have a nice little chat later about just how he managed to get in here in the first place."

The guard, now identified as Curtis, swallowed hard. "Yes sir."

Curtis pushed Jake ahead of him, prodding him toward the doors. Jake wondered how much trouble Curtis would get in for this perceived lack of diligence. As Curtis thrust Jake forward, the nearest party-goers were forced to move aside to permit their passage, and they did not look the least bit happy for the inconvenience. Their snide glares settled on Jake, and he noted several people who wore 'I knew that guy was going to be trouble' looks on their faces. Bodies parted before him, and the sounds of agitated murmuring followed behind him.

Jake eyed the serving tables.

"Can I at least make a plate before I go?"

No response. Curtis maintained a tight grip on Jake's arm as he escorted him back through the doors to the lobby. The walls muffled the orchestra music. The delicious smells faded with each further step. He pushed him past the two registration girls, who gaped open-mouthed at Jake like he was the bearded lady at the circus.

"You can probably let go of my arm now."

Curtis glared at him. "Not until you're safely outside the building. You won't be getting me in any more trouble tonight."

A stern voice called out to them from behind. "That won't be necessary."

Curtis stopped dead in his tracks and spun, and Jake was surprised to find Bernadette standing there, arms folded yet again across her chest.

"Miss Meullion, please go back inside," Curtis said.

"Absolutely not." If anything, her countenance became even more defiant. "You can go back inside. I'll see him to the door. I want to talk to him."

"No. Mr. Meullion gave me clear instructions."

"Unless you want me to tell my father about Morocco, I suggest you let me escort him from the building."

A long moment passed while Curtis weighed the pros and cons of each scenario. He finally sighed and then he released Jake's arm. Bernadette smirked, knowing that she had won the standoff. Curtis shot Jake a warning glance.

"If I see you in this building again-"

"I know, I know. You'll beat me so bad I'll wish I were dead. You'll make me rue the day I was born. You'll make me curse my mother for giving birth to me. You'll-"

Curtis's nostrils flared and he was in Jake's face so fast that they were nose-to-nose before Jake even registered the movement. "Just be gone from here." He flared his nostrils one last time and then stormed off.

Jake watched him go and then turned to Bernadette, smiling despite himself. She slapped him across the face.

"Ouch!" he cried. "What was that for?"

"For making me play my Morocco card against Curtis. I was saving it for something really good."

Jake rubbed his cheek. "You're nuts."

Curtis continued glaring at them from several yards away. Bernadette grabbed Jake's arm and led him around a corner and toward the main doors of the building, out of sight of the security guard.

Jake grinned. "So what happened in Morocco?"

"Shut up."

"You could have just let him do this and saved yourself the trouble, you know."

"I'm not taking you out of the building."

"Then what-"

She stopped abruptly in front of a bank of elevators, and pressed the button to go up. She paused there, waiting for the doors to open. Several seconds passed. Jake was sure that Curtis was going to come around the corner to check on them and catch them just standing there.

Jake scratched his head. "What exactly are you doing?"

A chime sounded and the doors slid open with a smooth swish. She gestured him forward, stepped in after him, and pressed a button to mark the twelfth and topmost floor. The doors closed, and the ascent began.

Neither spoke on the way up. A mechanical voice announced that they had arrived at their destination and the doors slid open again. They emerged into a wide reception area with two corridors extending out and away from it in different directions. Several offices lined both sets of corridors.

"Where are we going?"

"My office," Bernadette said.

"Why?"

She led him down the left corridor, past the first set of offices as well as a spacious cubicle-lined bullpen area. At the far end loomed a massive glass-wall conference room with two entrances. A large plasma screen rested high up on one wall before a heavy oak conference table. They proceeded past that to the largest office yet, situated in the rear corner of the building.

"I didn't want to have this conversation downstairs," she said by way of an explanation. "We'll have more privacy up here."

Jake shrugged and followed Bernadette into her office. He whistled when the full realization hit him that her workspace was bigger than his bedroom. The furniture was constructed of cherry-stained wood. A plush leather chair on one side and three smaller but equally tasteful chairs surrounded a wide wraparound desk. A separate conference area sported a rectangular table surrounded by eight more chairs.

Bernadette took her place behind the desk with the casual indifference of someone well accustomed to her wealth and who had never known any other existence. She gestured to one of the seats before the desk and he obliged. A hutch rose high behind her, lined with personal effects, such as family photographs, certificates, and vine plants.

"Tell me about my sister," Bernadette said without preamble.

"That's funny. I actually came here to try to get your dad to tell me about your sister. Nice office, by the way."

"It's okay," she said offhandedly.

"I guess it's easy to move up the ladder when your dad owns the company," Jake said.

"Are you implying something in particular?"

He realized his words could be construed as an insult, which was actually not his intention at all.

"No. I'm just putting my foot in my mouth as usual."

"Do you know where Elizabeth has been for the past eight months?" Bernadette said.

"No. But I've been investigating a situation that involves her. Most people seem to think she's missing. But I actually spotted her recently. The way I see it, someone must know something. And I want to know it too, because I really need to find her."

Bernadette watched him for a long moment. She leaned back in her chair and let out a drawn-out sigh. "So you've seen her? Where? When?"

Jake thought about that. Bernadette watched him expectantly while he considered his words. He knew Elizabeth was connected to Najac, on account of their working together, which indirectly linked her to the Myrtle Street voodoo cult. She also knew Faith Daelly. The fact that she was somewhere in New Orleans when she was supposed to be missing was also questionable. Factor in her father, Dennis Meullion, excavator of religious artifacts. He'd employed Najac and Elizabeth both. There was a connection there somehow as well. Jake wasn't sure exactly what to make of the man, other than the fact that he gave Jake the creeps. And now the way that Bernadette was looking at him was starting to give him the creeps too.

An odd sensation suddenly crept over him, and his first thought was that Bernadette had, unbeknownst to him, activated some hidden heater. A warm draft washed across his flesh, enshrouding and comforting him. He blinked and looked at Bernadette, who smiled coyly and then stood. She circled her desk and came to a halt right in front of him. She leaned over, enticingly, and lowered her face until her lips were mere inches from his own. His body heat rose considerably, like a fever, and a flush consumed his face and neck.

"I can make you talk," she whispered, and in that moment he was torn between two polar opposite urges: part of him wanted to throw her on her desk, tear her clothes off and have his way with her, while the other part experienced raw inexplicable terror on par with anything else he had experienced this week.

She took one of his hands into hers as she settled into his lap, nestling up against his chest. Her hair smelled so nice; he wanted so very desperately to run his fingers through it and feel the silky smoothness of it between each digit. Yet the immobilizing effect she exuded rattled his mind even as it stimulated his senses, and it repulsed him. He was like a hamstrung animal, paralyzed in front of a sexy predator. He loved the sensation. He hated the sensation.

She kissed him on the lips, delicately at first, then harder as her mouth lingered over his. He tasted her lip gloss and inhaled her musky breath into his own lungs. Her hand glided across his scalp and traced contours on his ear.

"Tell me about my sister," she repeated.

"I saw her at a murder scene the other day." The words sprang unbidden from within him. He willed himself to shut up, to say no more than that. But he was no longer in control, as though a part of Bernadette had burrowed into his cerebral cortex and now made those decisions for him. And before he knew it, more words tumbled out. "There was this guy named Najac, he was a member of some kind of voodoo cult and he was following me. Then a snake creature killed him. He called it a loa and said its name was Damballah. I saw Elizabeth at the scene of the murder, staring at me, but I didn't know it was her until later, when I saw pictures of the crime scene. Now I need to find her to see if she knows what's going on. For a while, I thought maybe her ex-husband killed her."

"You mean Dallas?" she purred into his ear.

"Yes. His fiancée was killed about a week ago. I was looking into that when I found out that his ex-wife had gone missing."

Bernadette sat up straight, pulling away from him in the process. The separation made him want to take his own life. He needed her close again. He had to have her close.

"Faith is dead?" Bernadette said.

"Yes," he said, still unable to control his own speech, but inwardly shocked to learn that Bernadette would even know the name of the fiancée of the ex-husband of her sister who she had not even been in touch with.

"I knew of her," she said. "Dallas and I have... kept in touch."

There was a heaviness to those words that Jake noted, but his yearning overpowered it. He reached out for Bernadette, to pull her back toward him. She obliged. All the while there was a part of his brain that screamed at him to run, to get as far away as he could. He ignored that warning.

"What else have you learned about Elizabeth?" Bernadette said.

"Just that she was working for your dad before she disappeared. That she abruptly came back to New Orleans to confront Dallas about getting engaged and then vanished."

"Do you know why her marriage fell apart?"

"No." He buried his face in her neck, and breathed in deep of her scent. She made no attempt to stop him.

"And that's all you know about her?" Bernadette said.

"That's it," he practically moaned into that delicate throat.

She suddenly pulled away and stood. He reached for her but she batted his hand away. He felt at first deeply wounded, but then that odd sensation that took hold of him started to fold back. He found that he could think clearly again. A horrified pang of dismay settled into his stomach.

"What did you just do to me?" He rose from his chair, frantic.

Bernadette smiled. "I'm a very charming woman, you know. I tend to get what I want from men, one way or the other."

He shook his head. "No. That went beyond womanly charm."

And then his eyes settled on something over her shoulder that he had not noticed before. A new feeling of dread came over him and he almost pushed her aside in his mad dash to examine a photograph on the hutch, depicting two young girls sitting together at a table in what appeared to be a quaint little café.

"What is this?" he asked.

Bernadette shrugged. "Me and Elizabeth as kids. It was taken right after my father married her mother. Why?"

Jake stared, open-mouthed, trying to process what he was seeing. The two girls in the picture did not look particularly happy to be seated near one another. Neither one smiled. Bernadette looked by far to be the more miserable of the two. But that was not what had caught Jake's eye and now held him so riveted.

"Why?" Bernadette repeated.

"No reason," Jake lied.

"There most certainly is a reason."

That warmth crept over him again and her fingertips brushed his arm. Against his better judgment, he turned to face her. She rolled her eyes. "Do we have to do this all over again? Why did that picture catch your attention?"

He had no will of his own. He opened his mouth to answer her honestly, but before the words could spill out and betray him, the door to her office burst open. They turned in unison to find Dennis Meullion in the doorway, a sardonic smile on his face. Several security guards lined up in the hall behind him.

"It looks like our little guest is still with us," Meullion said. "Most unfortunate."

Meullion stepped aside and the security guards came forward and seized Jake.

"Okay, okay, I'm leaving," Jake said.

Meullion laughed. "Oh, I'm afraid it's much too late for that now."

Twenty-seven

Curtis smirked from a few yards away as the wave of guards crashed in on Jake. Altogether there were six of them, including Curtis. Dennis Meullion remained off to one side of the doorway, an unreadable expression etched on his hard face. It all happened so fast, and Jake felt a sharp sting at his throat before realizing that one of the men had yanked the chain right off of him, snapping it.

"What are you doing?" Bernadette gasped.

"You may return to the party now," Meullion intoned.

"You can't just-"

Meullion silenced her with a cold stare that imparted all of the love and affection of a granite tombstone. She abruptly closed her mouth, defiance slowly giving way to the reality of her defeat. She cast one last glance at Jake, then shouldered past the crowd of men and stormed off in the direction of the elevators.

When she was gone, Meullion faced his prey once more.

"I'm glad we settled that," he said.

Jake wasn't sure what he was expecting. Perhaps to be roughly handled and thrown from the building forcefully. What he was not expecting was for Curtis to step forward and deliver a right hook that rocked his head back. Jake slumped against the wall. It had not been that long ago that the men in the truck had similarly brutalized him, and he was still sore from that attack.

Two of the nameless guards hauled him back into an upright position, just so Curtis could punch him again, this time in the stomach. A rush of air evacuated his lungs and the two men relinquished their grips, allowing him to double over and slump to the floor.

"Having fun?" Meullion gibed.

"Almost as much fun as I was having with your daughter a few minutes ago," Jake shot back.

"Hit him again. Harder."

Curtis stepped forward and walloped him where he knelt, and Jake cried out and fell over sideways on the floor, striking his head against the side of Bernadette's desk. The coarse fabric of the carpet scratched his cheek.

"I prefer my punch lines to be delivered with actual punches," Meullion said.

"Funny," Jake managed, gasping through the pain. "Since I don't see you throwing any punches."

Dennis Meullion chuckled, a low and throaty sound. "Touché."

At a gesture from their boss, two of the men again hauled Jake to his feet. They tossed him carelessly into one of the chairs, coincidentally the same one he had been sitting in when Bernadette had been doing that weird seduction trick. Meullion perched on one corner of the desk in front of Jake, neatly straddling the edge.

"Now, why don't you tell me what's really going on?" he said mildly.

"I got lost on my way to the bathroom," Jake said.

Meullion nodded and Curtis hit him again.

"That's really starting to get on my nerves," Jake managed. "I think I liked Bernadette's interrogation techniques better."

"A sentiment that I'm sure Mr. Lasserre shares as well," Meullion said.

Through the jumbled fog that his brain had become, Jake did not miss the insinuation.

"What?" he said, as a trickle of blood dripped off of his chin and spotted his shirt.

"Come on, Mister Wannabe Investigator. You don't know about Dallas Lasserre's tryst with Bernadette? She had him first, you know. Elizabeth should have known better than to go after him. Dallas didn't tell you any of this when you were pestering him?"

Jake tried to shake the cobwebs. "How do you know I spoke to Dallas?"

Meullion licked his lips. "Mr. Lasserre and I keep in touch."

Jake recalled that Bernadette had said almost the exact same thing about Dallas. What was going on, anyway? He really wished he could just go home and try to resume a normal life.

"I can do this all night, by the way," Meullion said. "If Curtis's hands get too sore to continue, the next man in line will gladly step up." He gestured to the closed office door, the drawn blinds, and the seven men surrounding Jake. The message was clear, Jake had nowhere to go and he was stuck in here with a lot of people who could and would hurt him. Maybe it was time to swallow what little of his pride remained. He had been defeated, there was no denying that now.

"What do you want to know?" Jake croaked.

"At last, some intelligence shines forth," Meullion said. A thin smile stretched his lips. "I want to know where the rest of *these* are?" Meullion dangled the silver chain in front of Jake's face. Jake considered making a grab for it but realized there was no way he could pull such a maneuver off in an enclosed space with this many people surrounding him. They would be on him way too quickly for such a feat to do him any good. He wasn't even sure if the chain would still work, since it had snapped when the guard snatched it off of him.

"The rest of them?" Jake said weakly.

Meullion sighed and nodded to Curtis again. Curtis kicked the chair Jake was sitting in, sending it crashing to the floor. Jake felt the impact and lay there stunned.

He wanted to make another wisecrack, but he hurt too much.

"The other artifacts," Meullion elaborated. "Don't make me drag it out of you. This hurts you far more than it does me."

Jake rolled clear of the wrecked chair and leaned against a wall, gazing up at the hostile faces leering back down at him. Not one shred of sympathy was to be found on a single one. He concluded that not only did they not mind doing dirty work, but that they enjoyed it. It was probably a prerequisite for working for Dennis Meullion.

"Look, I have no idea what you are talking about," Jake wheezed. When Curtis stepped forward again with a murderous glint in his eyes, Jake held out a shaking hand to ward him off. "I'm serious. I don't know what you're talking about. At all."

Curtis kept coming.

"Wait," Meullion said. Curtis paused, his disappointment palpable. He probably didn't even care about what Jake knew, he just wanted to keep pummeling him. Dennis pressed his lips into a tight line and clicked his tongue. "I assure you, Mister Presnall, this has the potential to end very badly for you. And I don't take kindly to being lied to. Where are the other artifacts?"

Jake pulled himself to a sitting position. He used the back of one shaking hand to wipe his face, and it came back dotted with blood. He could feel his lip beginning to swell.

"Look," Jake said. "That chain was given to me. I don't know anything about any more like it. Seriously."

"Imagine my surprise," Meullion said, "when just moments after I thought I had tossed you out of my party, I received a frantic phone call from one of my guards monitoring the cameras, ranting about a man in the lobby who had disappeared into thin air. Of course I had to have a peek at the footage myself. And there you were. And then you weren't." He looked at the chain he held. "You reappeared at precisely that same moment, inside the ballroom. All because of the power of this chain. And you expect me to believe that somebody just handed this to you?"

Jake gulped. Meullion knew about the power of the chain. "The man who gave it to me was dying. I'm sure you'd remember him. His name was Najac Petion."

Meullion stared at Jake silently for a few moments, appraising him, ascertaining the truthfulness of his words. "Yes, I knew Najac," he admitted. "He disappeared right before Elizabeth did. Along with several of my artifacts. One of which was this very chain I now hold. You can imagine why, having found it on you, I am suddenly very interested in your full disclosure."

Another piece of the puzzle, an explanation of sorts that had been tickling the back of Jake's mind, settled into place. He thought he was beginning to understand now. And just when he thought that this whole situation could not get any weirder.

"Something attacked Najac," Jake admitted. "He was dying, and he gave me that chain. That's why I have it. But he didn't give me anything else. I didn't even know that there were other chains."

"Oh, they're not all chains, my boy," Meullion said, grinning. "And the fact that you assumed so might make me lean towards believing your story. But what do you mean some*thing* attacked him?"

"You wouldn't believe me," Jake said.

"You wouldn't believe the things that I would believe."

"Fine. It was some kind of monster." There was laughter from some of the security force that surrounded Jake. He just went ahead anyway, not letting it deter him. "He was running with some pretty strange people.

I've been told it's a renegade voodoo god. Something that goes by the name of Damballah. Its body is covered in snakes."

Meullion chuckled.

"I told you that you wouldn't believe me," Jake said.

"Would it be overly patronizing of me if I said that I believe that you believe it?" Meullion asked. Jake did not respond. "But what of your involvement with Elizabeth?"

"There's no involvement," Jake said. "There was another victim before Najac. Her name was Faith Daelly and she was Dallas Lasserre's fiancée. I also found out that Dallas's ex-wife, your step-daughter, had gone missing before that. So I started trying to learn more about Elizabeth and realized she had been lurking around the place where Najac got killed. I came here tonight to ask you if you knew where she was. That's it. I swear."

Meullion drummed a fingertip on his cheek while he regarded Jake's story. He crossed one leg over the other, folded his hands, and placed them in his lap. "I believe you," he said. "At least, some of it. I think you have quite an imagination, and perhaps you're prone to hallucinations, but for the parts that concern me at least, I believe you."

"I'll just be going, then," Jake said, trying to rise.

"Not so fast."

Jake settled back down on the floor. "Can't fault me for hoping."

"Of course not," Meullion remarked. "But I can fault you for sticking your nose in my life and my business. And where, as I said, I am inclined to believe you, that's not enough. I need to be one hundred percent sure. I trust that you'll understand if I have a couple of my guys make certain that you are being completely honest. They are quite resourceful when it comes to extracting the truth from people."

Jake's stomach turned to ice, which was no small feat considering it still burned from Curtis's earlier gut punch. Before he could protest, he was rushed by a couple of the nameless cronies, who hefted him up and dragged him out of the office door. He tried to struggle, but they were stronger than he was, and they had the double advantage of having not had the crap kicked out of them. They were dragging him in the general direction of the elevators, but he was sure that they were not taking such a public route.

"Where are you taking me?" Jake gasped.

Meullion paced leisurely behind the men. "Service elevator that opens out back, behind the building. You will be transported to a much more secure location while I have somebody patch up the stains in Bernadette's office. You will be interrogated until such time as you spill whatever information you may yet be concealing or my guys decide you have already done so. I won't lie to you. It won't be pleasant."

A blind panic overcame Jake and he began thrashing against his captors. They reasserted their grips on him and one of the men reached back as if to strike him in the side of the head. At that moment Jake brought one of his legs up and kicked as hard as he could, aiming for the crotch of the man to his left. He felt the glorious contact and the man grunted, promptly releasing his grip on Jake and slumping to the floor.

Jake twisted free of the second man's grasp and half-staggered, half-ran toward the elevators near the front wall. He knew he would not have time to call the car and wait for it, but was hoping he would find the door to a staircase or perhaps a room that he could barricade himself within. Anything would be better than being dragged off to be tortured.

He only made it a few strides past the first line of cubicles before one of the other guards tackled him hard from behind. They crashed to the floor in a sprawled tangle of limbs. Jake tried to wrestle free but the man held him tight until another guard caught up and kicked him in the ribs. The pain blared throughout his body and then someone else kicked him from another direction.

Suddenly he was surrounded and kicks and stomps rained down upon him. He balled himself into a fetal position and did the best job he could of protecting the more essential parts of his body, like his head and face.

He thought it would never stop.

He thought they meant to kill him then and there.

When he heard what sounded like an explosion mingled with the shriek of about fifteen windows shattering, he didn't comprehend what it could be. Just more destruction, maybe. But then people started screaming and there came the sound of many muffled impacts around the large open bullpen. It sounded like somebody was literally ripping the entire building apart. Something like a wet tearing sound followed that, and then more screams. He thought he heard Meullion barking orders at somebody from far away. Curled up as he was, not daring to open his eyes or move his arms from their protective position over his head, he had no idea what any of it meant.

There was nobody kicking him now.

The screams and yelling and breaking and ripping continued. Tentatively he opened one eye, and then another. He ached all over. But something had changed and his life probably hinged on his actions over the next few seconds.

He rolled over onto his back. There was a large smear of blood on a nearby cubicle wall and one of the guards lay crumpled several yards away, unmoving. He heard a familiar slithering noise and something hissed from nearby as another set of footsteps echoed in his direction.

Jake twisted his head and looked down the corridor toward the front of the building.

The loa caught one of the guards by the neck and bashed the poor guy so hard into the nearest wall that his head actually whiplashed back, his neck breaking with an audible pop and then flopping as though there were no bones in it at all. Damballah's snake appendages writhed and gyrated in a chorus of movement all about the creature like some kind of grisly aura.

Jake watched, barely able to move. The creature turned toward him.

Twenty-eight

Rivera cursed and slammed on the gas at the same instant he cut the wheel and swerved around the slow moving grandma in the left lane, placing himself squarely into oncoming traffic. A car horn erupted and headlights from an encroaching SUV filled his field of vision as he jerked the wheel back in the other direction, cutting off the vehicle he had just passed. It was a narrow squeeze, and he might have even clipped the vehicle, but there was no time to dwell on that. His body was tensed, his shoulders clenched up tight against his neck. His knuckles were white on the steering wheel and his fingers burned from the pressure he was exerting on the plastic surface.

He pressed his foot down even harder against the gas pedal and the engine of the police issued sedan howled like a wolf in the night while the automatic transmission struggled to change gears.

On a level beyond the rational, which bordered more on the instinctual, he knew that Jake Presnall was in trouble. There was no doubt. Elizabeth Meullion, long thought to be missing or dead, was out and about, prowling about murder scenes. Najac Petion was connected to both her and the father, Dennis Meullion. There were things going on they could not begin to understand, and apparently voodoo murders and Holy Land archaeological digs were involved. And that little hothead brat had just taken off and placed himself squarely in the middle of it. No doubt about it, the kid was in over his head. Again.

Rivera could not get to the banquet quickly enough.

The next traffic light loomed in the distance, getting closer by the second as Rivera's vehicle raced toward it. The light was red. Cross traffic wove through the intersection, motorists just going about their business who had no reason to suspect that at any second someone was about to just career right through them. Bracing himself and holding his hand down on the horn, he sailed on through. He almost nailed a silver Honda Civic from the side, an impact that would not have been kind to either driver. Luckily, the car cleared Rivera's path just in time, escaping injury, but the car behind it did not get off so easy. That driver had to swerve, sideswiping another vehicle, setting off a chain reaction of screeching metal and squealing tires. Chaos filled Rivera's rearview mirror as he glanced up for only that one moment to see what he had caused. Hopefully nobody back there was hurt.

He had to park in a spot specifically marked "No Parking" outside the building by the street, but he had a special Police Permit for such occasions as this. He stuck the permit on the dashboard where it would be clearly visible, and made his way into the building. He stormed through the entrance corridor, past a bank of elevators, and into a spacious and elegantly decorated lobby. The two receptionists (or whatever they were) at the registration table gave him a wary eye, even after he identified himself as a police detective, and were of such little help that he questioned their purpose in life. He asked after their boss.

"Mr. Meullion? He's in the party," the blonde said.

"You're a cop?" the brunette said.

"Is he in trouble?"

Rivera dealt with their idiocy as long as he could tolerate, which was for about five seconds. He started asking about Jake, trying to determine if they had seen him. They had no idea who that was. He gave a description and they shrugged and looked confused. They looked at each other, as if thinking was a team activity, and came up with nothing.

"A lot of guys came to the party," one of the girls said.

"How about I just go in and look around?" Rivera offered.

They looked at each other again. Rivera was already turning in the direction of the double doors to the ballroom when a man, bloodied and panting, burst into the lobby from the other direction, near the elevators Rivera had just passed. The bloody man made it about halfway toward the tables before he fell. His eyes bulged. The girls looked alarmed, but not overly sympathetic.

The man favored Rivera and the two ladies with a stricken expression. Several other guests, who had been lulling about in the lobby, retreated back several paces. They clearly wanted nothing to do with whatever tomfoolery was going down.

"Snakes," the man said. "Its body. Covered with them." Then he passed out.

One of the reception girls giggled. Rivera didn't. This was the exactly the kind of thing that he had been afraid might happen.

Twenty-nine

One of the security guards made the unfortunate mistake of getting too close to the loa as it stalked Jake between the rows of cubicle partitions. From his angle on the floor, Jake could only see the top of the man's head over the distant cubicle wall. Damballah detoured, its snake appendages hissing, and cut the man off. Even though Jake had seen this monster in action on two other occasions, he couldn't help but feel shock and dismay at how quickly it ended the poor guy's life. Thankfully Jake was spared the visual, being unable to see the worst of it. But there was no mistaking the sounds. The guard let out a horrified cry, which was promptly cut off by a wet ripping noise. Something heavy hit the floor. And no more sounds came from that guy.

Jake knew he could not remain where he was. He had to drown out the protestations of about a dozen body parts that screamed at him as he rolled over and tried to crawl away. His body did not at all appreciate being forced to move. The body just wanted to lie there. Only Jake's mind seemed aware of how precarious his situation had become. He had to find a way to escape this. And he had to do so immediately, or it wouldn't happen at all.

That distinct slithering noise started up again, indicating that the loa was on the move. It was probably still ticked off at what he had done to it during their last encounter. His death at the thing's hands would not be glorious at all. He'd rather not experience it.

He crawled to the end of the narrow aisle and could see the front lobby area from his vantage point, about a million miles away. In the other direction, behind him, was the back wall, where the large conference room and Bernadette's office would be. He faced a dilemma. He could probably make it to the conference room and try to hide under the table or something, but how long would it be until the monster found him? On the other hand, the front lobby, with its elevators, would give him a real chance of escape. The obvious problem was that in order to get there, he would be heading back in the direction of the creature, which for now at least, was hidden from view.

In kindergarten the most difficult decision he had to make pertained to crafts projects: whether to use the liquid glue or that sticky paste that you applied with a stick? Why couldn't life still be that simple?

He decided to try for the front lobby. He had made it this far, probably on nothing more than blind luck. He would have to hope that this luck had not run out. He pressed himself low and tried to death crawl along the ground while making as little noise as possible. If he could only make it along the wall and get across any openings quickly, without attracting undue attention, he might make it.

The loa started tearing down cubicle partitions rather than going around them. Jake could not see the creature, but there was no mistaking the noise or what it meant. It was coming from just up ahead and to his right.

He decided to abandon the crawling strategy. He rose to his feet, but kept to a low crouch, hoping to remain hidden by the partition walls. If he hurried he might make it past the creature's path without being spotted, presuming he could keep himself hidden as he went. But at the rate the thing was tearing through the cubicles, there might not be anything left to hide behind after a few more seconds.

The thrashing, pounding sounds of destruction continued as Jake crouch-limped along the aisle. A stray thought popped into Jake's mind; what was that thing even doing here? Had it followed him? Or was it after one of the Meullions this time? That would be just his luck if that were the case, and Jake had just happened to be here for the attack. But those kinds of coincidences couldn't happen three times, could they? He had to face facts, the loa was here for him.

Just when Jake began to naively believe he might make it to the end of the aisle without incident, something hit him hard from behind.

Of course he assumed it was Damballah that had found him. He writhed and screamed, waiting for the sensation of a dozen snake bites, or the shredding of his body, or the bashing of his head against a wall, but instead a heavy weight just settled over him and somebody grunted with the effort.

He twisted and found it was Curtis who had tackled him.

"You're not going anywhere," Curtis said. One of his arms was pretty torn up, and blood was flowing freely from the wounds.

Really? He was worried about Jake escaping? With a snake monster about twenty feet away, hell-bent on killing them all, and nothing but flimsy cubicle walls separating them?

"It'll kill us both," Jake gasped. He did not try to fight, but rather attempted to continue his escape, clawing at the floor in a mad dash to freedom.

Curtis kept him pinned down and would not let him move.

"Idiot!" Jake screamed. "We gotta go! Do you want to die with me?"

He could hear the loa fast approaching. A menacing growl filled the air and it didn't take a genius to tell, from the sounds of things breaking, that the beast was headed straight toward their position.

"Really, man, can we settle this later?" Jake moaned.

It was no use. One simple glance at Curtis's taut face and frantic eyes provided all the confirmation Jake needed to see that the man was beyond reason. A temporary insanity plea could easily justify any atrocities he might commit in his current state. The sight of the beast and the ensuing killing of the other guards had rattled him to his core. He had already been half-mad with venomous glee from the beating he had dished out on Jake before Damballah had even shown up. In his current state, he was fixated on Jake alone, the threat he could understand. It was the kind of moment when it might have been nice for Jake to still have that silver chain around his neck.

The partition beside them disintegrated as the loa punched a thick arm through it and then ripped it apart the same way Jake might have ripped apart a sheet of paper, tossing the broken halves in either direction which in turn knocked down yet more partitions. The room suddenly looked much less like a bullpen filled with cubicles and much more like a wide open space filled with storm debris.

Curtis, straddling Jake, was the nearest and most convenient target. Damballah went for him first. The creature bellowed and struck a blow that knocked him several feet into the aisle, bending him over in the process. Jake immediately tried to crawl away. The loa lifted one of its mighty legs and Jake knew he was a half second from being stomped right through the floor. He had seen the damage this thing could do with raw power; it could probably send Jake through the ceiling of the floor beneath them.

Jake rolled aside as swiftly as he could manage. Desperation fueled the effort. The creature's foot shook the floor when it struck a moment later in the spot that Jake's spine had just occupied. Jake found himself lying on his back, between the creature's feet, looking straight up at its crotch.

What the heck? It always worked in the movies...

Aiming for that one delicate spot between the legs where no man ever wants to be struck, Jake punched upward with all the force he could muster.

Maybe he missed and hit a concrete wall. Or maybe the creature was using an iron plate to protect its delicate parts. More than likely, though, snake gods just didn't have that kind of equipment.

In any case, the blow definitely hurt Jake's hand way more than it hurt the creature. Damballah just stared down at him with a kind of curious expression on its dead features, while Jake's hand meanwhile felt like it had been broken in about a hundred and seventy-eight different places.

He scurried to hands and knees, regretting that during the course of the entire episode he had ended up facing away from the front lobby. He couldn't spare even the little bit of time it would take to pivot himself around, so he just took off in the direction he was facing, which took him back toward the conference room and Bernadette's office. He was dimly aware that Curtis was struggling to rise. Stubborn to the last, that one.

There was a tenuous moment as the loa turned around to track Jake's progress and it noted Curtis. The head security guard was panting, he was bloody, and he was having trouble standing, but he leveled his gaze at Damballah and returned the stare. To Curtis's credit, he did not shirk or run away screaming. He merely reached around to a holster on his side, withdrew a small firearm, and began firing rounds at the beast. Damballah roared, and it seemed as if at least some of the bullets struck the monster. The sounds of the impact possessed a muffled quality, like punching a pillow, but they did not penetrate the beast's skin. There were no holes in Damballah's body, no splashes of blood like at the voodoo house when Rivera had shot it. Why not?

Jake made a break for it as the creature made a beeline for Curtis. Say what you want about the idiot thug, the man was a very convenient distraction. Jake had the briefest glimpse of the man ducking for cover as the monster lunged, and there was another crash, a rattling of the wall, and a cloud of plaster dust. Jake took advantage of the diversion and changed course, making for the front lobby again.

Nothing could stop him now. He was going to make it.

It was precisely at that moment that his right leg gave out on him and he fell flat on his face.

In the mind-numbing, soul-searing, pain-filled eternity that followed, it occurred to him that he must have twisted the leg pretty badly when Curtis tackled him. The abrupt pivot when he stopped in his tracks and changed course for the lobby had been more than that leg could handle. Now he began the arduous task of rising to his feet again, knowing now what it must feel like to grow old and to have trouble moving at all. He could only hope that he would have the opportunity to grow old and have trouble moving.

Damballah had not re-appeared yet. Jake managed to regain his footing, but was unable to put much weight at all on the injured leg. So he limped along at what felt like the speed of ketchup creeping across a dinner plate. Stupid ketchup, always running and getting on all your food, even the stuff that you didn't want it on.

He made it about twenty feet and was beginning to think he might actually have time to get to the elevator, call the car, and ride it down to the first floor. Maybe he could just hop on a bus and go to Alaska or something. Hang out with Sarah Palin and do some wilderness hikes, possibly dial up Bristol and see what she was up to. Poach some salmon. Anything but get killed by a snake monster or an egomaniacal security guard.

But amidst a pile of what used to be some poor sap's workspace, now reduced to unglorified rubble, he spotted Dennis Meullion.

"Help me," Meullion said. He held out a trembling hand. He was partially concealed beneath the remnants of a computer desk and scattered equipment.

Jake almost kept going past him. But he had a crisis of conscience at precisely that instant. Could he afford to stop and help the man who had been about to have him tortured? Did he dare take the time to assist him and possibly give the loa all the time it needed to finish off Curtis and head his way? He looked down at that tight face, etched with pain, those same eyes that had so gleefully been about to condemn him to untold horrors just a few short minutes ago.

He should leave him. But he'd never be able to live with himself. Jake knew that he would never forget the day that he had just left someone to die. Even if that someone was a big jerk.

Jake bent down and started shoving debris off of the man, exposing the twisted legs that had been concealed beneath the desk. They were bent at unnatural angles. This man was not going to be rising again of his own power.

"Dude," Jake said.

A rivulet of blood trickled from Meullion's mouth. "Carry me. Do something."

"Carry you?" Jake knew for a fact he could not support two bodies with only one good leg. This was hopeless. He should not have stopped.

"I can't carry you," Jake said.

"Please," Meullion said.

And then Jake saw it; Clutched in the man's right hand, undoubtedly forgotten to him, Meullion grasped the silver chain that he had taken from Jake. He reached for it, but Meullion pulled his hand away. Jake reached again. Meullion pulled away again.

And so the fates of both men hung in the balance as an impromptu game of "Magic Necklace Keep-Away" began.

Jake lunged across Meullion's prone form, trying to pin the arm down and then attempting desperately to break the man's grip on the chain. Meullion did not even particularly seem aware of what Jake was doing or what he was trying to get, but was merely trying to thwart his attempts on principle.

The loa roared and started bounding toward Jake again. Jake had no idea what had become of Curtis. He was probably a liquefied pulp spread across the floor somewhere. Furniture smashed and flew in multiple directions as the creature batted things out of its way. Its sights were set squarely on Jake. And it was coming fast.

"Give me the chain!" Jake screamed.

Meullion continued to clutch desperately as though his very life depended on it. Finally, Meullion's grip slackened, the muscles in the limb growing weary from the struggle. Jake banged his hand, once, twice, three times against the floor and finally broke his grip. He snatched the chain and dove for cover around the corner of the pile of wreckage. The loa was upon him, snarling.

"I knew you'd abandon me!" Meullion shouted.

Jake ducked to avoid a swing of the thing's arm that would have probably decapitated him. Instead, it just smashed another hole into another wall. If this thing hadn't been trying to kill Jake, this could almost make a great drinking game: Every time the snake monster punches a hole in something, take a shot.

He scurried away, a frightened rat trying to evade a hungry cat. The creature was spinning around again, locking its sights on him.

The chase had brought Jake to a side wall that was lined with more offices. Most of the doors stood open. Jake ducked into the nearest one and slammed the door shut, heard the latch click. He dove to the ground just as a mighty impact completely blew the door off its hinges.

Damballah stood silhouetted in the doorway, and this time Jake had nowhere else to go.

But in the moment that passed after Jake slammed shut the door, he had been working feverishly at the chain, wrapping it around his neck. The clasp was broken, but he wound two ends of the chain around each other and pulled tight, like he was beginning to lace a pair of shoes. It wasn't pretty, but technically he was wearing the chain.

He had no idea if that technicality would impress whatever magical power governed the chain, however.

The loa started forward, its teeth gnashing together. Its powerful limbs were tensed for the killing blow. From his spot on the floor, Jake looked past the creature, said a quick prayer to whatever deity would listen, and did his thing.

He found himself out in the hallway again, free.

A howl of fury erupted behind him, the frustrated loa no doubt wondering what had become of its prey. Jake made his way back over to Meullion. For the moment at least, Damballah had no idea where he was, which gave him some time to work with. He breathed a sigh of relief; if that chain had not worked, just now, there would be nothing left to say. It would be over.

The last time Jake had tried to teleport away from Damballah, at the voodoo house, the monster had blocked his attempt somehow. What was different about this time? Was it because last time, the creature had been holding him up off the ground? Could it only block him from teleporting when it was physically touching him? That was another question Jake would be left to ponder if he got out of this alive.

"Knew you'd abandon me," Meullion said, as Jake crouched over him again.

"I wasn't abandoning you, idiot," Jake fired back.

Meullion looked at him dumbly.

But how in the world was Jake going to get Meullion to safety and somehow evade Damballah? He looked at the wreckage around the desk and realized that he had encountered either a moment of providence or just a cosmic prank to which he was the intended victim: The desk that had been smashed and under which Meullion had been trapped had had one of those waist-high rolling file cabinets attached. And the cabinet looked relatively undamaged, at least the wheels looked like they would still roll. It was probably large enough that he could get Dennis up on it, but the man would basically be draped across it like a towel on a clothesline.

Would it make a good gurney? Only one way to find out.

Jake pulled at the man, who was much heavier than he looked. Or maybe it was just the dead weight. He had heard that unconscious and dead people often seemed to weigh more. Dennis was neither unconscious nor dead; he just couldn't use his legs and so was no help whatsoever.

Jake tried to balance most of their combined weight on his one good leg, but even still he had to use the damaged one for balance, and the pain shot right up through his hip. He gritted his teeth and cried out, but he did not stop exerting himself, even though he felt that surely he was about to damage some internal part of his own body in the process.

Damballah had not emerged from the office yet. From the sound of it, the beast was tearing the room apart in a blind rage. Maybe it expected to find Jake hiding in one of the desk drawers or something. Hopefully it would keep itself busy for as long as Jake needed. If it came out of that office and saw Jake standing there, Jake would be a sitting duck.

Meullion howled in pain as Jake pulled and twisted.

"Shut up," Jake half-whispered, half-shouted.

He managed somehow to get Meullion sprawled out across the rolling cabinet. He was on his back, his useless legs dangling off one end and his head hanging off the other. It did not look at all comfortable, but was definitely better than he deserved.

Jake started pushing. He immediately regretted the squeak of the wheels as they tried to turn under the extra weight piled on them. The stupid little cabinet, not meant for tasks such as this, did not want to roll straight. It took a tremendous effort just to keep it on course and to keep it moving. All of this with only one leg for pushing. Their progress was painfully slow and altogether too noisy. Meullion cried out as Jake accidentally bashed one of his dangling arms against the wall before getting the cabinet back on course.

Damballah snarled and Jake knew it had spotted him. The roar was deafening. Meullion moaned where he lay. Jake turned to face his adversary just as it started forward.

Nowhere to go. Nothing to do. His only hope lay in abandoning Meullion, something he had already vowed to himself he would not do. So he faced the creature, tensing for what was coming.

A gunshot rang out. And then another. And then another. Jake could hear the blasts behind him as the bullets whizzed past his head and raced toward their target. Damballah stopped short as the bullets struck it.

Jake turned back and was surprised to see Detective Rivera standing in the aisle, gun in hand. His eyes swept the scene and returned to their target and he fired again.

"Don't just stand there, Presnall, get going!" Rivera shouted.

Jake did not need to be told twice. He started pushing the makeshift cart again. Rivera stood his ground, unloading his clip into the creature and then expertly ejecting the spent clip and inserting another.

Damballah was downright furious now. Jake passed Rivera and kept moving toward the elevators, when he heard what sounded like a tornado ripping through the office space. He knew that sound. In fact, the thought of what happened to Najac in the alley that night still haunted him. He spun around just in time to see the loa spit that noxious purple blast from its mouth.

Rivera never stood a chance; the blast enveloped him where he stood. Jake's last glimpse of the man was that of a hero; poised, determined, gun drawn and facing down evil. It was honorable, and noble, a perfect sacrifice, and there were no words. It hurt Jake worse than his leg. Not Rivera. Not like that.

"No!" Jake cried.

It was stupid, but it felt like he should stop and do something. But what? At the very least he should be permitted a moment to mourn. But he had no such time. It tore his heart in a way he would not have suspected, but he knew he could not stop. Not now. Not after that. So he kept pushing. And pushing. And pushing. He could not even spare a hand to wipe at the tears that ran down his cheeks; he needed both hands for pushing.

He fell just before he reached the elevators. His sore leg was throbbing so badly now that there were purple streaks in his peripheral vision and it seemed to his pain-ebbed mind that his knee was trying to detach itself from his body. He stumbled, and he went down. The force caused Dennis to fall off of the cabinet. He struck the floor with a small cry of anguish. They lay there together, right in front the elevators. Only the rolling cabinet remained upright. There was probably irony there somewhere.

He knew he did not have the strength to get up and get Dennis back on the cabinet. He was not even sure if he had the strength to get up at all. He rolled over onto his back and looked up at the ceiling. He was fairly sure it was the last sight he would ever see.

"Good lord, Presnall, can't you do anything?" somebody said. He looked over and saw Rivera's ghost. At least, it had to be his ghost, right? The real Rivera couldn't be standing there. Jake had just seen him incinerated. So much activity, so little time to process. The ghost slammed a heavy fist on the button to call the elevator and started dragging Jake toward the sliding doors.

"Not me," Jake said. "I have the chain. Get Meullion."

The ghost looked at the other man on the floor and grunted. He hefted him up with considerably more ease than Jake had been able to do. As the little ding sounded and the doors started to slide open, Rivera's ghost escaped with Meullion. He turned back just as the loa roared and started down the hallway again. Jake was still lying prone on the floor. The doors started to close.

"Use this!" the ghost screamed.

Something hit Jake in the chest and landed on the floor next to him. He was waiting to die and did not really care what it was, but he checked anyway. It was a small brown-colored sack, and it seemed familiar to him somehow.

Then he remembered it; the protective ward that the Mother had given him about eight thousand years ago. He grasped it in his hand and tried to make sense of it.

That had not been Rivera's ghost who had just saved Meullion. It had been the man himself. Rivera had the ward when the blast hit him. And it had protected him from the creature's power, just as it had Jake.

Say what you want about the Mother, but her wards worked. No doubt about it.

Jake laughed out loud and then the loa was there.

Something curious happened just then. The monster stopped, and just appraised him as he held high the small bag. For the first time, the creature seemed uncertain. Jake sat up tentatively and looked it right in the face, its teeth gnashing together menacingly, its nose slits contracting in time with its snarls, the bright jewel in its forehead glittering in the well-lit foyer.

Jake knew what he had to do. He just wasn't sure how to go about doing it.

He used the wall, one hand, and his one steady foot to scoot to a standing position, using the other hand to keep the ward out in front of him where the monster could see it. Damballah stood poised but did not strike. It seemed to be regarding him warily, as if waiting for some kind of opening to attack.

A small glass enclosure holding a fire extinguisher was mounted to the wall by the elevators. Jake worked at the latch to the box, never taking his eyes off of the beast. His hand shook.

Several things happened in rapid-fire succession.

First, the elevator dinged again. That made Jake jump. He could not help it. The uneasy tension and the way that Damballah was looking at him already had him uneasy, so that the sound of the chime caught him off guard.

Second, he dropped the ward. That was perhaps the most unfortunate part of it all. He was jumpy. He was focused on getting the latch for the fire extinguisher open and on keeping his eyes on the loa. Combine that with the fact that he was not in the best physical state to begin with, and yeah, the sack fell out of his hand.

Third, the beast lunged. That sucked too.

Fourth, the door to the enclosure finally came open and Jake suddenly had the fire extinguisher in his hand.

Fifth, the monster stepped on the ward just as it reached Jake. It made some kind of undefinable noise and then Jake swung the fire extinguisher with all of his might, connecting with the thing's face. Its head rocked backward and a startled grunt came out of it.

Sixth, the elevator doors opened and Rivera stepped back out into the foyer, still holding his gun. There was no sign of Meullion. He had probably deposited the man on another floor and then come right back up. He took one look at the loa and began firing. This time the bullets penetrated its skin, and that vile orange pus that passed as its blood erupted every which way.

Jake found himself on his knees. The swing with the fire extinguisher had thrown him off balance and he had fallen. His leg was never going to forgive him for this. The pain shot well past his hip and went everywhere. He was pretty sure he was crying again, but this time the tears were tears of pain, plain and simple.

But the ward was within reach. He grabbed it. The loa fell over onto its back before the reception desk. Its head left a dent in the paneled wood where it slammed into it. The beast was already trying to get back up. Rivera had spent his entire clip and was switching out again.

One of the snake appendages lashed out at Jake as he got close. He was crawling toward it, doing his best to ignore the pain. He held up the ward and the appendage coiled back on itself.

Jake knew better than to try to wrestle the beast. Whatever protection the ward offered him from the voodoo magic that had summoned this thing, he was still quite sure it was stronger than he was and would not allow him to just do what he needed to do.

That was why he grabbed the sack with both hands and pulled for all he was worth, tearing the leather where it was stitched together. Some of the powdery ash and bits of bone slipped out of it in the effort, but he managed to conserve most of it. He threw this in the face of the loa. The cloud of ash seemed to spread out in the air and completely engulf the monster. It wailed and started writhing. He hoped that would disorient it long enough for him to do what he needed to do.

Jake fell atop the beast, grabbed the jewel that was embedded in its forehead, and worked his fingers around it as best he could. His nails dug into the cold dead flesh and he had to fight down the repulsion that came over him and the urge to let the thing go and flee far from it. Instead of giving in to those urges, he tightened his grip, digging his nails in deeper, and started pulling for all that he was worth.

The creature shrieked, and snake appendages started shooting forward, and he felt first one, then another, then another, biting him. Their stings were hot sharp pinpricks in his flesh, but still he did not waver. It was now or never, all or nothing. Live or die.

The monster tried to use its strength to throw him off, but it was still weakened from the cloud of ash from the ward. The thing was in a great deal of pain, but who knew how much longer that would last? Jake twisted his wrist, using jerking motions to try to loosen the jewel.

Of course, if Jake was wrong about what he was thinking, he was going to die for nothing.

He was dimly aware of Rivera behind him, unable to fire more shots for fear of hitting Jake, unable really to do much of anything other than watch the wrestling match. He was yelling something at Jake, something about Jake being a suicidal idiot and a moron and other such things. Jake tried to tune him out.

He felt the jewel loosen in the beast's forehead. The wails turned more desperate and this time it got one hand around Jake's throat and started squeezing. The deprivation of oxygen was immediate. Even in its weakened state, the beast was still terribly strong. And Jake did not have the ward to protect him anymore. Now it was a race against time.

The gem gave a little more, sliding out of its perch a bit. Jake had thought it was just embedded in the flesh, but now he could see that there was some kind of prong or nail coming out of the back of it. This prong had apparently been driven into the thing's skull. It was not going to come out without a fight.

A curious blackness started to descend around Jake. It had been maybe twenty seconds since he had last taken a breath of air, and his usable supply of oxygen was about gone. His chest started to burn. But he kept pulling. The jewel worked just a little bit more free. He was now yanking with increased desperation. Something that looked remarkably like little fluttering butterflies danced at his peripheral vision, and a red haze began to descend over everything around him. He probably only had seconds left.

Just come out already!

In that moment he could sense he had reached the end of his rope. He was going to pass out any instant. His grip started to slacken on the jewel. Likely this would mean his death. Images of little Lucas and Missy and Bre and Miss Jerry flashed through his mind. He thought of Phil Latham, that old bastard, literally dancing on his grave. Probably at his funeral. In front of his family and friends.

Well screw that!

With one last twist and jerk, the jewel came free in his hand. Jake was in mid-tug and the sudden release knocked him backward. He fell and landed on his back, the jewel rolling several feet away and then coming to a rest nearby.

Other than Jake's ragged breathing, the pounding of his heart, and Rivera's cursing, it went eerily quiet in the office.

When Jake looked up there was a shimmer around Damballah's body. The ripples in the air resembled the heat waves that hovered over hot asphalt on blistering summer days, barely perceptible, but unmistakable. And that was it. The ripples vanished, and all that was left of Damballah was a blotchy corpse where the snake god had been. It was definitely a human corpse, and it looked like something that had been dead for weeks, yet curiously free from decay.

Rivera stepped forward and examined the body.

"What the hell?"

"Just a corpse," Jake said, staring down at it. "And not a very impressive one at that." Indeed, despite the fearsomeness of the monster during its reign of terror, the body before them possessed a certain ordinariness, completely unremarkable in every way. It could have been just any guy off the street. Likely, the presence of the indwelling spirit had been what kept the body from rotting. Jake half-expected it to just turn to dust before his eyes, which is what would have happened in the movies, filling the room with the sweet pungent aroma of deterioration. That never happened. Jake took several more deep breaths, then regarded Rivera.

"While you're here, I have something to show you," Jake said. Rivera looked at him, a mildly curious expression on his face.

Jake hobbled through the mass destruction that had once been a fully functional office environment, Rivera following close behind. Jake led him to Bernadette's office. Halfway there, he had to stop for a moment, as the world began to back away from him, as though he were viewing it through a large tunnel. His head spun. He was on the verge of passing out. But he kept going, keeping unconsciousness at bay for as long as he could. As the adrenaline wore off and plain old weariness kicked in, moment by moment the chore became more difficult.

But he did make it to his destination, and he did show Rivera what he needed to see.

Then, and only then, did he allow himself to pass out.

Thirty

He knew he was awake because he could smell some kind of generic disinfectant, like the bathroom cleaner often used in large office buildings. The aroma only partially masked another, more subtle scent, something broth-based, perhaps soup or stew.

He did not open his eyes for a time. He was enjoying the odd disjointed sensation, as if his consciousness had been separated from his physical being. He was free to listen and smell and think but there was no need to open his eyes or to move. It was somewhat comforting.

Footsteps approached and then moved away again, the gentle squeak of sneakers on a hard polished floor. Somebody entered his personal space and he could sense this person hovering just over him as the soft fabric of a loose cotton garment gently brushed his face.

About that time he noticed the gentle throbbing in the back of his head. His head rested on a soft pillow but the pain came from inside his skull, the remnants of an old headache or the onset of a new one. No telling. No matter. A gruff male voice spoke up, shattering the tranquility of the halfway state he had been enjoying.

"His eyelids are fluttering."

A female voice answered the male. "He's coming around."

A grunt. Then nothing for a while. He thought for a moment he would drift off to sleep again. But the time for sleep had past. The memories started flooding back. Damballah. Elizabeth Meullion. Magical necklaces. Hispanic thugs. Overturned delivery trucks. Purple death rays. Charred corpses. Nosey neighbors. Rude waitresses. Overpriced pralines.

Congealed applesauce clinging to walls.

His eyes popped open and the first thing he saw was Detective Rivera's mustache suspended nearby. A moment later his vision focused and he saw the rest of the detective clearly.

"Thank God," Jake muttered. "For a moment there I thought I was seeing a flying rat."

"What?" Rivera scolded.

"Nothing. Nevermind."

A moment passed. Then another. Finally Rivera broke the silence. "How are you feeling?"

"Why, I didn't know you cared," Jake whispered, finding his voice oddly hoarse.

Rivera straightened and adopted an affronted expression. "Damned if I do. I'm just covering my butt."

"You're kind of cute when you're pretending to be standoffish," Jake said.

Rivera studied him. "Well, your sense of humor survived, so I'm guessing the rest of you must be doing okay too."

"My head hurts."

"You banged it up pretty good. That's part of the reason you've been under so long. Not to mention all the snake bites. You're in the hospital."

"Hospital?" He should have known by the smells alone. That generic cleaner aroma. The broth. Two staple fragrances of hospital ambience. If someone ever created a hospital-scented candle, it would smell like bathroom cleaner and broth. He noticed the bowl of soup resting, untouched, next to his bed on a tray. He guessed someone had just recently set it there. The quality of the sunlight entering the room told him it must be mid-morning.

And then a moment later, he caught on to the other thing Rivera had said.

"Snake bites?" Jake almost sat up and screamed. Only the grogginess prevented him from doing so.

"Not to worry. They weren't venomous. I guess Damballah was more of your yard snake variety. You were pretty swollen, though. Luckily most of it has gone down."

"Crap," Jake said.

"You had a visitor earlier," Rivera said. "But you were still out of it. Older lady. Jerry Watters."

"Miss Jerry," Jake said. "I can't believe I missed her."

"Interesting lady."

"She's one of a kind," Jake said. "Ever since my parents... Ever since they... you know. She's been like a mother to me. I don't know where I'd be without her."

Rivera nodded. "It's good that you have somebody like that."

Jake closed his eyes and smiled. "Did you get to meet Missy?"

"Her granddaughter? That's some kid. I've never met anyone quite like her. Very full of life. And watching the two of them together, you would think they were actual mother and daughter. She really loves that kid."

Jake opened his eyes and looked at Rivera. "It's a mother thing, I guess. Never underestimate a woman's maternal nature."

Jake wondered if he had said something wrong. It was as if he had slapped Rivera in the face. The detective took a step back, a bizarre expression clouding his features, one that looked at once shocked and guilty, like he had been busted in the middle of doing something stupid.

Before Jake could ask Rivera what was the matter, the oversized hospital door creaked open. Bre walked in, little Lucas on her hip, and a crossword magazine in one hand. She didn't knock, just like at home.

"Good, you're awake," she said. "You really look like crap."

"And you look like a tramp," he said back, a faint grin spreading across his lips. Bre paid no mind to Rivera. Jake wanted to ask the detective if his comment had upset him somehow, but just then, his little nephew screamed to him.

"Uncoo!" Lucas chortled.

"Hey, man!" Jake called, and everything in his being wanted to reach out and envelop the child. "Come here!"

Bre plopped Lucas right down on top of Jake. He felt a surge of pain ripple up his damaged leg. "Ow! Hospital bed, Bre! Hospital bed!"

"Don't be such a pansy," she said, then, noticing the bowl of soup, added, "What is that garbage?"

Jake hugged his nephew tightly. "I missed you, little man," he said.

Lucas gazed up into his eyes. "Want eat."

Bre looked down at herself, the jean shorts that were barely more than glorified panties, the ruby-colored tube top that revealed more of her chest and midriff than would ever be considered appropriate, particularly in a hospital where it was conceivable that she might encounter a heart patient who might have some kind of cardiovascular emergency at the sight of her.

"And what do you mean I look like a tramp?" she said. "What's wrong with this?"

"Nothing, if you're going to audition for a Spanish soap opera when you leave here."

She stepped closer to the bed, handed him the crosswords book, and punched him on the shoulder. "You never know. I might meet a cute doctor."

"Glad my misfortune can provide fuel for your love life," he retorted.

Rivera watched the exchange with a back and forward volley of his head. Jake wondered only briefly if the big guy was noticing how she never once asked how Jake was feeling. Only someone who knew nothing at all about their relationship would find that odd.

The detective must have had his fill; he excused himself from the room. Jake realized he was sad to see him go because now he was all alone with his crazy sister and her overexcited toddler, and where Damballah had failed, between the two of them, they may just succeed in killing him.

"I'll be back to check on you," Rivera said before he left. "And don't forget, we still have business to attend to."

"We sure do," Jake agreed.

Rivera left.

Jake stroked his nephew's hair.

Bre folded her arms. "Okay, so tell me everything that happened."

Jake had no idea how to reply to that. "Would you believe that I walked into a door?"

Thirty-one

HappyGoLucky looked shocked when Jake and Rivera showed up at the homeless shelter, their faces grim. The run-down building hunkered on the edge of its lot, half-concealed behind a trio of pecan trees as though too self-conscious to show itself. Rivera explained to Jake on the way over that most such shelters were run by nonprofit organizations that relied heavily on donations for upkeep. HappyGoLucky's modestly sized room sported bare walls, a twin-sized bed, and a dilapidated old particle board dresser. The tile floors needed a good mopping. A black duffel bag rested on the bed. They found him in the process of packing up his belongings, which included a brand new pack of socks that the shelter provided.

Jake wasn't at all surprised to find Lita there.

The young girl wore khaki shorts and a sleeveless purple top that looked a tad too clean for someone who had been living on the streets. A guilty expression passed across her face for all of two seconds, before she masked it behind a blank stare.

"We've been worried about you. You disappeared on us," Jake said.

She bit her lip. "I'm sorry. I was scared. I didn't know what to do."

"So, to what do I owe the pleasure?" HappyGoLucky's tone indicated that he felt no pleasure whatsoever.

"Can't friends check up on friends?" Jake said.

"Friends. Hmmph."

It was Saturday. Both Jake and HappyGoLucky had been released from the hospital the day before. HappyGoLucky no longer wore nearly as many of the heavy bandages that had crisscrossed his body in the hospital. His left eye was still swollen and bloodshot, but time would heal that. He also had a sprained wrist and a noticeable limp, but it could have been much worse.

"So you ended up in a homeless shelter, huh?" Jake said.

"Nowhere else to go," HappyGoLucky said, a note of bitterness in his voice. "Our house on Myrtle Street is trashed. I have no money, no job. I came here just to regroup and get it together. How'd you find me?"

"A guy I know," Jake said, thinking about Corben. "He's been asking around, passing on your description. He knows a lot of the people that pass through these shelters. We figured if you or Lita popped up at any shelter in the city, we'd find out about it."

"Your friend must be pretty resourceful."

Jake thought about that for a moment. "You know, it is rather convenient the way he manages to get me where I need to be. Oh well."

"Well, good for you. You got me. Yay. Now have a nice life. It's been a blast. Literally."

"I see you packing up," Rivera observed. "Are you on your way out?"

"Can't stay here anymore. It's depressing as all hell. Guy in the next room just cries all day and talks to people that ain't there. Me and Lita, we're gonna chart a new course, see where life takes us." His face grew grim.

"Find a new voodoo house?"

He shook his head. "No way. I'm done with that stuff. It's nothing but trouble. Dark powers like that shouldn't be messed around with. Look what happened to us because of it."

"Hey, you're preaching to the choir, buddy," Jake said.

HappyGoLucky paused what he was doing and favored his two guests with a serious expression. "Whatever happened with Damballah?"

"We sent him back to where he came from," Jake said, puffing out his chest. "It was no contest really. We kicked his butt good."

Lita's face whitened at the mention of the monster.

"That thing didn't look like a pushover to me," HappyGoLucky said, and then rummaged in the bottom drawer of the small dresser. He withdrew some foodstuffs and threw them into his bag. "Looked like a killing machine."

"Yeah, well, now it's just some corpse on a slab somewhere."

Rivera chimed in. "If you don't mind, I've got a few more questions. About this voodoo stuff. I need to know a few things so I can get my facts straight."

"Shoot."

Rivera exhaled. Jake could tell that he did not enjoy this particular topic. "Isn't voodoo magic associated with bringing people back from the dead?"

"Zombification?" HappyGoLucky laughed. "Sure. It's a big part of Haitian voodoo practices. But I've never seen it done."

"Until now," Jake said.

HappyGoLucky stopped what he was doing and looked from Jake to Rivera and back again. "What do you mean?"

Rivera sighed. "When the loa finally left its host, the body that was left over looked like it had been dead for a little while."

"That doesn't sound right," HappyGoLucky said. "When Damballah left, the body should have returned to whatever state it was in when the loa first mounted it."

"Like the Mother, when Erzulie left her," Jake said. "Which is why we think the body was already dead when the loa mounted him."

HappyGoLucky spun his head to stare at Jake. "You don't honestly think?"

Jake scratched his chin. "Think about it. You're the one who told us that loas don't usually stick around very long when they mount a host, right? Maybe that has something to do with the host's mind, or consciousness or something. Maybe if a loa mounts a person who was already dead, there's less resistance."

"Except the loas aren't typically very interested in human affairs," HappyGoLucky practically pleaded. "Sometimes they stick around longer than others, but when they leave it's almost always because they lose interest. Even if it mounted a dead host, which I've never seen, and even if that made some difference, it wouldn't want to. You follow me?"

Jake reached into his pocket and withdrew the gem that had been stuck in the creature's forehead. He tossed it to HappyGoLucky, who caught it in one hand, then examined it.

"What is this?"

Rivera cleared his throat. "That was stuck in the creature's head. We think it bound him to his host, essentially trapping him there."

"That's the stupidest thing I've ever heard," HappyGoLucky said. "One of the most powerful loas in the world, trapped? By a little gem? You've got to be kidding me."

"Well, this is just conjecture," Jake said. "But suppose somebody figured out a way to do it. Maybe they were on a power kick. Maybe they wanted to see if there was anything to this voodoo stuff. Maybe they were intrigued about the prospect of bringing somebody back from the dead as a zombie."

"Voodoo zombies are not like what you see in George Romero movies," HappyGoLucky said. "They're not rotting corpses that eat the living. They're just people who have been killed by voodoo, then brought back after two or three days as slaves. They do the bidding of their master."

"Exactly," Jake said. "Except in this case the zombie that was slave to the will of its master was then infused with the power of a loa."

HappyGoLucky shook his head. "It's hard enough to summon a loa. And it's even harder to make a zombie, from what I've heard. And I've never heard of anybody trapping a loa. You don't know what you're saying. I can't imagine somebody making a zombie, summoning a loa, sending the loa into the zombie, and then trapping him there. Nothing like that has ever been done."

Rivera gestured to the gem in HappyGoLucky's hand. "Our perpetrator had help."

"This thing? I don't see how."

"Look," Jake said. "Let's just say that there are some items floating around that have powers of their own. If a person gets his hands on one of these items, then he would be able to do things that he would not ordinarily be able to do. I think you're holding one of these items now, and I think it was responsible somehow for trapping the loa in that body. As soon as I pulled it free, the loa left."

HappyGoLucky grimaced. "This is getting a bit crazy, even for me. Why are you even telling me this?"

"We can't let you go," Rivera said.

"Like hell. What do you think, I did it? I summoned the loa and bound it to that guy?"

Lita took a couple of steps away from the graying man. HappyGoLucky glanced down at her, something bordering on genuine hurt touching his eyes. He visibly deflated.

"Lita, no," he said. "They're full of crap."

"I wonder if this is crap," Rivera said. He opened the manila folder and threw a picture on HappyGoLucky's bed. Lita stepped forward despite herself, saw it, and then drew back again. HappyGoLucky glanced down and then back up.

"What in the world?" he asked.

"A murder scene," Rivera said. "The night your friend Najac was killed."

Jake knew the photo. He did not need to look down but he could not help himself. It was the same picture Rivera had presented to him on Thursday, the one that showed Jake sitting on his rump on a curb while crime scene investigators prowled about.

"So?" HappyGoLucky said.

"There's a woman in the background of this picture. Her name is Elizabeth Meullion."

Lita drew in a sharp breath. Rivera raised one eyebrow.

HappyGoLucky shrugged. "I'll say it again. So?"

"So until that picture was taken, Elizabeth Meullion had been missing for almost a year. Her family had not seen or heard from her. Nobody knew where she was or what happened to her. And then she pops up in this picture. At a murder scene, no less."

"Najac was killed by this Damballah zombie," Jake added. "And we didn't believe it was a coincidence that Elizabeth was there that night. A few days earlier, that thing killed a friend of mine. This friend was engaged to Elizabeth's ex-husband. So we knew Elizabeth was mixed up in this somehow, being connected to both victims."

"Sounds like you need to talk to this Elizabeth chick," HappyGoLucky said.

"Well, unfortunately, she seems to have disappeared again," Rivera said.

"So why are you trying to detain me?"

"We're not going to detain you."

"You just said you couldn't let me leave."

Rivera ignored him. He reached into his folder, took out another picture, and handed it to HappyGoLucky. "This one was taken from the office of Bernadette Meullion, Elizabeth's sister."

The man's face blanched.

And with good reason. It was the photo of the school-aged versions of Bernadette and Elizabeth sitting in the café. It was the picture that Jake had first noticed when Bernadette was trying to pump him for information, the object he had staved off unconsciousness for so he could show it to Rivera before he passed out.

There was something very wrong with the picture. But only a handful of people would have known what that something was. The problem stemmed from the fact that the picture had been taken years ago, when Bernadette and Elizabeth were kids. But despite this fact, there was no mistaking the eerie similarities between one of the girls in the photo and the one standing in the room with them right now.

"What the bloody hell?" HappyGoLucky said, catching it immediately. He turned the photo around so that Lita could clearly see it.

She responded the way Jake thought she would; she bolted for the door. Jake was ready, and before she had taken her third step, Jake teleported directly into her path, and she collided into him. The force of the impact was far greater than he expected, and he staggered. He managed to grab hold of her waist as he went down, and they both toppled to the floor.

HappyGoLucky still stared at the photo. His mouth hung open.

The girl in the photo, seated across from the kid version of Bernadette Meullion, looked an awful lot like Lita. In fact, she didn't just look like Lita.

She was Lita.

"Let me go!" Lita screamed. "Help! Help!"

Jake tried to keep her pinned to the floor, but she was squirming and pulling with more strength than any child should have been able to muster. She kicked, she clawed, and finally she bit him. He cried out, fumbling against her until he grabbed hold of one of her clammy hands. She tried to pull away but he held on for all he was worth.

"What exactly is going on in here?" a voice cried.

A man stood silhouetted in the doorway. This man was not terribly large, but he was not small either, and even a cursory glance his way revealed he was at least moderately toned. He wore the same style of clothing as many of the other derelicts who came to spend the night at the shelter. One of the multitudes of homeless people who needed help.

And the man did what any man would do, upon encountering a child being set upon by a grown man; he pounced on Jake, yanking and pulling at him in an attempt to free Lita.

Rivera tried to intervene, tried to command the Good Samaritan to break it off, but the man's single-minded focus was on saving a young girl and he paid Rivera no heed.

Amidst the fumbling, wrestling, twisting, and turning, Jake got hold of what he was aiming for, the so-called heirloom ring that Lita was always fingering. She gasped as his grip tightened on the piece of jewelry, but he was not to be deterred. She continued to resist, but with a final mighty twist and pull that made her cry out, the ring came free in his hand.

And just like that, Lita was gone; Elizabeth Meullion had taken her place.

The would-be rescuer gasped and let go of Jake, and drew back. Jake, despite the assurance of his conviction, was sufficiently shocked, so that Elizabeth was able to throw an elbow to his face. The blow hit home, and he saw stars as he fell to one side. Only Rivera remained in her path as she jumped to her feet.

She did not try to run past Rivera; she merely brandished a knife from somewhere on her person and slashed at him. Jake saw Rivera clutch his stomach and start to waver before Elizabeth shouldered past him, reaching the door and disappearing through it.

She could not be allowed to escape.

Jake rose to his feet on sheer determination, and rushed into the corridor beyond the door. Elizabeth had the head start on him, and was almost to the end of the corridor, gunning for the front door. She still held the knife; as curious bystanders happened too close, she slashed at them, driving them back.

Jake knew that he would have to time this right if it was going to work. He leaned into his stride, and dove, as though he meant to tackle the air in front of him. Elizabeth was several strides ahead, and the dive had no hope of connecting. But in mid-plunge, he tapped into the power of the chain to re-appear directly behind her. The plan worked; he struck her in mid-dive with the force of an open-field tackle, and she went down under his weight.

The first thing he did was grab the hand that held the knife, and he beat it against the floor until she dropped the weapon. She struggled so much that for a moment he feared that he might lose his grip, but then Rivera was there, his shirt bloody, handcuffs at the ready. Rivera put a knee in her back and wrested her arms behind her, before locking the cuffs around her wrists.

She continued to thrash, but there was nowhere for her to go. All at once she must have realized the fruitlessness of the effort, because then she went still. Rivera pulled her to her feet. Her breathing was heavy, and she looked at them both with obvious disdain.

Jake was glad to see that the bloody slash across Rivera's stomach was not very deep. It could have been much worse.

HappyGoLucky came near. A few bystanders stopped what they were doing to gape.

"How is it that I'm suddenly the one who has no idea what's going on?" HappyGoLucky said.

Jake stood, leaned over, rested his hands on his knees, and waited until he had caught his breath. Then he looked over at HappyGoLucky. "Stopping the loa zombie thing was only half the battle. We also knew we had to catch the one that summoned that thing in the first place. Here she is." He hooked a thumb toward Elizabeth.

"That's why we said we couldn't let you leave," Rivera added. "We meant that you couldn't leave with her. She would have killed you the first chance she got."

"Why?"

"The same reason she killed all those folks on Myrtle Street," Rivera explained. "To cover her tracks. Tie up the loose ends."

"Lita," HappyGoLucky pleaded with her, the look in his eyes begging her to say that they were lying, that she would never do such a thing.

Elizabeth winked at him. He choked.

"Why?"

"That's easy enough, once you know the background," Jake said. "I guess it all started when Daddy got Elizabeth a job overseeing one of his little archaeological digs. That's where she met Najac. My guess is they found something above and beyond the usual ceramic pot or chipped arrowhead. Is that right, Lita?"

She didn't say anything.

"Come on," Jake said. "This is the part where you explain your whole scheme to us, and then say something like, 'If it wasn't for you pestering kids and your little dog I would have gotten away with it!'"

She scoffed.

"Fine, have it your way then," Jake said. Turning back to HappyGoLucky, he continued. "So anyway, they must have found something big. Like, say, a cache of magical artifacts. I know, I know, it's starting to sound like bad science fiction, right? So something happens, there's some kind of falling out, I don't know. Najac disappears first. He steals a silver chain. Elizabeth disappears right after. Nobody knows why. Najac surfaces in New Orleans. Maybe to keep an eye on Dennis Meullion, who funded the whole expedition."

"A cache of artifacts? Where did you get that one from?" HappyGoLucky said.

"When I met Dennis, and he saw this chain around my neck, he recognized it immediately. And he kept asking me where the rest of the artifacts were. I said I didn't know. I didn't even know that there were any other artifacts. But he was willing to torture me to make sure I was telling the truth. That should tell you something."

"My step-dad can be a jerk like that," Elizabeth said.

Jake looked at her. Then something else clicked into place. "Wait a second," he said. "I think I get it now. If this had been some big happy coincidence, your father would not have known what my chain could do. But he did know. He specifically mentioned that when he saw me teleport he knew I had the chain."

Her eyes gleamed.

"Which means," Jake figured it out as he went along, "that he didn't find these artifacts by accident, did he? He was looking for them. He's been looking for them for some time. That's the whole reason for these digs he's been funding, isn't it?"

"You have all the answers, smart-ass, you tell me," she said.

"Whatever. I'm sure that's more or less it," Jake said. "Najac steals one of the artifacts, maybe more, whatever he can get his hands on, and then comes back here to keep an eye on your dad. Maybe he figures your dad has more of these artifacts. And maybe he's right. Maybe your dad's been digging these up for years. Hell if I know. But Najac's trying to find out. Then you show up looking for Najac, touch base with your family, find out that Dallas is engaged, you fly off the handle and drop off the radar. I just don't know how all that voodoo stuff fits in."

"He had connections," Elizabeth volunteered. "His people come from Haiti."

Jake mulled that over.

Rivera threw his two cents in. "So when you finally found Najac, he was already hanging out with those Myrtle Street people. And you disguised yourself with that ring, which also came from the cache, and infiltrated the group, is that it? Learned their secrets, that kind of thing. Figured out if you could use any of their teachings to your advantage?"

"I bet at first she was just trying to get close to Najac," Jake said. "She wanted to steal the chain back from him. Then she found out what those people could do, and she hung around. Najac never recognized you. I guess it was an easy scheme to pull off for someone with a ring that made them younger when they wore it."

"It makes me look younger," she said with a sneer. "It's just an illusion. That's why I wouldn't let anybody touch me."

Jake recalled Lita recoiling from him when he had tried to hug her on Myrtle Street. He recalled HappyGoLucky in the hospital, telling them how he suspected she had been abused because of the way she avoided physical contact with everybody.

Jake gestured to the tiny gem that HappyGoLucky still clutched in trembling fingers. "Somehow you figured out how to raise a zombie. I'm guessing you had plenty of connections in the voodoo community by that point. And you just said yourself that Najac's people came from Haiti. Maybe he knew how to do it. Maybe you got him to share that information. I don't know. I don't care. But you looked like a kid. People let their guards down around you. You kept your eyes and ears open. You learned a lot of their secrets. You managed to make a zombie, and then send Damballah into the zombie, and that little gem that you nailed into its forehead trapped it in there some kind of way. I'm guessing it came from the same cache of artifacts that this chain, and your little youth ring, came from."

She just smirked. "You give me a lot of credit. You must think highly of me."

"Well, it's just amazing how many things started to fit together once I puzzled it out," Jake said, a sarcastic tone resonating in his voice. "Like how when I met your father and sister, he called her Bernie. I'm guessing when you were a kid, he called you Lita. I can't believe I didn't think of it sooner, that Lita is a nickname for Elizabeth. And then there was the little Spanish Inquisition that tried to filet me in the back of a delivery truck. I guess that was your doing too."

"Hypothetically speaking," Elizabeth said, rolling her eyes, "It's possible that I knew Luis. It's possible that he used to do jobs for my dad. Dirty jobs. It's possible he would have done a job for me if I offered him enough money. It's possible that I sent him after you to get the chain back, since you kept getting away from Damballah, and you wouldn't leave with me that night in the alley when I tried to reason with you."

"He said he was sent to warn me to keep my nose out of other people's business."

She laughed. "It's also possible that was just a ruse, when in fact he meant to kill you and take the chain off of your neck."

Jake shivered.

Rivera scratched his head. "You didn't need to have Faith killed," he said. "I get why you killed Najac, why you went after Jake. Why you went after those people on Myrtle Street. You wanted to get back what you thought was yours. Cover your tracks when you were done. It's psychotic, but I get it. But Faith?"

She was not immediately forthcoming.

Jake huffed. "Come on, don't go silent on us now," he said. "It has something to do with your little love triangle, doesn't it? You dad told me that Bernadette had a little fling with Dallas herself. He broke your heart, didn't he? Killing Faith was just your way of breaking his heart in return, is that it? You already had this slave zombie god at your disposal. Why not send it after the woman that was about to marry the man who broke your heart? Give it a little trial run?"

Elizabeth appeared to have lost all interest in speaking.

"Come on, share your feelings with us," Jake said. "It isn't good to keep those things bottled up. Ask Freud. Look where it's gotten you this far."

Elizabeth actually smiled. "You have a lot of nice theories. But is that what's going to go on my arrest report? Using voodoo to send a zombie assassin after my enemies? Do you honestly expect to put me away on that?"

Jake did not have an answer for that. He stammered, at a loss for words. But Rivera was ready. The detective stepped forward.

"Well, not exactly. But the way I see it, we've got you for attempted murder on a police officer." He held up one bloody hand to illustrate the point. "Then we'll go back over the evidence from the crime scenes, see if we can't link you to them with DNA. All we need to do is show that you were present both times. I think we can establish motive in both instances. I think that's a pretty good start, don't you?"

Elizabeth's smirk faded. "I'm done speaking."

"I bet you are," Rivera said. "And I've got witnesses that can testify that you spoke freely and never once asked for a lawyer. So now I'm going to read you your Miranda rights and put you under arrest, okay? We wouldn't want you getting free on a technicality."

Jake smiled as Rivera read Elizabeth her rights.

Thirty-two

Homicide Detective Lester Rivera, Jr. had seen things that only two weeks ago he would not have thought possible. He watched a man teleport. He faced down some weird snake thing that apparently had been a zombified corpse indwelt by the spirit of a snake god. He had almost been killed by it. But he had stood up to it, and, along with Jake Presnall, had conquered the thing.

And he had managed to capture the person responsible for all that trouble. Elizabeth Meullion was currently sitting in a holding cell, dressed in an orange jumpsuit.

That was nothing.

Now for the hard part. It was time to face his wife.

Rivera entered through the back door into the kitchen, a nondescript brown package tucked under his right arm. The small table, where his wife spent most of her time, was unoccupied. He ascended the steps to the second floor, and found Maxine at the computer in their bedroom, sorting columns of numbers in her spreadsheet program. Her fingers flew across the keyboard with a speed and skill that defied reason. One of her many talents, he realized. He held the package tighter and waited for a pause in her typing that did not come.

She either was unaware that he entered the room, or did not care.

He was guessing the latter.

He cleared his throat uncomfortably. She did not acknowledge the sound. He cleared his throat again. From his position in the doorway he had a clear view of the back of her head and the slant of her shoulders, as if the weight they bore had grown so obtrusive that she could no longer hold them straight.

She did not slow down, and he realized this was going to be even harder than he had imagined. He deserved that. He did not know where to start. Maybe he should just take it from the top.

"I think I get it now," he said.

Her fingers kept pressing keys, like hikers following a familiar path.

"The reason I missed your luncheon on Wednesday was only in part because of my caseload. The truth is, I really didn't care all that much." She did not slow her pace but he noticed that her head tilted slightly, as if she was listening but trying to not be obvious about it.

He rested one hand against the doorway, like someone who needed assistance to continue standing. Or maybe he just wanted to feel something that was firm and unyielding. "The simple truth is I just didn't make it a priority. But then again, you knew that already."

She was still not acknowledging him. But she was typing much more slowly, giving him the impression that she was at least listening.

"I guess I've resented the youth center all along," he admitted. "I resented how much time you spent working there, I resented how much time you spent at home doing youth center stuff, and in time I came to resent you."

She stopped typing, all pretenses forgotten. But she still did not turn to face him.

He continued. "I guess I saw something on this case I've been working on. I probably won't communicate this well, you know I'm not a speaker. But I caught a glimpse of what being torn from your loved ones can do to a person. This kid, Jake, he lost both his parents, and he... it was years ago but you can still see how much it hurts him. And this lady, Jerry, and her love for her granddaughter. We need families. It's practically written in our DNA. And Jake, he latched onto Jerry like a mother."

He shook his head. "I think you might know a thing or two about kids adopting mothers. You adopted a whole pack of surrogate children, didn't you?"

Rivera was trained to notice slight variations in body language. It was a handy skill to have during an interrogation. You could tell a lot more sometimes from how someone was standing, sitting, slouching, or pacing than you could from what they were saying. Maxine was probably not even aware of the minute bobbing of her shoulders. She was trying really hard to keep herself steady.

He sighed. "I met this lady the other day, this surrogate mother. She has a granddaughter, and she's fiercely protective of her. But it wasn't until someone made a comment about not underestimating a woman's maternal nature that I realized what was wrong with me. And then I saw. I resented you for distancing yourself from me and burying yourself in that youth center. But the youth center was never the problem. I see that now. And you did the only thing you could do, being married to such an insensitive and unsympathetic jerk."

Her back shot upright, a spastic lurch that caused her to bump her knee on the computer desk.

"Yeah, I said it," he said. "You buried yourself in your work to get away from the pain. You allowed those children that you helped to be a substitute for the children we could never have and I was too dense to catch on. You were all alone in the world until you took them on."

She turned slightly, as though she meant to face him. But a last bit of resistance prevented her from turning all the way around. So she stopped herself, no longer looking at the computer, but not yet looking at him either. He could only see her face at an angle, a portion of one cheek and the corner of her forehead.

"When the fertility treatments failed, I should... I should have realized how hard you took it. That the part of you that so desperately wanted to be a mother wasn't going to just take it lying down. I wasn't there for you. You weren't choosing the youth center over me. You were choosing the youth center over emptiness."

Rivera felt twin hot trails on his face, one on each cheek. Two tears rolled downward, one from each eye. The sensation was completely unfamiliar to him. He could not recall the last time he had cried.

"I'm sorry," he said simply.

She must have heard the emotion in his voice, the first genuine emotion in months, must have immediately understood what it meant for him to allow her to hear that, because suddenly she was on her feet, spinning to face him and taking a step toward him all in one graceful, elegant motion.

He was struck by the beauty of this woman he had been married to, her thin lips, her sparkling green eyes, the little button nose that decorated her face like an afterthought. Those eyes were puffy now, red-rimmed and springing forth with their own glistening vertical trails.

Before he could muster another word, she was in his arms.

Her body felt light and delicate. Her skin, mocha-colored and smooth, was soft to the touch. He caught a whiff of her tangerine-scented shampoo. She did not say anything, and he followed suit, letting their silence say all the things that the English language could never convey. He lost track of how long they held each other in that way.

When they parted she smiled up at him. "This doesn't fix everything. We have work to do, you know. To get back to where we were."

He wiped at his face with the back of one of his sleeves. "I know."

She grinned mischievously. "What's in the box? A bribe?"

He took the package out from under his arm. "I'll show you." Together, they went back down to the kitchen. He set the brown box down on the counter. "Open it."

She carefully undid the packaging, parted the flaps, and removed a small, bubble wrapped object. She unrolled the wrapping, and let out a soft little whimper when she saw what it was.

"This kid, Presnall," Rivera explained. "Well I guess technically he's not a kid, he just acts like one. Anyway, he told me about this little place in the Quarter he found, that sells things like this. I figured we had to have one."

She held the object up, and nodded her approval.

He stepped forward and gently pried it from her fingers. She did not resist him.

It was a tiny statuette of a ballerina, similar to the one Maxine had placed on the counter all those years ago. This one stood with her arms raised over her head, one leg stuck out in a nimble pose that reflected serenity and control.

He placed the new figurine on the counter, and turned it so that it was facing the old one.

"Now she has a partner," he said.

Thirty-three

It had been years since the last time Jake purchased flowers for a girl. On that long ago but not-forgotten occasion, he had been after a bouquet of roses to give to his then-girlfriend, Tonya Rigney. The roses were a failed attempt to salvage a relationship that ended up dying anyway. Something had changed, she said, and she felt they were no longer romantically compatible, and they settled for friendship instead of romance.

Tonya was married now, and Jake was carrying wildflowers instead of roses. He reminisced about Tonya all the way to the cemetery.

The grave marker would not be installed for several more weeks, but Fleur had given him directions to the appropriate grave. She had not been at all happy to see him at the bistro again, but had relented when he explained his reasons for the second visit. Now he kneeled down at the grave, clutching the flowers. A granite chalice was bolted into the stone slab that covered the grave, and into this he placed the bouquet, arranging it as neatly as he could manage. He would need to go into the mausoleum area, find a sink, and get some water to pour into the chalice.

He plopped to the ground beside the slab. The sky was almost impossibly blue and the sweet scent of freshly mown grass hung in the air. The cemetery was vast, and the tall stone gate that surrounded the whole place managed to filter out most of the sounds of a world going on around him. An unseen robin chirped, one of the few sounds that actually reached his ears. He found it strange that he should find so much peace out here, surrounded by the dead. A few scattered clouds rolled lazily across the sky. Magnolia trees dotted the graveyard at random points, and it was under the shadow of one of these that he now sat.

An ant crawled up his pants leg; he plucked it off.

"We got her," Jake said at last. "I don't know if you care about that where you are, but we caught her. Your killer."

The only response came from the rustle of a soft breeze through the leaves of the magnolia trees.

He sat there a while longer. He was not sure what else there was to say, or even if there was a point to saying anything. Surely the body in the ground could not hear him, and if there was a spirit that had once been Faith floating around somewhere, such a spirit could probably hear him just as well from his own living room as from the cemetery. But there was something special about being here, in this place, and he knew it. Everybody knew it. If that were false, then why did so many people even bother visiting cemeteries at all?

Besides, he was in no hurry. Nothing awaited him at home but an empty house. He had no job to rush off to. Sooner or later he would need to address that, for the bills were going to keep arriving, heedless of his employment situation. In a strictly worldly sense, things had never looked bleaker for him.

So what was that warm and fuzzy feeling coursing through him?

The cemetery turned out to be a great place to just think. His mind wandered, and he knew what it was that had him feeling so chipper; for the first time, he was actually living. Day after day he had followed the same boring routine: get up, go to work, come home, pay bills. Occasionally there was room in his schedule for video games. But that was no kind of life. The blood lab and his game console had been a kind of screen, keeping him from seeing the vastness of the world. Damballah and Elizabeth Meullion, despite their evil intentions, had ripped him from that monotony, and for a while he had been doing something worthwhile.

Was he supposed to just go back to his old life now? Find another job? Go back and play video games? He had a freaking teleportation necklace, for crying out loud!

Jake stood. He would figure this out. He would determine what came next for him. However his new life turned out, it would not look at all like the old life. He was done with that. What good was a virtual life on a video game console, anyway? Eventually you have to turn the console off and then the only world you have to live in is the real one.

He entertained the notion of using his new ability to help people. Not to be a superhero, that would be cheesy, but maybe he could be a private investigator. He could solve the problems of others, like he had done with Detective Rivera by bringing Elizabeth Meullion to justice.

The sound of padded feet crunching the grass behind him brought him around. He turned and saw Dallas Lasserre with two of his Labradors. The dogs sat on their haunches and remained perfectly still by their owner's side.

Dallas clutched his own bouquet of flowers; a dozen red roses. His eyes locked on Jake, then looked past him at the little chalice with the wildflowers sticking out of it. He puckered his lips a little bit as he sucked air through his teeth.

"Guess I should have gotten here sooner," Dallas said. "Now I have to go find a vase."

Jake suppressed a laugh. "I'm sorry for all of this. For your loss."

Dallas shook his head up and down. "Thank you."

"I'll just leave you two alone, then."

Jake strolled across the grass. He made it about ten feet before Dallas called after him, and he turned to face the man he had so recently suspected of murder.

"Detective Rivera says you were a big help in catching Elizabeth."

"I did what I could. I just wish it hadn't happened at all."

Dallas sighed. "I'm not making excuses for her. God knows I hate her for what she's done. But she's had it rough. The way her stepfather and sister treated her while she was growing up... I could tell you some stories that would make your hair stand on end."

"I've caught a vibe with them," Jake admitted. "Elizabeth was the outsider in their family, wasn't she?"

Dallas could only nod. He had no words with which to elaborate, no sobering explanation that would put it all back in order. Jake watched him, noted the warring emotions vying for control of his face. First he sucked in a breath and exhaled slowly, as though fighting a great big sob. Then he locked his jaw and one side of his face curled up in a snarl. He finally just bit his bottom lip and shook his head, grief giving way to anger giving way to cluelessness.

For a long moment they just stood there facing each other with the grave of Faith Daelly between them like a stone-faced chaperone.

"I was a jerk to you back at your place," Jake said.

"Yeah."

"Sorry about that too."

"Least of my worries."

Jake looked down at the freshly churned mud where the coffin had been covered the previous week. He hesitated, another question on the tip of his tongue, but he was unsure whether or not it was appropriate to ask it.

"Out with it," Dallas said at last. "I can tell you have something else on your mind."

Jake chewed his lip. He shoved his fists down inside the pockets of his jeans. "Dennis and Bernadette both said something about keeping in touch with you."

A bitter little laugh slipped out of Dallas's throat. "Keeping in touch? Sure. If you count the veiled threats I've been getting every couple of months since Elizabeth went missing. And the people that I catch following me around from time to time. I'm sure they work for Meullion. I'm sure he had them tailing me to try to find out if I knew where his step-daughter was."

He shook his head and stared off at the distant cemetery gate, his eyes glistening.

Jake knew enough to figure out that Meullion had certainly not been looking for Elizabeth for her sake. He had merely believed she knew something about his stolen property.

"Dennis mentioned that you had a thing with Bernadette?" Jake said. He knew he was starting to step into murky waters, that this other man was likely to tell him to mind his own business.

But Dallas Lasserre surprised him.

"Yes. I met Bernadette first. We dated for a while. I met Elizabeth through her. But then Bernadette and I broke up."

"Because you started seeing Elizabeth?"

"Absolutely not. At least a year went by before I bumped into Elizabeth one night at a restaurant in the city. We had always been friendly. We decided to get together to catch up. It started innocently enough. But things progressed. Elizabeth assured me that she had told Bernadette about us, and that Bernadette understood."

Jake watched Dallas's face. "And did she?"

"Supposedly. But things were always tense whenever Bernadette was around. Deep down, she was furious at Elizabeth for dating me. Then Elizabeth and I got married. That was the icing on the cake."

Jake nodded. "I understand the marriage didn't last long."

This time, Dallas actually laughed. "That's one way of putting it. No sooner did we come back from our honeymoon, then Bernadette showed up at the house one night when Elizabeth was out. I knew I shouldn't have let her into the house. Next thing I knew, we were..."

Dallas trailed off. Jake waited for him to continue. When the moments ticked by and he began to suspect that Dallas had said as much on the topic as he intended to say, Jake prodded him.

"You were what?"

"Together."

"Together?"

"Intimately."

Jake nodded. "Oh. I see. Charming woman, empty house. I get it."

Dallas dropped his head and his chest heaved. "No, I don't think you do. I didn't want to do anything with that woman. I've been tempted before. I used to play football, after all. I can resist temptation. That wasn't temptation. That was something else."

Jake's heart skipped a beat. He recalled all too well what transpired between himself and Bernadette at her office. "What do you mean?"

"It was like I wasn't even the one in control anymore. I just did whatever she said. I didn't want to, but that didn't matter. The whole time, my mind was screaming for my body to back off. I felt warm and flushed, dizzy, disoriented. I'd accuse her of drugging me, except I hadn't had anything to eat or drink. Needless to say, Elizabeth walked in on us. The divorce wasn't long after."

Jake stood there, his feet rooted to the spot, feeling like he was going to start hyperventilating any second.

Dallas met his eyes. "I can imagine how that sounds. I probably sound like any other guy would sound in that situation, making excuses."

"No," Jake said. "I believe you. I've met the woman. And I had a similar experience with her. Too similar."

"What's that supposed to mean?"

His mind raced. Was there more to the story? Was this the point in the movie where you start to wonder if there is going to be a sequel? Or was it just as simple as saying that Bernadette was irresistible?

"I don't know yet," Jake said at last. For a long moment, silence reigned between them. Then Jake offered his hand. Dallas shook it. There was nothing else to say.

"I should leave you to it," Jake said.

Dallas turned to the grave. Jake turned to go. There was no extended farewell. Just two men parting, one mourning his fiancée, and the other wondering what tomorrow would look like.

As he left that tranquil place, Jake wondered where he went from here.

And he smiled.

He'd go anywhere he wanted.

A NOTE TO THE READER

Word of mouth recommendations are the best friends of authors. If you enjoyed this book, please consider telling others about it. Your support is invaluable, needed, and so very appreciated.

To stay up to date on new projects from this author, including release dates of upcoming novels such as Jake Presnall's all-new adventure arriving in 2014, please visit the author's website: http://www.eslermedia.com

You can also find the author on Facebook. http://www.facebook.com/EslerMedia

Smashwords Profile: https://www.smashwords.com/profile/view/EslerMedia

ABOUT THE AUTHOR

George Esler knew he wanted to be an author from the time he was old enough to hold a pencil. As a child, he drew comic books on tiny notepads and gave them to his mom to read. As he grew, he tried his hand in everything from superhero stories, to slasher horror, to science fiction and fantasy. If it had magic, superpowers, or a masked killer, George was all over it.

In 2012, after a lengthy hiatus from writing, George decided to get serious again about his craft. In April of that year, he began working on the first draft of a book that would go on to become "Line of Sight." George's deepest passion in writing is to use the power of the written word to create fictional worlds that he can share with others, who then get to live and eat and breathe and play in these places that once existed only in his own imagination.

George was born and raised in New Orleans, Louisiana, where he lives with his beautiful wife and his two adorable daughters, who outnumber him 3-to-1.

www.ingramcontent.com/pod-product-compliance
Lightning Source LLC
Chambersburg PA
CBHW052042240626
47153CB00006B/2193